FAIR PLAY

A Novel

By
MRS. E. D. E. N. SOUTHWORTH

AUTHOR OF

"The Trail of the Serpent," "A Skeleton in the Closet,"
"Nearest and Dearest," "The Lost Lady of Lone," Etc.

A. L. BURT COMPANY

PUBLISHERS　　　　　　　　　　NEW YORK

POPULAR BOOKS
By MRS. E. D. E. N. SOUTHWORTH
In Handsome Cloth Binding
Price per volume, - - - - - 60 Cents

Beautiful Fiend, A
Brandon Coyle's Wife
   Sequel to A Skeleton in the Closet
Bride's Fate, The
   Sequel to The Changed Brides
Bride's Ordeal, The
Capitola's Peril
   Sequel to the Hidden Hand
Changed Brides, The
Cruel as the Grave
David Lindsay
   Sequel to Gloria
Deed Without a Name, A
Dorothy Harcourt's Secret
   Sequel to A Deed Without a Name
"Em"
Em's Husband
   Sequel to "Em"
Fair Play
For Whose Sake
   Sequel to Why Did He Wed Her?
For Woman's Love
Fulfilling Her Destiny
   Sequel to When Love Commands
Gloria
Her Love or Her Life
   Sequel to The Bride's Ordeal
Her Mother's Secret
Hidden Hand, The
How He Won Her
   Sequel to Fair Play
Ishmael
Leap in the Dark, A
Lilith
   Sequel to the Unloved Wife
Little Nea's Engagement
   Sequel to Nearest and Dearest
Lost Heir, The
Lost Lady of Lone, The
Love's Bitterest Cup
   Sequel to Her Mother's Secret
Mysterious Marriage, The
   Sequel to A Leap in the Dark
Nearest and Dearest
Noble Lord, A
   Sequel to The Lost Heir
Self-Raised
   Sequel to Ishmael
Skeleton in the Closet, A
Struggle of a Soul, The
   Sequel to The Lost Lady of Lone
Sweet Love's Atonement
Test of Love, The
   Sequel to A Tortured Heart
To His Fate
   Sequel to Dorothy Harcourt's Secret
Tortured Heart, A
   Sequel to The Trail of the Serpent
Trail of the Serpent, The
Tried for Her Life
   Sequel to Cruel as the Grave
Unloved Wife, The
Unrequited Love, An
   Sequel to For Woman's Love
Victor's Triumph
   Sequel to A Beautiful Fiend
When Love Commands
When Shadows Die
   Sequel to Love's Bitterest Cup
Why Did He Wed Her?
Zenobia's Suitors
   Sequel to Sweet Love's Atonement

For Sale by all Booksellers or will be sent postpaid on receipt of price.
A. L. BURT COMPANY, PUBLISHERS
New York

FAIR PLAY

CHAPTER I

THE FOUR BELLES OF BELLEMONT

"God created woman, a living soul, worthy to stand in His presence and worship Him, and if it were only from the reverence she owes Him she would never degrade herself to be any man's slave! God endowed woman with individual life—with power, will and understanding, brain, heart and hands to do His work; and if it were only in gratitude to him, she should never commit the moral suicide of becoming the nonentity of which man's law makes a wife!"

She was a splendid creature who uttered this heterodoxy, a magnificent and beautiful creature! She spoke fervently, earnestly, passionately, with blazing eyes, flushed cheeks and crimsoned lips that seemed to breathe the fire that burned in her enthusiastic soul.

She was the most brilliant of a group of four lovely young girls who were seated on the fresh grass, in a grove of magnolia trees on the south banks of the James.

Before them flowed the fair river, fringed with wooded shores and dotted with green isles, all sparkling in the early sunlight of a June morning.

Behind them, from amidst its ornamented grounds, arose the white walls of Bellemont College for young ladies.

The first day of June was the annual commencement of the college. And these four young girls, all dressed in purest white robes with rose-colored wreaths and sashes, had sauntered out together and grouped themselves under the magnolia trees to wait for the ringing of the bell which should call them to the exhibition room.

Four more beautiful young creatures than these could scarcely be found in the world. They were called the Four Belles of Bellemont. They would have been belles anywhere and borne off palms of beauty from all other competitors. Yet beautiful as each one was, the four were not rival belles; because, in fact, each one was of a totally different style from all the others. They might be said to represent the four orders of female beauty—the blue, gray, hazel and black-eyed woman.

So far were they from being rivals, that they were fast friends, banded in an alliance for offense and defense against the whole school, if not the whole world!

Britomarte Conyers, the man hater, the woman's champion, the marriage renouncer, first in beauty, grace and intellect, was, as I said, a magnificent creature—not in regard to size, for she was not so tall as the blue-eyed belle, nor so full-fleshed as the hazel-eyed one; but magnificent in the sense of conscious strength, ardor and energy with which she impressed all. She felt and made you feel, that if her earnest soul had been clothed with the form of a man, she would have been one to govern the minds of men and guide the fortunes of nations; or, woman as she was, if law and custom had allowed her freer action and a fairer field, she would have influenced the progress of humanity and filled a place in history.

Britomarte's present position and prospects were not very brilliant. She was the orphan ward of a maiden aunt, who had sent her to this school to be educated as a governess; and a hard struggle with the world was all that she had to look forward to; but certainly, if ever a woman was formed to fight the battle of life without fear and without reproach, it was this brave, spirited, energetic young amazon.

In this quartette of fair girls the second in merit was certainly Erminie Rosenthal, the daughter of a Luther an minister. Erminie was about the medium height, with a well-developed, beautifully rounded, buxom form; splendidly moulded features, blooming complexion, softly shining, hazel eyes, and a shower of bright, auburn ringlets shading the sweetest face in the whole group.

The third in this bevy of beauties was Elfrida Fielding, the daughter of a thriving farmer. Elfie was small, slight, and elegant in figure, and dark in complexion, with a rich crimson flush upon cheeks and lips, and with black eyes, eyelashes and eyebrows, and jet black hair, cut short, parted on the left side, and worn in crisp curls like a boy's. Elfie was the wild sprite, the mischievous monkey, the fast little girl of the party. She was lively, witty, impulsive, excitable, fickle, and had an especial affinity for—anything and everything in its turn, and an especial mission to engage in—anything and everything that turned up.

Fourth and last among the four belles of Bellemont, though certainly first in social position, was Alberta Goldsborough, the daughter of a wealthy merchant in Richmond, and the heiress in her own right of a rich plantation on the James. Alberta was tall, slender and dignified, with classic, marble-like features, dazzlingly fair complexion, light golden hair, and light blue eyes. She was a statuesque blond beauty.

The four belles, languidly reclining under the magnolia trees, had been discussing as schoolgirls always do when they get together out of the sight of their teachers—first the highly important subject of dress; Elfie exclaiming indignantly at the outrage of being obliged to wear rose-colored trimmings, when maize or cherry suited her brilliant brunette beauty so much better; and Alberta placidly adding that she herself would have preferred pale blue or mauve as more becoming to her blond complexion. Erminie made no objection to the uniform, which was perfectly adapted to her blooming loveliness; and Bruomarte was too indifferent to the subject to join in the conversation. But when their talk turned upon matters of secondary importance, namely love and marriage, and they had talked a great deal of nonsense thereupon, then Britomarte broke forth with the words that opened this story.

"Are you right, dear Britomarte?" questioned Erminie, lifting her soft, sunny, hazel eyes to the face of the speaker, with a loving, deprecating reverence, as though asking pardon for doubting that any word of her oracle could be less authoritative than those of Holy Writ. "Are you quite sure that you are perfectly right?"

"I am," answered Britomarte, firmly.

"But is not man's law of marriage founded upon God's?" timidly persisted Erminie, laying her hands upon the lap of her idol.

"No! Those who say that it is, repeat a falsehood, invented by man and inspired by Satan! The law of marriage founded on the law of God, indeed! There is not a line or a word in the books of Moses or the gospels of Christ to justify the base assertion! Pray, were the glorious women of the Old Testament, Sarah, Rebecca, Rachel, Esther, Deborah, Judith, Jael—women who ruled with men—had talked with God and His angels—or were the divine women of the New Testament, Mary, Elizabeth, Anna—the mother of the Christ, the mother of the Baptist, the Prophetess of the Temple—were any of these, I say, the mere nonentities that man's laws makes of married women? Never! And more I say! Any man who approves of the present laws of marriage that take away a married woman's property and liberty, and even legal existence—any man, I say, who approves those laws is a despot and despoiler at heart, and would be a robber and murderer if the fear of prisons and scaffolds did not hold him in restraint! And any woman who disapproves these laws, yet dares not express her disapproval, is a slave and coward who deserves her fate!"

"Britomarte, dear, how warm you are. Your cheeks are quite flushed. Take my fan and try not to get so excited," said Alberta, coolly, presenting a pink and spangled toy to the ardent amazon.

"How can I be cool? I cannot, I will not want it,"

answered Britomarte, waving away the proffered article.

"But, Britomarte, love," murmured Erminie, leaning upon the champion's lap, and lifting her soft hazel eyes to the champion's proud face, with that appealing gaze with which the loving plead with the fiery, "Britomarte, darling, 'Wives, obey your husbands,' are the words of Holy Writ!"

With an impatient gesture Britomarte pushed off her worshiper, exclaiming:

"Paul said that! He was a dry old lawyer, a bookworm and a bachelor! What did he know about it? And besides, if he had been like Jacob, a married man with two wives, and two handmaids, and twelve children, I would not take the word of the old apostle any more than I would that of a modern preacher, unsupported by the law of Moses and the gospel of Christ! And man's legislation upon marriage has been guided neither by law nor gospel!"

"Bosh!" exclaimed Elfie, whom neither pastors nor masters had been able to break of the use of slang. "Let the poor wretches make all the laws in their own favor, if it amuses or helps to deceive them. They like it, and it don't hurt us! We needn't trouble our heads to keep their laws, you know! Let who will bother themselves about women's rights, so we have our own way! And anything we can't bluster or coax out of our natural enemy ain't worth having! Why, law! girls, the creatures are easily enough managed when you once get used to them! Why, there are no less than three governors at Sunnyslopes—one pap and two uncles; but who do you think, now, rules the roost at Sunnyslopes?"

"You do, when you are at home," suggested Britomarte.

"You better believe it, my dear! Why, law, girls, I can wind pap and uncles round my finger as easily as I can this blade of grass," said Elfie, suiting the action to the word with a mischievous sparkle in her bright black eyes.

"Well, for my part," said the fair Alberta, coolly playing with the

ever I shall be engaged to be married, it will, of course, be to the proper sort of person. And papa will see that proper settlements are drawn up between us, and that my own fortune is settled upon myself to spend as I please. In that way I shall secure all the rights I care about. I must have a splendid establishment, with costly furniture, and carriages, and horses, and servants, and dresses and jewelry, and unlimited pocket money. And so that I have all that, my husband may do all the voting and make all the laws for both of us."

"Yes!" exclaimed Britomarte, bitterly, "it is you and such as you, Alberta, that retard the progress of woman's emancipation! If there were no willing slaves, there could be no successful tyrants! You are quite willing to sell your liberty for lucre—to become a slave, so that your chains and fetters be of gold!"

"Yes, these ornaments are rather like handcuffs, are they not?" said Alberta, slightly raising her eyebrows as she displayed the priceless diamond bracelets on her wrists. "But I do not see the justice of your words, Britomarte, since I certainly do not intend to sell my hand for money, but only to have my own inherited fortune settled upon myself."

"For which simple price of justice you are willing to concede your most sacred civil and political rights!"

Alberta shrugged her shoulders "I don't know what you mean," she said. "I speak to you of pocket money, and you answer me with politics. Bah! why should I care, so that I have a fortune to spend independent of my future husband? For just think what a trouble it would be to have to ask him for money every time I wanted to go shopping!"

"Oh! a horrid nuisance! I think I shall follow your example, Alba! I shall get pap to settle the niggers, and the money, and the old blind mare, and all the rest of the personal on me by myself, so that my natural enemy, whenever I shall fall into his hands, can't take it from me. In return for which I will promise to keep in my sphere, and not run for constable nor Congress," said Elfie.

"You are bad if as far as you " " " Britomarte, earnestly, "but you don't go far enough. A girl with property is often married only for that property. And if her husband should be a prodigal and squander it, and bring her to want, or if he should be a miser and hoard it, and deprive her of the comforts of life, she has no redress. Therefore, it is well that a woman's property should be settled upon herself, and that she should be independent of her husband, at least as far as money can make her so. What do you say, my dear?" she inquired, turning to Erminie.

Erminie hesitated, the bright bloom wavered on her cheeks, and then deepened into a vivid blush. She dropped her long-fringed eyelids over her soft eyes, and answered, gently:

"I am glad I am not rich; very glad that I have nothing at all of my own. Now I go to my dear father for everything I want, and it is sweet to receive it from his hands; for he never refuses me anything he can afford to give, and I never ask him for anything he cannot spare."

And the Lutheran minister's daughter paused thoughtfully, as if in some tender reminiscence of her absent parent.

"But we are not talking about papas—we are talking about hubs," exclaimed Elfie, impatiently. "We are cussing and discussing the best means of offense and defense against our natural enemies, meaning our future hubs—poor wretches!"

"I know," said Erminie, gravely.

Then, turning her soft eyes, that had strange mesmeric power in their steady tenderness, upon the face of Britomarte, she continued:

"And, as I am not rich, as I have nothing at all of my own, no one will ever marry me for anything else but affection. And, as I find it so sweet to depend on my dear father, who loves me, I shall find it very sweet also to depend on another who shall love me—ah! if only half as well as he does!"

"I hope you will remain with your father, my darling. Fathers may be trusted with their daughters—sometimes. The same cannot be said of lovers or husbands," said Britomarte, earnestly, and laying her hand caressing upon the bright head that leaned against her bosom. "Yes, I hope you will never commit that spiritual suicide of which I spoke."

Erminie gently lifted her head from her queen's bosom—every motion of the fair girl was gentleness itself—again she hesitated, and the bloom wavered on her face and settled into an intense blush, as she softly said:

"I do not agree with you, dear Britomarte I cannot. Nor do I like discussions on this subject. It seems sacrilegious to speak so irreverently of the holiest mysteries in nature, for such, indeed, I deem love and marriage; and it seems like unveiling the holy of holies in one's own sacred bosom to give one's thoughts and feelings about them. Still, when that, which to me is a divine truth, is assailed even by you, dear Britomarte, I must defend it, if necessary, by laying bare my own heart."

"Defend it, then, my love. Come on! I shall mind your fencing about as much as I should the pecking of an excited turtle dove," said the amazon, with an indulgent smile.

Yet again the bloom wavered and flickered on Erminie's sensitive cheek as she murmured, softly:

"I have been thinking of all you have said this morning; I have been listening to my heart, and it has told me this: To lose self in the one great vital love a true wife finds in a true husband is not moral suicide, as you say, but the passing into another life—a double life—deeper, sweeter, more intense, and more satisfying than any known alone. To be content to be guided by his wisdom, and upheld by his strength, and comforted by his love—to have no will but his will, which she makes her own—this is not to be a nonentity, or weak, or silly, or childish, but to be identical with the husband's greater life—to be wise, strong, womanly. She passes into his life, becomes part and parcel of it. In losing herself she finds herself; in giving herself away she receives herself again —transfigured! Oh! Britomarte, I am not intellectual like y   ly tells me, that the true wife and the true husband are one—one being on this earth, as they will be one angel in heaven," said the gentle girl, forgetting her timidity in her enthusiasm.

"Bosh!" cried Elfrida Fielding, in disgust, tearing and throwing away the withes of grass she had been winding around her fingers, emblematically of her method of managing natural enemies.

"Bah!" yawned Alberta Goldsborough, shrugging her shoulders.

"Have you seen many such unions in your short life, Erminie?" gravely inquired Britomarte.

"No, I have not; but I know that all unions should be such! As for myself, I do not think I shall ever love; but I do know that I shall never marry unless I shall be sought by one whom I can love with all my heart, and soul, and spirit; whom I can honor almost as I honor my Creator; and I can obey in word and deed, with such perfect assent of my will and understanding, that to obey his will shall be to have my own way!—one who shall be to me the life of my life, the arbiter of my fate, almost my God! Yes, that is what I feel I want, and nothing else in the universe will satisfy me! That is what every true woman wants, and nothing else in the universe will satisfy her! Oh! Britomarte—you who are woman's champion—you greatly bewray woman when you ascribe to the coercion of coarse human laws that divine self-abnegation and devotion which is the instinct and inspiration of her own heart!" exclaimed Erminie.

"The dove pecks sharply—her little peaks are keen," said Britomarte, smiling. Then, speaking more gravely, she added: "Women might be such angels, my darling, if men were such gods; but you will find few women willing to be so devoted, and fewer men to deserve such devotion. Men do not believe in women's voluntary self-abnegation, and hence they coerce them by what you call coarse human laws, by what I call unjust, despotic, egotistical laws. I return to my point, darling. I hope that you will never marry."

"I do not think I ever shall, since it is likely

that I shall ever meet with any one such as I have described," said Erminie.

"Oh, no, that you will not, my dear," said Elfie; "but you will think you have met such a prodigy, and that will be all the same to you. You will some day run against some commonplace John Thompson or Tom Johnson whom you will take for a Crichton or a Bayard. You are booked for a grand passion, my dear. It is in your system and it must come out. It would kill you if it was to strike in. I pity you, poor child, for that thing don't pay. I know all about it; I've been all along there!"

"You, Elfrida?" exclaimed Alberta, with unusual interest, for her.

"Yes, me, 'Elfrida!' You had better believe it!"

"Tell us all about it."

"I am going to. Well, you see when pap first brought me to this school to finish my education, we stopped in the city a few days to fit me out and show me the sights. One night he took me to see an opera. Hush, girls! I never was inside of an opera house before in my life; and you better believe I was dazzled by the splendor and magnificence around me, and found quite enough to do to gape and stare at the gorgeous decorations of the house and the beautiful dresses of the ladies, until the curtain rose. Then, whip your horses! The opera was 'Lucia di Lammermuir,' and the part of Edgar Ravenswood was performed by Signior Adriano di Bercelloni."

At the mention of that name Britomarte became attentive.

"Now, whether it was the jaunty bonnet, with the heron's feather, or the crimson tartan plaid, or the black velvet tunic coat, or the white cross-gartered hose and buskins, or the music, or the man, or all together, I don't know; but I fell over head and ears in love with Edgar Ravenswood. Heavens! how I adored him! Don't frown, Britty. And, ah! how I hated Lucia, who had the divine happiness of being wooed in strains of heavenly music by Edgar Ravenswood! And on! how ardently I̶ a great prima donna, and play Lucia to that exalted being, Edgar. Alba, if you smile that way I'll bite you."

"How did it end?" inquired Ermmie.

"I'm going to tell you, Minie. I went home with my head in a whirl; I had Bercelloni on the brain. Pap wanted me to come into the dining room and take some supper. But faugh! After the divine life of music, buskins, love, heron's feather, romance and Ravenswood, the mere idea of eating was revolting to the last degree! But I made pap promise to take me to the opera the next night. 'Why, daughter, you are music mad,' he said. 'I am very fond of music, pap,' I answered. Law girls! he believed it was only the music! Our paps are very simple-minded people. Or else they have learned so much wisdom in their age that they have forgotten all they knew in their youth. Don't you think so, Alba?"

"Yes, but never mind about the old gentleman. Tell us of the signior."

"Well, instead of feasting on a vulgar supper, I went to bed to feast on memories of the divine life of the opera and on hopes of living it over again on the next evening. Ah! how I worshiped the Signior Bercelloni! Ah! how I detested the Signiora Colona! Ah! how I aspired to be a famous prima donna! I felt capable of dying for Bercelloni, of choking Colona, and of running away from pap to become a prima donna. I was in the last stage of illusion, hallucination, mania! Don't glower at me so, Britty! or I can't go on. Ah! if our paps did but know, it is not always safe to take every one of us to such places!"

"Indeed, it is not!" exclaimed Britomarte, so earnestly, so bitterly, so regretfully, with so dark a shadow overhanging her face, that little Elfie paused and gazed at her in dismay, faltering:

"Why, Britty, what is the matter? Surely, you never——"

"No, no," said Britomarte, recovering herself with an effort, "I was never at an opera. Go on. How did it end?"

"How did it end? As a Court of Jew's rock ends,

of course. It streamed up from the earth a blazing meteor, aspiring to the heavens! It fell down to the ground a blackened stick, to be trodden under foot!"

"Ah!" sighed Erminie, in a voice full of sympathy.

Elfie laughed, and went on:

"But to leave the hifaluting and come down to the common. It was very late when I got up next morning, and pap was as late as I was. And when we sat down to the breakfast table we found a party sitting opposite to us who were as late as we were. I didn't look at them. I was still in a dream, living in memories of the past evening and hopes of the coming one. In so deep a dream, that I didn't know whether I was breakfasting off an omelette or stewed kid gloves, until pap stooped and whispered to me: 'Daught., there's Signior Adriano di Bercelloni sitting opposite to us.' I woke from my dream and raised my eyes to see. Was it Bercelloni? I looked and looked again before I could be sure. Yes, it was he! But oh! my countrymen, what a change was there! How like, yet how unlike my gorgeous hero of the evening before! His head was bald! his face was bloated! his form was round! Ugh! His eyes were red! his nose was blue; his teeth were yellow—ugh! ugh! He had a great plate of macaroni and garlic before him and a great spoon in his hand, with which he shoveled the mess down his throat, as a collier shovels coal into a cellar—faugh! Whatever he had done to himself to make him look so differently on the stage I don't know. But the sight of him *au natural* made me sick and cured me."

"And so that is the end of the story?" inquired Alberta.

"No, not quite. On one side of him sat a swarthy, scrawny signiora, who was the wife of his 'buzzum.' And on the other sat an equally swarthy and scrawny signorina, who was the lovely pledge of their wedded affections. And that's not all either, Alba. That evening pap said, 'Well, daught., shall we go to the opera to see the Signior Bercelloni play 'Fra Diavolo?' I answered, 'Thank you, pap. I had rather not.' And so we went to church instead to hear the celebrated Rev. Mr.—What's-his-name? Law! you know who I mean."

"Did you fall in love with him?" inquired Alberta.

"Not as I know of! He may have had 'a very beautiful spirit,' as some of his admirers say, but, if so, it was clothed with a very unattractive person. Next day pap brought me here to school, and I have been here ever since, except when I have gone home for the holidays. Now, sisteren, I have given in my experience at this love feast for the benefit of Sister Erminie Rosenthal, and I hope she will profit by it. And now, I think, that is all."

Alberta and Erminie laughed, but Britomarte looked very grave as she said

"No, Elfrida, that is not all. I have a sequel to your story, but I will not tell it to you now. I will tell you this, however: The old glutton who revolted your taste at the breakfast was Signior Adriano di Bercelloni, the elder, and the father of Signior Adriano di Bercelloni, the younger, whom you saw play Edgar Ravenswood."

As Britomarte spoke, Elfie gazed at her with open eyes and mouth in silent amazement.

"They have the same name, and they bear a strong personal resemblance to each other, modified by the difference of age and temperament; but they never play the same parts. How could you imagine, my dear, that there could be any arts of the toilet, or effect of the stage, that could transfigure that coarse old creature into the hero of an opera?"

"I don't know. I thought toilet arts, and stage effects, were almost miraculous. But what astounds me is the cunning of the gay old receiver, my pap! Now, I wonder if he didn't see my infatuation from the beginning! I wonder if he didn't show me the old one, and let me deceive myself, on purpose?"

"Of course, he did," opined Alberta

"But how came you to know anything about them— so much about them, I may say, Britty, dear?" Elfie inquired.

"I said I had a sequel to your story; but I cannot tell it now," replied Britomarte, very gravely. Then, after a thoughtful pause, she added: "I think it wrong—oh! very wrong—in parents and guardians to take young, inexperienced, impressible girls to such places. If they love music, let them have as many concerts as they please, but no operas, and no plays—except, perhaps, a few of Shakespeare's best historical plays."

"How old are you, Britomarte?" suddenly inquired Alberta.

Britomarte paused as though she could scarcely answer that question at a moment's warning; and then she answered:

"I am eighteen. Why?"

"You talk as if you were eighty—that's all."

"I have had enough to age me," said Britomarte, putting Erminie's caressing arms from her neck, and rising, and walking away, as if to conceal, or overcome, some strong and deep emotion.

"Britomarte speaks bitterly," said Elfie, in amazement.

"She has good reason to do so," replied Alba, meaningly.

"What reason?" inquired Elfie and Erminie, in a breath.

"Law! don't you know? Have you never heard?"

"No."

"Then I don't know whether I ought to tell it. It seems unfair to do so. It seems, indeed, like speaking ill of her family behind her back. She might not like it," said Alberta, hesitating.

"Then, don't do it," urged Erminie.

"Do!" insisted Elfie.

"Well, you see, I never knew a word of it myself until last Easter holidays, when I was home on a visit, and heard it by the merest accident. For you know she never mentions a word about her family."

"No, never; except sometimes to allude to the maiden aunt who pays her school bills. But do tell me! Is it anything bad?" eagerly inquired Elfie.

"Yes, very," replied Alberta, with a shudder.

"And to think you should have known the secret

ever since last Easter and kept it from us!" exclaimed Elfie, with a reproachful look.

"You see I kept it to myself for her sake," explained Alberta, with an apologetic smile.

"Keep it so still, Alberta," earnestly urged Erminie. "If you have become possessed of any secret that you think Britomarte would not like to have divulged, it would be disloyalty to your friend to divulge it."

"Bosh! It is all among friends, so what's the harm? Go on, Alberta. I am on thorns until I hear all about it. Was it a murder, or a forgery, or a bigamy, or an elopement, or an—or what was it?" eagerly questioned Elfie.

"It was neither of these. It was something far more— Where are you going, Erminie?" Alberta suddenly broke off in the middle of her sentence to ask of her fair companion, who had risen and was walking away.

"I am going out of hearing of a secret that my friend might not like me to know," answered the true-hearted girl, leaving Alberta to tell Britomarte's mystery to her only willing listener.

CHAPTER II

THE MAN-HATER'S LOVER

ERMINIE sauntered slowly down the winding footpath leading through the magnolia grove to the acacia avenue, on the banks of the river. She had not gone far when, a few paces in advance of her she saw Britomarte walking alone.

Not wishing to intrude on the amazon in her dark hour, Erminie was turning away, when Britomarte by some means became aware of her presence, and looked back with an expression of ineffable tenderness, and beckoned her to approach.

The gentle girl went to the brilliant amazon's side, and was encircled by her arm.

"Thanks for letting me come, dear Britomarte," she

murmured, lifting her soft, hazel eyes to meet the gaze of the splendid dark-gray orbs that were shining down upon her.

"My bonny love, I never wish to avoid you. In my darkest hour you are ever welcome to me," answered the man-hater, in the soft tone and with the sweet smile she ever used in addressing this best-beloved of her soul.

"Thank you! Thank you, dearest Britomarte!" Erminie exclaimed, kissing the hand of her friend. But, then growing grave, she added, "Oh, my dearest love, I am so sorry you are such an intense man-hater! Your wholesale hatred makes you so unjust! It is the one dark spot on the bright disc of your clear, warm, strong, sunlike nature! All men are not brutes, dearest Britomarte."

"Then they are imbeciles! There is but one division."

"What! Do you mean that all men are either brutes or idiots?"

"All!"

"Oh! Britomarte, how can you—can you—say so, dearest? You had a father!"

Dark as a thundercloud grew the beautiful face of the amazon; harsh, curt and strange were the words of her reply.

"Yes; I had a father with little claim upon my love, and less upon my honor. Never name him to me again."

Erminie was appalled.

Britomarte stopped in her walk and sat down at the foot of a tree, as if overshadowed by some dark destiny.

Erminie sank down at her feet and laid her head on her lap.

Both were silent for a time, and the only sounds that broke the stillness were the whispering of the leaves above their heads, the hum of the insects around them, and the ripple of the river below.

Erminie began to sob softly, while Britomarte laid her hand gently on her pet's head.

"Britomarte, dearest, I am sorry that I hurt you; I

would not have done it for a kingdom, if I had known it."

"I am sure you would not, darling!—sure you would not! Say no more about it, love; but tell me of your own father, who cannot come under my severe category because I do not know him; and tell me of that wonderful brother whom you idolize so much, and whom I have never seen."

"My father and my brother," murmured the minister's daughter, as at the memory of cherished home affections—"my dear father and dear brother! Ah! Britomarte, if you had known them you would never have been a man-hater! When you do know them you will cease to be one!"

"Then a miracle will be performed," said the beauty. "But tell me, are they coming to the commencement?"

"I am not sure. That is to say, I know that one of them will come to fetch me home, for my father wrote to say so; but I am not sure which. Perhaps both may come. I hope they may. I want my dear father to be present to-day. A triumph is no triumph to me unless he witnesses it; and oh! I am so impatient to see my dear brother. I have not seen him, you know, since he left us, five years ago, for Gottingen."

"Your brother is studying for holy orders, I think you told me."

"Oh, yes. He has a genuine call to the ministry of the gospel if ever any man had one in this world. He has sacrificed the most brilliant prospects of earthly success to obey that call."

"How is that, my dear?"

"Oh, why you know he is my father's only son, and except myself, his only child, for there are but two of us, my brother and myself. Justin is ten years older than I am, however, since I was but sixteen in May, and he will be twenty-six in August."

"Yes; but about the sacrifice he made, my dear?"

"I am telling you. My dear brother and myself are the only children of the house of Rosenthal. My father's family is not what is called a marrying family. Father has two bachelor brothers, who are the great woolen importers. Uncle Friedrich has the Berlin house and Uncle Wilhelm the New York house. They offered to take Justin into the business, and bring him up as their successor, but he felt this call to preach the gospel, and he declined their offer."

"It was a great sacrifice," said Britomarte.

"It was; but our dear father encouraged him to make it. Oh, there are very few like our father; and Justin is worthy to be his son! He has come home to stay now! And he is to be ordained this coming autumn! Oh, Britomarte, you must come and visit them, and go with me to see his ordination."

"I shall be pleased to do so, my dear! Listen! Yes, the bell is ringing! We must go and take our places on the platform. I suppose many of the friends of the pupils have arrived. What a pity it is they cannot see their charges until after the ceremonies," said Britomarte, rising to retrace her steps towards the college buildings.

"Yes; it is a pity; but I suppose their earlier meeting is prohibited to prevent confusion and delay. I saw Alba's parents roll by in their open barouche as I came down here. And there are Elfie's father and two uncles riding up on horseback. And my dear father and brother, or both, will be here presently. But, Britomarte, who is coming for you?"

"No one. No one ever does come, nor do I wish that any should. I am contented, darling."

"You are self-reliant! But, dear Britomarte, I will be near you, so do remember that one will watch your ordeal with as much interest as father, mother, sister and brother, all combined, could do; and will mourn over your defeat, or rejoice over your victory, more than over her own."

"I do believe it, my darling! And therefore I take pleasure in assuring you that you shall have cause only for rejoicing. I shall achieve a victory, Erminie."

"Yes! I never doubted that! I was always sure of that. What is your theme, dear Britomarte? You will not object to tell me, now that the reading is so near."

"My

at any period, if you had asked me to do so. My theme is the 'Civil and Political Rights of Woman.'"

"What a tremendous subject! Britomarte, dear, you will be sent to Coventry by all the professors."

"Perhaps! But do you think I shall go there?" laughed the beauty.

By this time they were approaching the college through the roseries, as the terraces, adorned principally with these beautiful flowers, were called. On the upper terrace they made a turn to the left, to avoid the carriages that were continually rolling up to the front entrance, depositing their freights and rolling off again.

The two friends entered a side door, and found themselves in a large ante-room, in which were assembled all their schoolmates in the festive school uniform of pure white muslin dresses, pink ribbons and rose wreaths.

And among them walked Alba Goldsborough, the blond beauty and wealthy heiress, and Elfrida Fielding, the bright little brunette country girl. These two girls walked apart, with their arms around each other's waists, conversing in confidential whispers.

"They are still talking of Britomarte!" said Erminie, indignantly to herself, and as she looked at them her suspicion was confirmed; for as soon as they saw her with Britomarte they ceased to talk, and began to look embarrassed. But before the quartet of friends could meet, the great folding doors, separating the ante-room from the exhibition hall, were thrown open, and two of the teachers appeared to marshal the pupils to the scene of their approaching ordeal.

Promptly and quietly they fell into line and marched into the hall—a spacious room of the Corinthian order of architecture, fitted up as a temple of the muses—the nine muses being represented by nine statues supporting the arches separating the platform from the part of the hall occupied by the audience.

This platform was provided with rows of benches covered with crimson cloth, for the accommodation of the pupils.

Up the side stairs leading to this platform the line of pupils marched. They seated themselves on the benches in good order, and then surveyed the scene before them.

The hall was crowded with a large number of spectators, among which were to be seen distinguished learned professors, noted preachers and the heads of neighboring colleges. But the great mass of the audience consisted of the parents and guardians, friends and relatives of pupils and teachers

Alberta Goldsborough, the wealthy heiress, recognized her stately papa and fashionable mamma, and saluted them with a cold, young-ladyish bow as she sank into her seat.

Elfrida descried, seated away back in an obscure corner, the three honest country gentlemen whom she saucily designated "one pap and two unks." And she audaciously kissed her hand to them with a loud smack as she popped into her place.

Erminie discerned, near the middle of the crowd, her revered father and idolized brother, and exchanged with them a bow and smile of recognition and joy. But, oh, fate of Tantalus though she had not seen her father for ten months, nor her brother for five years, she could not either approach or speak to them; she could not even turn to Britomarte and point them out; she could only bow and smile, for silence and decorum were rigidly enforced upon the pupils on the commencement day at Bellemont College.

Britomarte, with her sad eyes wandering over the assemblage, saw not one familiar face. But Britomarte was almost alone in the world.

The ceremonies of the day began.

Now, as there is nothing in this wearisome world half so wearisome to an uninterested spectator as a school exhibition or a college commencement, and as this anniversary at Bellemont partook of both characters, I will spare my readers the details of the proceedings and discuss the whole affair with as few words as possible.

Professors preached and pupils prosed on the platform; visitors fanned themselves vigorously, or yawned behind fans of every description, from the plain palmleaf to the scented sandalwood, in the hall.

Teachers and scholars were alike in the highest state of exultation and—the deepest degree of fatigue.

The audience politely pronounced the affair to be very interesting and—heartily wished it over

In fact the exercises of the day were only redeemed from the most ordinary monotony by the reading of Britomarte Conyers' theme—"The Civil and Political Rights of Woman."

At Bellemont College the themes were not read by the writers, because in that immaculate institution it was deemed unladylike for a young lady to stand upon a platform before a mixed audience and read her own composition aloud, and it was also thought that the embarrassment which a young writer would be likely to feel in such a position would seriously mar the delivery and detract from the effect of her theme. So it was arranged that all the themes should be read aloud by the professor of elocution to the institution, whose highly cultivated style would certainly improve the poorest composition, and do full justice to the richest He "lent to the words of the poet the music of his voice."

He read with great effect Britomarte Conyers' essay on the "Civil and Political Rights of Woman," in which the author bravely asserted not only the rights of married women to the control of their own property and custody of their own children, but the rights of all women to a competition with men in all the paths of industry and a share with them in all the chances of success—in the mechanical arts, in learned professions, in commercial business, in municipal and national government, in the camp, the field, the ship; in the Senate, in the Cabinet, on the Bench, and in the Presidential chair. She supported her argument with the names and examples of the noteworthy women of all ages and countries—women, who, in despite of the obstacles of law, precedent and prejudice, had distinguished themselves in every field of enterprise ever j   d l   clear, warm, strong, brilliant article; and, like all works of genius, it received an almost equal share of enthusiastic praise and extravagant blame. It was excessively admired for the strength, beauty and ingenuity of its argument, and bitterly censured for the heterodoxy of its doctrines.

Among those who listened to the reading was Justin Rosenthal, the brother of Erminie, who, seated beside his father, gave the most earnest attention to the argument.

At its conclusion, he turned to the elder Rosenthal, and said:

"That is the most original, outspoken and morally courageous assertion of right against might that has been made since the immortal Declaration of Independence! And that it should have been written by a schoolgirl seems almost incredible. A rare, fine spirit—a pure, noble heart—a clear, strong intellect she has. I wonder who she is?"

"I do not know," replied Dr. Rosenthal, for Erminie's father was a D. D.—"I do not know; but I do know that her argument, though ingenious, is wrong from beginning to end."

Later on was announced the name of the successful candidate for the medal to be awarded for the best English theme. The medal was awarded to Britomarte Conyers, for her essay on the "Civil and Political Rights of Woman."

"Britomarte Conyers, then, is the author of that theme you admire so much, and is the young lady you are so curious to see. I congratulate you, Justin! Miss Conyers is your sister's most intimate friend. You will have an opportunity not only of seeing her, but of forming her acquaintance under the most auspicious circumstances," said Dr. Rosenthal.

"Nay," smiled Justin, "I do not know that I care to follow up any such acquaintance with the young champion of womankind. I merely wish to see and judge her as a rather singular specimen of her sex."

It was at the school ball of the evening that Justin Rosenthal was presented to Britomarte Conyers, whose personal beauty and grace made as deep an impression on his heart as her genius had made upon his mind. At the same time and place Colonel Eastworth, a distinguished son of South Carolina, was introduced to Erminie. And thus two of our young friends met the persons who were destined to exercise the most powerful influence over their futre lives.

The next morning the school broke up for the midsummer holidays, and the pupils went their several ways. Elfrida Fielding went with her father and uncles to Sunnyslopes. Alberta Goldsborough accompanied her parents to the Rainbows, their waterside villa. And the Rosenthals, with Colonel Eastworth and Britomarte Conyers, embarked on the steamer bound for Washington.

CHAPTER III

A MYSTERIOUS LETTER

The barouche containing Dr. Rosenthal and his party reached the steamer in such good season that the two young ladies had time to go down into the cabin and choose their berths from among those left vacant, and to make all arrangements for their comfort during the voyage. They took two berths in a stateroom together, unpacked their traveling bags, laid their toilet articles in order upon the little shelf below the tiny looking-glass, and then returned to the deck.

They sat down on the side that still looked toward Bellemont College, whose white walls arose from amidst green foliage on the crest of a gentle hill at a short distance up the river. Half in joy at work accomplished and freedom gained, half in regret at leaving the school where they had been so happy for so many years, and teachers whom they had loved so well, the young friends gazed upon their late home.

The gentlemen of their party meanwhile walked up and down the deck, wondering when the steamer would start, and complaining of the impatience, and restlessness of their restless and impatient sex, until, as they passed near the two young ladies, Justin Rosenthal left his companions, and, with a bow and a smile, as if asking permission, or apologizing for taking it for granted, seated himself beside Miss Conyers.

Britomarte would have given a year of her life to have repressed the blush that mantled over her cheek and brow as Justin took the seat beside her.

His first words were well chosen to set her at ease.

"The scenery of James River is quite new to me, Miss Conyers. We came down from Washington by railroad to Richmond, and thence by stagecoach to Bellemont. I look upon this fine river for the first time," he said, not, as before, fixing his eyes upon her, but letting them rove over the bright waters of the James and the verdant hills beyond.

Britomarte only bowed in reply. She would have given another year of her life for the power of controlling the unusual tremor that seized her frame and made it dangerous to trust her voice for a steady answer in words.

Justin, still letting his eyes rove over the river, and rest here and there upon particular points of interest in the scenery, spoke of the beautiful effects of the shining light and shade as the clouds floated over the sun's disk and their shadows passed over the hills.

And Britomarte merely answered "yes" or "no," until, indignant at the influence that was growing upon her, she suddenly erected her haughty, little head with an impatient shake, and said:

That she could not appreciate the minutiæ of river scenery; that only the ocean in its grandeur and might could awaken her admiration.

At this moment Dr. Rosenthal called to his son, and Justin, with a bow, left the side of Britomarte.

"Why, Britty, dearest! I always thought you loved river scenery," said Erminie, when they were left alone together.

"So I do, as a general thing, but I don't care about it to-day," answered Miss Conyers.

"Well, Britty, dear, I never knew you to be capricious before."

"Nature has given me no immunitiy from the common weaknesses of humankind."

Erminie looked so hurt at the curtness of her friend's words and manner, that Britomarte suddenly took her hand and tenderly caressed it.

Erminie, touched by this new proof of love, was encouraged to press Britomarte to go home with her to the parsonage.

Miss Conyers caressed her and thanked her, but reiterated her resolution to go to Witch Elms.

"Ah! don't, ah! don't—don't go to that horrid place, dear Britomarte! You don't know what it is! They say—that the place is haunted."

"Of course, they say every isolated old country house is haunted."

"But—forgive me once again, dear Britomarte—are you expected or desired there?"

"I do not know. My old aunt has never written to me. The half-yearly payments for the schooling, for which I am indebted to her, always have been forwarded by her agent in Washington. On each occasion I have written to her a letter of thanks, but I have never received an answer."

Just then a boy rushed up with a letter for Britomarte.

She opened it wonderingly, and turned to the signature.

Her face was suddenly blanched to the hue of death, and she reeled, as though about to fall.

"Britomarte, dear Britomarte, what is it? Any bad news?" anxiously exclaimed Erminie.

But Miss Conyers raised her hand with a silencing gesture, and arose to go down below. She trembled so much as she moved, that Erminie started forward to attend her. But with a repelling motion the pallid girl stopped her friend, and hurried alone on her way.

All the morning the Thetis steamed down the river. At the dinner hour Erminie was very glad of the excuse to go down into the stateroom she occupied in common with Britomarte, to take off her bonnet and mantle, and brush her hair, to go to the public table.

She o

Miss Conyers was lying on the upper berth, with the curtains drawn down before her.

"Britomarte, dear Britomarte, how are you? Can I do anything for you?" murmured Erminie, stealing to the berth and cautiously lifting a corner of the curtain.

"No! don't speak to me' leave me!" was all that Miss Conyers replied, and in a voice so hoarse as to be nearly inaudible.

Pale with pity and with awe, Erminie dropped the curtain, and sank into the one chair their little den boasted.

She sat there quite still, and forgetting to prepare for dinner until the bell clanged out its invitation to the table and aroused her from her trance of trouble.

Then she hastily arose, threw off her bonnet, shook back her auburn ringlets, and hurried out to join her father and his friends, who were on their way to the dining-room.

Much concern was expressed by them that Miss Conyers was not able to come to dinner.

Once again in the course of that afternoon Erminie went to the stateroom to implore Britomarte to take some refreshment.

Then Miss Conyers suddenly drew the curtain back, and turned upon the intruder a face so pale and ghastly in its grief and horror that Erminie shrank back appalled.

"Don't you see that it takes the whole power of my will to hold body and soul together until I get to New York?" she demanded, in a voice husky with suffering.

"To New York!" repeated the panic-stricken girl.

"Yes—I can do no more I cannot eat, or drink, or talk—much. I can only manage to live until I get there. Leave me."

"Oh! Heaven of heavens, what has happened to you, Britomarte!" exclaimed Erminie, as she turned, unwillingly, to leave the stateroom.

Miss Conyers did not divulge what had upset her, but pleaded headaches for absenting herself from the table. Erminie was much t cc t nor was she taken into the confidence of the sullen and solitary mourner.

In due time the Thetis landed at her pier at Washington.

And the great bustle of arrival ensued.

"My dear Miss Conyers," said Dr. Rosenthal, "I understand from my daughter that you have positively declined making us a visit; but now, at the last moment, let me prevail with you to make us all happy by consenting to go home with us at least for a day and night, if no longer, to rest before you go farther."

"I thank you very much—more than I can express But it is not in my power to accept your kind invitation. Urgent business compels me immediately to go to New York I know that a train leaves in an hour from this. And I must drive to the station instantly"

Miss Conyers embraced Erminie, who was bathed in tears, and then turned to shake hands with Mr. Justin Rosenthal.

But, raising his hat with a grave bow, Justin said:

"I will see you to the station. Eastworth and my father are a sufficient bodyguard to Erminie."

And before the beautiful man-hater could object, he had taken her hand and was leading her from the boat.

He placed her in a carriage, entered and took a seat by her side, and gave the order to drive to the Baltimore railway station.

All this was done in spite of Britomarte's tacit protest He did not, however, obtrude his conversation upon her. The drive was finished in silence.

On their arrival at the station, he procured her ticket, checked her baggage, and then placed her in one of the most comfortable seats in the ladies' car.

Even then he did not leave her, but remained stationed by her until the shrill, unearthly whistle of the engine warned him to leave.

Then, bending over her, he took her hand and whispered low

"Miss Conyers, I never utter vain or hasty words What I speak now, I speak earnestly from the depths of my heart. In me you have a friend through good report and time and eternity. I have never spoken these words to any human being before this; I never shall speak them to any other after this. Good-by; we shall meet again in a happier hour."

CHAPTER IV

THE WITCH OF WITCH ELMS

AFTER seeing Britomarte well on her way, Justin walked thoughtfully home to the parsonage.

Days passed; but no news came of Miss Conyers Eastworth remained at the parsonage, wooing the minister's daughter—never with compromising words, but with glances more eloquent and tones more expressive than words could ever be. For if his words were only, "The days is beautiful," his tone said, "I love you!" his glance said, "For you are more beautiful than the summer's day." And Erminie! how entirely she believed in him; how devotedly she loved him; how disinterestedly she worshiped him.

"If I could in any way add to his fame, or honor, or happiness, how blessed I should be! And oh! if he should go away without ever telling me what I could do to please him, how wretched I should become! Ah! he may meet more beautiful, more accomplished and more distinguished women in the great world than ever I can hope to be; but he will never meet with one who could love him more than I do!"

Such reveries as these, scarcely taking the form of words, even in her thoughts, engaged the young girl constantly.

In the midst of this trouble came letters from the Goldsboroughs. One from Papa Goldsborough to Papa Rosenthal, inviting him, his family and his guest to come down to the Rainbows on a visit for the season; and another from Alberta to Erminie, urging her to use her influence with her father to induce him to accept the invitation and be at the Rainbows to spend the approaching Fourth of July.

No interference on the part of Erminie was needed.

Dr. Rosenthal, with the concurrence of his son and his guest, wrote to Mrs. Goldsborough to say that he and his party would be at the Rainbows on the evening of the third proximo. And as this letter was dated on the thirtieth of June, there were but two days left to prepare for the journey.

As soon as this letter was written and posted and fairly on its way, Ermmie went to look for her brother in the library, where, in study, he passed his mornings.

"Justin, do I interrupt you?" she inquired, in a deprecating tone, as she opened the door and found him at his books.

"No, my dear, you never do," replied Justin, closing the volume in his hand and drawing forward a chair for his sister.

"Justin, I want you to do something for me this afternoon, please," she said, as she seated herself.

"What is it, dear?"

"Oh, Justin, it is now four weeks since Britty went away, and we have heard nothing from her, and we do not know where to address her."

"Well, my dear?"

"And to-morrow evening we start for the Rainbows, to be absent from the city for the whole remainder of the season."

"Yes."

"But, Justin, I cannot, indeed I cannot bear to go away without first trying to find out something about my dear Britomarte."

"Well?"

"And so I wish you, if you please, to get a carriage and take me across Bennings Bridge to Witch Elms, to ask about her."

Justin could refuse his sister nothing, so the carriage was ordered and Witch Elms was reached after a tedious drive through a heavy rainstorm. The entrance was stoutly barred, but the travelers were at last admitted and shown into a wide parlor, the door being instantly shut and locked upon them.

Justin, amazed by this proceeding, began to search around

The person who had admitted them had left them in total darkness, so it was no easy matter making one's way about. At last Justin came to a flight of stairs leading upward, and bidding his sister take his arm, they ascended.

On reaching the upper hall, Justin whispered:

"Listen; do you hear anything?"

There was an unmistakeable murmur proceeding from some dark room in their vicinity, and then an angry voice spoke aloud:

"Why, the foul fiend, then, didn't you take them in to see the old woman?"

The muttering voice made some reply, to which the loud voice responded:

"Bosh! What danger? That's all over now. The verdict of the coroner's inquest settled that. Suicide. Nothing more likely. After that there was nothing more to be said."

A blaze of lightning that flashed through every chink and crevice of the shut-up old house, and a crash of thunder that overwhelmed all other sounds, stopped the talk of the unseen companions.

Then the muttering voice was heard again, saying something offensive to the interlocutor, though inaudible to the listeners, for the loud voice replied:

"Drinking; no, I have not been drinking! At least not more than is good for me! The moment any one takes a deep breath and shows a little fearlessness, you think they've been—drinking! Go and look after the people you have left in the hall so long, and take them up to see the old woman. That is, if she wants to see them. You must humor her; but as for the girl——"

Again the murmuring voice intervened, but the loud voice broke in:

"I tell you she must be got out of the way! Now go look after these visitors below."

A sound of shuffling feet was heard, and Justin whispered to Erminie:

"Little sister, there's something wrong here, but we must not seem to have been listening." And, so saying, he hurried her down the stairs, as fast as the darkness would permit him to do with safety. Arrived at the foot, he waited some few minutes, and then he sang out as loud as he could:

"Hallo! waiter! porter! footman! major-domo! man-of-all-work! whatever or whoever you are! where are you? Come, let us in; or let us out!"

"I am here, set fire to you! Couldn't you be quiet for five minutes, while I was gone to tell the old lady?" answered a growling voice from the hall above. And at the same time a person, bearing a dim light, began to descend the stairs.

He was a man of about thirty years of age, of gigantic height; but with a small head, and closely-cut black hair, and a beardless, or else closely-shaven, dark-complexioned face; a man you would not like to meet on a lonely road on a dark night. He was dressed from head to foot in a closely-fitting suit of the dust-colored coarse cloth that has since become so well known as the uniform of the Confederate army.

"Couldn't you be easy for five minutes, while I was gone?" he growled, as he reached the foot of the stairs.

"Your minutes are very long ones, friend!" laughed Justin.

"You want to see the old lady, you say?"

"I wish to see Miss Pole."

"Come along, then," said the man, stopping to snuff the candle with his fingers, and then leading the way upstairs.

Justin, still holding his sister closely under his arm, reascended the stairs.

By the light of the candle carried by the man before him, he saw that this part of the old house seemed entirely unfurnished. The floors were bare and rough, and broken here and there, and the walls were disfigured by torn paper and fallen plastering.

This hall of the third story was neatly papered and comfortably carpeted, and well lighted by a small, clear lamp hanging from the ceiling. A large window at the end of this hall was also curtained.

The smooth-chinned giant in the dust-colored clothes opened the nearest door to the right, and said,

"Go in there."

With Erminie tucked under one arm, and his hat in his hand, Justin entered the room.

It was a neatly-furnished sitting-room, lighted, like the hall, by a small, clear lamp, hanging from the ceiling.

Under this lamp stood a large, round center-table, covered with flowered green cloth, and laden with books, bookmarks, hand-screens, smelling-bottles, a small open workbox, and, in short, all the paraphernalia of a lady's table.

Beside it, in a large resting-chair, with her feet upon a foot-cushion, reclined a very old lady, bent with age, and trembling with palsy. She was wrapped in a light-colored French chintz dressing-gown, and her shaking head was covered with a fine lace cap, whose deep borders softly shaded her silver hair and withered face.

"You've come to see me?" inquired the old lady, in a shrill and quivering voice.

"Yes, madam; I hope to see you in your usual health," said the young man, bending his head.

"To business, sir," snapped the old lady. "I suppose you come from Trent, my agent?"

"No, madam; I——"

"Then, what did you come for? I receive no visitors except upon business," interrupted the old lady, impatiently.

"Pardon us, madam. We are friends of your niece; and not having heard from her for some weeks, and being on the point of leaving the city for the season, we came here to inquire about her."

"About—whom?" demanded Miss Pole, in a shrill, impatient voice, as she began to tremble with excitement.

"Your niece, Miss Conyers."

Shaking violently, the old lady moved her hand to the bell and rang it.

The weird handmaid appeared.

"Nan, Nan, show these people downstairs, and tell Dole to see 'em out! and to mind how he sends unwelcome visitors to me again!" exclaimed the old lady, shaking more and more violently with growing excitement.

"I hope I have given you no cause for offense, madam," said Justin, deprecatingly.

"Offense! off—offense!" stammered the old lady, with her head nodding fast between palsy and anger. "How dare you mention the name of Britomarte Conyers in my presence?—a toad! a beast! a snake!" And at every epithet she spat with spite. "Show 'em out! show 'em out! show 'em out, Nan!"

"I am very sorry, madam, to hear you speak in this intemperate manner of your niece. I have the highest respect for Miss Conyers," said Justin, gravely.

"Go! go! go!" sputtered the old creature, letting fall her cane, and seizing a book, which, with all her trembling strength, she launched at the offender. But, of course, the missile fell wide of its mark.

Erminie, shocked, amazed and terrified, clung to the arm of her brother.

"I wish you a better spirit, Miss Pole," said Justin; and, bowing as courteously as if he were leaving the presence of a queen, who had conferred upon him a grace, he passed out of the room with his sister.

CHAPTER V

THE RAINBOWS

NEXT day the party sailed down the Chesapeake to the Goldsworths' seaside home, a beautiful spot on the eastern shore called the "Rainbows." Here they were received by Albert Goldsworth, who bade them a hearty welcome.

Erminie was surprised and delighted to learn that Elfrida Fielding and Britomarte Conyers had promised to join the party by the end of the week.

The meeting between Britomarte and Erminie was a very affecting one. Miss Conyers was clothed in deep mourning, but gave no reply to the inquiries made by the others respecting her life

When pressed by Erminie she simply said:

"Darling, I have lost some one; I have suffered; but my heart is not broken, else I should not be here. That is all that I can tell you, for there is good reason why I cannot tell you more. I hate mystery, my pet; but this mystery—and I acknowledge that it is one—is none of mine. Ask me no more."

Miss Conyers was certainly the most brilliant woman in the circle of beauties gathered together at the Rainbows. Nothing but her poverty, obscurity, and the mystery underlying her life, prevented her from being the belle of the seaside villa. But poor, obscure and even questionable as was her social position, she excited the admiration of the men, the jealousy of the women, and the interest of all.

Justin Rosenthal loved Britomarte Conyers with a depth and earnestness of affection and a singleness and persistence of purpose very rarely experienced in this world of many distracting attractions and conflicting interests.

To win her as his wife was just now the first object of his existence, an object which he determined to accomplish before he should undertake any other enterprise—so as to get the affair off his mind, he said, and also that they two might commence the work of the world together as man and woman should.

And Britomarte? Well, it would have been almost impossible for any other woman, and it was difficult even for her, to conceal from the deeply-interested, keenly-searching eyes of her lover the true state of her affections. Britomarte loved Justin; but she combated that love with all the strength of her strong will.

The summer was fading into autumn; the season was waning to its close; the guests at the Rainbows were preparing to leave—many being anxious to get back to town to be present at the milliners' great openings and examine the new styles in fall bonnets.

In truth, Mr. and Mrs. Goldsborough were not very sorry to see their party breaking up It had not, indeed, afforded them that full measure of satisfaction which their princely hospitality deserved. Two cir cumstances especially annoyed them—the growing friendship between their sole heiress, the fair Alberta, and the Signior Vittoria, a penniless young Italian professor, who was also a guest at the house, on the one hand, and the manifest attachment between their nephew Albert and Farmer Fielding's pretty daughter.

And very much relieved they were when the sensitive young Italian—who was neither adventurer nor fortune-hunter, nor willing to be considered such—feeling the social atmosphere near the presence of his entertainers rather chilly, took the hint that his welcome was worn out and bowed his adieus; and also when Farmer Fielding placed his little girl on her pony and carried her off to Sunnyslopes.

Elfrida had entreated Britomarte to go with her to her mountain home, urging that the country was ever most beautiful in the autumn, when all the woods were clothed in colors more gorgeous than the robes of Solomon in all his glory.

Miss Conyers had declined the invitation with thanks and with the explanation that her plans for the autumn were fixed.

So Elfrida, with a sigh, left her friend.

But what of Britomarte? Where would she go from this temporary home? Not certainly to Witch Elms, since there the doors were fast closed against her entrance. Where, then, could she go? What means had she to go anywhere? What, then, were the plans of which she spoke? And how would she carry them out? Who could tell? Not even her lover!

Justin knew well enough what his own plans were, and how he should carry them out.

Three days before the day appointed for his own party to leave the Rainbows, Justin sought a private interview with Britomarte. He knew where to find her; for by this time he was well acquainted with all her favorite haunts. It was late in the afternoon, and he was sure she would be found on "Lond's Rock," a point of land between Crystal Creek and Bennett's Bay, extending out into the Chesapeake—a solitary desert, though so near the peopled villa, and only frequen

So down a narrow path leading through the thick woods that lay below the house, he wandered till he came out upon the bluff overhanging the beach. Along the bushy bluff, now burnished bright in the late sunshine of the waning summer and the fading day, he went toward the tip of that long point, extending like a giant's arm out to the sea.

As he approached, he saw that she was sitting on the rock, with her hands clasped upon her knees, her face turned seaward, and her black dress was very conspicuous upon the glistening white stone at the extremity of the point.

So absorbed was she in thought that she remained totally unconscious of Justin's proximity until he picked up her bonnet, which had fallen to the ground, and handed it to her, saying:

"Excuse me, Miss Conyers, but the tide is creeping in, and, if left there, it will get wet; and even you, if you remain here much longer, may be cut off from return, for you must be aware that at high water this point of land is covered by the sea, with the exception of this rock, which, for the time, becomes an island."

"Thank you, Mr. Rosenthal. I know that; but there is an hour of grace left. Pray, did you come here to remind me that twice a day Lond's Rock becomes an isolated fastness?" said Miss Conyers, raising her large, brilliant, dark-gray orbs to his face.

"No, Miss Conyers; it was for something more serious—more important—more imminent, indeed, than that," said Justin, gravely, seating himself beside her. "It would be bad," he continued, "if the rising tide, before you should become aware of it, should cover the point and cut you off from the land, and leave you alone upon this rock for twelve hours of darkness; but the evil would be temporary. You are brave enough to overlive it, and the night would end in morning, and your road lie open for your return. Britomarte! dear Britomarte!—there is an isolation more to be dreaded for you, because more fraught with fatal consequences, than that I have named could be!" said Justin, trying to regulate the deep emotions of that passion which was thrilling in every inflection of his earnest voice. "Oh! Britomarte——"

"Hush! do hush, and go away!" she exclaimed, hastily interrupting him.

"No, no—I must speak! I have been silent long enough! Dear Britomarte, you must hear me now! You cannot have mistaken the meaning of my devotion to you in all the months we have passed together here. You——"

"Nor could you have failed to perceive that such devotion was very unacceptable to me! I thank you, of course. It was very complimentary to me, no doubt, and I—was very much honored, indeed. But, as I said before, it was unacceptable, and you must have perceived that it was so."

"Britomarte, I love you. Oh! that I could make you feel the real meaning of the phrase when uttered by truthful lips. All of life, or death—all of heaven or hell—seem to hang upon the words. I love you! Britomarte, from the first moment that I saw you, something in your face powerfully attracted me. It was not your beauty, dearest, though you are beautiful; it was something deeper than that. It was the soul looking from the face! I love you with my whole heart and soul, once and forever! And if it were possible that I should lose you, Britomarte, I should never love again! And now, lady, I have unveiled my heart before you. I love you as men loved in those old heroic days when for woman's smile solemn vows were made and deadly perils braved. Now tell me, dearest, dearest—what I can do to deserve——" His voice faltered for a single instant, and she took swift advantage of the pause to answer hastily, and even harshly.

"You can do nothing! I never can accept your suit! Pray, to begin with, are you aware that I am a girl of very obscure birth?"

"That is nothing to me, beloved——"

"That I have not a penny——"

"I have more than enough for both, Britomarte!"

"And, worse than all, that the shadow of a great shame is thought to rest upon my life!"

"How should that affect your personal merit, or my appreciation of it? Come, darling, come! I never can be less than your lover! let me be more! accept me for your husband!"

"For my master, you mean! that is what 'husband' signifies in your laws!" said the man-hater, coldly turning away, as once more Woman's Rights throttled and threw down woman's love.

"No! Heaven forbid! I could no more be a tyrant than I could be a slave! My soul abhors both! And if in your own soul there is one quality that attracts me more than all the others, it is your impassioned love of liberty. I sympathize with it, my beloved! I have no wish to rule over you as a master! I could not, indeed, endure the love of a slave! Or if one must serve, let it be the stronger. I wish only to cherish you as my beloved wife, to honor you as my liege lady! Come, darling!"

But Woman's Rights had her heel upon the neck of woman's love, and Britomarte coldly answered, as she walked away:

"I do not know, for my part, how, in this age and country, with the old barbarous laws of marriage still in force, any sane, honest man can look a woman in the face, and seriously ask her to be his wife! For their own honor, I wonder men do not set about and remodel their disgraceful laws before they do anything else! As for me, if these days were like the 'old heroic days' of which you just now spoke, when men braved deadly perils and wrought great works for woman's smile, I would have every woman lay upon her suitor the holy task of reforming the laws as the only possible condition of her favor!"

"I will take up the gauntlet you have thrown down," he said. "I will look into these offensive statutes that were made, by the by, some centuries before I was born, and for which, therefore, I do not see that I can be held individually responsible——"

"But you are responsible for them," warmly interrupted Britomarte. "Every man who lives under them, marries under them, sees women robbed and oppressed under them, without rising up to oppose them, is as much responsible for them as if he, and he only, had originally enacted them!"

"Granted that this is in a measure true! It shall be so with me no longer," smiled Justin "I will examine these, and wherever I conscientiously believe they need reform, I will labor zealously with pen and tongue to reform them. But, in the meantime, as I cannot give my whole mind to any subject—not even to that—until my heart is set at rest, Britomarte, dear Britomarte! be my wife! and we will labor together lovingly, zealously, in all good works!"

"I cannot! I will not! Do not ask me again! In the 'old heroic days,' you are so fond of quoting, a true knight performed his task before he ventured to sue for his reward."

"And then?—and then, Britomarte?"

"He did not always get it," answered the man-hater.

Justin bowed gravely to her and smiled quietly to himself.

They were walking away from Lond's Rock, where, indeed, they had already lingered too long; for the tide was now rising rapidly, threatening to cut off their retreat from the main.

CHAPTER VI

BRITOMARTE'S PLAN

"But what then will you do, my child? I am an humble minister of God, even in his beneficent aspect of Father to the fatherless. As such I invite your confidence; trust in me."

These words were spoken by the old Lutheran clergyman to the beautiful man-hater, as he bent kindly over her, holding her hand, on the morning after their departure from the Rainbows.

They were on board the Leviathan and within a few miles of Washington.

He had been urging upon her the oft-repeated, oft-rejected invitation to make his house her home. For the last time she gratefully declined the offered hospitality.

"But what then will you do, my child?" he resumed, seeing that she remained silent and thoughtful. "Your old grandaunt has most unnaturally renounced you; nor indeed, if she had not, would Witch Elms be a desirable home for you. The people that Miss Pole retains around her, and the rumors that are afloat about the place, make it particularly objectionable as a residence for a young girl."

"I will become a missionary," answered Britomarte, stoutly, and neither prayers nor commands could move her from this resolve.

The Board of Foreign Missions were in want of teachers to join a company of missionaries whom they were about to send out to Farther India, and she had made up her mind to offer her services.

Britomarte, after leaving Dr. Rosenthal, went down into the cabin to put up her effects, to be ready for landing.

Erminie was already there, engaged in making similar preparations; but as soon as she saw Britomarte she threw herself into her friend's arms and burst into a passion of tears. The prospect of separation from her queen was almost insupportable to the minister's gentle child.

"If it were only in pity for me, Britty, you might not leave me! I have no mother, nor sister, nor any one in the world but you! In mercy to me you might come with me!"

"My darling—no one? Why, you have your father, your brother, and your lover," said Miss Conyers, gently caressing her.

"Oh! I mean no woman! It is so sad for a girl to have no woman friend. I feel it so. And yet it is not for myself either that I grieve, but for you who have neither father, brother, nor lover, as I have!"

"No, thank Heaven!" exclaimed the man-hater, fervently; and then, with a softened manner, she added: "But about your lover, my darling, since you are afflicted with such a nuisance—tell me, before we part."

"Yes, I wished to do so. I have no secrets from you, dear Britomarte. Well, then—we—we are engaged," murmured Erminie, with hesitation and blushes.

"You and—Colonel Eastworth," muttered Britomarte, slowly and in dismay. "Erminie, darling, it is customary to congratulate a friend on these occasions; but I—I cannot do it."

"Oh, Britomarte! you will surely wish me joy!"

"With all my heart and soul, I pray you may have lifelong happiness, my dearest one!" said Miss Conyers, with a quivering voice.

"My dears, my dears, are you ready to go on shore?" called Dr. Rosenthal from the head of the cabin stairs.

"Yes, papa dear!—Oh, dear Britomarte, think again! come home with me!" pleaded Erminie.

"No, my darling! We must part here. Give me your parting kiss in this cabin, not on deck before all the men," said Miss Conyers.

Erminie threw herself into the arms of Britomarte, and clung long and wildly to her bosom, until a second and a third summons from Dr. Rosenthal compelled her to let go her hold.

Then the two friends went up the stairs together.

The three gentlemen were waiting to escort them on shore.

Dr Rosenthal placed his daughter in the carriage that was waiting for her; but when he would have led Britomarte to the same place, she courteously thanked him, and said that her way lay in another direction, and that she would go on foot.

Justin came forward and said:

"You will let me see you safe to the place where you are going?"

"No, thank you," she replied.

Justin argued, pleaded, insisted, but all to no purpose. And at last she said.

"Mr. Rosenthal, since you compel me to say it, your attendance would be an intrusion."

"Then I have nothing more to urge, Miss Conyers. We will meet again."

"'At Philippi,' ghost of Cæsar? Good by, Mr.

Rosenthal," laughed Britomarte, waving her hand.

Justin bowed and left her, to enter the carriage where his party were waiting.

And Britomarte watched the carriage drive off and roll out of sight, and then she drew her black veil before her face, and walked on her way alone.

CHAPTER VII

BRITOMARTE EMBARKS

BRITOMARTE possessed a few jewels of value. These she had never worn or shown. She now took them to a jeweler on Pennsylvania avenue, and sold them for enough to defray her expenses to the city from whose port the missionary company was to sail.

On arriving at that city, she found a cheap boarding-house, and then sought out the secretary of the Board of Foreign Missions, and offered her services to go as teacher with the company they were about to send to Farther India.

The secretary required testimonials, which Britomarte immediately submitted. And then, after a little business and investigation, her services were accepted.

Miss Conyers then devoted all her time and attention to making preparations for a sea voyage that was to last several months.

The missionaries were to sail on the first of October, in the great East Indiaman, Sultana, bound from Boston to Calcutta; but their destination was Cambodia.

When her preparations were completed, Britomarte wrote to her friend Erminie, informing her of all the particulars of the projected mission, and asking her for the last news of their own fellow-graduates.

Quickly as the post could return, Miss Conyers received an answer from the affectionate girl.

And now that the missionary measure seemed irrevocable, Erminie did not distress her friend by any vain lamentations over her own loss. Little womanlike, she praised, glorified, and ι˙˙˙ ˙˙˙ over her friend, and bade her Godspeed. She wrote that her brother Justin had just been ordained a minister of the Gospel, and that he was to leave them soon for distant duty; but she did not say where he was going.

"So, then, our paths diverge forever, thank Heaven!" exclaimed the man-hater, as she read this part of the letter, but, indeed, her heaving bosom, and quivering lips, and tearful eyes did not look very much like thankfulness.

Erminie further stated that Colonel Eastworth had taken apartments at a first-class hotel in the city, with the intention of passing the ensuing winter there.

Of their late classmates, Erminie wrote:

"There is the mischief to pay down in Henrico. It seems Vittorio Corsoni sued for the hand of Alberta Goldsborough, which was indignantly refused him by her father. Next he was refused admittance to the house by her mother; after which Miss Goldsborough, chancing to meet her lover in the streets of Richmond, coolly informed him that if they could not see each other in her own home, they could do so at the houses of their mutual friends, and at the same time announced that she should spend that evening with her schoolmate, Eleanora Lee. That evening you may be sure that the Signior Vittorio lounged into Judge Lee's drawing-room to pay his respects to a former patron.

"In this manner they contrived to meet everywhere where they were both acquainted, until at last, oh, Britomarte, they eloped! You don't know how shocked I was to hear it, and how ashamed I am to have to tell you! But you asked me for news, and I will keep back nothing.

"They made for the nearest point to cross into Maryland, where they could be legally married, notwithstanding she was under age. But Mr. Goldsborough, with two of her uncles, pursued and overtook them before they had crossed the boundary and seized both, as he had a right to do.

"Vittorio, they say, was dreadfully agitated, and even drew

But Alberta was as cool as ever, and bade him put up his sword and yield for the time being; for that, though their marriage was delayed, it was not prevented.

"Mr. Goldsborough talked of prosecuting Vittorio in a criminal court for stealing an heiress and minor. But Alberta calmly assured her father that in doing so he would only be degrading his future son-in-law, and by consequence his only daughter, for that she was resolved to give her hand to Vittorio upon the very first opportunity after she should become of age.

"Whether or not this announcement influenced Mr. Goldsborough's conduct I do not know; it is certain, however, that he did not prosecute Signior Vittorio; but he brought Alberta here, and placed her as a parlor boarder in the Convent of the Visitation, where, behind grates and bars, she is secure from a second escapade.

"Mr. Goldsborough did not call on us until he had left his daughter in the convent, and then he only stayed long enough to tell us these facts before he left for Richmond. I called at the convent to see Alberta, but was refused a sight of her. She is, in truth, no less than an honorable prisoner there.

"And that is not all the trouble in Henrico County. I have a letter from Elfrida Fielding, in which she tells me all her secrets with the utmost candor, requesting me also to tell you, whom she supposes to be somewhere in our reach.

"Now, who would have thought that wild little monkey, Elfie, would have acted, in similar circumstances, with so much more prudence and good sense and good feeling than has been displayed by our model young lady? Yet so it was.

"Elfie has had a proposal from—whom do you think?—young Mr. Albert Goldsborough, who was intended for his cousin; but as she ran away with the flute-playing Italian, of course he could not be considered bound to her; so he followed the bent of his inclinations, and offered his hand to Elfie Fielding.

"The proposal was in every point of view a most eligible one for Elfie, and much better, she says, than she had any reason to expect. The young suitor was handsome, amiable, intelligent, and possessed a large fortune, and last and most he had the favor of his intended—but—he differed in politics with Elfie's 'pap and two unks.'

"Now you know what it is to differ in politics in these days—you have read how gray-haired Senators take each other by the throat in the Senate Chamber. You have seen how it sets father against son, and mother against daughter; how it parts lovers and divides families; pray Heaven it may not some day come nigh to divide the Union!

"Elfie's 'pap and two unks' are enlightened, far-seeing and progressive men. Elfi's lover is a conservative, and believes in the eternal stability of 'institutions' and the infallibility of the powers that be, etc. Elfie's lover had he lived in the first year of the Christian era in Judea, would have been a Jew, and helped to crucify Christ. Had he lived in England at the time of the civil wars, he would have been a royalist. Or had his presence enriched the earth at the time of our own Revolution, he would have been a Tory.

"Now, you know, of course, it is an irreconcilable difference between Elfie's 'pap and two unks' on the one hand, and her lover on the other. But Elfie won't run away with him, as he wishes her to do. She tells him plainly that he must convert her 'pap and two unks', or be converted by them, before she will endow him with her hand and the reversion of the old gig, the blind mare, niggers and other personals to which she is heiress; for, though she don't care a pin for politics herself, she will have peace in the family.

"I have here quoted Elfi's own words. Now, who would have given that little monkey credit for so much wisdom and goodness?

"And in the meantime you see Mr. Goldsborough has his hands full between his cool, determined daughter and his self-willed, refractory nephew; both of whom, instead of marrying each other, and keeping the family estates together, to please their friends, have taken the liberty to choose partners for life to please themselves.

"But after all, as these marriages are not yet consummated, who knows but that young Mr. Goldsborough may 'see his own interest,' as the phrase goes, and persuade Alberta to 'see her own duty,' as the other phrase goes, and that they may yet marry and unite the two great branches of the great house of Goldsborough.

"But, oh, I am wrong to write so lightly on such sacred subjects. How hard it is, dear Britomarte, to keep from sinning with one's tongue and pen! I hope that all these lovers will be true to themselves, and to God, who is the Inspirer of all pure love. I hope they will wait patiently until they win their parents' consent and the reward of forbearance."

There was much more of Erminie's letter, too much to quote. Sometimes the effervescent spirits of her youth would break forth in some such little jest as the above, and then she would quickly repent and piously rebuke herself for such levity.

Her letter closed in one deep, fervent, heartfelt aspiration for Britomarte's happiness.

Britomarte's tears fell fast over this letter. This man-hater would like to have persuaded herself that she wept over the thought of the lifelong separation from her bosom friend, or over the frailties of Alberta, or over the troubles of Elfie, or over anything or anybody rather than over the memory of Justin Rosenthal. Erminie had written freely of Alberta and Elfrida and their lovers; but she had mentioned her brother only to say that he had been ordained and was going away. And Britomarte could scarcely forgive her friend for such negligence. The name that was written in the letter, "Justin," she pressed again and again to her lips, while her tears dropped slowly and heavily upon the paper. Suddenly, with a start, she recollected herself, and to punish herself for a moment's weakness, she deliberately tore up the letter and threw it away.

In the omnibus that was to take her to her steamer she was introduced in form to Mr. Ely and Mr. Breton and their wives. These, with herself, were the five missionaries that were to go out to Farther India.

The two young women were crying behind their veils. They were strangers to each other, and all but strangers to their husbands. One had come from the West, and one from the South, to marry these young men, and go out with them to India. They had now been married but a few hours, after an acquaintance with their intended husbands of but a few days. In a fever of enthusiasm they had left all the familiar scenes and all the dear friends of their childhood and youth, to join their hands with strangers and go out to a foreign land, to live and labor among heathen No wonder they wept bitterly behind their veils as the omnibus rattled over the stony street and under the drizzling sky.

On the pier was a crowd of the church members, consisting of men, women and children, in omnibuses, in cabs, and on foot, the latter having large umbrellas hoisted, all waiting to see the missionaries off

Beside the pier was chained a large boat, waiting to take the voyagers to that magnificent three-decker East Indiaman that rode at anchor about half a mile out in the harbor.

In less than fifteen minutes they were alongside of the great behemoth of a ship that lay upon the waters like some stupendous monster of the deep.

An officer stood upon the deck as if waiting to welcome them, and some sailors were letting down a rope ladder from the lofty deck to the boat But to attempt to climb up the side of that ship by that means seemed like trying to crawl up the front of a three-story house by the rainpipe. The two brides were frightened nearly out of their senses at the bare thought.

But Britomarte volunteered to go first, and she set her foot on the lowest, slack rung of the ladder and took hold of the side ropes and began to climb. Mr. Breton followed close behind her, to keep her from falling, and also to keep her skirts in order, and Captain McKensie bending from the deck and holding down his hand to help her up on board

So Miss Conyers safely boarded the ship and soon the whole party stood on deck and waved a last adieu.

Two brother ministers who had so far accompanied the voyagers went back in the smaller boat; but before she had reached the pier, the signal gun was fired and the Sultana stood out to sea.

CHAPTER VIII

A LOVER'S PERSISTENCE

It was the fifth day out at sea; Britomarte had a stiff attack of *mal-de-mer*, but had not been so sick as to be unable to enjoy the witticisms of the Irish stewardess, Judith Riordon, or the pleasantries of the good-natured Captain McKenzie; but the spell of dirty weather that had ensued after crossing the bar was now over, and Britomarte climbed the stairs, made her way carefully across the deck and seated herself on one of the coils of rope stowed against the bulwarks.

Her eyes wandered over the scene.

What a grand, sublime and glorious round it was! This boundless sky! One vast circle of air above; one vast circle of water below. Not a bird to be seen in all the air, not a sail to be seen on all the sea.

Their own lonely ship was the center of this circle and the only one within it. The solitude of this scene was even more stupendous than its vastness.

Gazing, Britomarte sank into thought, then into dream, then almost into trance.

What past life was the beautiful man-hater living over again in that self-forgotten reverie?

Whatever it was, it wrapped her whole soul in an abstraction so profound, that she did not hear the approach of a footstep, though that step rang clearly and firmly upon the deck, nor did she see the form that stood beside her, though that form sheltered her from the sun's spray that had begun to wear clothing; nor did she become conscious of the intruder's presence until he stooped to her ear and breathed her name:

"Miss Conyers!"

She started and looked up.

Justin Rosenthal stood before her, looking tenderly down into her face.

In the first shock of surprise she gazed at him with widely dilated eyes, as though he had been an apparition from the unseen world, and she seemed to think that she was in a dream, or that she had lost her reason. Then, as the certainty, the reality of the presence rapidly grew upon her—as she became conscious that it was he, himself, Justin Rosenthal, her lover and her beloved, that was standing before her—an overwhelming rush of joy filled her soul; and before she had time to control her countenance, this joy beamed and radiated from every feature of her beautiful face! It was as if the womanhood kept bound and captive in the lowest depths of her heart by pride and principle had suddenly burst her chains and looked forth in liberty and light. It was but for one instant this womanhood showed itself, for in the next the man hater reasserted her supremacy, and put a strong guard upon her countenance.

"Well?" said Justin, answering her various changes of countenance with a trusting smile.

"You here!" she exclaimed.

"Yes."

It was but a word, calmly spoken; but it told everything.

"Why are you here?" she demanded sternly.

But that assumption of sternness came too late. He had seen the transient flash of an exceeding great joy on her face, and even if he had ever entertained any doubts of her real feeling toward him, those doubts were now forever dispelled.

He seated himself beside her, and then answered:

"You ask me why I am here. I am here because I love you, have faith in you, and hope to win you as my wife."

"As your slave, you mean! Pray, do not," ex

claimed the marriage renouncer, with burning cheeks and flashing eyes.

"No, no, Britomarte; but as my wife and equal; and if not so, as my wife and liege lady, for if one must serve, let it be the stronger. I have said all this to you before."

"So this, then, is the 'distant duty' you were to go upon when you were ordained and went from home," said Miss Conyers, sarcastically.

"Yes."

"And Erminie never explained! It was not like her to be so reserved with me."

"My sister was in honor bound to keep my secret."

"But why should your action in this matter have been kept a secret? It seems to me that honorable actions need never be kept so."

"That is a mistake. Sometimes they must. My intended voyage was kept a secret because I thought, if you discovered that I was to be your fellow-voyager, you would never embark on this enterprise."

"That I never should have done."

"And your valuable services would have been lost to the mission," said Justin, with a slight smile.

Her eyes flashed fire. She came down upon him with a trenchant scorn in her next words.

"We sailed on Tuesday. This is Saturday, the fifth day out, and we have not seen anything of you until this morning! Pray, do you consider it conduct worthy of a gentleman to come secretly upon the ship, and remain in hiding like a fugitive convict for four or five days?"

"I beg your pardon," said Justin, good-humoredly, "but you are wrong in your promises. I did not come secretly on the ship. I engaged myself as clerk to the captain, who is an old friend of our family. The first day, it is true, I kept out of sight, lest, if you happened to see me, you might take flight and go back on the pilot-boat."

"I verily believe that I should have done so."

"Certainly you would; and, as I said before, your valuable services would have been lost to the mission. To obviate such a misfortune, I have kept out of your sight, and in the captain's office, where I occupied myself in arranging his books and papers until the pilot went back. After which, as it was quite impossible you should swim back to the mainland, I did not mind showing myself at the table. But, unfortunately, you were seasick, and I could not see you until this morning."

"But was it right, was it manly, was it honorable, to follow me in this manner?" scornfully questioned the man-hater.

"Yes, Miss Conyers, it was all that," said Justin, gravely. "I told you in the beginning that I loved you with my whole heart and soul, for time and for eternity; that I should make it the first object of my life to win you, letting wait all other business that might be incompatible with the pursuit of that object. I do not say I could not live without you, for I have a sound, strong constitution, and could endure a great deal of suffering for a great length of time. But I do say that I do not choose to live without you. So much do I love you, so hopeful I am of winning you."

"You are very arrogant and presumptuous to say so!" with which she left him.

Justin, though he had embarked on the same ship with Britomarte, had no intention of playing the bore. It was enough for him just then that she was near. She rarely spoke to him, and only then with the most frigid politeness.

So the days passed away without incident, till, one morning, the lookout announced land in sight, and everybody rushed on deck, but only the faintest speck could be discerned on the horizon.

In an hour, with the aid of the glass, they made out Table Mount, and in two hours they could see the whole line of coast, with its bold headlands and deeply indented inlets. A few hours more of sailing brought them to the entrance of Table Bay, under the shadow of Table Mount.

The ship dropped anchor just as the sun touched the horizon. The sailors were all busy with the rigging. The missionary party hurried forward to view the novel

them, walked aft, and leaned over the taffrail, to bid good-night to the last sun of the old year, as he sank beneath the wave.

Justin Rosenthal followed her, and stood by her side for a few minutes, watching in reverent silence the rich crimson light fading from the western horizon; and then he said, quietly:

"It is gone! Will you please to take my arm and allow me to lead you forward? The captain will not send a boat on shore to-night; but to-morrow morning we shall all have an opportunity of visiting the colony. In the meantime, the view of the town and its vicinity, from this anchorage, is well worth looking at. Will you come?"

"Thank you—yes," said Miss Conyers; and she permitted him to draw her hand within his arm, and take her forward, where all her companions were grouped together, gazing upon the new sights before them.

The view, as Justin Rosenthal had truly said, was well worth looking at. First of all, the bay into which they had put was vast enough to accommodate any number of ships, and, indeed, a very considerable number rode at anchor within it. Before them lay Cape Town, nestled at the foot of Table Mount, whose perpendicular sides rose up behind it; while on either hand, like giant sentinels to guard the entrance of the port, stood the barren crags of Lion's Head and Devil's Peak. A little back from the shores were sunny, green hills and shady grove trees, among which, half hidden, stood beautiful villas, built in the old Dutch style, with flat roofs and painted walls and broad terraces.

The newly-arrived voyagers remained on deck, gazing on this scene with never-tiring interest, until the short, bright twilight of those latitudes suddenly sank into night, and the stars came out in the purple-black heavens, and the lights shone in the streets and houses of Cape Town. Then they went below to the supper that had long been waiting; and afterward they turned in for the night.

As soon as they were awake in the morning, the whole party arose and dressed, and hurried up on deck to take another look at the harbor, the shipping, the town and the mountain.

"So this is Africa!" exclaimed Mrs. Ely, gazing in open mouthed wonder upon the scene before them; "and only think—as long as we have been expecting to get here, now that we are here, I feel as if I was in a dream. Africa! Why, law, you know, though I always studied the map of Africa at school, and read about it in geography, I never seemed to realize there was such a place. It always seemed to me only like a place in a story, just as the Happy Valley, or the Cave of Despair. And I am sure it is as strange for me to be standing here, looking at it, as if I suddenly saw before me the Island of Calm Delight, or any other place that was only in a book. How queer! Africa!"

"I think your feeling is a more common one than would be generally acknowledged," replied her husband. "Used to express nd to our senses" the Real, like the Ideal only exists for us in our imaginations."

"What astonies me," said Mrs. Preton, "is to see here, at the most southern extremity of the most barbarous grand division of the earth, a town with houses, and a harbor with shipping, so much like the seaports of our own Christian and civilized native country. Why, law, only for that great mountain behind the town, and those two great rocks to the right and left, that stand like Gog and Magog, to guard the port, one might think we were in New York Bay, and looking in upon some of the old Dutch quarters of the city."

"Yes," said Mr. Breton, "for harbors and shipping have a certain general resemblance all over the world. So also do seaport towns. And this town with its Dutch style of building, does certainly resemble some of the old portions of New York. But it resembles still more the seaports of Holland, with canals running through the middle of all the principal streets, as you never see in ours."

"Oh! canals running down the middle of the streets! How queer! Like Venice."

"Oh! not Venice,

all canals—the walls of the houses rising straight up from the edge of the water. But here the canals only run down through the middle of the most important streets, and there are beautiful sidewalks, well shaded by lofty trees, before the rows of houses, each side. But you will see all these things when you go on shore. And there is the breakfast bell."

While the others talked, Miss Conyers and Mr. Rosenthal stood side by side, perfectly silent, and letting their eyes rove over the sea and land. And now they turned and followed their companions into the saloon.

While they were breakfasting, the sailors were getting out the yawl boat, so that when they came on deck again, they found it waiting. They made haste to prepare themselves, and were soon ready. The gentlemen handed the ladies carefully down into the boat. The captain, who was going on shore with his passengers, joined them; and the sailors laid themselves to their oars and pushed off the boat.

"In African waters—only think!" said Mrs. Breton, who did not seem to be able to get over her astonishment at finding herself in such a, to her, mythical place.

They rowed cautiously past British men-of-war, past East India merchantmen, past Dutch traders, past Chinese junks and the shipping of all nations that rode at anchor in the harbor; and then past the fortifications, and past the custom-house, near which they landed.

As they brought nothing into the town but what they wore on their persons or carried in their hands, they had no business with the receivers of duty; so they went on into the town. First they found the usual crowd that day and night haunt the piers of seaports—only in this place the crowd was smaller as to number and greater as to variety than is commonly to be met with, for here were English, Dutch and Portuguese colonists, and Hottentot, Kaffir and other natives, besides a sprinkling of strangers and visitors from all parts of the world.

Through this crowd they went up a narrow street,

and turned into a broad avenue, beautifully shaded with poplar, oak and pine trees, and built up on each side with handsome houses in the Dutch style of architecture, having gaily painted fronts, flat roofs and broad terraces.

Here the captain paused to point out to them the way to the South African College, and left them, and went in pursuit of his own business.

Mr. Ely and Mr. Breton had letters of introduction to Professor John of that institution, and thitherward the whole party turned their steps. It was a long but pleasant walk. The novelty of everything around them, and the strangeness of seeing so many old familiar objects of their own native land and home mixed up with so much that was new and foreign, beguiled the time, so that they were unconscious of fatigue until they reached the college building.

The professor was within, and received them in his private study—a comfortable room, carpeted, curtained, and fitted up with chairs and tables, desks and bookcases, like any European or American gentleman's library.

Professor John was a pleasant little old man, in a dressing-gown, cap and slippers. And very cordially he arose and welcomed the party to Africa.

"To Africa!" echoed Mrs. Ely, who seemed in a chronic state of amazement—"it seems like saying—'to the moon.'"

"Well, my dear young lady, it is rather an outlandish place, and in the same quarter of the globe as the mountains of the moon!" said the Professor, who was something of a humorist.

He offered them refreshments, consisting of the rich Constantia wine of the colony, and biscuits, cold fowl, cake, fruit and so forth. And, when they had eaten and drank and rested, he showed them over the college—into the library, museum, classrooms, refectories and dormitories. And, when they returned to his study, he sent a messenger to procure a carriage to take them around the town.

CHAPTER IX

A VILLA IN CAPE COLONY

From the South African College they drove out of town in the direction of the Wynbey Hill to a beautiful villa in the English style of architecture, closely shaded, with the brilliant native trees of the colony grouped with the imported old familiar trees of the mother country, and surrounded with gardens laid out in the English fashion. To the owner of this lovely home, the Rev. Mr. Burney, of the Presbyterian Church, Mr. Ely bore letters of introduction for himself and his whole party. And when their carriage had rolled through the beautifully ornamented grounds and up the poplar-shaded drive to the front of the villa, he left his companions in their seats and alighted and went in to present his credentials to the master of the house.

He was welcomed by Mr. Burney with that cordial hospitality which must be peculiar, I think, to colonists all over the world; but is perhaps most peculiar to those of the Cape of Good Hope.

He insisted that Mr. Ely should immediately bring in his whole party; and to enforce the execution of his plan, went with that gentleman to the carriage and put his head in at the window and shook hands with all its occupants, and then had them all out of it and in his own drawing-room before they knew what they were about.

Then he sent for his wife and daughters and presented them to his visitors.

"Mrs. Burney, Miss Burney, Miss Mary Burney."

And then he presented his visitors to his family:

"The Rev. Mr. and Mrs. Ely, my dears. The Rev. Mr. and Mrs. Breton. The Rev. Mr. and Mrs. Rosenthal."

"Miss Conyers—the young lady's name is Conyers," whispered Mrs. Pretor, in her ear.

But all the hurried, low-toned conversation the un

fortunate host heard only the names, and he corrected his mistake and made matters worse by exclaiming

"Bless my life and soul, yes! I beg your pardon, sir and madam." Then, turning again to his family group, he presented the young people over again as—"My dears, the Rev. Mr. and Mrs. Conyers."

Britomarte's cheeks were scarlet. But Justin smiled with perfect self-possession and some little amusement as he shook hands all around, saying as he did so:

"I am not so happy. The young lady by my side is Miss Conyers; but it is not the fault of Justin Rosen that, at your service, that she is so."

The good minister uttered another.

"Bless my life and soul!" And then he laughed and stretched forth his hand, saying: "But you see the mistake was so natural on my part. Here is a party of missionaries on the way to India! And here is one young couple and here is another young couple; and here are two more young people, and what so natural as to take them for a third young couple? But I beg your pardon, Miss Conyers, I am sure!"

"And he 'won't do so no more!'—will you, papa dear?" said Miss Mary, who seemed to be the privileged romp of the family.

"Indeed I will not; until you give me the right," laughed the minister.

Miss Conyers responded by a grave, severe bow; she could not easily recover her equanimity.

But Justin begged to assure his host that he, for his part, suffered under no sense of injury.

Mr. Burney laughingly replied that he should imagine he did not.

And so the affair passed off.

When the party were all seated comfortably in the easy chairs and on the sofas of the drawing room, that looked so exactly like their drawing rooms at home that they could almost have supposed themselves transported by magic back to America, their host, with his hands upon his knees and his head bent eagerly forward said:

"You

"No. We sail on Saturday."

"Bless my life and soul!" exclaimed this good man, who was given to imploring benedictions upon his own head. "You sail on Saturday, and this is Thursday. Well, well! You must make the most of your time and we must make the most of you. You must remain with us while the ship is in port. Not a word now! I will take no denial."

Nor did he, and, indeed, it required very little persuasion to induce the voyagers to share Mr. Burney's hospitality. The intervening days were spent delightfully in sight-seeing, and it was with real regret they bade the good people adieu and returned to the ship.

For two weeks they were blessed with fine weather and a fair wind.

Then, when the moon was at the full, there were indications of a change. The wind gradually died away, or rose and blew in fitful puffs, and sank again. The ship, with all her canvas spread whenever it could catch the faintest breeze, made little or no progress. The weather grew intolerably hot and oppressive. The sun blazed down from a cloudless sky with consuming fierceness. The ladies were driven from the deck to seek shelter from the burning heat in the deep shades of the cabin, where they remained all day, or at least while the sun was above the horizon. After sunset they ventured upon deck to seek a breath of fresh air, which they very seldom found even there, for the atmosphere seemed oppressed with some deadly element that made it almost unfit for inhalation. And even the reflected light of the moon seemed to be reflected heat as well, and Mrs. Breton declared it looked as hot, and felt as hot, as ever the sun did in her own native clime.

The crisis came; the wind fell lower and still lower, and then the fitful puffs that had served to carry the ship forward a knot or two an hour, ceased altogether; the sea sank; and the ship lay like a log upon the glassy sea, under the burning sky.

Day and night for nearly a w   h this dead calm continued, with most depressing

The heavens wore an ominous aspect. The sun had set, and every ray of his light had faded from the western horizon; yet the whole sky seemed to be illumined with supernatural light—a bronze-colored glare that made the moon and stars look pale and dim, and that was reflected by the sea, until the whole sphere seemed smoldering on the eve of bursting into a conflagration; while ever, at short intervals, came that low, deep, distant sigh, moan or sob, across the waters. As if in sympathetic answer to this mysterious sound of distress, the ship began to creak, groan and roll. And the whole circle of the sea began to boil up into a white foam.

The seamen also were very active and busy. Some were reefing the top-sails; some were setting storm stay-sails; others were closing the portholes; and others again were securing the fastenings of the lifeboats.

"There's something wrong a-brewing," said Mrs. Ely to Miss Conyers, as they walked after Mrs. Breton, who had hurried to the stern where the anxious men stood grouped around the wheelhouse.

"What is coming, Captain McKenzie?" inquired Miss Conyers.

"Not much, I hope, my dear young lady; but I would recommend you and your companions to go down into the cabin."

Even while the captain spoke, the dull bronze-colored glare grew darker and darker, and in the gloom the ripples of the sea gleamed in phosphorescent light, and the air was filled with a sulphurous odor.

"Will there be a hurricane?" Miss Conyers was about to ask, but in pity for Martha Breton, who was an exceedingly timid woman, she forbore the question.

"Oh, take me down, please! I know there's something dreadful at hand; and I don't see my husband anywhere at all! Please, take me down!" pleaded poor Martha.

Miss Conyers would have much preferred to remain on deck to watch the coming of the hurricane that she felt was a'mo-

trembling friend she drew poor Martha's arm within her own, and led her towards the cabin. They had scarcely reached the top of the ladder before the wind suddenly arose out of the northwest with a great blast, and then as suddenly fell, leaving the ship rolling from the impetus.

Miss Conyers hurried her helpless companion down the ladder and into the cabin.

"Oh, Britomarte, I know! I know! The captain and all of them expect a terrible storm! I saw it in their faces! and see how hard the sailors are at work making preparations to meet it! And only think, they have not even thought of supper, though it is past the hour! Not that I care for supper now! I am too frightened; but I know if there were not great danger, they would not forget it, or neglect to serve it"—and, oh! what a blast was there!" cried Martha Breton, as another gust of wind suddenly sprang up and blew with great violence for a few moments, and then again as suddenly subsided

"You had better let me help you into your stateroom; where you can lie down on your berth and be quiet; and no doubt presently the stewardess will bring us some tea, which I will take in to you," said Miss Conyers

Meanwhile on deck all was anxious preparation to meet the danger. Some of the men were aloft, relieving the masts from everything that could cumber the action of the ship or be reft away by the wind. Others were seeing to the chains. Others again were clearing the deck from the lumber sent down from aloft. The captain, with two men, was at the wheel. The wind that had at first sprung up in fierce and fitful gusts now blew steadily, but with great and increasing violence, from the northeast, driving the ship furiously through the boiling waves. The sea, risen to a great height, dashed over the decks at intervals, carrying off all light matter that had been left there, and threatening at every return to wash off the crew. So strong and fierce was the wind, so high and heavy the sea, that it was all the man at the wheel could do to keep the helm.

As the night advanced the tempest increased in fury, the wind blew in fiercer blasts, howling and shrieking around the ship as if all the accursed spirits in Tartarus had been let loose; had there been a square of canvas up, it must have been split to pieces; the very masts were bent like reeds. "Alps on Alps" of waves arose and broke in death-dealing blows upon the deck; scarcely any hour passed in which some unfortunate seaman was not torn from his holdings and swept overboard, and the utmost precautions taken could not prevent the waves rushing into the cabin, to the unutterable horror of Mrs. Breton, who could only gasp and sob, while even Mrs. Ely exclaimed in affright:

"We shall be drowned! Oh, my Heavens, we shall be drowned! drowned here in the cabin like blind kittens in a tub!"

"Ah, thin, bad luck to the kittens! I wish meself they were drowned entirely, for sure it was themselves as brought this hurricane upon us, as the saymen foretold!" exclaimed Judith, the stewardess, who had only heard, in the din, something about drowning and kittens. At every wave that came rushing in, Mrs. Breton went into a spasm, and Mrs. Ely cried out for mercy, though before the words had left her lips, the wave had left the cabin.

At last one, heavier than any that had preceded it, broke into the cabin prostrating all its inmates, and then rushed out again.

"We are lost! Heaven and earth, we are lost!" cried Mrs. Ely, as soon as she could get her breath.

"Ah, be calm, we are immortal spirits; we cannot be lost! Think of that, and brace yourself to bear whatever comes! At worst it will be but a stormy passage to the other world!" said Miss Conyers, earnestly.

But her companions were unnerved beyond all hope of being strengthened.

And still, as the awful night deepened, the wind blew in more furious gusts, bending the masts like rods, the sea rose in higher waves, beating the ship with more

and the lightning blazed with a more deadly glare. The ship was driven furiously through the darkness, and clear out of her course, and no one on board had any distinct idea of where she was.

So the night of horrors wore on.

"Oh, for daylight! oh, Heaven, for daylight!" was the frequently aspirated prayer in the dark cabin. And, "Oh, for daylight! oh, God, for daylight!" was the unuttered prayer on the quivering deck.

CHAPTER X

THE ROCKS

ALL things have an end. That awful night passed at last. Daylight came, slowly enough, through the heaped black clouds that rolled upon the heaving waves below and reached unknown heights in the sky above.

So darkly and gloomily came the morning, that it seemed not so much the dawning of the day as the fading of the black darkness. Night grew paler in the cabin, and the scared inmates could see in the waning darkness the wan faces of their companions rising up and down with the tossing of the ship.

And soon after daylight came that startling cry from the man on the lookout—that cry which is so often a sound of rapture or of despair, because it is a herald of life or of death. Ah, Heaven! it was now a knell of doom.

"Land ho!"

"Where away?"

"On her lee bows!"

"Thank Heaven!" fervently breathed Mrs. Ely, to whom the words conveyed no other idea than that of a good landing place, where they could all leave the dreadful ship, and go on shore in safety.

Mrs. Breton lifted her prostrate head, and ventured to draw a long breath.

Miss Conyers never moved or spoke; too well she

knew the deadly meaning of the words she had heard—"Land ho!" "On her lee bows!"—when the ship was being driven before the wind at such a furious rate. Silent and breathless she sat, and waited for what should come next.

The voice of the captain rang clearly out above the roar of wind and wave.

"Luff! Luff!"

Too late! Another instant and the doomed ship was lifted high on the top of an enormous wave, and carried forward and cast down with a tremendous shock that crashed and tore through all her timbers from keel to quarter-deck, while she shuddered in a death agony, impaled upon the horns of the hidden rocks!

The passengers in the cabin were tossed up and thrown down by the concussion. They were jarred and shaken, but not seriously hurt. They quickly recovered themselves; and all the women except Miss Conyers were surprised and pleased to find that the ship, which had been tossing and pitching with such tremendous force for the last twelve hours had now become nearly motionless.

But there was a great deal of rushing about and calling out among the men on deck, and Mr. Ely and Mr. Breton started and ran up to see what it all meant.

"What is the matter? Have we landed anywhere? Oh, I suppose of course we have, but with what a stunning shock! It is bad enough when a river steamer strikes the pier too suddenly; but I declare this quite knocked the breath out of my body; and, besides, it was so unexpected! I didn't know that ships ever did come quite up to piers and I did not even know we were near any place. What port is it likely to be, do you know, Miss Conyers?" inquired Mrs. Ely.

"I do not know where we are. We shall hear presently, I suppose," replied Britomarte. But too well she knew where they were not—in any place of safety.

"Anyhow, I am very glad to be still. I know that," answered Mary Ely.

Martha Breton, who was often of her

senses by slight or imaginary dangers, was now quite cheerful in the midst of the real and appalling peril of which she was fortunately unconscious. She got off the floor and into a chair and began to smooth her disordered hair and dress and to call out to Judith to light the lamps; for though it was daylight, it was still very dark in the cabin.

"And you know we have got to dress and go on shore," added poor Martha.

"Ah, bedad, yes! sure we've got to go somewhere," wailed Judith; but she got up and lighted the cabin lamps.

Meanwhile the commotion on deck increased. Suddenly again the captain's voice was heard above all other sounds:

"Launch the lifeboats!"

And the rushing of many feet on the deck increased, mingled with the rushing of many waters around the ship.

"Lord betune us and harm, the lifeboats! Mary, star of the say," and so forth, and so forth, said Judith, wailing lamentations and muttering litanies.

"Are we to go on shore in the boats? I thought the ship itself had landed and touched the pier," said Mrs. Ely, rising to go to her stateroom to put on her bonnet.

"Well, I suppose we shall know what port we have touched sooner or later," laughed Mrs. Breton, so glad to know that the ship stood still, and to believe that she was about to leave it for the shore.

Britomarte neither spoke nor moved. She knew, if her companion did not, that death was imminent.

The commotion on deck grew furious; it seemed almost as if a mutiny had sprung up among the seamen; too well she knew the meaning of that commotion; the crew were seizing the lifeboats. Again the voice of the captain was heard near the companionway:

"Mr. Bates! see to getting the women in the cabin up on deck immediately—they must first be saved!"

Miss . . . . reply.

"Save l' ? . a . of Heavens! From what? From

what are we to be saved, Britomarte?" exclaimed Mrs. Breton, suddenly seized with terror.

"How strangely you look, Britomarte! Your face is as white and as hard as marble! Oh, dear! oh, dear! what is the matter? What has happened? What are we to be saved from? Tell me! tell me quickly!" cried Martha Breton, wringing her hands in the extremity of distress.

"Oh, Heaven, do you not know, then? The ship is wrecked on the rocks! The crew are leaving her in the lifeboats!" said Miss Conyers, solemnly.

"Oh, no, no, no! Oh, don't say that? Oh, mercy!" screamed Mrs. Breton, wild with horror and despair.

"Be firm! For Heaven's sake, be firm! Be a woman! Let these men see that we can brave death with the best of them!" said Britomarte, for you see the ruling passion was "strong in death."

"I don't care what they see! Oh, dear! oh, dear!" wailed the poor woman.

"What is all this fuss about?" cried Mrs. Ely, coming out of her stateroom equipped in bonnet and shawl for her landing.

Before any one could answer her, there was a rush of many feet down the companion ladder, and several men entered the cabin, which was still too dark to enable the occupants to recognize the new comers. But Judith hurried out of Mrs. Breton's stateroom with a lighted lantern, and then they saw that the visitors were Justin Rosenthal, Terrence Riordan, and the two young missionaries.

Mr. Ely and Mr. Breton each rushed to the rescue of his wife.

Riordan hurried his daughter up the companion ladder.

Justin Rosenthal came to the side of Britomarte Conyers.

His face was very pale, but his voice was firm as he hastily addressed her.

"The ship is a total wreck, the crew are about to abandon
women.

"I will go with you on deck," she answered, calmly giving him her hand.

The other women of the cabin had been taken away by the men that had come for them.

Justin and Britomarte now followed them up on deck.

But oh! what a scene of unparalleled horror and desolation met their appalled sight! The sun was just struggling up above the horizon through masses of black and ragged clouds; the thunder and lightning had ceased, and the wind had died away, but the infuriated sea still foamed with rage, and rose in mighty waves, and roared above the ship and fell in thunder over her decks. The ship, a mere shattered wreck, lay impaled upon the sharp rocks that had penetrated her keel; her bows were under water, and the waves dashed over her every minute, threatening to divide her amidships, but fortunately, her stern was lifted high out of the sea, and wedged in a ravine or crevice of the rocks; heavy clouds and fogs rested on the tempestuous ocean, and no one could see where the land lay, if indeed there was any land near, or anything else but this chain of sunken rocks which had proved a reef of death to the fated ship.

The lifeboats were all launched, and the crew were crowding into them.

Captain McKenzie stood, pale and stern, by the starboard gangway, seeing to the lowering of the women into the boats. Mrs. Ely and Mrs. Breton were let down into one, and Judith Riordan into the other.

"Hand the other girleen down! Sure we'll save the women, the craytures! but as for the other passengers, faix they must take their chance along with the ould ship itself! troth, they'd swamp us all if we was to have thim in here," said Mike Mullony, the carpenter's mate, who, in this hour of confusion worse than chaos, and horror worse than death, had seized the command of the boat he was in.

On hearing these dreadful words that doomed their husbands to death, the two unhappy young wives began to scream and sob and pray to the crew; and to stretch out their arms in an agony of yearning to those beloved ones who had grown so dear to them on their voyage, and who now stood fixed and livid with despair upon the quaking deck.

Sick at heart at this sight, Miss Convers turned away and walked as rapidly as she could up the inclined plane formed by the leaning quarter deck, to the stern of the ship, where she stopped, looking down upon the "hell of waters" beneath her.

Justin Rosenthal stepped hastily after her and stood by her side.

He stood a moment silent, livid, and breathing hard, like an animal spent in a long chase; but in his eyes burned the intense fire of a love victorious over horror and despair. Then he suddenly seized her hand and nearly crushed it in his convulsive grip, as he whispered hoarsely, in a voice vibrating with the strong passion of his soul—stronger than death and the grave:

"Woman! spirit! we are on the immediate brink of eternity! I love you more than life in this world or the next! I love you more than all created things in earth or heaven! Tell me, in this last mortal hour! tell me before we part—Britomarte—that you love me."

She looked him in the face and met his eye; she raised her hand and pointed upward, as she answered in a low and thrilling voice.

"We shall meet there! I will tell you then!"

Her answer seemed to satisfy him; a ray of joy inspired and exalted his countenance; once more he crushed her hand in all too strong a grasp, and then he stooped and said:

"Come! your companions are all in the boats. Let me take you to them."

"And you?"

"They are leaving me in the ship! no matter! Come!"

"Why do they leave you?"

"There is no room in the boats! Come! come! there is not an instant to be lost!"

"No! I will return . . . . . . remain with the wreck! . . . . ," she answered, with that iron resolution that he seldom ever saw in any other human being.

"But it is your duty to try and save your life! Heaven and earth! there is no time to argue this point! The ship is doomed! the boats are leaving her! Come!" he rapidly and eagerly exclaimed.

"My mind is made up! I will share the fate of— the ship!" she answered, calmly.

"Then I will save you whether you will or not!" he cried, hastily laying hands on her.

"Stop! Don't dare to use force with me, Mr. Rosenthal!" she exclaimed, in a tone that made his hands fall from her person as if they had been struck off.

"But Heaven of Heavens! there is no time—not an instant of time for persuasion! The ship is sinking, I tell you!" he cried, breathing hard.

"Then I will sink with—the ship," she persisted.

"But why? oh, why?" he demanded, quickly, scarcely able all the while to keep his hands off her. "Why? why?" he pleaded. Perhaps he hoped that in this last awful hour she would give him a supreme proof of love, and say that she was resolved to stay to share his fate. And perhaps "to share his fate" was her strongest motive for wishing to remain on the wreck; but if so, she gave a weaker one; she said:

"Because I would rather at once sink with the ship, and meet a quick and easy death, than take the chance of life amid the horrors of the lifeboats. I will stay here, and wait my fate."

"Then, before Heaven, I will not permit you to do so! You are mine by the right of the strongest love man ever felt for woman, and I will dispose of my own as I please," he exclaimed, throwing his arms around her, and lifting her up as easily as a child would lift a kitten. He bore her down to the starboard gangway, from which the last lifeboat was just putting off.

"Stop!" he shouted. "Men! seamen! some of you help to lower her down! Some of you take her as I let her go! Riordan!—Mullony!—hold up your arms!"

"Be'ad, an' I m self will do that sure! Let 'er go!" excla'm d .1 .e standing up in the boat, and spreading his arms, to receive the form that Justin was preparing to lower down.

Too proud, or too fragile to struggle with superior force, up to this instant Britomarte had been quiet enough; but now, as he was letting her go, she turned with a half-suppressed cry and clung to his breast. But he tore her away from that hold, and dropped her into the strong arms of Mike Mullony. And then, stepping back upon the deck, he waved his hand for them to push off.

But oh! what a cry of unspeakable anguish came up from that boat, as Britomarte started to her feet, and stretched forth her arms yearningly, longingly toward him, exclaiming:

"Justin! With you! Take me! My beloved! my beloved!"

But he waved his hand to Mike to take charge of her, and turned away, white as death.

And it was an insensible form that Mike Mullony laid gently in the lap of Judith Riordan, who, with his own wife, Biddy, were the only other women in that boat; Mrs. Lly and Mrs. Breton being in the other one.

While Britomarte lay still in that swoon, the boat was put off from the side of the ship. There were on board of her, besides the crew and the women, the ship's doctor and the supercargo. And oh! in the midst of all their selfish anxiety for the preservation of their own lives, and their natural sorrow for their companions left behind to perish, what grief they also felt in abandoning the brave ship that had so gallantly borne them through such a waste of waters, the good ship that had so safely brought them through such tremendous storms, and that had only succumbed at last to the overwhelming power of winds and waves! Aye, they grieved remorsefully for her as for a human being, deserted at her utmost need, and left alone to die.

When Britomarte recovered from the deep, death-like swoon that had held her life in abeyance, the boat w..
and n..

ness. Her first thought was of her lover—her first act to raise herself on her elbow, and with her eyes to sweep the horizon in search of the abandoned wreck.

Yes, there it was yet—distant and dimly seen—but certainly there, with the bows under water, and the stern wedged up in the crevice of the sunken rocks, and the sea breaking over it as before; while all above were dark and driving clouds, and all below foaming and heaving waves. The boat made very little head way over this heavy sea. Britomarte never took her eyes from the wreck. As she gazed on all that remained of the good ship, the sun suddenly burst through a black cloud; and some shining object on the stranded stern caught the rays and lighted up the wreck, like a star of hope.

"Save him! oh, God of Mercy, save him!" was the perpetual, though unuttered cry of her heart.

"Spake to me, ma'am! Look at me!" said Judith Riordan, coaxingly. "Don't be setting your eyes out on sticks, and twisting your head around like Lot's wife, looking after that wreck. God save the craytures that were left behind, for we could do nothing for thim! Sure this boat wouldn't howld another sowl! And the other boats were as heavy laden, and they left the ship first. And Lord knows what's become of them, for I don't see one of them! though troth, this fog to the landward swallows up every object, so it does. Ah, well, thin, sure I have been praying for the poor sinners left on the wreck, and saying the litany of the 'Star of the Say' ever since we left thim there! And I'll aven go at it again."

And Judith opened her little book and went at it again, muttering her litanies in a half audible voice.

Miss Conyers paid no sort of attention to her. She also was breathing earnest prayers for the salvation of one left to perish, while she strained her eyes for a sight of the wreck that was often hidden from her view by the rising of some great wave that threatened to carry it down, and as often loomed again through fog and spray to assure her of its continued existence.

"Oh! if it can but hold together for a few rays, some

ship may pass and take him off! Oh, if this dreadful sea would but subside! Oh, God have mercy on me and save him!"

Such was the constant burden of her thoughts and prayers.

There might have been others left on the wreck with Justin Rosenthal, but she scarcely remembered their existence; she thought only of him!

There was appalling danger surrounding herself and her companions in the boat, but she hardly cared for it, she suffered only for him!

Now, in this awful hour of doom, all the depths of her soul had been opened up, and she knew how strongly, how ardently, how devotedly she really loved him—how entirely he possessed her life!

Meanwhile, the danger to the boat and its crew was imminent. The sea ran high and heavy, threatening every instant to swallow them up. The shore, toward which they were blindly struggling, was covered with clouds and fogs that might hide, for aught they knew, more frightful perils than those from which they were trying to escape.

What this shore was, no one had the least idea. For twenty-four hours before the storm no observation had been taken and no reckoning made, and during the storm, the ship had been driven some hundreds of miles out of her course, so that no one knew on what rocks she was wrecked, or to what land this struggling boat was tending. The wind, that had fallen at sunrise, now started up from another quarter, and blew directly off the fog-hidden land. This soon cleared away all the mist and revealed a rugged, rockbound coast, more terrific in its aspect than the sea itself.

And the sea was growing darker and wilder every instant, and the boat was tossed like a cockle shell on the mad waves. They lowered the little sail to prevent the wind capsizing the boat, and they took to the oars and worked hard through the heavy seas along the shores, keeping as well as they could off the rocks, and watching for some opening to effect a landing.

One of the men had a pocket compass in his possession, and he took it out and set it, and saw that they were rowing northward.

The sun was sinking down through a bank of clouds behind the land, when the boat's crew, still striving with the wild waves and rowing northward, saw that they were coming to a point that seemed to be the most northern extremity of some island.

"If we can once round the point," said one of the sailors, "we can get under the lee shore, and may manage to make a landing."

"We must give it a wide berth, then, if we double it at all; the current around that point would suck the boat down to destruction in no time," said another seaman.

They turned a little off and struck out to sea, meaning to give the point with its fatal maelstrom "the wide berth" that their comrade recommended.

The sun went down and night gathered, and all was hidden from her view.

The boat's crew labored on through the darkness of the night, the beating of the wind and the roughness of the sea, striving to round that point and get under the lee shore of the land. But as night deepened the sky grew darker, the wind higher, and the sea wilder. It was a miracle that the boat lived from moment to moment, through several hours of that dread death struggle, but while they strove for life, they expected only death. They made what blind preparations they could to meet the greater calamity, when the boat itself should be lost. The men were strong swimmers, as well as good sailors and good oarsmen. Some of them took the oars, while others fastened what life preservers they had at hand on the persons of the helpless women.

Miss Conyers objected

"Pray, don't," she said. "It will be but a prolongation of the death agony. I had rather drown at once and have it all over, than beat about for hours in this wild, dark sea, and perish miserably at last."

"Bedad, though, there's a chance of life at last! And sure I promised the masther to try and save ye, and faix I'll do it! Help me here, Terry!" said Mike Mullony, and with the assistance of Terry Riordan, the father of the Irish stewardess, he invested Miss Conyers with the life-preserver.

Not an instant too soon!

There came roaring onward an enormous wave that lifted itself high above and fell with annihilating force upon them. And in an instant the boat was gone, and the souls that had intrusted themselves to her were struggling in the mad sea

Britomarte almost lost her senses in this shock of doom; and then she found herself in the wild waters, kept up indeed by the life-preserver, but dashed hither and thither, a helpless creature, at the mercy of the waves. And the night was appalling with the howling of the wind and the roaring of the waters and the shrieks of the drowning men and women!

In this scene of horror unutterable, Britomarte was beaten about, now driven out to sea, now dashed in towards the land; and through all one sublime thought exalted her soul above all the despair of the situation

"We are immortal souls and cannot be destroyed! We are spirits and must live forever!"

At last she felt herself lifted up by an enormous wave, that, roaring as in triumph over its prey, bore her forward with great velocity and threw her with deadly force upon the shore; and with the shock she lost her consciousness.

CHAPTER XI

LADY ROBINSON CRUSOE

WHEN Britomarte awoke from that deadly state of insensibility into which the tremendous mental and physical shock had cast her, her recovery seemed like coming back to life in the grave. At first she did not know what sort of creature she was, or what state of existence she had come into. Neither memory nor thought

bodily sense of uneasiness, as the air again inflated her collapsed lungs, and the vital current resumed its flow through her damp, chilled and heavy limbs; and a mortal sense of vague despair, impossible to analyze.

Instinctively she turned over and tried to rise; faintly she perceived that the palms of her hands were deep in the moist sand, and that they went deeper as she bore her weight upon them in her efforts to get up. And thus she discovered that she was on the ground.

At length, after several fruitless attempts, she succeeded in lifting herself to a sitting position. And then she looked blindly around. But nothing was to be seen. All was dark as pitch. And nothing was to be heard except the thunder of the sea upon the coast—a sound that impressed her senses like some dimly remembered knell of doom.

She put her hands up to her head, and tried to struggle forth from this state of mental dullness and confusion. She tried to think and remembed who she was, what had happened, and how she came to this hades of darkness and desolation! In vain! as well might a new-born infant try to recall the events of its pre-existence, supposing it ever to have had one. With all her striving to come forth from chaos, she could only arrive at a dim, mysterious consciousness of infinite loss and eternal despair. Was she a disembodied spirit, then? Was this really hell? Had she come to it? And for what sin? No, but such spirits had not flesh and blood, as she felt too sensibly that she had.

What then?

The ceaseless beating of the waves upon the shore was a familiar and suggestive sound, and troubled her with glimpses of memory that flitted in and out of her mind like ghosts in a graveyard.

It was a trifle that at last struck the electric chain of association, and restored her to herself. In her blind movements, she touched the inflated life-preserver that was fastened around her waist. And instantly, with a shock of returning life, the whole scene of the catastrophe flashed upon her memory. And she knew that she was cast away upon that dreary coast on which the lifeboat had been struggling all day long, and far into the night, and on which it had finally been wrecked!

But whether this coast was a part of the mainland or of an island; whether it was barren, or clothed with vegetation; whether it was uninhabited, or peopled with cannibals, she did not know and she did not care; or what deadly perils and cruel sufferings from the ruthless savages, or from protracted starvation might await her there, she did not know and did not care.

Instantly, with the flash of memory had come the knowledge of her one great sorrow, the loss of her lover and her beloved! Yes, in this awful hour of doom, Britomarte knew that she loved Justin with an earnestness that outweighed her hatred of his whole sex and her devotion to the sacred rights of her own.

And the cry of her broken heart arose wildly on the dark air, amid the profound stillness of that strange land!—a cry of bitter anguish, not for the fate of all her late companions, too probably perished in the sea, not for the feeling of her own horrible state of danger and desolation worse than death, but for despair at the loss of him whom she loved as only such souls as hers have power to love.

"Gone! gone! gone! Gone out of my way forever! Oh, this is the sorrow I dreaded worse than all others in this dark world! the only sorrow I ever really dreaded! life without him! And now he is gone forever, without one good word from me to let him know how I loved him! Ah! Heaven, how I loved him!" She wrung her hands and tore her beautiful hair and then flung her arms on high, and cried out again, in the frenzy of longing:

"Justin! Justin! My lover! My beloved! Where are you? Where are you in all space? Are you near me? Can you hear me? Oh, is there no way of piercing the veil? of getting to you, or drawing you to me? Oh, come to me! Oh, hear me! I am telling you what no power could have ever drawn from my lips, Justin, while you were in the flesh! Justin! I am telling you how I loved you! How I loved you! I want to have died with you on the wreck! I did, Justin! I did, though I would not confess I loved you! I meant to have died with you! Oh, why did you not let me? I cannot, cannot outlive you! Once you said, though you loved me so much, you could live without me, because you were so strong to suffer! But I! oh, now I know that I am not strong. I cannot live without you! and with the memory of my bitter unkindness to you! Justin! Justin! Oh, spirit! wherever you live in boundless space, speak to my spirit!"

She was indeed almost insane in her frenzy of grief, remorse and despair. And but for her deep religious principles, in her fierce anguish she would have run down through the darkness and cast herself headlong into the sea, that she still heard thundering upon the beach.

At last, exhausted by mental and physical trials, she sank down upon the ground and covered her face with her hands, and sat there in mute despair during the remaining dark hours of the night.

Day dawned in that strange place at last.

She lifted up her bowed head and looked around, feeling in the midst of all her misery the same sort of weird curiosity that causes a criminal on his way to the scaffold to look with attention at every object of interest in the range of his vision.

She saw the eastern horizon growing red behind a grove of tall, dark trees, but what sort of trees they were she could not tell. She arose to her feet and stretched her chilled and benumbed limbs and took off her life-preserver. Her clothing had dried upon her, but it had a harsh feeling and a stiff set, and a scent of the sea water. Her hair, too, was loose and flowing; combs and pins had been lost in her recent battle with the waves. But she cared little for all these circumstances. A feverish thirst consumed her and she walked on in search of some spring or stream of fresh water.

Day broadened over the unknown land, showing her an undulating and variegated country of hill and valley, plain and forest. The ground was covered with a coarse, rank verdure, and starred with many strange wild flowers. She merely glanced at these as she rambled inland in quest of a fountain to quench her burning thirst.

She walked some distance, fearless and careless of what unknown wild beasts or wilder men might intercept her progress and destroy her life. She often sank exhausted on the ground; and arose and recommenced her journey, driven onward by the fiery thirst that seemed to scorch up her very lifeblood.

She came to that grove of tall dark trees behind which she had seen the sun rise in the morning. She found them to be a grove of cocoa palms, and as she entered under their umbrella-like shades she was startled by a chattering over her head, and at the same time a missile was launched at her, that missed its mark and rolled at her feet.

She stooped and picked it up. It was a cocoanut. Raising her eyes at the same time, she saw a monkey perched in the tree above her, grinning and chattering with mischievous delight, and preparing to launch another nut at her. So she hurried from under that tree and out of the way as fast as she could. She carried off the monkey's gift with her, thinking that if she could not find fresh water, she would try to break the nut and drink the sweet milk.

She passed through the grove of cocoa palms and came out upon a gently declining plain that descended to the seaside; so she knew that she must have crossed the narrow point of land and come out at the part opposite to that upon which she had been first thrown.

The upper part of this plain was covered with a thick growth of what seemed to be a coarse reed or bamboo, or what might be a species of sugar cane. Britomarte had never seen the sugar cane growing and so she could not judge of it. She broke off one of the straight stems and placed it to her lips and found it to contain a sweet juice, which she sucked with avidity to moisten her dried lips. But this only seemed to increase her thirst; and as yet she had found no fresh water, nor could she hope to find any so near the seashore; but with a fragment of rock she contrived to break the cocoanut and drink the milk. Still that did not quench her thirst; so she once more turned her steps from the sea and walked inland, though by another route than that by which she had come.

She entered another thicket of unfamiliar trees, which were not, however, cocoa palms, but some unknown growth of that country. It was a picturesque thicket, with rocks and grottoes, clothed with luxuriant vegetation that grew in the crevices or wherever there was a root-hold of soil.

Suddenly she heard a welcome sound, the gurgling of some spring or stream of water. Following the sound, she came to a rock, from a fissure in which trickled a small, clear fountain. She hastily made a scoop of her hand, and caught and quaffed the precious liquid eagerly. And when she had quenched her feverish thirst, she bathed her face and hands, and dried them with her handkerchief, which she found safe in her pocket. While she was so employed she heard a sudden rush and whirr of wings, and looking up, she saw that a large flock of strange birds, of beautiful plumage, had made a descent and settled among the branches of the trees over her head. She watched them for a little while, and then passed out of the thicket, up upon a sort of tableland that occupied the center between the two shores of this long peninsula, as she supposed it to be. She walked on she knew not, cared not whither. Her burning thirst sated, and that physical suffering allayed, she again experienced heavy mental trouble. She walked on in a purposeless way, until, happening to glance downward she saw before her a strange looking little animal, in size and shape not unlike our young native pig. But on being observed, it started and scampered away. She went on and crossed the elevated plain and came to another thicket and passed through it and came out upon the sea coast again. And here she sat down in the collapse of despair.

"It is only to wander here until I shall be massacred by the savage natives, or destroyed by scarcely more savage beasts of prey, or else until I drag out a miserable remnant of existence, and perish slowly of famine and exposure, or of sorrow and despair, more terrible than physical suffering! How long will my strength hold out to live and suffer? Not long, I hope and pray, since it would be to no perceptible good end! Ah, well, it cannot last forever! 'Time and the hours wear out the weariest day!' This is a dreary season; but this also will pass away. Time is but a small portion of eternity, and flesh but a transient condition of the spirit; I am an immortal spirit, living in eternity, and I cannot die or be lost, and sometime—somewhere—I shall meet him! Let me think of that and be strong!"

While thus she reasoned herself out of her despondency and nerved herself to endure the horror and desolation of her condition—a horror and desolation not even to be imagined by any one who has only known misery in the midst of their own kind, in the reach of human sympathy—she suddenly heard a cry —a sharp, wild, piercing cry, between a howl and a shriek and a wail—a cry of anguish and defiance and ferocity!

She started and listened.

It was repeated again, wilder, higher, fiercer than before.

She hoped—she truly did—that it came from some rapacious beast of prey, mad with hunger, which would set upon her and make short work of her and of the "dreary season" she dreaded so much.

It was reiterated in almost human tones.

How intently she bent her head and listened.

"Ow-oo! ow-oo! ow-oo!" it screamed.

Human tones, yet not articulate sounds.

"Och-hone! och-hone! och hone!" it hallooed.

A sudden light dawned on Britomarte's mind. She knew that these last sounds were never heard off the "Gem iv the Say," except from some "exile of Erin." She immediately arose and hurried down the beach in the direction from which the cries proceeded.

And there, upon the sands, dangerously near to the water's edge, lay the form of Judith Riordan. The life-preserver was still around her waist, but she lay flat upon her back with her kicking and fighting the air, and her voice lifted and howling dismally. And with good reason; for she seemed unable to get up and run away from the spot, and the tide was coming in rapidly, and with every advancing wave threatening to overwhelm and drown her.

Miss Conyers hurried to her side and knelt down, exclaiming eagerly:

"Oh, Judith! Judith Riordan! Thanks to Heaven that you are saved!"

"Yis, thanks to Hivin, and small thanks to any of yez, laving me here be meself to be drowned entirely. And where are the lave of yez, at all, at all?" demanded the Irish woman, crossly.

"The rest of us? Oh, Judith, I don't know You are the first one that I have seen! Oh, Judith! I fear—I greatly fear—that all the others have——"

A huge wave came rolling and roaring onward, breaking at their feet and showering them with spray.

"Ah, bad luck till ye thin, why don't you drag me out of this, itself? Sure the next one will carry me off entirely!" screamed Judith.

"Oh! Judith, poor girl, can't you help yourself at all? Are you so badly hurt as all that?" inquired Miss Conyers, as she took hold of the woman's shoulders, and putting all her strength to the effort, slowly and laboriously dragged her a few feet from the water's edge and let her down a moment, while she, Britomarte, stopped to breathe and recover.

"Am I hurt so bad as that? ye ask me Ye bether believe that same! Sure and I'm thinking ivery bone in me body is broke, so I do! Ah, bedad, here come another say. Sure if I'd been left where I was, it would have took me off entirely. Och! drag me further out iv this——"

Even while she spoke, the advancing wave broke, and tumbled down, a shattered avalanche of water, at their feet, covering them with a shower of spray.

When it had fallen back, Britomarte once more took hold of her companion, and with painful efforts succeed

CHAPTER XII

LEFT TO HIS FATE

AND now let us see what in the meantime had become of Justin, left with his few unfortunate companions to perish on the deserted wreck.

After he had forcibly torn Britomarte from him and dropped her into the outstretched arms of Mike Mullony, and had heard her last despairing cry, and had waved his hand for the lifeboat to be pushed off— he abruptly turned away that he might not have his resolution shaken by the imploring words and gestures of her whom he loved more than life; for he did not know that with the cry still upon her lips she had swooned away in the arms that had received her.

He climbed with difficulty up the inclined plane of the half-submerged quarter-deck to the stern, which was lifted out of the water and wedged tightly in a cleft of the rock at an angle of about forty-five degrees, more or less.

There he turned and stood nearly waist deep in water, holding onto the shrouds of the mizzen mast to keep from being carried off by the waves.

The sea that continued to break over the wreck with tremendous shocks, did not, however, rise far above the foot of the mizzen mast; though every wave that thundered over the quaking deck shook the wreck to its keel, and nearly swept the man from his hold ings.

Yet there he stood, intently watching the receding lifeboat and silently praying for her safety, as she labored through the heavy sea.

And even when she was lost to sight, in the deep fog that enveloped the distant, unknown shore, he continued to gaze after her, until an enormous wave broke over the ship, burying him up to the neck in water and almost tearing him from the holdings where he clung with all his strength.

As the wave fell back a terrible cry arose from the sea.

Justin, clinging still to the shrouds, bent his head forward to see whence it came. And to his horror and grief, he saw a man's hand and arm strike up for an instant through the foaming wave and then sink out of sight.

"Great Heaven! Who is it? Which of my friends has been swept off?" cried Justin, gazing in sorrow upon a calamity that he was powerless to prevent.

But the arm arose no more, and Justin turned his head to look over the portion of the deck that was still above water to see what had become of his companions.

There were but three of them—Mr. Ely and Mr. Breton, whom the sailors had refused to receive on the heavily-laden lifeboats, and Captain McKenzie, whom they would willingly have taken off, but that he regarded it as a point of honor to remain with the passengers whom he was unable to rescue.

Justin, looking all over the deck, saw nothing of these men. Until the moment he had heard the cry of the drowning man, he had been so much absorbed in watching the fate of the lifeboat which contained all that he loved most on earth, that he had quite forgotten his companions in misfortune. Now, however, he looked around for them with great anxiety. One of them was lost—carried off the deck by that last great wave—that was certain; but which one? Was it either of the two young missionaries who with himself had been abandoned to destruction, or was it the brave and loyal McKenzie, who voluntarily shared the fate of those whom he could not save?

It was impossible as yet to tell; for, look as he might, Justin could see neither of his companions.

He tried to think when and where he had seen them last, and he recollected that it was on the starboard gangway, where the three stood near together when the first lifeboat, containing, besides a portion of the crew, the two young missionary ladies, was preparing to leave the ship. He himself had turned away and followed Britomarte to the stern, and his whole attention had been given to her until he lowered her into the second lifeboat. And after that he had seen no more either of the missionaries or the captain.

Now what had become of them? One was drowned; but where were the others? Justin asked himself the question, and looked about for the answer in vain. They were nowhere in sight. They were not on deck, that also was certain. It was possible that the two survivors might be in the cabin, which from the position of the wreck was as yet a place of safety. He called aloud with all the strength of his sonorous voice, which rang out clearly above the thunder of the waves:

"Ely!—Breton!—McKenzie!"

"And but the sounding sea replied,
And fast the waves rolled on."

"McKenzie!—Breton!—Ely!" he called again; but called in vain.

"Oh, the roaring of the sea drowns my voice, I suppose, so that they cannot hear me; but as soon as it is safe to let go these shrouds, if the wreck holds together, I will go down into the cabin and look for them. Great Heavens! Now I think of it, it must have been McKenzie who was lost. He must have remained on deck. He never would have hidden himself in the cabin," thought Justin, with an access on of sorrow, for he esteemed the brave and loyal captain far more than he did the well-meaning but rather weak-minded young missionaries.

In his eager look after his companions, he had ceased to watch the waves, and so he had not observed that the sea arose no higher; that the last great wave was the climax of its swell, and that now it seemed to be gradually subsiding.

His anxiety to search the cabin was now greater than ever; for he "hoped even against hope" to find the good and brave Captain McKenzie safe within its shelter. He waited and watched his opportunity to try to re... the cabin.

When the sea had gone down a little, and the waves

came with less force, but long before it was quite safe for him to leave his holding, he let go the shrouds, and began to climb the inclined deck, holding by anything that he could lay his hands on, until he reached the cabin door. It was a feat of gymnastics to get down the companion ladder, and when he had safely reached the bottom, he inadvertently lost his footing, and slid all the way down the leaning floor, until he was stopped by the opposite partition.

There he arose to his feet, stood ankle deep in water, and looked around. But he could see nothing; it was nearly dark in the cabin, the dead-lights being up, as they had been put at the commencement of the storm. He listened; but he could hear nothing except the beating of the waves that still broke over the wreck, though with decreasing force. Again he called out:

"McKenzie! Breton! Ely! Where are you? For Heaven's sake, answer!"

But there was no reply. His anxiety became intolerable.

He climbed the leaning floor again, and scaled the companion ladder, and with great difficulty succeeded in taking down the dead-lights and letting daylight into the cabin.

Then he returned to the cabin, and clearly saw its condition.

From the foot of the ladder, the floor inclined at an angle of about forty-five degrees. The highest part near the ladder was free from water, commenced around the pedestal of the center-table, and became deeper as the floor was lower, until at the partition wall it was two feet deep. The chairs and all the movable furniture had slidden down the sloping floor, and lay half submerged and piled against the wall. The doors of the staterooms were open, and the furniture within them was in the utmost confusion. And yet everything there—the women's clothing, hanging on the pegs or dropped upon the berth; the little workbasket, scattered books, but it was of desolate life, for all was chaos—still life, for not a living creature was to be seen.

A shock of alarm, almost of conviction, that his three companions had been lost, struck like an ice-bolt through his heart. He went into all the staterooms, one by one.

They all exhibited the wild disorder he had partly seen through the open doors; not only that of small sleeping apartments hastily evacuated, but that consequent upon the hurricane. The two staterooms to the right and left of the companion ladder, being in the highest part of the leaning cabin, were comparatively dry; the other two, lower down, were partly submerged.

No human being was to be found, either; but on the upper berth of the spare staterooms lay Judith Riordan's cat, quietly and comfortably nursing her three kittens. On seeing Justin's face leaning over, she began to purr with delight. What a contrast was this picture to all the desolation around?

But Justin turned away, sick at heart, to prosecute further what he felt would be a vain search for his missing friends.

The dining cabin was on the deck above, but it had been so continually swept through by the tremendous seas which had broken over the ship, that it seemed scarcely possible any living creature should have found refuge there; yet as a forlorn hope, he went thither to seek them.

And what a scene of destruction met him there!

The sea, that had fallen considerably, no longer swept through it, but everything was shaken together in the maddest medley. The table which had been laid for the supper which poor Mrs. Breton so greatly lamented the loss of, was standing in its place, for it was a fixture, and the glasses that were fitted in the swinging rack above the table were also safe, but everything else was thrown out of place and smashed to atoms, or piled up in the lowest part of the leaning floor. In the highest part of this cabin were two doors leading into two large staterooms; the rig... ...s the captain's private room, the left-hand one was the doctor's. Justin opened the door of the captain's room, but found it unoccupied. A sound of pitiful whining and barking came from the doctor's room. Justin opened the door, and found the doctor's little dog, who leaped upon him with the wildest demonstrations of delight, but otherwise this room, like the captain's, was unoccupied.

And now the anxious dread became a fatal certainty—his companions were all three lost!—swept from the deck by that last overwhelming wave! But yet, stay—one hope remained. They were not on the wreck, that was certain; but they might have been taken off at the last moment by the first lifeboat that had left the ship. They might have been so taken off without his knowledge, for he had left them standing on the starboard gangway, near the boat in which the two young wives were wildly pleading with the crew to save their husbands; the two young missionaries shaking with agitation in this crisis of their fate, and the captain pale with passion, and stern in his determination to share the fate of his abandoned ship and passengers. So he had left them to follow Britomarte and take her to the other boat, and he had not seen them since!

They might have been saved by the relenting boat's crew, but, if so, who was the castaway that he had seen and heard in the uplifted arm and voice for one instant before he—the castaway—was whelmed in the sea?

Again came the overpowering conviction—it was the brave McKenzie who was lost. The young missionaries had probably been taken off at the prayers of their wives; for sailors have a soft place in their hearts, or heads, for the woes of women, and will risk much to alleviate them; and so they had probably consented to risk the swamping of their heavily-laden boat by the additional weight of the two young husbands rather than listen to the sobs and cries of the two heartbroken young wives. But Captain McKenzie had chosen to remain on the wreck with his one abandoned passenger—Justin Rosenthal; and he

—the gallant McKenzie—had been swept off the deck and was lost!

Such was the conclusion that Justin came to. And at the thought he sat down and dropped his head upon his hands and sobbed aloud; for, you see, as I have often said before, the bravest are always the tenderest.

The doctor's little dog, unable to endure such an appalling sight, to him, as a man's distress, jumped and whined around him in sympathetic grief and terror.

At length Justin lifted up his bowed head and tried to bring reason and religion to the relief of his great regret. He reflected that the death of so good a man could but have been a quick passage to eternal bliss—a blessed fate compared to that which awaited himself, left to perish slowly on the abandoned wreck, or that which attended the fugitives in the boats, exposed to battle with the elements, and perhaps with hunger and thirst for days, upon the bare chance of saving their lives.

Somewhat strengthened by the first clause of his reflections upon the eternal destiny of the brave and good captain, and very much distracted by the counter irritant of his anxiety for the fate of the lifeboats, Justin Rosenthal arose to leave the dining cabin, the little dog jumping and barking around him.

Just as he went out on deck, the sun broke through a mass of black clouds, and striking upon the brasses of the stern, lighted up the whole wreck in a perfect blaze of glory.

It was the same "star of hope" that had been seen by Britomarte, from the lifeboats, just before the wreck disappeared from her view in the distance. For it must be remembered that the wreck, being much the larger object of the two, and being hoisted high upon the rocks, was visible to the boat's crew long after the boat was lost to Justin's sight.

By noon the sea had fallen so much that the whole length of the deck from stem to stern was above the water; and Justin was enabled to take note of the actual condition of the ship.

She rested . . . fted

high and wedged tight in the crevice of the rocks, and her deck inclined at a great angle. Her bows were very much broken and her keel was gored by the sharp points of the rocks upon which she had struck and where she was fast fixed. Her hold must have been full of water, which would have sunk her but for the fact that she was high and fast upon the rocks; that with the rise and fall of the waves the large leaks let out the water as easily as they let it in.

Justin went down to the lower deck and examined the forecastle, which he found in an even greater state of chaos than the cabin and the saloon had been. Everything was saturated with sea water.

From there he went into the storeroom, which he found in the same condition. All the provisions that could be hurt by salt water were totally ruined—except a few articles that, being in water-tight receptacles, remained uninjured.

Feeling faint from long fasting, Justin broke open a tin canister of biscuits and sat down to satisfy his hunger upon that dry fare. The little dog that had trotted after him wherever he went, as if afraid of being left behind, now stopped and stood on his hind legs and began to beg as his poor master, a little Dutch doctor, had taught him to do. Then, perceiving that his new master did not notice him, he began to expostulate in short, impatient barks.

Justin threw him some biscuits, and, leaving him to nibble them, went to the upper deck.

How rapidly the sea had fallen! The jagged rocks upon which the bows of the ship rested were laid bare. The wind had changed, and blew directly off that distant, unknown shore, rolling the fogs out to sea and towards the wreck. While Justin strained his eyes to make out, if he could, what sort of shore it was, he felt something rub against his ankles and heard a mew.

He glanced down and saw the poor cat, who was rubbing her furry sides against his limbs, and mewing piteously, and gazing up into his face with that helpl...

tion in their need seem to pray to the human for relief.

"Poor little animal!" said Justin, stooping, and gently stroking her fur. "Poor little companion in wretchedness! You look up in my face with your perplexed eyes, as if you think I have the power, and ought to have the will, to help you. But you are half famished, and I have nothing but a biscuit to give you. And, as you are not granivorous, it is not your natural food."

And he broke up the biscuit and scattered the pieces on the deck.

And pussy, granivorous though she was not, pounced upon the fragments as if they had been so many young mice, and devoured them all before she returned to her kittens.

Then Justin found his way to the cabin, and threw himself upon one of the berths in Britomarte's abandoned stateroom.

For some hours he lay, not sleeping, but thinking of her, and praying for her safety. Then, as even convicts sometimes sleep the night before their execution, he, Justin, notwithstanding his own great personal peril, and his excessive anxiety for Britomarte's fate, fell asleep, and slept long and well.

CHAPTER XIII

ON THE ISLAND

When he turned out of his berth next morning he noticed that the cabin was entirely free from water, from which circumstance he judged that the waves had quite subsided.

He climbed up on deck to take a look at the prospects there. He found that the ship was high and dry upon the rocks, and that the water in her hold had run out.

The sly

and the sun shone down upon a sea as calm as the inland lake.

In the pure atmosphere the distant land could be distinctly seen, with its rugged white line of rockbound coast in strong relief between the deep blue sky and deep blue sea.

But as Justin dropped his eyes upon the intervening space between the land and the wreck, an exclamation of surprise and joy escaped him.

What he saw there was rescue! was safety! It was what could not have been seen at any other period since the gale, for at no other such period had the sea been so low as it was now. What he saw, then, was an extremely long and narrow chain of rocks, reaching out from the distant shore to the point upon which the ship had been wrecked. It was a natural causeway, extending from the land far out into the sea. When the sea was high, this causeway was deeply covered with water, and thus the ship, when driven so far out of her course, had struck upon it and had been wrecked. But now the sea had fallen; and the causeway was above water; so that any expert walker and climber might pass over it almost dry shod to the land.

Justin was not one of the sort who stand idle and indulge in speculations while there is anything to do. He knew that the first thing for him to do was to try to reach the shore by that causeway.

He knew that there was no danger of the ship breaking up just yet; unless there should be another hurricane, which was not to be expected, at least until the next change of the moon. He knew also that while she held together, the ship afforded a safer place of refuge than the unknown land might offer; for on the ship there was nothing to injure him, while on the land he might fall into the hands of cannibals. And in that case what could one man do against a whole tribe? Still, he considered, that unless he would perish in the sea when the ship should break up, that unknown land, with all its hidden dangers, must sooner or later be his own, and he thought the sooner he ventured the better.

With this resolution he went into the captain's private cabin to look for a small telescope, which he felt sure was there, and which he wished to use in surveying the causeway and the shore. He found it and came out. The little dog jumped down from the doctor's berth, where he had nestled himself in his accustomed place to sleep, and began barking and jumping up and wagging his tail by way of a morning greeting to his new master.

Justin patted his head, and then went out on deck, followed by his little four-footed companion.

The ship had struck at right angles with the chain of rocks, so that the starboard gangway was towards the shore. There Justin stood and adjusted his glass to view the far-reaching causeway and the distant land.

But, even with the aid of his telescope, he could discover little more than he knew before. He could only more distinctly ascertain that the causeway was a chain of rocks leading to the shore—a road that would be covered with water at high tide, and be entirely bare at low tide; and that the distant land presented only a rock-bound and forbidding aspect.

While he was still gazing, he felt something claw at his boots, mewing pitifully; and the next instant he heard a shrill barking, and spitting, and clapper-clawing. And he looked down to see the cat and dog engaged in a fierce combat, in which the fur flew plenteously.

Justin separated them, lifting the cat up in his arms, and giving the dog an admonishing kick. Then he took them both down into the storeroom and fed them apart.

While he was busy in this humane duty, he was greeted by a dismal sound—a prolonged "Ooom mow'" that he knew must come from the captain's cow. He followed the sound until it led him to her pen, which was between decks in the stern, a position that had saved her from being drowned, as the stern was lifted at such a high angle upon the rocks. Justin had no sooner reached the cow pen, then he was greeted by a perfect

in that part of the ship. The hens clucked, the ducks quacked, the sheep baa'd. and, above all, the pigs squealed as if they would have squealed themselves to death, and their hearers to deafness.

All these animals had been saved by their position from drowning, but they were in great danger of starving.

Justin went back to the storeroom, and found an ax. and broke open several boxes of grain; and then went to the fresh water butts, and drew water, and mixed food, and carried it to the pens, and fed the famished creatures.

Then he set a pan of milk in the cabin for the cat. After which he filled a little basket with a day's provisions for himself, and put a pair of revolvers in one pocket and a small telescope and a pocket compass in the other. Then he put on a broad-brimmed hat, and took in his hand a stout walking-stick, called the dog to follow him, and went carefully down the leaning deck to the bows of the ship, that were nearly on a level with the rocks. With one bound he sprang from the ship to the causeway. The little dog jumped after him.

The causeway was high and dry above the sea, and long and narrow in its course, and irregular and rugged in its aspect.

Walking on it would have been very dangerous, either to a reckless or a timid pedestrian.

But Justin was at the same time careful and fearless, and he and his little companion went on safely enough, though often slowly and with difficulty; for often a deep chasm cut the causeway across, and then Justin would be obliged to stop and consider the best way of getting over it, and then, with the aid of his walking-stick, he would have to descend very carefully down one side, and using his stick for a leaping-pole, throw himself across the isthmus at the bottom, and then as carefully ascend the other side.

Sometimes the little dog would follow him well enough, tripping down the first side, swimming the isthmus at the bottom, and climbing up the other side; but at other times a steep or

the stream at the bottom very rapid, the little dog would come to a dead halt, and stand whining miserably, and Justin would have to turn back, and take him up in his arms, and carry him over.

Thus Justin was two hours in going the distance between the ship and the shore.

As he neared the shore, the causeway became wider and higher, until it began to assume the aspect of a cape or promontory, and so it continued to rise and widen until, almost unawares, Justin, with his dog, found himself ascending a rocky hill, in character almost a barren mountain.

In this ascent he found his walking stick of great service in getting a purchase upon the difficult ground; but he found his little dog a great trouble to him; for he—the dog—was tired, and would often stop and whine as persistently to be taken up and carried as any spoiled child.

And Justin always indulged him, for he was much too kind hearted to leave his little four-footed companion behind. Another hour's painful toil brought Justin to the top of the mountain, which he judged to be about a thousand feet above the level of the sea. The summit was as bare of vegetation as the ascent from the causeway had been; so that Justin, from his point of observation, had a very extended view of the landscape. He took out his telescope, adjusted it, and took a sweeping view around the horizon.

He found that the land was on all sides surrounded by the sea, and that he was on an island oblong in shape, and as well as he could judge, about twenty miles in length by about ten in its utmost width.

The lofty hill, or mountain, upon which he stood, was the highest point upon the island, and was situated near the southern end—the long causeway upon which the ship had been wrecked being the extreme southern point. And, though this mountain was barren on the side descending towards the interior, it was fringed with beautiful trees and gemmed with sparkling fountains. The center of the island was ve   yards

the extreme north the land descended and narrowed to a sandy neck of not more than a mile in width from sea to sea; but this neck was thickly wooded with the tall and graceful cocoa palms.

Having observed so much, and the time being now about two hours after noon, Justin, who was "sharp set," from his long and toilsome walk along the causeway and up the mountain, sat down and emptied his basket in preparation for his midday meal. It was but a simple luncheon of cold bacon, ship biscuit and milk, but he and his little dog enjoyed it very much.

Having finished his meal, he began to descend the mountain, with the purpose of exploring the island as far as he could that afternoon, and of spending the night upon it, if he should find a convenient place of repose.

He designed to return on the next morning to the ship to feed the animals and make preparations for bringing away all that was likely to be useful to him in this strange land, which he foresaw would probably be his home for as long as he should live in this world.

With the aid of his stick he slowly descended the difficult mountain side. About half way down he stopped at a fountain to assuage his thirst. The little dog, who had kept close to his heels, followed his example, and lapped lower down the stream.

Then Justin resumed his journey, and continued it without interruption until, near the base of the mountain, the little dog startled a covey of splendid oriental birds that burst up from their cover, deafening him with their explosive cries, and dazzling him with their gorgeous colors, so that the whole thing affected him something like the sudden lett'ng-off of fireworks would have done. The little dog took the affair as a personal affront, and continued to bark himself hoarse long after the winged fireworks had disappeared in the distance. Justin pacified him at length, and they went on. As they reached the foot of the mountain, the sun sank behind the horizon.

Justin sat down to rest and reflect.

"Night before last on the deck of the ship, pudding

before a terrible hurricane; last night alone upon the wreck, in the midst of the stormy sea; to-night on an unknown and what seems to be an uninhabited island. What next, I wonder! Well, I earnestly thank God that my life has been preserved! But what has become of her—of Britomarte, whom I forced to leave the ship? Oh, would to Heaven I had permitted her to remain! She would have been even now by my side! And now—where is she? Where? Shall I ever meet her again on this side of the grave? Ah, Heaven, who can answer any of those questions?" he groaned, and unable longer to sit still, he got up and walked forward, still followed by his faithful little four-footed friend. He walked on and on through the woods at the foot of the mountain, while twilight deepened into night, and the stars came out in the purple-black sky; then he sat down and rested for a little time, while the dog coiled itself up and went to sleep at his feet. Then he got up again and resumed his walk, followed still by his sleepy but loyal little adherent.

He walked on until the moon arose, when he discovered that he had come out upon the seacoast, through the grove of cocoa palms that he had seen from the mountain top.

CHAPTER XIV

A MEETING BY MOONLIGHT

Britomarte conducted her frightened companion to the thicket of woods and grottoes where she had found the spring.

She made her sit down on a fragment of rock under a spreading tree, and then she went to the spring and found a large leaf, which she doubled up in the form of a cup, and caught some water, which she brought to the woman, who drank it eagerly.

"Ah, thin! bless the Lord for giving us water itself! Sure, there's nothin'

thirst is upon one!" said Judith, gratefully, drawing a long breath.

Britomarte brought some wild plums and cocoanuts which she saw growing, and gave them to Judith.

At first the woman was too frightened by the chattering of monkeys and the growls of hidden forest fiends to open her mouth; but Britomarte overcame her fears and she ate and drank with avidity.

Miss Conyers made a meal of the plums she had gathered.

But Judith, now that her appetite was satisfied found another source of trouble.

"Sure, the sun is setting, and it will soon be dark! And Lord kape us, where will we slape?"

"It is a lovely summer evening, Judith. And there is a deep, dry grotto in the thicket that we have left. We will stay here through the twilight, and through the dark hours before moonrise, and then we will go to the grotto and sleep."

And there they sat through the short twilight, and through the long, dark hours that intervened before the moon arose. The moon arose, a glorious, golden globe, illumining with its rich, soft light the broad expanse of sea, and the strange, wild land, with its stately palm trees.

Britomarte sat gazing with something like calm enjoyment upon the exceeding beauty of the scene. Sleeping, or forgotten in this quiet hour, seemed all her sorrows.

Judith gradually fell to nodding and snoring

She was awakened with a vengeance.

A grim footstep came crunching through the pebbles on the beach.

With a scream, Judith started to her feet.

Miss Conyers also arose and listened

And almost at the same instant Justin Rosenthal appeared before them.

"Lord kape us—it's his sperit!" gasped Judith, who was too panic-stricken to turn and fly, but stood with her face blanched as white as snow, and her mouth and eyes distended with terror.

Almost at the same instant! Britomarte, gazing upon each other in incredulous astonishment and unspeakable joy. For an instant they stood thus, and then their joy broke forth:

"Saved! Oh, thank God! thank God!" exclaimed Justin, holding out his arms toward her.

She extended her hands. She could not speak; the overwhelming tide of joy had deprived her of the power.

But he caught her to his bosom; and she dropped her head upon his shoulders, and burst into a passion of tears and sobs.

"Oh, my own! my own!" he cried, "my beloved! my peerless treasure! This is the very happiest moment of my life! How dearly purchased with shipwreck and the loss of everything else!"

Still she sobbed upon his shoulder, unable to make any other reply.

"You are with me! I have you, and I care for nothing that can befall me that does not part us!" he continued.

"And I'm left out in the cold entirely," said Judith, who had gradually recovered from her panic and recognized the apparition as Mr. Rosenthal in the flesh.

"Britomarte! Love! love! Do you know how happy I am? Speak to me, love! I have not heard the sound of your voice yet, except in sobs. Speak to me, my own, only love!" whispered Justin.

"Oh, I am so glad, so glad, that you are saved! Oh thank God! thank God! Oh, in what words can I thank God enough!" exclaimed Britomarte, with an emotion that shook her whole delicate frame.

He caught her closer to his bosom, and bent down his head over hers until his lips touched her forehead and his auburn locks mingled with her dark brown tresses.

"God bless you for every sweet word you have spoken, oh, my dearest! my dearest!" he murmured.

But it was not until her great passion of joy had somewhat exhausted itself that she recollected herself, and gently attempted to withdraw from his embrace.

But of course he held her fast; until at length she said, ever so kindly, but ever so firmly:

"Let me go, please. I am not quite sane, I think. Oh, I am so glad, so glad you are safe! Thank God with all my heart and soul! Oh, thank Him forever and ever! I do not care that I am shipwrecked on this foreign shore now!" she added, earnestly.

"Nor I; not one whit. I rather like it," agreed Justin, as he sat her down upon a ledge of rocks and took a seat by her side.

"No more would I, if I had Fore Top Tom foreninst me, and daddy, and could get me tay, and toast, and mate, and granes rigalar," muttered Judith, dropping into her old place

"I was so overjoyed to see you safe, that I forgot to ask how you were saved, or where your companions are," said Justin.

"My companions! Ah, Mr. Rosenthal, how selfish I was to forget them for a moment! They are all lost! Our boat foundered in that last gale! Only myself and Judith Riordan chanced to be saved by having life preservers on, and by being cast ashore by a wave. Our companions are lost!" said Britomarte, solemnly.

"Lost!" repeated Justin, gravely.

And a deep silence fell between them—a reverential silence in tribute to the dead, taken away so awfully; a long silence, broken at length by the voice of Judith, who, reminded of her losses, recommenced her howling.

"Lost!" again repeated Justin. "Well, God's will be done. All our grief will not restore them to us. And, much as I lament the calamity, I am too happy in this hour of reunion with you to feel inconsolable at any circumstance whatever."

"How were you saved? Though I am so glad to see you saved that I have scarcely room to feel curious about the manner," said Miss Conyers.

"When the storm was over, and the wind and the waves had fallen, the ship was left high and dry upon the rocks, in a crevice of which the stern was tightly wedged. These rocks formed the extremity of a long chain, or natural causeway, extending from the land far out into the sea. When the subsiding of the sea left this chain bare, I passed over it to the land. And here I am—your lover and servant, to work for you and defend you, through life and unto death!"

"Again and again, and forever and forever, thank God that you are safe! But for the rest——"

She paused and hesitated.

"Yes, for the rest—for the rest, Britomarte?" he eagerly repeated.

"Do not speak of it now, or here! It would be scarcely generous or like yourself to do so."

"It would not be like myself to do anything repugnant to your feelings!" said Justin, a little abashed; then recovering his self-possession and dignity, he added, slowly and thoughtfully, as if he weighed every word before he uttered it:

"We three persons—being two women and one man—are cast here upon this unknown and uninhabited island, where we may remain for years, or even for the term of our natural lives; for, however little we do know of it, we know that it is out of the course of ships, since our own ship was driven very far out of her course before she was wrecked upon its shores. There are no habitations here, nor any of the commonest conveniences of human life. All these have to be provided by labor—hard manual labor such as women cannot perform—such as men only can accomplish. This being so, Miss Convers, while ever we remain together on this island, whether it be for years or for our lives, I will serve you with all the honor a subject owes his queen, and all the love a brother bears his sister. Let us close hands upon that."

"Willingly," said Britomarte, giving her hand. "Be —not my subject, for that savors too much of the old folly—be my brother, and as my brother I will love and honor you infinitely! I will pray God to bless you always."

"Agreed! But this compact is to last so long as we remain on this island," said Justin.

"Yes."

"And when we are rescued, if ever we should be; when is you a g y should see you so—then, Britomarte—then I shall sue for some nearer and dearer tie than that which unites the most loving brother and sister!"

"Mr. Rosenthal! Justin! why will you advert to this forbidden subject? I esteem and honor you beyond all men, because you are an exceptional man! but I tell you I esteem and honor you only as a good and noble brother! In no other light can I ever regard you. You know what my principles are, and what my frequent declarations have been: that I never will become the wife of any man while the present unjust laws of marriage prevail," said Miss Conyers, earnestly."

And while she spoke these cold words, the sound of other words—uttered in her wild agony, at that bitter moment of parting were echoing through his memory —"Justin! Justin! With you! My beloved! My beloved!"

And he saw again the outstretched arms and the wild, appealing gaze with which she had uttered them. Had she forgotten them? or did she wish to ignore them? He could not tell. But he felt, of course, that honor and delicacy forbade him to allude to them, or even to the joy with which he received them—all these circumstances being "proof as strong as Holy Writ" that she loved him as no sister ever loved a brother.

Now he answered her cold words as calmly as she had spoken them:

"While we remain on this island I will never even ask you for a promise or a hope of the sort, and this is the last time I will ever allude to the subject. But now you should have some repose. I can understand why you should deem it prudent to watch the night out rather than sleep, in this strange land, which might, for aught you knew, be infested with wild beasts; but now that I am here to defend you, there is no reason why you should not sleep in peace."

"I was not afraid to go to sleep," replied Miss Conyers, a little proudly; "but my companion here refused to go in ·· ·· · · · ·· · ·· ·· ·· I not think it ·· · ·· · · · · ··)

"It was like you to think of others first; but now you can both seek shelter and sleep while I watch. There is a fine grotto that I passed in my rambles over the island, which I think would afford you a safe place of refuge for to-night. To-morrow better shelter shall be provided."

"I thank you earnestly," said Miss Conyers. "That grotto was the place of shelter I first wished to go to. Come, Judith."

"Sure, and I'll not budge a fut unless the gentleman promises to stand at the hole all night to keep off the wild bastes!" said the woman, defiantly.

"I promise that, Judith. I had a good night's rest on the wreck last night, and so I can very well afford to lose this night's sleep," replied Mr. Rosenthal.

Britomarte objected strongly to Justin's proposed watching; but he succeeded in convincing her that he could watch without inconvenience. And so they all went to the grotto in the thicket.

Justin spread his great coat on the floor to make a bed for Britomarte, and then he bade her good night, and went out and took up his stand as sentinel before her rude bower.

CHAPTER XV

MAKING THE BEST OF IT

WITH the earliest dawn of morning Justin withdrew from his post and went and gathered some loose, dry sticks, and piled them up before the hole of the grotto and but a short distance from it. Then he took some matches that he had brought in his pocket, and kindled a fire to protect Britomarte and her attendant from the approach of any beast of prey; for it is well known that no wild animal will ever venture to come near a fire.

Then leaving his sleeping charge he took up his stout walking staff and hurried away as fast as he could go in the direction of the cane-brake. His wish and in

provisions for Britomarte's breakfast, and to return with them to the grotto before she should awake and miss him from his post.

Knowing now the way so well, and being relieved from the trouble of looking after the little dog, that he had left sleeping at the feet of Britomarte, he made much faster progress over the distance between the island and the ship than he made on the preceding day.

He plunged straight ahead through the thicket, without the slightest regard to briers and brambles. He passed over the mountain with more haste than care; but finally he reached the landward end of the causeway with safety as well as with swiftness.

Then he set out to walk across the causeway to the ship. He hurried on without much respect to discretion, dropping himself down the steeps; with the aid of his walking-staff, which he used as a leaping pole, flinging himself across the chasms; and running on all the level places until he reached the ship and jumped upon the leaning bows, which were down upon the level of the causeway.

He found the ship very much in the same condition in which he had left it, and in which it might remain for an indefinite length of time.

He found also plenty of work to do, and he hastened to do it. First of all, the poor cat met him on the deck, with every demonstration of delight a dumb creature could make. That was his welcome. But, of course, she had lapped up all the milk he had left for her in the cabin, and she wanted more.

He went immediately to the pens to look after the condition of the animals, and he found that they also had consumed all the provender he had placed there for them, and they were clamorous for a new supply. He hastened to the storeroom and mixed mashes and brought to the pens and fed all the creatures plentifully. Then he milked the cow and fed the cat. For even in his eager impatience to get back to the island with provisions for his own subsistence, he could not neglect the sacred duty of providing for the brutes of

these poor dumb brutes, which were so utterly helpless and dependent upon his kindness.

These duties faithfully discharged, he passed into the storeroom to attend to the business upon which he had especially come. He looked up a large basket with a cover, and he proceeded to fill it with parcels of tea, coffee, sugar, biscuit, butter, bacon, pepper and salt, and a bottle of milk. Next he went to the pens again and found the hens' nests, and collected about a dozen fresh eggs, which he also added to his store.

Then he ascended to the dining saloon, and from the mounds of *debris* there he picked out a few knives, forks and spoons, and cups, saucers and plates, that had escaped the general crash, and put them in with the provisions. And he took a tablecloth and folded it and laid it over all the contents of the basket, which was now quite full, and upon which he shut down and fastened the cover.

Next he went down into the caboose and looked up a teakettle, a frying-pan, a teapot and a coffee-boiler, and tied them together by the handles and hung them upon a pair of tongs, which he slung over his left shoulder. And with his heavy basket of provisions on his left arm, and the handle of the tongs in his left hand, and his stout walking-staff grasped in his right hand, he left the wreck and set out upon his return to the island.

Britomarte was up and about when he returned.

"Good morning, sister; I hope you rested well," was his cheerful, smiling greeting, as he carefully set the basket down and dropped the cooking utensils, and stretched his cramped arms.

"Thanks to your kind guardianship, very well," said Britomarte, cordially.

"You are staring at that basket, Judith," said Justin, laughing. "Well, I have been to the ship, and brought off some provisions for breakfast. The greater part of the ship's stores are spoiled by the wetting they got in the storm, but still there is a considerable quantity which here it just so, aped injury."

The breakfast was very leisurely eaten. It was a pleasure to linger over that *tête-à-tête* meal; and it was prolonged as much as possible.

When it was over, Britomarte and Justin withdrew from it, leaving Judith to her undisputed privilege of washing up the service.

"The first thing to be done," said Justin, as they walked apart, "is to provide shelter. There is no time to be lost before it is done. The grotto, it is true, is better than the open sky, and it is well enough at night."

This grotto was at the inland base of that long mountain that Justin crossed in coming from the causeway to the center of the island. It was entered by a hole about seven feet high by three broad. Around this hole, and up the entire side of the mountain, the whole surface was richly clothed with a thicket of shrubs and saplings wherever they could find root hold in the soil between the rocks, and it presented a most beautiful appearance. In front of the grotto was the small natural opening in the woods, where our little party had made their fire and eaten their breakfast.

Passing in through this hole of the rock, or doorway of the grotto, as it might be called, Justin and Britomarte found themselves in a spacious cave, of oval form and great natural beauty. The floor was nearly level, and the walls rose in the form of a dome, in the top of which was a fissure that let in the sun; and floor and walls were all of the most brilliant white stone, that reflected back the sunlight with the luster of frosted silver. The whole size of the place was about that of a large family drawing-room.

"It is a palace for a fairy!—a bower for a queen!" said Justin, in admiration.

And then they turned and left the grotto to look after Judith.

CHAPTER XVI

SAVING THE STORES

"THE next thing to do," said Justin, as they joined Judith at the fire, "is to get all the stores from the wreck. After I have secured them I may bring away as much of everything else that may be useful to us as I can move before the ship breaks up."

"It is a great labor that you propose for yourself," said Britomarte, gravely.

"An absolutely necessary labor, and therefore to be undertaken and accomplished," replied Justin, smiling.

"You must let us take our share of the work."

"My dear—sister, I mean—the task will be much too laborious for you. The causeway over which all these things have to be brought is no macadamized avenue, I assure you."

"For all that, Justin," you travers'd it yet, and you know that I must make the attempt. If I fail I shall very quietly yield the point and leave all the labor to yourself alone."

"Well, well," said Justin, laughing, "You are 'queen o'er yourself' and all things else here. You must work your own will."

"And sure, here's meself, wid me two hands to the fore, ready to fetch and carry wid the best uv yez."

"Thank you, Judith, I had certainly counted on your help," said Mr. Rosenthal. "And now—sister—shall we set forth?" he inquired, turning toward Britomarte.

"If you please," said Miss Convers.

Justin looked up through the trees toward the blazing sky. For though this was January, yet they were in a climate where that month answers to our July.

"It is very hot and growing hotter, and I dare say you did not bring a bonnet with you when you landed on this island?" he inquired, with a droll look.

"I dare say I did not," smiled Britomarte.

But

"Bonnet?" she echoed. "Sure mine was lost itself in a fray fight wid the say!—Bonnet? Faix, it was all I could do at all, at all, to kape the hair itself on me head, let alone bonnets!"

"Then we must improvise some defense for your heads against this sun," said Mr. Rosenthal, looking around. "Ah! I have it! the palm leaves! nothing could be better!" he exclaimed, starting off in a run through the thicket toward the grove of cocoa palms.

"Ah! sure, what would we do without him, at all, at all! Troth, we hadn't aven a dacent meal's victuals till he come to our relaif, so we hadn't. Sure, we'd perish intirely only for him," said Judith, looking gratefully in the direction where Justin had disappeared.

The man-hater did not reply. There was no controverting Judith's words. Perhaps also they expressed Britomarte's own thoughts. What, indeed, though one was brave and the other strong, could these two women have done for self-preservation, left alone on this desert island, without the help of the one man Providence had sent to their assistance?

Justin soon returned, bearing large palm leaves, which, with some natural dexterity, he doubled and shaped into a rude sort of hoods, more remarkable for utility than for beauty.

"There," he said, "they are not in the latest Parisian style of ladies' bonnets, I am afraid, but they will keep the sun off, and to do that is the purpose for which they were formed. I hope we may all answer the end of our creation as well."

When they were about to start, the little dog, seeing symptoms of a move, began jumping and frisking around them, to testify his approbation of the journey and his willingness to share it.

"No, you don't, my fine little fellow. I have had enough of crossing the causeway with you. I had rother carry a two-year old child at once. We'll leave you here," said Justin, looking about for some means of confining the dog.

To "leave him" there was easier to say than to do. They might have tied him to a tree, only they had neither rope nor chain. Or they might have shut him up in the grotto, only they had no door to close against his exit.

At length a bright idea struck Justin. He took his handkerchief from his pocket, rubbed it well upon his own face and hands and laid it down on the ground, and called the little dog, and said:

"Fidelle! Fidelle!—watch it!"

And the royal little creature ran and put his fore paws upon it and stood looking "faithful unto death" with all his might.

"Come—we can go now," said Justin. "Our way leads up the mountain, immediately over the roof of your grotto, sister; and the ascent is steep and rugged; and although you are not a very ancient lady, I think that you will find this staff serviceable, indeed, indispensable," he added, handing to Miss Conyers a stick that he had cut for her use in climbing, and which she received with a smile of thanks.

He gave Judith a similar staff, and then they all set forth.

They ascended the mountain in a much shorter time than might have been expected.

When they reached the tableland on the summit, Justin found a fragment of rock that would do for a seat, and advised Britomarte to sit down and rest.

Then he took out his telescope and adjusted it, and invited her to take a survey of their little kingdom—

"For this island is our kingdom, my sister'—

"'We are monarchs of all we survey—
  Our rights there is none to dispute;
From the center all round to the sea
  We are lords of the bird and the brute.'

"But how much happier we are than was poor, solitary Robinson Crusoe, or his prototype, old Alexander Selkirk!" said Justin, placing the telescope in her hands, as she arose and stood beside him. "Rest the glass upon my shoulder to steady it, and then look," he added, placing himself in a convenient position as a telescope

She adjusted the instrument according to his advice, pointing it toward the wreck, which she saw distinctly wedged in the cleft of the rock at the end of the causeway.

"Poor ship! I lament her fate almost as if she were a human being doomed to death. For, of course, she is doomed. She must break up sooner or later," said Britomarte.

"Yes, sooner or later," replied Justin, contemplatively; "and it seems even the greater pity, because, as she lays now, she is really not injured beyond repair, were the means of repairing her at hand. However, she will hold together the longer for being hurt no worse."

Britomarte now lifted the end of the telescope from Justin's shoulder, and, taking it in both her own hands, supported it thus while she made a survey of the whole circle of the horizon. Some minutes passed in this review, during which no one spoke. Britomarte was the first to break silence.

"A wilderness surrounded by the sea; a desert in the midst of the ocean! It is magnificent—it is sublime in its utter isolation and perfect solitude!" she said, lowering her glass.

"It is," answered Justin, relieving her of the telescope. "Yet let Providence give me the time, strength, and opportunity and this wilderness shall bloom and blossom as the rose, this desert become a beautiful home. This island shall be a new Eden, of which we shall be the new Adam and Eve. Yes! for all that has come and gone, we shall be very happy her—Sister!"

He brought himself up with a jerk by this last word. His fancy had been running away with him, until he saw the clouds gathering upon the man-hater's brow, when he suddenly pulled up with—"Sister!"

"Shall we go on?" asked Britomarte.

"Certainly, if you are rested," replied Justin.

And they resumed their journey, going down the mountain side toward the causeway.

"I think that we had all the necessaries and comforts, and many of the luxuries and elegancies of life on board of our ship, had we not?" inquired Justin as they went on.

"Yes, of course, but you have some reason for asking that question, or rather for reminding me of those things. Now, what is your reason?" inquired Miss Conyers.

"Merely to follow up your answer by assuring you that you shall have all those necessaries, comforts, and perhaps luxuries and elegances still."

Britomarte looked up at him inquiringly.

"Nearly all these things remain yet upon the wreck. If it will only hold together for a month, I can, by diligence, convey them all to the land, and store them here. There is a chest of carpenter's tools in the forecastle; and there are building materials enough on the island. I can build you a very fair little house, and furnish it comfortably with the furniture I shall rescue from the cabin and staterooms of the wreck. There is also a large assortment of grain and garden seeds, which poor Ely was carrying out with him to try the experiment of growing them on Indian soil. I will try the more promising experiment of planting them on your island. And then there are the animals to stock your farm! The cow, the pigs, the sheep, and the poultry—if I can only get them over the causeway. This—the removal of the animals—will certainly be the most difficult part of our enterprise. But if it is to be effected by any amount of labor and perseverance, I will effect it."

"Sure, sir, did ye say as Cuddie is saved, the crayture?" inquired Judith, who was tugging on after them as fast as she could.

"Cuddie!" echoed Mr. Rosenthal, with the air of perplexity.

"Yes, sir, sure—Cuddie, the captain's cow itself, the crayture! I was asking you is she saved sir?"

"Oh, yes," laughed Justin; "I milked her this morning for your breakfast, you know, Judith. And oh! by the way, I fed your cat and kittens, too, Judith. They, also, are quite safe."

"Ah, thin, bad luck to thim! Are they safe is it, af er

wish they'd been drowned, so I do, the day I brought them on the ship to bring destruction on us all! Ah, bedad! we'll lave them where they are, and not bring a bit of them off at all, at all!"

"But that would be cruel, Judith. And as for myself, I shall not leave the smallest living creature to perish on the ship, if any effort of mine will save it."

"Ah, thin, sure would ye bring thim divil's imps on the land to bring us to disthruction over agin'!"

"People can't be brought to destruction 'over again,' my good girl."

"Oh, can't they though, nather! Sure ourselves was brought to disthruction once be the shipwrack, and we may be brought to disthruction over again be wild bastes or ilse be cannibals! Whist! Lord kape us! where are yez a-going to at all, at all?" gasped Judith, breaking off suddenly in her discourse, and stopping short in her progress upon the brink of one of those chasms that cut the causeway across.

"Don't be frightened, Judith. Stand just where you are until I help Miss Conyers over to the other side, and then I will come back for you," said Justin, who was carefully supporting Britomarte in her difficult descent down one side of the steep.

When he had lifted her across the stream at the bottom, and helped her to climb the other side, and seen her safe upon the top, he returned to fetch Judith.

"Troth, I've heard tell iv the divil's highway, but niver saw it before; and sure this must be itself!" said Judith, as she gave her hand to Mr. Rosenthal, and clambered awkwardly down the descent.

When he had convoyed Judith safely to the other side of the chasm they all three resumed their walk. Several of these chasms they crossed in the same manner. And finally they reached the ship, which remained in the state in which Justin had left it.

Mr. Rosenthal handed Miss Conyers on deck, and then helped Judith up beside her.

Britomarte looked around with sorrowful reminiscences of that dire calamity which had separated her from all her late companions.

"I never expected to tread these planks again! It seems strange to be here! It seems almost wrong to be here! as if we had no right to be alive, now that all our fellow voyagers are lost! I cannot rejoice in being saved, remembering their destruction!" she murmured, sadly.

"We do not know that they have been destroyed. I think it highly probable that the boat which first left the ship's side—the boat containing the missionary party—was saved," said Justin, with the purpose of consoling her.

"Why do you think so?"

"Because it was the most seaworthy boat of the two, and it was manned by a more knowing crew, and finally, because they had sense enough to sail for the open sea instead of making for that fatal rock bound coast upon which your boat was wrecked."

"Oh, Heaven grant they may have been saved!" fervently exclaimed Britomarte.

"Oh, the poor ould ship! Oh, me poor ould daddy! Oh, me darlint Fore Top Tom! Are yez all lost intirely? Drowned in the dape say? Oh me fine ship! Oh, me good daddy! Oh, me gay Tom! Ow-oo! Ow-oo! Ow-oo!" cried Judith, sitting down upon the deck, flinging her apron over her head, rocking herself to and fro, and howling dismally.

And as she was howling not only from an acute feeling of grief, but also from a profound sense of propriety, there was not the least use of any one's attempting to console her.

Britomarte laid her hand gently upon the woman's head, and kept it there a moment as a tacit assurance of sympathy, and then passed on.

To get into the cabin she was obliged first to climb up the leaning deck, and then go round to the companion ladder and climb down.

Justin helped her as much as she would allow him to do.

Looking around upon the empty cabin and the vacant staterooms, lately the scene of her and her fellow-voyagers,

realization of the awful calamity that had befallen them.

She wondered why it was that she could not weep! but she really could not! the feeling of awe overpowered the feeling of grief, and, besides, the pressure of necessity was upon her—the necessity of immediate action.

She went into the stateroom and changed all her clothing, and from her good stock of wearing apparel, which she found in excellent preservation, she selected two more changes; then she took her sewing materials—needles, thread, scissors and thimble, and her little toilet service—combs, brushes, soap and towels, and she rolled all these articles up together in a compact little parcel, and tied it up with pocket handkerchiefs. And while doing this, she experienced a feeling of compunction for taking off anything for her own individual comfort only, when so much needed to be carried off for the general good. But then, again, she reflected that the common decencies of life, no less than her own inclination, made it absolutely necessary that she should provide herself with the means of personal neatness and cleanliness.

By the time she had made up her little parcel, Judith, who had finished her performance on deck, and so satisfied her sense of what was expected from her, came stumbling down the companion ladder.

And Judith's cat and kittens, recognizing their mistress, jumped out of the spare stateroom and ran up to her, purring and lifting their little tails, and rubbing their sides against her feet.

But Judith made short work with them all.

"Ah, thin, get out iv me way, ye divil's bastes Sure, if it wasn't bad luck to kill cats, I'd haive the whole iv yez into the say, so I would!" she cried, lifting them one by one upon her foot, and tossing them away as fast and as far as she could.

And then she went in turn to all the staterooms except Britomarte's.

"Sure, I suppose I may help meself to everything that ou des'n. wan, here? ... . that you won't take lies betwane meself and the say. And if meself don't take it, the say will. And the rightful owners will niver want it at all, at all! Say, ma'am?"

"Judith," said Miss Conyers, doubtfully, "if I understand what you mean by so many 'selfs,' you are asking my leave to take what you want from this cabin?"

"Sure, yes, ma'am, that's just what I mane itself!"

"Then I have no right either to give or withhold leave. Here we have equal privileges, and you must do as you please; or, rather, you must act according to the dictates of your own conscience."

"Sure, ma'am, I know betther than that intirely. Sure, I'm not going to act according to the dictates iv what's-its-name, nor anything else, at all, at all. I'm going to do as ye bid me. Faix, meself knows we are both depinding on the gintleman to save us from perishing intirely. And, troth, ye can wind the gintleman around yer finger, so ye can; and so, bedad, it behooves me to do as ye say, since he's king and you're quane."

"So," thought the man hater to herself, "what power I possess in virtue of superior intellect and education goes for nothing with this, my only female companion; but what power I possess, through my interest with this one able-bodied male creature, is all in all, because, forsooth, we are both dependent upon him (with his physical superiority) to save us from perishing. Why, the physical superiority is a quality he possesses in common with the ox and the ass! Yes, but the ox and the ass have not physical superiority united to intellectual power as he has. A drove of oxen or asses could not save us, as this one man can! Bah! nature has been very unjust to women, and that is the sacred truth! She should have given us strong bodies to match our strong hearts and heads!'"

"And ye have niver tould me whether or no I may take what I like," said Judith

"Then I tell you now: Judith, help yourself."

"Thanky, ma'am! Sure, it's a privilege I niver had before in all me life; but, thanks to the shipwreck I have it now! Sure, it's an ill wind that blow's nobody good," said

ginning to rummage over that poor woman's finery with great satisfaction.

Mary Ely, having been the daughter of a wealthy merchant, had as large and as rich a stock of wearing apparel as any woman in the middle class of life could wish to possess; and Judith overhauled it with great enjoyment.

"Ah, what an illigant shawl!" she cried, holding up a fine, large camel's-hair wrap. "What an illigant shawl entirely to wear to mass! What would Fore-Top Tom think iv me in this? And, sure, won't it astonish them all whin I wear it! Father O'Neil may talk as much as he likes about the lilies of the field and Solomon in all his glory; but, sure, I'll wear this shawl to mass if I have to make up for it wid a thousand 'Hail Marys.' But, sure, there's no mass nor no church on that baste iv an island, and I should only wear it for them wild bastes to grin at. But, ah, what a darlint iv a green silk dhress, and how beautiful it will go with the shawl, sure' Look, ma'am!" she exclaimed, rushing up to Miss Conyers, and holding up the shawl in one hand and the dress in the other for inspection.

Britomarte turned away, revolted at the woman's exhibition of thoughtlessness or heartlessness. If one of the common enemy had acted as Judith did in this matter, Britomarte would have poured upon him the full measure of her scorn and indignation; but with her own sex she was ever most merciful and forbearing.

"Look, ma'am—oh, look! the beautiful red shawl and the green silk dhress Sure, ye niver set eyes on 'em before' She'd niver be wearing the like iv these on the deck, to be spoilt intirely wid the salt say wather. Look, ma'am," persisted Judith, too much absorbed in her own delight to observe the pained expression of Miss Conyers' countenance

"Oh, Judith! how can you! Don't—don't!" was all that she could reply.

But it was enough; for in an instant the consciousness of her own seeming want of heart flashed upon Judith's mind and quite overwhelmed her with remorse. She dropped the finery, flung herself down upon the floor in a sitting position, threw her apron over her head, and began to rock her body to and fro, crying:

"Oh, the baste that I was! Oh, the haythen I made iv meself! Oh, the divil I was turning into wid me vanity and hardness iv heart! To be enjoying ov the property before iver graving for the dead! Oh, the poor young craythur, cut off in the bloom iv her youth! Sure, she was the core iv me heart and the light iv me eye! But I shall niver see her again—niver! She's gone! gone! gone!—lost in the salt say wather! Ow-oo! ow-oo! ow! Och hone! och hone! och-hone!"

And Judith set in for a regular bout of rocking and howling—not by any means in the spirit of hypocrisy, but as a matter of business, from a sense of duty, and with a feeling of some little sorrow which she was conscientiously trying to increase.

Miss Convers liked this performance quite as little as she had the other; but, as she was not a habitual fault-finder, she said nothing.

Meanwhile, on deck Justin had collected together as many stores as the united strength of himself and party could carry to the shore.

And now he came down the companion ladder, and inquired:

"Are you ready to return, sister?"

"Quite," answered Miss Convers. Then turning to her companion, she said: "Come, Judith, my good girl, compose yourself, and make your bundle. We have got to go on shore."

"Is the gintleman ready?" inquired Judith, dropping her apron from her head and revealing a red, swollen, tear-stained face.

"Yes, Judith, and waiting. Let me help you up."

"Thankee, ma'am! Sure, I wouldn't throuble ye, only me limbs bend under me wid the graif I'm faling for the poor young craxture who has left me her clothes!" said Judith, trying hard to feel as badly as she said she did.

Nevertheless, she was very particular in making up her bundle of could afford Mr. Rose Conveying a part of the stores that he had gathered together. But at length she managed to tie her bundle on her back and take a box of tea on her head. And so she followed Mr. Rosenthal and Miss Conyers, who were both laden with as much as they could carry.

CHAPTER XVII

MYSTERY

WE must leave our three shipwrecked voyagers on the desert island, and return on the wings of thought to look after their friends left behind at home.

While the missionary ship had been sailing toward the sun and toward the reef, our ship of state, our beloved nation, was also sailing toward the sun and toward the reef—toward the glorious sun of emancipation, toward the fatal reef of disunion. I shall not burden this light and simple story with the politics of the Civil War. I shall only allude to it where it immediately concerns the people of whom I am writing.

When, in October, the missionary ship sailed from the United States disunion was not dreamed of, except by a few leading politicians. But after the election of Mr. Lincoln, in November, and before any overt act of secession took place, it is now well known that secret meetings were held in Washington, Richmond, Annapolis, and all the principal cities in the border States, to take measures to prepare the people of these States to act promptly and in concert when the opportunity for seceding should present itself. But the foremost object of this conspiracy was to muster into Maryland and Virginia a secret military force strong enough to seize and occupy Washington, and prevent the President-elect from taking his seat there.

Among the most active, secretive, and persevering of these conspirators was the accomplished scholar, soldier   .   .   .   .   .   .   o you, my re   .   .   .   .   voith.

You know already that during the greater part of the summer of that year he was in Washington, ostensibly on a visit to his father's friend and his own old tutor, the retired Lutheran minister. In September he left the city to return to his home in the South. In October he reappeared in Washington, and took rooms in one of the best hotels most frequented by Southern gentlemen. But while he made Washington his headquarters, he went on frequent journeys to Charleston, Richmond, Annapolis, and other cities. And not even to his betrothed did he ever mention the object of these sudden journeys.

Such was his manner of life until the first of December, when, as usual at the meeting of Congress, the city became crowded with visitors. All the boarding houses and hotels were full of people, and very full of discomfort.

Colonel Eastworth, a constitutional sybarite and epicurean, escaped as often as he could from the crowded rooms and scuffling meals of his "best hotel" to the quiet fireside and dainty table of the Lutheran minister's home. Colonel Eastworth was certainly no petulant fault finder; yet in his close intimacy with the family of his betrothed, he sometimes let fall half laughing expressions that betrayed how ludicrously uncomfortable he was when in his quarters at the "best hotel."

Dr. Rosenthal, in his earnest German nature, considered betrothal almost as sacred as marriage, and looked upon the betrothed lover of his daughter as already his own son. And so, one day when they chanced to meet in the Capitol library, and the colonel was unusually sarcastic on the subject of hotel living, the minister said:

"Now, see here, Eastworth. We have a very large house, with four rooms on a floor, and sixteen rooms in all, counting basement and attics, and only myself and my daughter and our two servants to occupy them. Now, as you are to pass the whole winter in Washington, what should hinder you from coming and stopping with us?"

"Thanks

stantial evidence to the contrary notwithstanding—I did not mean to angle for and draw out this invitation," laughed the colonel.

"Don't I know that you didn't? But you will come?"

"It would be too great a trespass on your kindness."

"Nonsense! not at all! You are one of us! You are my son. And really, now, Eastworth, I want you to come."

"A thousand thanks! I shall be too glad to do so! I accept your kindness as frankly as it is offered."

"That is right. And now I will go home and tell Erminie to have fires lighted in your rooms, to air them comfortably for you against your arrival. She will be glad, I know. But—when shall we expect you? This evening, shall it not be?"

Colonel Eastworth hesitated, smiled, and then replied

"This evening? Yes, if you please, if it will be convenient for you. There is really no reason on my part for delay."

"Nor on mine! nor on Erminie's! nor on the servants'; I do not wish to boast of our housekeeping, Eastworth, but I take pleasure in telling you that we are always prepared to receive our friends. And if to-night we should be surprised by the sudden inroad of a tribe of cousins as numerous as a Scotch clan, it could not put us out in the least. There, now! come when you like! Come home with me now, if you choose, and send a messenger to the hotel to direct your servants to pack up your property and follow you!" said the minister, cordially.

"Many thanks! but I must return to my room first. I will join you at your tea table."

"Very well! Then I will expect you," said the minister, as cordially as if he himself had received a favor.

They parted for a few hours. Colonel Eastworth, for many reasons deeply gratified with this project, returned to his hotel to prepare for his removal to his new quarters.

Dr. Rosenthal, pleased with the thought of giving pleasure to others, hastened home to inform his daughter of the plan and to get ready for his guest.

Erminie was delighted. It had come to this pass with the minister's gentle child—that she only seemed to live in the presence of her lover; and to have him always under the same roof with herself seemed to be the perfection of happiness. She could ask no more than that of earth or heaven. And what comfort she took in preparing for his arrival! Colonel Eastworth, like most middle-aged gentlemen of a certain class, was an epicure, and his betrothed bride knew it. First, she went to the kitchen and gave the cook very particular directions concerning the preparation of certain dainty dishes sure to delight the fastidious palate of the expected guest. Then she called the housemaid, and went to get the spare rooms ready for his accommodation.

Dr. Rosenthal's house was a large, square, brick building, standing in its own grounds which, even in winter, looked very bright and cheerful with its many evergreens. There were long vine-shaded porches before every floor in front of the house, which was of three stories, with basement and attic. There was a large hall running from front to back through the center of each floor, and having two rooms on each side. The basement contained the kitchen, laundry, servants' rooms, and cellar. The first floor contained, on the right hand of the broad entrance hall, the long drawing rooms, connected or divided at will by sliding doors; and on the left hand, the family library in front, and the dining room back.

The second floor contained, on the right of the hall, the minister's private apartments, consisting of a bed chamber and a study, and on the left, Erminie's bed room and private sitting room.

The third story comprised two suites of spare rooms, neatly furnished and well kept, for the accommodation of visitors.

To this third floor, Erminie, attended by her lady's maid, repaired. She opened the front windows of the left suite the beautiful parlor, while her attendant knelt down before the grate and began to light the fire, which was always kept ready for kindling. Everything was in such exquisite order that there was but little else to be done than to warm and air the rooms. But when the fire was burning brightly, Erminie drew the sofa up one side of the hearth, and the easy-chair up on the other, and placed a footstool and a sofa-stand before each. Then she went down into the library, and brought up the magazines of the month and the papers of the day, and placed them on the center table. And, finally, she went to the conservatory and gathered a few choice winter roses and geraniums and placed them in a grass-green Bohemian vase, and brought it and set it on the mantelpiece, where the fragrance of the flowers filled the room.

Then, leaving the handmaid to prepare the adjoining bedchamber, she went down to put a few graceful finishing touches to the arrangements of the drawing-rooms, library, and dining parlor.

Next to the delight of a mother preparing for the visit of her son is the delight of a girl preparing for the comfort of her betrothed lover.

Erminie shared her father's religious belief in the sacredness and inviolability of betrothal; and she seemed to herself little less than a wife, making ready for the reception of her husband.

She ordered the tea table to be set in the library; and never was a tea table more exquisitely neat and dainty in all its arrangements than this which was prepared under the immediate supervision of the minister's daughter. She knew that the library was the favorite room with their visitor as well as with her father and herself. And never before did it look more inviting than on this evening when it was made ready to receive their most welcome guest.

When Erminie had seen these arrangements completed, she contemplated the effect with a smile of satisfaction, and then went to make her own toilet.

Colonel Eastworth came in good time. Erminie's quick ears   the carriage wheels as they turned into the gate and rolled up the avenue toward the house.

Dr. Rosenthal himself went out to receive the guest and show him up to his rooms.

Erminie, who had been so very busy in preparing for him, was now seized with a strange timidity, which prevented her from going forth to welcome him. But she rang for the housemaid to show Colonel Eastworth's servant where to carry his master's trunk, and then she went back to the library and sat down to wait until her father should return with her lover.

In a few minutes they came downstairs and entered the room.

Erminie half arose to receive her betrothed. She saw his look of appreciation and approbation as he glanced around the room before his eye fell upon herself, and he advanced toward her.

"This looks like a little paradise, after the pandemonium in which I have lately existed. A paradise, of which my lady is the Peri," he murmured in a low voice, as he lifted her hand, and, bowing over it, pressed it to his lips.

Erminie blushed beautifully and murmured something in reply, to the effect that she hoped he would be happy with them.

"Humph!" thought the good minister to himself—"that is all very high toned, I dare say; but for my part, I had rather seen him kiss her openly and heartily, as an honest sweetheart and betrothed husband should! but, then, very likely he is right and I am an old-fashioned fogy!"

"Are you ready for tea, papa dear?" inquired Erminie, with her hand upon the bell.

"Yes, pet—quite; and so is Eastworth. Have it in directly."

Erminie rang, and tea was immediately served. Everything was in perfect neatness and taste. Colonel Eastworth's favorite delicacies were on the table. Erminie presided over the urn. And the pretty parlor maid waited on the table.

"A beautiful contrast to the hurly burly of the hotel or—

"You should not be too hard upon the hotels. How is it possible they should be any better than they are, in their present overcrowded state," said the charitable minister.

And then their conversation left the hotel grievance and turned upon more agreeable subjects.

When tea was over and the service cleared away, Erminie brought out Gustave Doré's illustration of "Don Quixote," and laid the volume on the table.

It was a rare work and a new purchase; and it had cost the good minister a round sum to import it from Paris. But Erminie had expressed a wish to possess it; and her father never denied his beloved daughter anything that she wanted which it was possible for him to procure. So here it lay upon the table; at this time, perhaps, the only copy of the work to be found in America.

Colonel Eastworth had never seen it; so Erminie had the delight of being the first to show it to him.

There are perhaps about a hundred large plates— each plate being a perfect work of art, to be studied separately and carefully, and with ever-increasing appreciation and enjoyment of its truthfulness to nature and richness in humor.

In the examination of this book the hours sped quickly away, so quickly that ten o'clock, the regular bedtime of the quiet household, came and passed unheeded.

But if the striking of the clock did not disturb our laughing party, something else soon after did—the ringing of the street doorbell.

Dr. Rosenthal himself went out to see what this very late summons might mean.

It was the penny postman of his district. And the minister started; for this was an unheard-of hour for the penny postman to present himself.

"Yes, doctor, it is I," said the man, handing a letter to the minister. "You see, it came by the late mail, and, being a foreign letter, I thought it might be from your son who went out to the Indies, and I thought I wouldn't keep you waiting for it until the regular delivery to-morrow morning, but I would just step around with it to-night."

"A thousand thanks, my friend! It is from my son! It is in his handwriting. A thousand thanks! this is a real act of kindness, which I shall never cease to remember," said the minister, earnestly, as he received the letter.

"Oh, don't mention such a trifle, doctor. Good night, sir," said the kind-hearted penny postman, taking himself off.

"Erminie, my dear, here is a letter from your brother!" exclaimed the minister, bursting into the library with all the vehemence of a schoolboy.

"Oh!" cried his daughter, jumping to meet him.

And for the time being Colonel Eastworth was "left out in the cold."

"Ah! pray excuse us, sir! Have we your permission?" inquired the minister, suddenly recollecting himself and bowing to his guest.

"Oh, certainly, certainly! Am I not one of yourselves? Pray do not mind me," replied Colonel Eastworth, smiling, and then turning his whole attention to Gustave Doré, which lay still before him.

Dr. Rosenthal opened the letter; and then the father and daughter held it between them, bent their heads over it and read it together.

It was the first letter they had received from Justin —a letter that he had written and mailed at Porto Praya. It merely told them of the ship's prosperous voyage and safe arrival at Porto Praya, and of the well-being of all the passengers.

"I hope you have had good news from my friend Justin and his party," said Colonel Eastworth, as they joined him at the table.

"Excellent! They have had a very prosperous voyage as far as Porto Praya, with every prospect of a continuance of fine weather, thank Heaven! There, you can see what he says if you will take the trouble to look over his letter," said the minister, putting the paper into the visitor's hands.

"Thanks," said Colonel Eastworth, with a bow. Then he

look over the letter again with him, and opened it, saying, with a smile:

"I know, of course, that you cannot read this too often."

"I believe you read my thoughts," answered Erminie, with a beautiful flush. "And—I do wish I could read yours as well," she added, gravely.

"I wish you could, my dearest. You would know then, for yourself, how perfectly I love you," he replied, in a low whisper.

"I know that already. I never for a moment doubted your love. What, indeed, but perfect love could draw you down to me?" murmured Erminie, in a voice tremulous with emotion.

"God bless you in your faith, my dearest! But why, then, do you wish to read my thoughts?" inquired Colonel Eastworth, with a sidelong glance toward the minister, to see if he was attending to their conversation.

But no—Dr. Rosenthal was deep in the study of Gustave Doré.

"Why do you wish to read my thoughts, Erminie?" repeated her lover.

"Oh, I do not know. Sometimes when you have been here spending an evening alone with me, you have been so moody, so grave, so thoughtful, so absent-minded, so utterly oblivious of all around you; so utterly oblivious even of me," replied Erminie, sadly.

"Of you! Never, Erminie. Never, for an instant, better angel of my life!" exclaimed Eastworth, warmly, though still in a suppressed voice. Then he paused and reflected for a few moments, and then he said: "Sweet girl, I am no longer a young man, and middle age brings with it trials and responsibilities with which I do not wish to burden your gentle heart. No, Erminie, I am no longer a young man. I remember sometimes with pain, and with grave misgivings—ay, almost with despair—that I am your senior for full twenty years!"

"Oh, why do you say that? I never knew and never asked myself whether you were thirty or forty, or fifty! But I do know that I—I—" She broke down in the sweet confession she was trying to make, and dropped her head and hid her face upon his shoulder

He encircled her waist with his arm, and stooped to whisper something.

Dr. Rosenthal glanced up over the tops of his spectacles, muttering to himself:

"Humph! so that is the way in which they read my son's letter;" and then he bent his head still lower over Gustave Doré, and became still more absorbed in study.

"Then you do not love me the less because, like Othello, I am somewhat 'declined into the vale of years?'" Eastworth asked.

He spoke so low as scarcely to break the dead silence of the room—a silence which was so profound, that when the mantel clock began to strike it sounded like an alarm.

"Eleven o'clock! Bless my soul! Erminie, ring for the bedroom candles!" exclaimed the doctor, rousing himself.

Erminie obeyed. The housemaid appeared with three wax candles in three little silver candlesticks

"We have no gas in the bedrooms. I consider it unhealthy. Good night," said the doctor, as he lighted a candle and handed it to his guest.

CHAPTER XVIII

ERMINIE'S TRIALS

On the morning succeeding the domestication of Colonel Eastworth in the family, Erminie, restless with excess of happiness, arose earlier than usual

She went down into the library to open and air it, and to have the fire lighted and the table set for breakfast under her own supervision.

And half an hour later, when Dr. Rosenthal and Colonel Eastworth entered the room, a very pleasant scene greeted them.

The r

up the amber-colored hangings, the gilded picture frames, the glass bookcases, and the silver service of the breakfast table. The fire burned clearly in the polished grate, and by its side sat Erminie in her soft white merino morning dress and rich auburn ringlets.

She arose with a smile to greet her father and her lover.

Her father kissed her fondly and then took up a morning paper and appeared to become absorbed in its contents.

Her lover drew her away to the sunny window and whispered:

"My dearest, I recognized your loving care in every single arrangement for my comfort in my rooms last night. I knew it was this dear hand that wheeled my sofa in its place, and set the footstool, and even cut the leaves of the magazines upon the table. Shall I thank you for all this? No, sweet girl, I will not mock you so. But do you know, Erminie, that I sat up last night turning over all those magazines, merely because these dear fingers had touched them all?"

"I am so glad that you can be pleased with anything I can do for you, for, oh, it is so little I can do," she murmured, softly.

"You can love me! You do love me, and that love of yours makes your slightest act for me a priceless service!" he replied, fervently pressing her hand to his lips.

"Hallo, Eastworth! what's this? what's this? what's this? What on earth are they about in the Senate?" suddenly cried out the old minister, staring at the paper in his hand.

"What is what, sir?" inquired Colonel Eastworth leaving the side of Erminie and going to join her father.

"This! this!" said the old minister, pointing emphatically to a lengthened report of the previous day's debate in the Senate. It was a warm debate between the Union and the Secession factions. Eastworth looked from the paper to the face of the reader, and his face grew dark.

"I am afraid, sir," he said, "that you do not look

into the papers very often to keep up with the politics of the day."

"No, no—I do not; I never did and never shall. I always let the opposing parties fight out their own battles, having such firm faith in the glorious destinies of the country as to feel well assured that the very worst of them can never succeed in bringing it to ruin. My eyes only happened to fall upon this debate by chance. But, I say, this looks a little serious, doesn't it—as if they really mean secession, eh?"

"I think the Southern States really mean it, sir." said Eastworth, gravely.

The old minister reflected a moment, and then laughed, and threw the paper aside, exclaiming

"Pooh! pooh! Eastworth! Nonsens ! A few crafty and unscrupulous politicians, who are willing to sacrifice their country so that they may rise into transient notoriety upon its ruins, may rant as they please, and a few hot-headed boys, who are ready for revolution or excitement of any sort, at any price, may be led astray by their sophistries. But the Southern people at large, with their whole-hearted attachment to and pride in their country—never, Eastworth, never, it is all talk, all dream, all moonshine! Nonsense! Erminie, ring for the breakfast, my dear."

The old Lutheran minister was no politician; he was a philosopher and bookworm; but he was not alone in his incredulity. Even up to this late period, it was very difficult to make any sane man, not infected with the madness of the day, believe in the possibility of disunion.

Breakfast was served. But for some reason or other, the social morning meal did not pass off so cheerfully as it might have been expected to do. And as soon as it was over, Colonel Eastworth excused himself and went out.

Colonel Eastworth came home to the late dinner He was grave, absorbed, absent-minded. He sometimes shook off this pre-occupation, but it was with an evident effort. There was no danger that he should talk politics with his host; he was very, very reticent on all public subjects.

After dinner they withdrew to the drawing-room, where coffee was served, and then Dr. Rosenthal took his pipe and went off to his study to smoke and read.

Erminie was left alone with her betrothed. A sort of shyness, that she never could get rid of, when left *tête-à-tête* with her lover, induced her to rise and open the piano. She sang and played, one after another, his favorite songs, and in many of them he joined his voice to hers. At length she struck into the old, yet ever new, beloved and all-inspiring "Star-Spangled Banner." She had sung the first stanza, and was striking into the chorus with all her heart and soul, expecting him to join her with all the ardor and enthusiasm of his Southern nature, when suddenly he laid his hand upon her shoulder—his hand, that shook as with palsy:

"Not that! not that! Oh, my dearest—not that, if you love me!" he exclaimed, in a voice that shook as much as did his hand.

She ceased playing, and turned around and looked at him in meek surprise. She had never before in all her acquaintance seen him moved from his gentlemanly self-possession; but now he was terribly shaken. She was alarmed.

"Why? Why may I not sing the 'Star-Spangled Banner?'" she faltered.

"I cannot bear it! My dearest, I cannot! Strong man that I thought myself, I cannot!" he exclaimed, with the same half-suppressed, tempestuous emotion.

"But, why? Tell me why?" she persisted, with affectionate earnestness. "You have fought gallantly for it; you have shed your priceless blood in its defense; you have won immortal fame under it. Oh, why, then, may I not sing the praises of that glorious banner, so doubly dear to me for your sake?"

He was frightfully agitated.

"Oh, hush, Erminie, hush!" he cried.

"Ah! what has disturbed you so—what?" she exclaimed, rising from the piano and standing by his side.

"Some day, better angel of my life, I will tell you

all. Not now! I cannot bear to do it; nor could you bear to hear it."

"I can bear all things—all things for your sake! Try me—try me! Say, is your trouble now connected with the dear old flag?"

"Yes, it is connected with——" He paused, and then, with a spasmodic effort, added—"the dear old flag! But enough! 'Old things shall pass away, and all things shall become new!' We shall raise a banner, Erminie, in the blaze of whose young glory the old stars and stripes shall pale and fade, as the stars of night at the rising of the sun!"

"Oh, what do you mean? What are you about to do?" gasped Erminie, in a low voice, as she turned deadly pale.

"'Be innocent of the knowledge, dearest chuck, till you approve the deed!'" he answered, smiling and throwing off the gloom that had gathered around them.

And in good time he did so; for the door opened quietly, and the old doctor, who had finished his pipe, sauntered into the room, to spend the rest of the evening with his children, as he called these two.

Many more evenings did the betrothed lovers spend alone in that drawing-room. But not again did Erminie attempt to sing the "Star Spangled Banner," and not again did Colonel Eastworth lose his self possession, or hint darkling at the "coming events" that cast their shadows over his spirit. As the scene of that evening was not repeated, Erminie let its memory fade from her mind and she grew tranquil and happy in the society of her lover.

But Colonel Eastworth was neither happy, nor even tranquil. An honorable gentleman, a patriotic citizen, and a distinguished soldier, who had won ever living laurels in the service of his country, and now a State's Rights man, conscientiously plotting her ruin, his mind was torn by the struggles of what he called a "divided duty," and likened not unaptly to the martyrdom of dismemberment by wild horses. Nor did the society of his betrothed bride tend to soothe him.

He was too readily

tiful child to bear the close intimacy of her constant companionship with anything like calmness—unless he could be permitted to marry her immediately.

One evening they were as usual alone in the drawing-room. She was seated at the piano, singing his favorite song. He was bending over her, turning the music, but thinking far more of her than of anything else. She was singing the refrain of that song so full of wild, sad, almost despairing aspiration:

> "Beloved eye! beloved star!
> Thou art so near, and yet—so far!"

He bent lower over her, until his quick breath stirred her bright auburn ringlets. As she ceased singing, he whispered, in a voice vibrating with intense feeling:

"'Beloved star! Thou art so near, and yet—so far!' Oh, my dearest! Oh, Erminie! do you know—do you know what my trial is! To be with you every hour of the day, your betrothed husband, sharing the same home, sitting at the same fireside, mocked with the appearance of the closest intimacy, yet kept at the sternest distance! Oh, Erminie! I cannot bear it longer, love! The period of my probation must—it must be shortened! Say, love! shall I speak to your father once more? Shall I implore him to fix an early day for our union?"

The color deepened on Erminie's cheek; and she hesitated a few moments before she replied:

"We are very happy now! we are together almost all the time. What more can we require? My dear father is very much opposed to our marriage taking place before two years. And why should we hurry him? Surely, surely you do not dream that in these two years I shall change toward you?" she suddenly inquired.

"No, my angel, no! I dream nothing of you but to your honor! I know that you are truth itself! But I cannot wait two years to call you mine, my love! I must—I must have your consent to speak to your father and implore him to shorten the time of our betrothal."

"I was very happy," said Erminie, thoughtfully, "but I cannot be so any longer if you are discontented, for your discontent would be mine. Speak to my dear father, if you will."

"Thanks, dearest, thanks! I will lose no time," he said, and he pressed her to his bosom for a moment, and then hurried out of the room to look for Dr. Rosenthal.

He found the Lutheran minister in his study, sitting in his easy-chair, enjoying his pipe, and enveloped in a cloud of aromatic smoke.

"Ah! is it you, Eastworth? Sit down; take out your pipe—I know you carry it about you—and try some of this tobacco; it is prime," said the doctor, cordially, pushing another easy chair toward his guest, and setting his box of tobacco near to his hand.

"Thanks," said Eastworth, availing himself at once of all his old friend's invitations, as the quickest method of conciliating him.

There was silence for a moment, then Colonel Eastworth said abruptly.

"Sir, I have come to speak to you about your daughter."

The old minister laid down his pipe and turned to the speaker. The name of his daughter was powerful enough, at any time, to bring him all the way back from the past and fix his attention on the present.

"Yes, well, what of Erminie?" he inquired, anxiously.

Colonel Eastworth reflected for a moment, and then plunged headlong into the subject.

"I would submit to you, sir, respectfully, but very earnestly, that an engagement of two years will be intolerably tedious to me. I come to entreat you to shorten the period. There is really no reason why we should not be married at once. I love your daughter devotedly, and I am so blessed as to have won her affections. My means are ample and I shall be only too happy to a[...]"

that you may please to name. My character and position, I hope you know, are unimpeachable."

"All that is true, Eastworth—quite true!" said the old doctor, taking up his pipe and putting it in his mouth, and puffing away leisurely.

"Then, sir, let me hope that you will reconsider your decision, and allow the marriage to take place soon," pleaded the colonel.

"No, Eastworth. She is much too young to be married yet. Think of it!—she is not yet seventeen! Her youth is an objection to her marriage that cannot be set aside, Eastworth, by any agent except time. You must be patient, my friend."

Nor could further pleading move the old man.

Colonel Eastworth rejoined Erminie in the drawing-room. She looked up inquiringly as he entered.

"Your father is obdurate, my sweet love! I cannot win his consent to my wishes, upon any terms," he said, with a profound sigh.

"Then we must be patient My dear father is very good to us in all other respects; in this also, perhaps, though we do not know it," replied Erminie, gently.

"It may be so, love," said Eastworth.

"And you know that if our engagement were to last ten years, or twenty, and if, in the meantime, you should travel to the uttermost ends of the earth, and I should never see or hear from you, I should still be true to you—yes! true as truth!"

"I know it, my only love! And I shall soon put your truth to a terrible test!"

"Put it to any test! to any!" exclaimed Erminie, rashly, in her great faith.

CHAPTER XIX

ANOTHER LOVE CHASE

On the morning succeeding the conversation related at the close of the last chapter, Erminie was seated at work in her own room, and singing as she sewed, when the house maid entered and laid a card before her.

"'Vittorio Corsoni,' our Italian professor! Where is he, Catherine?" inquired Ermine, with her eyes on the bit of enameled pasteboard that bore the name she read.

"I showed him into the drawing-room, miss; which he says he would very much like to see you for a few minutes, if so be you can do him the honor," replied the girl.

"Certainly, Catherine—our ex-master! I will go at once," said the minister's daughter, rising.

Always dressed with exquisite neatness, Ermine had no occasion to keep her visitor waiting. She followed the maid down the stairs, and passed into the drawing-room.

The young Italian professor was seated, leaning back in one of the easy-chairs. He looked haggard and careworn, but quite as handsome and interesting as ever, with his long, curling black hair, large, luminous, dark eyes, and slight and elegant form.

Ermine walked straight toward him. She liked the young Italian, who was, indeed, a great favorite with all ladies. He arose to meet her.

"I am very, very glad to see you, signor," she said, cordially holding out her hands.

He bowed over them as he took them.

"I called to-day, Miss Rosenthal, to pay my respects to yourself and your learned father, and also to make some inquiries after——" His voice faltered and broke down, and then, after an inward struggle for composure, he added, huskily—"one who is infinitely dearer to me than my own soul!"

Ermine pitied this lover. How could she help it? She said, gently:

"After Alberta Goldsborough?"

"Yes, my dear Miss Rosenthal. I have heard no word of her since our violent separation in the latter part of September, and this is January. I have used every means to soften the hearts of her parents, but all in vain! I have written them many letters, but they have been returned to me unopened. I have besieged their house.

denied admittance, and once I have been threatened with the police! I, a Corsoni! But, in the pursuit of my dear love, I would suffer any ignominy that would not touch my honor!"

"I will tell you all about her. I see no reason in the world why you should not know. Alberta is a boarder at the Convent of the Visitation."

"Thanks! a thousand thanks! It is much to know where she is. I can at least walk outside the walls and gaze up to the windows in the hope of seeing my queen love. Perhaps I may be permitted to write to her. Perhaps I may have the divine happiness of being allowed to call on her!" exclaimed the excitable Italian, springing up.

"Oh, no; do not hope it. I am sorry to discourage you, but I know that she is permitted to correspond only with a few trusted friends, and that all her letters and her correspondents' letters pass through the hands of the mother superior. And she is allowed to see only a certain small number of visitors upon fixed days, and in the presence of one of the sisters," said Erminie.

The young professor heaved a profound sigh, and inquired:

"Have you the great happiness of being one of the blessed number who are permitted to visit this angel?"

Erminie could not restrain a smile at the hyperbolical language of this lover as she answered:

"Yes, I am allowed to visit her; but only in the presence of one or two of the sisters."

"Then, my dear Miss Rosenthal, may I entreat you to be our good genius and convey one little, little message to my love?" said Corsoni, clasping his hands imploringly.

"I am very sorry to refuse you, signior; but, even if it were right for me to take your message, I should not be allowed to deliver it," answered Erminie, very gravely.

"Ah! what an unfortunate man I am! Miss Rosenthal, if you cannot take a message, since you would not be permitted to deliver it, can you not take one little, little letter? You could easily deliver a little, little letter unknown to the sentinel sisters," entreated the lover, again clasping his hands and bringing his beautiful eyes to bear upon her with all the force of which they were capable.

"I cannot, signior! I am very sorry to refuse you, but I cannot. It would be a very great breach of faith on my part to do as you wish me. I am trusted by Alberta's parents, and I must be faithful to my trust," said Erminie, seriously.

"You draw hair-breadth lines of distinction, my too good Miss Rosenthal," said the signior, rising, in ill-suppressed displeasure, to take his leave.

"Have faith and hope, and the patience that springs from both, signior. In time all will be well," said Erminie, gently.

"I thank you, my much-too-good Miss Rosenthal! I will have faith and hope; but I will have no patience! I will not wait for time; but all shall be well because I will make it so! Good-morning, my very much-too good young lady!"

And Vittorio Corsoni, with a deeply-injured look, bowed himself out.

Erminie, smiling at the Italian's half-suppressed vehemence, went upstairs to her needlework.

Corsoni, after leaving the Lutheran minister's house, walked rapidly to a cab stand, threw himself into a carriage, and gave the order.

"To the Convent of the Visitation."

And the carriage started.

He reclined back in his seat, looking grim, moody and sardonic, until, at the end of about three-quarters of an hour, the carriage reached to within a hundred yards of the convent wall. There he stopped it, got out and dismissed it, and continued his way on foot, until he reached the front of the convent. There he walked up and down before the building, gazing up at the windows and debating with himself whether he should boldly go up to grand entrance and ask to see Miss Goldsborough, with the great probability of being refused and suspected and watched, or whether he should wait and see

ing her by stratagem. The first plan suited him well, except in the small chance of success it offered; and the second plan would have suited him, for his Italian spirit delighted in stratagem, but that his impetuous nature detested the process of waiting.

While he was thus debating with himself, he noticed the front door open, and little girls, singly or in twos and threes, and then in larger numbers, issue forth and hurry away in various directions.

And he easily divined that this hour was the midday recess of the institution, and that these children were the day pupils going to their respective homes in the neighborhood for dinner, and that in an hour or two they would return for the afternoon session of the school

And that "second plan" which had been vaguely forming in his mind, immediately took distinct shape and color, and sprung to maturity.

He hastened to the nearest restaurant and ordered luncheon for himself. And while it was being got ready he asked for writing materials and wrote a letter. Very soon he dispatched his luncheon, and then, with his prepared letter in his hand, he started once more for the convent. On his way thither he stopped at a confectioner's and bought a quantity of French candy, with which he filled his pockets.

When he got back before the convent walls he found, as he had expected, the day pupils returning to school for the afternoon session. They came in as they had gone out—singly, or in twos or threes, or in larger numbers.

Vittorio stood under a tree, apparently engaged in reading a newspaper, but really in watching the countenances of the returning children. Nearly all had gone in, and Vittorio began to despair of the success of his plan. At length all seemed to have gone in, for not another one appeared, and the door was closed, and Vittorio quite despaired of the success of his plan. But, as he was turning away, with a most heartbroken expression of countenance, he met a beautiful little girl of about nine years of age, dressed in deep mourning, and carrying a satchel of books. He knew that she must be a day pupil of the convent school, and that she was behind time. This little girl, meeting the handsome, melancholy and most interesting young Italian, looked up in his face with that wistful expression of sympathy which is so often seen in the faces of children when they are contemplating the troubled brows of older people.

Vittorio Corsoni knew in an instant that he had met the sort of little girl for whom he had patiently waited.

He immediately addressed her:

"My dear child, are you a pupil of that convent school?"

"Yes, sir," answered the tiny woman, gently, while her wistful face seemed to say, "Poor fellow! what can I do to help you?"

"Do you know a young lady who boards there by the name of—Miss Alberta Goldsborough?" he inquired, in a low voice.

"Oh, yes, sir," she answered, quickly, while her speaking face expressed the thought, "Oh, this is the sweetheart she is hidden from!" For you may be sure, my readers, that there are very few secrets in this world; and the real reason why Miss Goldsborough had been sent to that convent school was whispered about among the older pupils, and this little girl had heard of it; and all her sympathies were with the lovers.

"You love Miss Goldsborough, of course, and would do anything to make her happy, I am sure," said the Italian, in a persuasive voice, fixing his large, lustrous, melancholy eyes with mesmeric effect upon the sensitive child's face.

"No, I do not love her so very much. She is so still and proud," began the truthful child.

"That is because she is ill-used and unhappy, my dear," said Vittoria, persuasively, keeping his beautiful, sorrowful eyes fixed upon the little girl.

"I am unhappy, too! I have lost my dear mother!" said the child.

"Have you, my darling? T͟ ssed

Mother of Christ be your mother, and comfort you," said Vittorio, plaintively.

"But that does not make me sullen! And although Miss Goldsborough will not let me love her much, I do think I would do anything to please her; and I do know I would do anything in the world to please you, so you wouldn't look so very, very miserable!"

"Would you, my little angel? You are a little angel of goodness! Would you take a letter from me to Miss Goldsborough?"

"Oh, yes, sir, that I would!"

"And could you give it to her—secretly?"

"Oh, yes, sir, I know I could!"

"Without any one but herself seeing you do it?"

"Oh, yes, sir!"

"Then, little darling of my eyes and heart, will you take this to her?" said Vittorio, handing his prepared letter to the little girl.

"Yes, indeed, I will, sir! and nobody shall know anything about it but Miss Goldsborough," answered the child, with her countenance all radiant with the delight of delighting, as she hid the letter in her bosom.

"I shall be here this evening, when the school is dismissed, waiting to see you. Will you bring me the answer to that letter?"

"Oh, yes, indeed, sir, that I will, if she writes it and gives it to me."

"Thanks, little Seraph! And now look here! here are some delicious French bonbons—whole boxes full of them. Take them, my dear, and share them with your schoolmates," said Vittorio, emptying his pockets of their sweet contents.

CHAPTER XX

SUCCESS IN THE CHASE

ALBERTA GOLDSBOROUGH had been a pupil in the convent school for somewhat less than four months. In all that time she had not once heard from her lover.

She bore her trial with great stoicism, disdaining to complain, and doing all that was required of her with quiet indifference. She made no friends either among the teachers or the pupils. She was, as the little girl dscecribed her to be, proud and still. She felt sure that some time or other Vittorio would, with his Italian craft, succeed in discovering her retreat and effecting her deliverance. And she calmly awaited the time.

Julie McKnight, the little girl whom Vittorio had intrusted with the letter to his ladylove, watched all the afternoon for an opportunity of delivering it to Miss Goldsborough. Chance favored her. She was sent by her class mistress into one of the small music rooms to practice her lesson on the piano. As she passed on the long hall, flanked on each side by a row of such rooms, she saw the door of one of them open and Miss Goldsborough seated at the piano. The child cast a hurried look up and down the hall, and, seeing no one near, she slipped in and thrust the letter into Alberta's hands, whispering eagerly:

"He gave it to me outside. You are to answer it, please, and give me the answer to take to him. You had better make haste, please, and write it and give it to me before we have to go down in the classrooms again. I am in the music room, number seven."

"Thanks, my dear——" began Alberta; but the little girl did not wait to hear thanks. She was off like an arrow.

Miss Goldsborough opened her letter and read:

MY OWN AND ONLY LOVE: I have but a few minutes to write to you in; if I would seize the earliest opportunity of getting this letter into your hands I must have it ready in a quarter of an hour. After long months of unremitting and unavailing search, I have but just learned the place of your incarceration. Oh, my beloved, my adored, my worshiped queen, you know that I would die to deliver you. Events are on the wing, sweet love, that may separate us—it may be for years, or at most be forever, unless we meet and unit

time nor opportunity to explain further. Let is suffice for me to say that I will be on the watch outside the north front of the building every evening from six o'clock p. m. to six a. m. I will have a carriage and horses waiting near, but out of sight. Dear love! if you can effect your escape from the inside of those jealous walls I will secure your safety on the outside. Or if you will give me a hint as to how I can further aid your deliverance, I will risk my life—nay, more —my eternal salvation to serve you. And always, for time and for eternity, I devote myself body and soul to your service. VITTORIO.

Alberta read this with flushed cheeks and beaming eyes. Before she had finished it her plan was formed. Ever since she had been in the convent all the senses and faculties of her mind and body had been on the alert to discover the best means of escape. And she knew them and she might have availed herself of them long before, but for this one consideration—she was ignorant of the whereabouts of her lover, and she was destitute of any other refuge. Out of the convent, where could she have found Vittorio, or where could she have gone for shelter? These unanswered questions held her captive as bolts and bars could never have done.

But now, if she should make her escape, Vittorio would be outside waiting to receive her. And her resolution was taken immediately.

She had no proper writing materials at hand. But she took an end of a pencil from her pocket and tore the blank page from Vittorio's letter and wrote her answer. It was very pithy:

Be at your post to-night and wait till you see me.

She turned his envelope inside out and put her answer into it, and took it into the little music-room where the child, Julia McKnight, was practicing.

"You will give this to the gentleman as you go home," she said, handing the letter to the little girl.

"Oh, yes, that I will, Miss Goldsborough. I am so

glad you wrote the answer to his letter. He will be delighted to get it," replied little Julia, hiding the letter in her bosom.

These two could not remain long together. Their interview was altogether against the rules of the school, where the elder and the younger pupils were not allowed to associate, except in the presence of their teachers.

Now, as soon as the affair that had brought them together was thus far concluded, they separated, the cold Alberta warming with gratitude enough to stoop and kiss her ardent little friend before leaving her.

Alberta returned to her own room. And when the inspecting sister came around she found the two pupils diligently practicing at their respective pianos.

When the hours for study were over for that afternoon, and the day pupils were dismissed, little Julia hurried away to deliver the letter to its destination.

Alberta, in furtherance of her plan of escape, went to the large apartment known as the recreation room, where the boarding pupils always spent their play time in bad weather. The windows on one side of this apartment overlooked the north road, where she had warned Vittorio to be upon his post. When she entered this room she found many of her schoolmates assembled, and the question, "What shall we play?" eagerly discussed among them.

"I will tell you," said Alberta.

"What? what?" demanded the girls, pressing around her in much surprise that the still, cold Miss Goldsborough should move in any play.

"Hide and seek. It is a fine, exhilarating play for a cold winter afternoon," said Alberta.

"Yes, that will be just the thing," replied the girls.

To the ever-increasing astonishment of her companions, Miss Goldsborough engaged eagerly in the play, but not successfully at first, for she caught no one. At length, however, when the afternoon deepened into night, and the gas was lighted, and the snow was falling very fast, Alberta succeeded in finding the hiders.

"Now, mind!"

"you must act fairly, and go quite out of sight, and refrain from watching me. I mean to hide where none of you have hidden before. "You will have great difficulty in finding me, but I assure you it will be good fun when you do find me. Don't come back until I call 'Whoop!'"

"No, no, we won't, Alberta!" exclaimed several of her companions in a breath.

And they all hurried out into the passage.

Alberta stole behind them, and not only closed the door upon them, but silently slipped the bolt. Then she went to the only other door of the room, which was at the opposite end, and she drew the key from the other side and locked it fast. Having thus secured the room, she went to the north windows. The green linen blinds were drawn down, and the outside shutters were closed. She stopped at a window at the extreme end of the row, and the most out of the range of vision of any one who might, at a later hour, force an entrance into the room, and she lifted the blind, but did not draw it up, and she hoisted the window and opened the shutters. It was dark as pitch outside, and snowing fast; it was a terrible night to take the road in. But what will not a self-willed girl, bent upon her own destruction, venture? She leaned far out of the window and peered into the darkness, but she could see nothing except the falling snow.

Then she ventured to call softly:

"Vittorio! Vittorio!"

There was no response. After a minute she called again, but with no better success. She paused another minute, and then called for a third time:

"Vittorio!"

"I am here, my love—I am here!" answered a hushed and vehement voice below the window.

"I have called you three times," she said.

"I must have been at the other end of my beat. I have been pacing the whole length of this building from one end to the other, and looking up to those windows—oh, how longingly!"

"Is all clear below this?"

"Yes, dear love."

"Then wait there. I will be with you in a moment," she said, and she withdrew from the window.

Her schoolmates, who had grown impatient at her long delay in hiding, were now clamoring for admittance at the closed door, which, however, they did not know was fastened.

"Why don't you 'whoop' and let us in? Haven't you hid yourself yet?" inquired one and another.

"No," answered Alberta, going up to the door—"not quite yet; I shall in a minute. Don't you be in such a hurry, and don't come in until I whoop."

"Make haste, then," exclaimed several of the girls in a breath; "it is cold out here."

"I will," said Alberta. And she went to the peg where her own everyday bonnet and shawl hung, and she took them down and put them on. Next she turned off the gas, leaving the room dark.

Then she went to the window, pushed it up as high as it would go, got upon the sill, letting the blind drop behind her to hide her means of exit, and took a clear leap down to the sidewalk below. It was a fall of about eight feet, and she came down with a severe shock but with whole bones.

"My own! my own! are you hurt?" exclaimed her lover, in the extremity of anxiety, as he picked her up.

"I—let me recover myself! No, I am not hurt," answered Alberta, confusedly.

"The carriage is round the corner. Let me lift you and bear you to it."

"No, I can walk very well now, if you will give me the support of your arm," answered Miss Goldsborough.

He drew her hand through his arm, and carefully conducted her to the waiting carriage.

How long her school companions remained outside the door of the recreation room, clamoring to come in, or when their patience became exhausted, or how they effected an entrance, or whether they gave the alarm, or who first discovered her flight, Alberta never knew and never cared.

Her

mediately to the dwelling of a clergyman, where, with the special license Vittorio had taken care to provide, they were married; for in the District of Columbia there is no law to prevent a minor marrying, without the consent of parents or guardians, at any hour.

From the house of the officiating clergyman they went to a hotel, where they remained until the next morning, when they took the boat to Richmond.

You see Vittorio Corsoni, with all his faults, did not shrink from facing his father-in-law. In the Italian's creed, love was law, and in his inmost soul he was unconscious of having done a great wrong.

But there was no chance of Vittorio's meeting Mr. Goldsborough in Richmond just then. The very boat upon which the newly-married pair embarked, and which had reached the Washington wharf late on the evening before, had brought up Alberta's father on a visit to herself. As it was too late for him to see his daughter that night, and as the hotels were almost uncomfortably crowded, the old gentleman decided to quarter himself upon his good friend, the retired Lutheran minister.

It seemed that Erminie had been booked for surprises that day, and that the tribe of cousins or friends as numerous as a Scotch clan, of which her father had jestingly spoken, were really beginning to pour in. She had scarcely curtsied Vittorio Corsini out, before a cab rolled up to the door and her two uncles, Hans and Friedrich Rosenthal, got out of it.

Hans had suddenly come from Germany the day before, and they had both come on to see their brother Ernest, the retired Lutheran minister.

Erminie welcomed them with the warmest affection, and showed them into a spare room, where she hastened to have a fire lighted, and to make them comfortable; and then she dispatched Catherine to the Congress Library to look for her father and tell him of the arrival of his brothers, so that he might hurry home. The old Lutheran minister came with the messenger, his face beaming with joy, and embraced his brothers warmly in his earnest German manner.

Colonel Eastworth did not appear until the six

o'clock dinner, when he was introduced to the strangers. He was, as often now, moody and preoccupied; but even he could not long resist the influence of that cordial spirit of love which seemed to pervade the Lutheran minister's family.

It was some time after they had had tea in the library, and had gone into the drawing-room, and it was while Erminie, her uncles and her lover were at the piano, singing some of the finest selections from the German operas, that the doorbell rang and Mr. Goldsborough was announced.

Old Dr. Rosenthal started up with the agility of youth to welcome his friend.

Erminie stopped singing and playing, and turned around with a frightened look. Her first impression, that came quick as lightning at the sight of Mr. Goldsborough, was that he had come to Washington in fierce pursuit of Vittorio Corsoni; but she arose to receive her father's guest, with all the calmness and courtesy she could command.

Mr. Goldsborough's first words somewhat allayed her fears.

"You look surprised and even shocked to see me here so unexpectedly, at this late hour, my dear young lady, but you will be pleased to learn that I have come to withdraw your friend, my daughter Alberta, from her convent school," said Mr. Goldsborough, cordially shaking her hand.

"I am very glad to see you at any hour," replied Erminie, smiling

"Thanks! The boat was behind time in getting in, or I should not have been so unseasonable in my appearance," added Mr. Goldsborough.

"You are not unseasonable at all, my old friend. It is not eleven o'clock. And we had not begun to think of retiring. For, you see, here are my two brothers, just arrived, and one come all the way from Germany! Let me present them to you: Mr. Hans Rosenthal, Mr. Friedrich Rosenthal—Mr Goldsborough."

The Virginia gentleman bowed with old-fashioned ceremoniousness as the sons of the Lutheran minister

chants were introduced. And then he sat down and became one of the party.

"Have you supped?" hospitably inquired the young mistress of the house.

"Yes, my dear, on the boat. Give yourself no trouble," said Mr. Goldsborough, with a bow.

"I am very glad that you are going to take my favorite, Alberta, out of the convent," said the doctor.

"Yes! my doing so before the half-yearly term has expired may seem very capricious; but, in fact, it is not so. There are grave reasons why all we Virginians should gather all the scattered members of our families under our own State roofs. The progress of public affairs makes it imperative that I should take my daughter home, or risk the being separated from her for a long and indefinite period. I believe that I am speaking among friends and sympathizers here—the presence of Colonel Eastworth in this house, indeed, assures me that I am. And I know, also, that my esteemed host, although not a native of the country, has been a citizen of the South for many years. I may, therefore, say that Virginia will certainly secede from the United States, and that she is now arming herself in defense of her right to do so."

No one answered for a while. But the speaker caught the eye of Colonel Eastworth, who was looking at him with a steady and meaning gaze, that was intended to convey the impression that the subject must not be pursued, and must never be resumed in that house.

At length, after a thoughtful pause, Dr. Rosenthal spoke; but he spoke rather wide of the mark; for though nothing could have been plainer than the words used by Mr. Goldsborough, and although Dr. Rosenthal understood the meaning of those words, yet he strangely misunderstood the position assumed by the speaker. He honestly supposed that the Virginian gentleman, in speaking of secession, spoke of it only as deprecating its evils. This was very apparent in his answer:

"You say that Virginia will certainly secede from the United States, and that she is even now arming herself in defense of her right to do so! Nonsense, Goldsborough! Don't alarm yourself! There is, certainly, an epidemical madness in the air, and a few leading statesmen have caught it. South Carolina has gone, it is true! She took the malady in its most malignant form. Let us hope that she will soon get well and come back. But Virginia secede! The gallant Old Dominion go! Never, Goldsborough! Don't distrust your native State, my friend! She is as loyal to the Union as you are, or as I am! And, Heaven knows, I love this country, which has fostered me for forty years—I love her as truly and as deeply as if I had been born her son! And should this madness of secession become general, and should she have a civil war forced upon her, I, with my three score years, will take up arms in her defense as promptly as you, Goldsborough, or as Eastworth, or any other loyal and gallant son of her soil would do!"

What a speech was this for the brave and true-hearted old man to make to a couple of conscientious, but unsuspected secessionists, who were his honored guests.

Neither of them answered a word, they found that they had mistaken their man; for this was really the first definition of his position that the Lutheran minister had ever thought it worth while to make, and Eastworth had supposed him to be indifferent on the subject, and Goldsborough, seeing one of the strongest spirits of secession an inmate of his house, had really believed him to be one of that party. They were silent from surprise.

But Emmie was a picture! She turned upon her father, beaming with love, admiration and enthusiasm as she exclaimed:

"Right, my dear father! I love to hear you speak so. And I myself would strap the sword to your side and place the musket in your hand, and follow you to the field, if you would let me, to dress your wounds if you should be hurt, and nurse you if you be sick, and to risk my life with yours and die with you, if need should be!"

"The   grave

and good girl! and there are millions of your countrywomen like you! for you are a native American citizen, my Minie, although I am not," said the Lutheran minister, patting his daughter on the head. "But there will be no necessity, let us hope, for all this self-devotion! The clouds of secession gather rather thickly and darkly just now, but they will be dispelled—they will be dispelled," he added, walking away to the fireplace.

Colonel Eastworth took the vacant place beside Erminie, and stooped and whispered very low·

"And what will become of me, my Minie, when you shall follow your father to the field? Where shall I be, and who will care for me?"

"You will be with my father, and I will care for you both! Surely you will stand shoulder to shoulder with my father, in defense of our beloved country! And as surely I shall be near to minister to you both!" answered Erminie, looking up with surprise.

As the hour was late, the party now separated and retired to their respective rooms.

The last thought of Colonel Eastworth, in sinking to sleep, was:

"It will come to this—that my beloved Minie must choose between her loyalty and her lover—and her lover will be quite sure to triumph!"

CHAPTER XXI

ELFRIDA'S ARRIVAL

As soon as the early family breakfast was over, Mr. Goldsborough got ready to go to the convent to fetch away his daughter.

"You will bring her immediately here, I hope?" said Erminie.

"Oh, of course—of course he will," added Erminie's father.

"Thank you both. I certainly intend to call with

Alberta before leaving town," replied Mr. Goldsborough.

"Call with her? Bring her here and make a visit with her. You surely cannot mean to take her direct from the convent to the country without giving her a sight of the city!" exclaimed the old doctor.

"We must leave Washington this evening at the latest. The necessity for our return is imperative!" answered Mr. Goldsborough, gravely.

"I suppose you are anxious to get back to stem with all your strength this tendency to secession, or should you not succeed in that, at least to take care of your family interests, threatened by State politics. Well, perhaps you are right," said the unsuspicious old minister.

Mr. Goldsborough's face flushed scarlet, but that might have been from the efforts he was making to draw on a very tight glove, or even from the compression of the very thick woolen scarf that was wound around his throat as he stood there booted and great coated, and ready for his start. He answered not a word, but took his hat from the rack, bowed, and went away.

The snow that had been falling all night long, lay deep upon the ground, and was falling fast still.

The old doctor shut the door quickly after his departing guest, and came back into the library with a renewed appreciation of the comforts of his own fireside.

Erminie ran upstairs to get ready her best spare room for the reception of Alberta; for though Mr. Goldsborough had said that he must leave Washington with his daughter on that same evening, Erminie entertained hopes that he would change his mind, and pass the day and night with them.

While she was busy having the fire lighted, the bed linen changed, and the water brought up, thinking all the time how comfortable and happy she would try to make her friend Alberta, whether her stay should be short or long, she received a hasty summons from her own father.

She ran downstairs to the

unbounded astonishment, she saw Farmer Fielding and his daughter Elfrida. They had just been admitted by the servant, and were shaking hands with Dr. Rosenthal, who had come out of the library to receive them.

"I am so glad, oh, so glad to see you, my darling Elfie!" exclaimed Erminie, running and catching her little friend in her arms, and kissing her a dozen times before she even thought of the elder visitor When she did recall his existence, she turned toward him with a blush and a smile, saying:

"Excuse me, Mr. Fielding. I am very happy to see you. How do you do?"

"Thank you, Miss Minie, I do as well as any man can in my circumstances. I have been——" began the farmer, but he was cut short by the doctor, who finished the sentence for him in his, the doctor's, own way.

" 'Exposed to a snowstorm, and I am wet and cold;' that's what he would say, my Minie. Come right up into my room, farmer, and change your clothes at once."

"Thank ye kindly, no. I'm not wet. We came in a covered wagon as far as the Drover's Rest, close by here, and only walked the little bit from there here. Bless you, we do look powdered over pretty well, but it's all on the outside. It don't penetrate like some things do, doctor. No, Miss Minie; the circumstance to which I allude was the being turned out of my home by a lot of lunatics, who are also trying to turn the Government upside down!" said the farmer, beginning to unbutton his overcoat as he stood.

Erminie and her father stared up in silence for a moment, and then exclaimed in surprise, and at the same instant:

"Driven out of your home, Mr. Fielding!"

"Yes, driven out of our home—nothing else. Ask my girl, here!"

"Yes—that was it!" broke in Elfie. "Old Virginny was made too hot to hold us—literally too hot. In short, our houses were burned over our heads, and we should have been burned in it if we hadn't made good our escape."

"You shock me beyond measure!" exclaimed the minister, in consternation.

"Oh, my dear Elsie, what a misfortune! How did that happen? But don't try to tell me here, my darling. Come up to my room and change your clothes first," said Erminie, in deep sympathy.

"Oh, no. I can just take off my hood and cloak and overshoes here, if you please, and let your maid carry them away. I am dying to tell you all about it. Let us go into that pleasant looking room, there. I dare say it is your usual sitting-room," said Elsie, nodding her head toward the open door, while she impatiently tore off her hood and cloak and kicked off her overshoes.

"It is our library, and a favorite room with us all," replied Erminie, pushing the door wider open and leading the way.

The room was empty. Colonel Eastworth had left the house soon after Mr. Goldsborough went, and the doctor's two brothers, Hans and Friedrich Rosenthal, were up in the doctor's snuggery enjoying a good smoke.

Erminie placed chairs round the fire, and the party of four drew up to it.

Erminie and her friend sat on one side of the chimney, and the two gentlemen on the other.

"First of all, though, have you had breakfast?" inquired Dr. Rosenthal, while Erminie placed her hand upon the bell, ready to ring and give orders.

"Oh, yes, thank ye; we had a very good breakfast at the Drover's," replied the farmer.

"Then tell us all about this affair," urged the doctor, earnest in his sympathy and eager in his curiosity.

"Ask my girl here; she'll tell ye. She knows a deal more about it than I do," said the farmer.

"Tell us all about it, Elsie, darling," said Erminie, affectionately.

"Oh, don't you be afraid but what I'll tell you all about it. I've been dying to do so ever since it happened.

"The burning of your father's house, my dear?" exclaimed Erminie, in horror.

"No, but the provocation of those who did burn it. The first public act of my life resulted in getting our house burned over our heads! Encouraging, wasn't it? It was all my fault!"

"It was all her glory, she should say. Miss Minie!" put in the farmer.

"That's a mere matter of opinion, pap. The glory or the shame of my act is an open question that will be settled in quite opposite manners by opposing parties. The Secessionist will call it an act of treason! The Unionist will say it is an act of patriotism! The first will call me a wretch; the second will say I am a heroine. All I say about the matter is, that it was all my doings, because I am a self-willed little party, who don't like contradiction."

"I see I must tell the story myself," put in the farmer. "Well, I suppose you know there is a pretty strong secesh feeling down here in Virginny?"

"I have heard so, I am very sorry to say," replied the doctor.

"Bless you, yes; and down our way—— Whew! Why, as far back as last Christmas, when our Virginia boys, who were at college in Washington, came home for the holidays, they made their boast that when they went back to Washington it would be behind the 'red-cross' banner (whatever in the deuce's name that might be), to the sound of drum and bugle, and with swords and muskets to take the city. Bosh! I let the lads talk. I didn't even think it worth while to contradict them. I only thought they were a little more inflated with gas than ever college boys usually are, and I considered their blowing it off a necessary process."

"I heard the talk of Secessionists very much in the same spirit. I could not believe it real," said the doctor.

"Yes; but the jest has become very serious now. The madness has spread, and is spreading. Our neighborhood is a regular hotbed of secession. A few weeks ago I had occasion to go to Winchester with my two brothers. It was a lawsuit that took us there. In fact, we were subpœnaed as witnesses in the great case of Trowbridge *versus* Kay, and we had to go, and the case detained us there more than a fortnight. I will just observe here that on our road to Winchester, we noticed at every public house, post-office, blacksmith and country store, and at ever so many private houses, banners raised, and bearing such mottoes as these: 'Secession,' 'The Southern Confederacy,' 'No Compromise;' 'State's Rights,' and so forth. I didn't see one Star-Spangled Banner in the whole route! Well, meantime, you know, I left my little Elfie at home, with no one to protect her but the negroes. Bless you, I thought she was as safe as safe could be! Now you tell what happened after I went away, Elfie, for you know more about it than I do," said the farmer, turning to his little daughter.

"I knew he'd break down in the story. He'd better let me told it from the first. Well, when pap and my two unks had gone and left me alone, with the old blind mare, the cow, the pigs and the darkies, I got into mischief the first thing.'"

"Of course you did," said Dr. Rosenthal, laughing. "'When the cat's away the mice will play.' But what particular species of mischief did you get into?"

"Ah! 'thereby hangs a tale,' and not a mouse's tail neither. Well, seeing so many strange new flags flying round, I thought I would just hoist the old one, for fear people might forget its existence. The only difficulty in my way was that I hadn't an old one to hoist."

"But mark you what she did!" exclaimed her father, proudly.

"I made a raid upon our drawing-room and best bedchamber. There were red moreen curtains hanging up in one and white cotton in the other; so I took down the curtains red and white, and tore them into strips, and sewed them together like the stripes of the dear old flag! Then I took my blue merino dress and cut out the square for the stars. Then I cut the stars and sewed 'b   ,   '. 'I wa tv uty f   ' long by eight 'r   ⸺   ⸺   ⸺ eight stripes and a hundred stars, and it took me a whole fortnight to make it! When it was done, I had a misgiving that it was over regulation size, and that there were more stripes than was lawful, and more stars than States; but I wasn't sure, for I had forgotten all about my geography and history; and, besides, I thought if I had made a mistake it was certainly on the right side, and at worst, it was only a prophecy of the future, for the dear old flag is bound to grow and increase; and if she isn't entitled to a hundred stars now, she will be when we have annexed South America and the rest of creation! So I resolved to let my flag fly as I had made it."

"But where could you expect to find a staff strong enough to bear it?" inquired Dr. Rosenthal.

"This was my second difficulty. And I was at my wits' ends for a little while. However, there was a tall Lombardy poplar tree growing before our house. So I made Ned, our man of all work, take an ax and go up that tree and shred off all its branches, until it stood up a bare pole—tall, straight and strong, as the mainmast of a three-decker. The stumps of the limbs that were lopped off made very good holds for the feet and hands in climbing. I made Ned take the flag up to the top of that pole and nail it there, so that it might never be drawn down!"

Here Elfie's father nodded approvingly toward his host, as if claiming admiration for his daughter, while little Elfie went on.

"Well, they did let Sunday go by without making any very violent demonstrations against the flag. They confined themselves to hooting and howling. But bright and early Monday morning three ruffians came to the house and rapped. I hadn't left my room, so I looked out of the window and saw who they were and guessed what they came for, and I called down to Ned, who slept in the hall, not on any account to open the door. And then I went and hoisted the window and asked what they wanted.

"'We want that blamed flag down!' roared one.

"'It has no business here! It shall come down!' howled another.

"'Serve you right!' said I.

"'Send out your beastly black man to haul it down!' growled the third.

"'Do you good,' I observed.

"They didn't seem to see the point of my answers, for the first one that had spoken broke out into a terrific volley of imprecations, that was enough to raise the hair up off my head, only it didn't! And then he ordered me to have the flag lowered.

"'You're another!' I said.

"Then all three began to curse and swear in a horrible manner. And I began to sing as loud as I could:

"'Three blind mice! they all ran after the farmer's wife!'

"Then, still cursing and swearing, like a crew of pirates in a sea fight, they went to the flagpole and began to climb it. Seeing which, I went and got father's gun, examined it and found it all right. It was a double-barreled gun; and I carried it to the window and rested it on the sill and pointed its muzzle toward the top of the pole. The three men had reached it then, and were tearing away at the flag to get it loose.

"'Come down!' I shouted, 'or as sure as I live I will fire!'

"They answered me with curses. Now, I am no sharp-shooter, so what followed was all owing to chance. Using the window sill as a rest, I trained the gun as well as I could, pointed it toward them, and pulled the trigger. And simultaneously with the flash and the report one of the men uttered a fierce yell, and fell to the ground. Oh, Heaven, Minie what a tremendous revulsion of feeling I experienced when I thought that I had killed a man! I do not know whether I could have fired again. However, the two others did not wait for the discharge of the second barrel. They slid down that pole like monkeys, and ran off like quarter horses, leaving their wounded upon the field. Then I laughed. I could not help it. I sung on':

"'See how they run! see how they run!'

"And then, in my excitement, I blazed away at them with the other barrel. But they were so far off that only one of them got struck, and in the back, and with a spent ball, for I saw him stop suddenly, with a great howl, clap his hands behind him, bend backward, and then run faster than before."

"I call that a brilliant victory," said Farmer Fielding, nodding toward his friends.

But the Lutheran minister and his daughter were too gravely interested in Elfie's narrative to express any admiration of her feat.

"I am not proud of the victory," said Elfie, candidly. "I was delighted with it—elated with it—but not proud of it. How could I be? For it is true, I was one girl against three men, yet I had the great advantage of fighting behind my entrenchments, while they were exposed. I had also firearms, which they had not. No, I don't think I have any reason to vaunt myself for this easy victory."

"But the man you shot from the pole! Oh, my dear Elfie, I hope—I hope he was not killed!" said Erminie, clasping her hands in the earnestness of her anxiety.

"As soon as the other two men had run away, I set the old gun up in its place, and ran downstairs to the hall, where I found my faithful Ned guarding the door with an old blunderbuss.

"'Miss Allfrida!' he said, 'I told you we'd have a fight for the old flag, and we's had it; and it won't be the last, nuther. They're gone now, but they'll come back to-night in stronger numbers.'

"'I don't care, Ned.' I said; 'come one, come all, this house shall fly from off its firm ground as soon as I!'

"And then I told him to open the door, for I wanted to go out and look after our wounded prisner. Lor', Minie, when I went up to him I thought he was dead, sure enough! He was lying on his stomach, with his head, arm and leg doubled under him. Ned was frightened, too.

"'Goodness gracious me alive, Miss Elfie; he's done for; and the constables will do for us!'

"'Turn him over, Ned,' I said.

"Ned turned him over, showing a ghastly face turned up towards the sky. I ran into the house, and brought out a pitcher of water and a bottle of whisky. And we dashed the water in his face; but with very little effect. Then Ned opened his clenched teeth with an oyster knife, and I uncorked the bottle and poured the whisky down his throat. Bless you! he swallowed it like mother's milk. Did you ever see a baby suck in its sleep? Well, that's the way that fellow sucked, in his unconsciousness. When the bottle was empty, and I drew it from his mouth, he opened his eyes and began to stare around.

"'You'll do!' I said

"And then I told Ned to call one of the field negroes to help him, and to bring the wounded man in, and lay him on pap's bed, and then go for the doctor. When the man was moved, oh! he shrieked out, I tell you. And when the doctor came and examined his injuries, he found that my shot had passed through his shoulder, and the fall from the flagpole had broken his leg. So you see his injuries, though serious, were not fatal. Later in the day his friends came, in a large wagon, with a feather bed and blanket in the bottom of it, and took him away. They 'cussed sum,' and threatened loudly to have me arrested and sent to prison for life. I assured them that I was justified in what I did, and that the law would sustain me, and they knew it. Finally they went off, vowing vengeance against all our tribe"

"Were you not terrified by their threats?" inquired Dr. Rosenthal.

"Not then! I was too mad! But, after I had calmed down and saw that it was growing late and night was coming on, I began to feel uneasy; because, you see, there was no one to guard the house but myself and old Ned and old Cassy! So, very early in the evening, I fastened up the house, bolting and barring every door and window. And I loaded three double-barreled guns, and made other preparations to meet the assault. And I went up into the attic to watch the app   . And, I t   , that,

I was glad when I saw pap's wagon coming down the road!"

"Yes," put in Farmer Fielding. "The case of Trowbridge *versus* Kay, closed that very morning, and my two brothers and myself were at liberty to come home. My two brothers, however, decided to stay over that evening, to attend a Union meeting, got up to make some little stand against the progress of the Secessionists But I was anxious about my girl, and so I resolved to come home, and in good time, too, for I found her fortifying the house to withstand an assault. I was so astonished that my breath was suspended! But she soon told me what had happened; and I soon had reason to see the prudence of her preparations, and also their inefficiency!"

"What a dreadful state of things!"

"You would think so if you had been at our house that night!"

"What night was that, by the way?"

"Why last Monday night, of course."

"Oh, certainly—yes! I recollect Miss Elfie's naming the day."

"It is a day to be remembered in the annals of my domestic life. Myself and my girl sat up and watched. But, for all that, I did not believe that our own old neighbors would pull the house down over our heads, merely because we were loyal to the old Union and the old flag. But what will not maniacs do? Myself and my brave girl watched until near daybreak, when, thinking that all was right for the time being, and that we would not have an attack that night, we separated, and went to bed, to get an hour or two of repose before breakfast. I had been some time asleep when I was rudely awakened by a terrific yell—such a yell as a band of painted savages, armed with firebrands and tomahawks, might roar forth in surprising a peaceful home.

"I sprang up and rushed to the window and threw up the sash and looked out. The eastern horizon was quite red, and by its light I saw a crowd of men armed with guns, pistols, swords, pitchforks and a variety of weapons, gathered around the house. As I bent out

FAIR PLAY

to look down, I saw a quantity of straw, shavings and dry brushwood piled around the posts that supported the porch. The moment they saw me they saluted me with a perfect howl of rage.

"'Come out of that, you——' Here followed a volley of profane and indecent imprecations and vituperations—'come out of that house with your devil's imp of a daughter, unless you wish to be burned alive inside of it!'

"Before I could reply, my brave girl, who had heard the row, was by my side. She put a gun into my hand and said,

"'Pap, I have called up Ned, and he can do good service. Now you take this gun, and fire into them from this window, and I will fire from the other. And we'll keep it up as long as the ammunition lasts; and then we'll die game, pap'

"I turned to answer my girl, to tell her not to show herself at the other window—to be careful; but she was gone—she was already before the other window, and training the gun so that its muzzle should be in a line with the crowd below. I did the same at my window. We fired at the same moment, and our fire was answered by a roar of rage and a discharge of musketry. The shots rattled against the front of the house, and shivered the windows, shutters and sashes. I trembled for my girl.

"'Elfie, for Heaven's sake, leave the window! fall flat upon the floor,' I said

"'Not if I know it, pap,' she answered, 'not while I have a shot left to send at the enemy.' And, so saying, she blazed away with her other barrel

"I did the same with my other; and again we were answered by a volley of musketry; and again the shot rattled against the walls, and split the timber of the window frames I saw my brave girl fall, and, in an agony of terror, I threw down my gun, and ran and raised her up

"'I'm all right, pap,' she said 'It was only my gun kicked and knocked me down; and, now, if you don't load up and let 'em have it again, you are no pap of mine! I'll assist you

"But, notwithstanding her words, I bore her into a back room, where she would be safe from the shots; and, even as I carried her away, I saw the smoke and flames rising from the outside of the house, and heard the rioters roar forth with many fierce curses:

" 'Come out of that, or be burned alive in it '

"I laid my girl on the bed, in the back room, and hastened to my own room, where I secured my little money and valuable papers. While I was hiding them about my person, old Ned came to the door and whispered:

" 'Massa, massa, for de Lord's sake, come away! Take Miss Elfie my main force, if she won't give in any other way, and come! I'm got the wagon and horses at the back door.'

" 'Ned,' said I, 'come with me to Miss Elfie's room, and tell her the state of affairs.'

"And we went to my girl's room, and I got her clothes, and ordered her to dress herself quickly, and threatened if she did not do so, to take her just as she was.

" 'Oh, if I am to contend with foes outside and cowards inside, of course I shall have to evacuate! And I will do it decently!' said my girl. And she got ready very quickly, and went down the back stairs to the back door, where Ned had the wagon ready. And I put my girl into it and got in beside her; and Ned mounted the driver's seat, and we set off by the back road and made our escape. And here we are! But if it had not been for the thought of my dear, brave girl, I should have stayed there and defied the mob to the utmost!"

"If it hadn't been for the thought of me' Well, now, I like that! That's cool!" exclaimed Elfie; "especially when, by your own showing, pap, if it had not been for you and Ned and the kicking gun, I should have stood my ground and died game, or driven off the assailants on the last occasion as I had done on the first I'm sure I did very well on that first occasion, when I hadn't you to help me, pap! But on the last' Well, what could I do with fiery-hearted foes outside

ing to get out; and my very weapon recoiling upon me and kicking me down! I tell you all what! I fought against fearful odds on every hand! Joan of Arc herself would have given in under such circumstances! Not that I would, if it hadn't been for that cowardly pap of mine!"

"I don't think either you or your papa have reason to be ashamed of your conduct on that occasion. 'What could you 'gainst the shock of hell?'" said Dr. Rosenthal.

"Well, anyhow, I know what I'll do next time. If ever I find myself in command of a domestic castle in siege, I'll lock pap up in his bedroom till the fight's over. You hear that good, don't you pap?" said pap's daughter, saucily.

"But, Elfie, my darling, where have you left that good old negro who rescued you from the burning house?" inquired Erminie.

"Oh, he's all right. He is at the Drover's."

"You know, Elfie, he would be quite welcome in our kitchen. Our servants would take care of him."

"'Thanky, honey,' as Ned would say; he is very well where he is. Besides pap and I haven't come to quarter ourselves upon you so suddenly. We only wanted to see the smiling faces of friends after having seen the frowning faces of so many foes. That is all. Presently we intend to go out and look for a boarding-house where we can stop for the present."

"Indeed, you will do no such thing, Miss Elfie! In the first place, there are no boarding houses but what are already crowded. In the second place, here is my house, open to receive any of my friends at any time, and especially wide open to welcome any number of friends for any length of time, who have suffered from their devotion to this Union which has fostered me for nearly fifty years! So, friend Fielding, you will please make yourself at home where you are," said Dr. Rosenthal, with earnest sincerity in every word, tone and look.

Farmer Fielding put out his sturdy hand and shook the fat fist of the good doctor, as he replied:

"Thank ye, minister! for thy press. I accept your

kind invitation, the more especially as I shall be backward and forward from here to Virginia, and sha'n't like to leave my little girl alone in a boarding-house. Thank ye, kindly, minister! We'll stop with you a bit, until we can turn ourselves round."

"That's settled, then! And now I am happy to tell you that to-day you will meet an old friend of yours here," said Dr. Rosenthal, cordially.

"An old friend of mine? Humph! I should like to see one besides yourself. Nearly all my old friends have become Secessionists, and are no longer friends of mine!"

"Ah! but this one hasn't. He is loyal to the Union, and is very much disturbed in his mind on account of the spread of the Secession spirit through his native State. I am speaking of Mr. Goldsborough, of Richmond," said the unsuspicious old man.

"Goldsborough! One of the rip-stavingest Secessionists in the State—one of the moving spirits of secession!—a leader among them!" exclaimed Farmer Fielding.

"Who, Goldsborough?"

"Himself."

"Are you not mistaken?"

"Not a bit of it! He has been stumping the State, making secession speeches in every congressional district. I heard him make one, in our neighborhood, at the Bull's Head Tavern. Who do you think replied to it?"

"I don't know, I am sure. I am so astonished to hear that Goldsborough is a Secessionist that I am filled with perplexity."

"Why, Vittorio Corsoni answered him. You know that there is no love lost between Goldsborough and Corsoni; and Goldsborough being a Secessionist might have been cause enough to make Corsoni a Unionist; though I have observed that naturalized foreigners, who have been protected by our Government, have been among the most zealous in its defense, and if this matter ever comes to blows, they will strike good ones."

Just as the door-bell rang violently, and when the

servant ran in haste to see the cause of the noisy summons. Mr. Goldsborough burst into the house, and then into the library. His face was inflamed, his features distorted, and his eyes flashing with passion.

"For Heaven's sake, Goldsborough, what has happened?" exclaimed Dr. Rosenthal, rising, in alarm.

"What? She has gone! Fled from the convent!" roared the enraged man, throwing his hat upon one chair, and his gloves upon another, and without noticing any one in the room, except his host; "yes, brought dishonor upon all her family! And may the curses of——"

"Hush!" said the minister, laying his hand gently upon the lips of the speaker; "no curses, Goldsborough. Sit down quietly and compose yourself, and tell us all about it. See, here is Mr. Fielding and his daughter, your old friends."

"How do you do, Fielding? How are you, Miss Elfie? I beg your pardon for not seeing you! But you will not wonder at a man being blind with rage when his only daughter has disgraced herself and her family," said Mr. Goldsborough, gruffly enough, as he coldly shook hands with Elfie and her "pap."

"Oh, no, Mr. Goldsborough, not so bad as that! Young people will sometimes choose for themselves, you know. And though their choice may be indiscreet, and even unfortunate, it need not be disgraceful. Try to calm yourself, and make the best of it! The young man is something of a monkey, to be sure; but I believe him to be a well meaning monkey!" urged the farmer.

And all party politics seemed for a moment forgotten in the interest felt in this domestic calamity.

"Sit down, Mr. Goldsborough! Do sit down and compose yourself! And let us hear the details of this flight," entreated the doctor.

"No, I cannot sit down! And I will not compose myself! I will pursue the abductor of my daughter, and shoot him wherever I find him."

"But how do you know who was the abductor, if it comes to that?" inquired the farmer.

"Oh! I know! Perceval! And I swearing to

the description of this Corsoni, was seen lurking around the convent all day yesterday! Besides, you know, she would have run off with no one else! Good-by, Fielding! Good-by, Rosenthal! Young ladies, your servant!" said Mr. Goldsborough, seizing up his hat and gloves, and leaving the house before the startled company had recovered from their astonishment.

CHAPTER XXII

ANOTHER TRIAL FOR ELFIE

All unknown and unsuspected by the good Lutheran minister, his house became the headquarters of consultation, and he became involved in a network of circumstantial evidence that at a later period might have brought him before a military commission, or placed him on the scaffold.

He had discovered that Mr. Goldsborough was a Secessionist; and for that reason he was very glad to get rid of that gentleman's presence; but he knew that Farmer Fielding was a good Union man, and he believed that Colonel Eastworth was as loyal as himself—Ernest Rosenthal.

Colonel Eastworth, over and above his strong love for the Lutheran minister's beautiful child, had another great motive for remaining the guest of Dr. Rosenthal; it was this: That under the cover of one who was so well known to be a stanch and loyal man, he might, with less suspicion and more safety, perfect certain plans. Under this roof he daily and nightly received many visitors with whom he held long interviews in his own rooms.

Dr. Rosenthal never dreamed of inquiring into the motives, conduct or character of his guest's visitors. They would come at almost any hour of the twenty-four, ring the bell, inquire for Colonel Eastworth, and be shown up to his rooms, either to see him, if he should be in, or to wait for him, if he should be out.

And Colonel Eastworth was out

pecially in the evening. At length, so well were his plans organized that his co-conspirators knew very well at what hour to call and find him in; and he would be in his rooms all day busily writing and sending off letters, or receiving visitors, and half the night he would be out. Erminie saw but little of him at this period.

One evening, when he came into the drawing room, before going out, she gently rallied him on what she gaily called his "going on."

"Where are you off to now?" she inquired, with affectionate freedom.

"Dear love, the lodge," he answered, after some little hesitation.

"I don't believe the lodge meets every night! And you are away every night!" she gaily remonstrated.

"Dear love, this lodge does meet every night," he answered, seriously.

"I declare, one would think, to see and hear you, that you nightly met conspirators who were darkly plotting 'the ruin of themselves and kind!'" laughed Erminie.

But how little she dreamed how much truth she had spoken!

Colonel Eastworth also laughed—a strange, unnatural laugh—that chilled Erminie's blood; and then he kissed her and went away.

Most of Colonel Eastworth's visitors were strangers to the old minister's family, and even to the rest of his staying guests.

But one morning Eltie had a great surprise. She was running downstairs, singing, "Gay and happy," when suddenly she met, face to face on the stairs, her lover, Albert Goldsborough, who had just been admitted and was on his way up to Colonel Eastworth's rooms.

"Eltie!" he cried, stopping short and staring at her.

"Well, I do think! Where did you come from?" she exclaimed, stopping and gazing at him.

"I had no idea that you were in this house," he said, meaningly.

"And I had no notion that you were coming to it. So you don't follow me here?"

"No, I came to see Colonel Eastworth."

"It appears to me that there are a great many people coming to see Colonel Eastworth. I don't know anybody that sees so many people, except it is that old door-keeper at the White House! But you won't see Colonel Eastworth this morning. He is generally in, holding a levee in his rooms all day long; but this morning the queerest-looking fellow that ever I saw came after him and carried him away."

"What sort of a looking fellow, Elfie?"

"A great, tall, broad-shouldered man, with little, tiny head. They got in a carriage together I heard him tell the coachman to drive to Benning's Bridge. Now, that is four miles from this, and, if they are going any distance over that bridge, they won't be back till evening."

"Humph! humph! humph!" muttered Albert, reflectively.

"However, as this house is certainly Liberty Hall, you can stop and wait for him," suggested Elfie.

"I am not altogether sorry to miss him, just now that I have met you, dear Elfie. My business with him can wait till evening. And I wish so much to talk with you, Elfie. Oh, I am so glad to see you! It is such an unexpected pleasure. Are you glad to see me, love?"

"I had a little rather see you than not, perhaps."

"No more than that?"

"No—no more than that."

"But I am happy—so happy to meet you."

"Happy, are you? Well, you don't look so; and, indeed, I haven't seen anybody look happy for the last six months. Of all the glum wretches that ever existed, all my fellow creatures are getting to be the glummest. Happy! if that is your happy look, I wonder what your dismal one is like."

"Nonsense, Elfie dear, this is no time for raillery. 'Great events are on the wing.' Men have heavy responsibilities just now, as you must know, living in this house. I said I'd talk to you on the stairs, dear.

Is there no place where you can take me for a quiet tête-à-tête?" inquired Albert.

"Yes; there is the library and the drawing-room, both unoccupied at this hour."

"Take me to the place where we shall be least liable to interruption."

"Come to the library, then," said Elfie, leading the way thither.

When they were seated before the fire, Albert inquired·

"How long have you been here, Elfie?"

"For several weeks. Ever since our house was burned over our heads."

"Your house burned over your heads!" exclaimed Albert, in astonishment.

"Yes, and we would have been lynched if we had not made our escape."

"Well, the violence of these Unionists in Virginia is certainly as horrible as anything in the Reign of Terror."

At the word "Unionists" Elfie stared. Then, as it dawned upon her mind that Albert was a Secessionist, that he took her for one, and that he supposed her house to have been burned by the Unionists, she grew very pale, but in the interests of her country she kept silent, and involuntarily she played the spy. This with her bitter experiences of secession persecutions, and with her keen perceptions, had led her to suspect the loyalty of Colonel Eastworth, and of all those strange visitors who came to see him in his rooms. But up to this time her suspicion was not strong enough to justify her interference in any way. Now however, by certain words and tones of her lover, her suspicions were strengthened; and, in the interest of her host, as well as of her country, she instinctively kept silent, and involuntarily played the spy.

"Yes," continued Albert, "the outrages of the Unionists are really beyond belief, though, as yet, I have never heard of their burning any house except yours."

Still Elfie kept silent. She would let him betray himself

ing, not even for the sake of her country, to invite a confidence which she did not intend to keep. If Albert was a Secessionist, and mistook her for one, and under that mistake volunteered certain communications, the revelation of which would be important to the interests of her country, Elfrida would listen to him, but she would say nothing to draw him out.

"Why did the Unionists burn your house?" indignantly demanded Albert.

"The men who burned our house did so because we differed with them in the matter of States' rights," diplomatically answered Elfie.

"Oh! of course! that is understood as the remote cause; but what was the proximate cause, the immediate provocation to such an outrage?"

"We raised a flag that was obnoxious to their feelings!"

"Exactly! In my neighborhood they have torn down every secession flag that has been raised, and sometimes tarred and feathered the owners! But I tell you what, Elfie, their day is nearly over! But you must know that, living in this house. We can never be sufficiently grateful to Dr. Rosenthal. His services to the good cause are so important that I have no doubt he will be rewarded with a high position in the administration of the government in the rising young Confederacy!"

Elfie listened, but said nothing.

"Ah!" she thought, "he knows that Dr. Rosenthal's house is made the rendezvous of revolutionists, and he believes that Dr. Rosenthal is cognizant of the fact. Colonel Eastworth could enlighten him on that subject; but then, Colonel Eastworth is absent."

"And now, Elfie—dear Elfie—knowing what a true-hearted and brave-spirited little heroine you are, I am going to tell you something. It is not quite a secret, Elfie, else I would not confide it even to you. It is known to all the leaders of our party; it is well known to Eastworth, and to the gentlemen that visit him; it is known to your host; and very likely it is known to you also. If it is, you can speak and save me the trouble of telling you."

FAIR PLAY 171

"No," said Elfie, "I know nothing; I suspect a great deal."

"Then I will tell you. Indeed, your sufferings in the good cause entitle you to the same sort of confidence that would be given to a man; and your presence in this house is a sufficient indorsement of your reliability. Besides, you can be of the greatest use to us. You can be, and I am sure you will be."

"I would lay down my life if it were required of me in the good cause," said Elfie, compressing her lips and growing deadly white; for in Elfie's bosom there was a terrible conflict going on between her love and her loyalty.

"They are making great preparations for the pageantry of the inauguration of their President, Elfie," he continued, with a laugh.

"Yes," said Elfie.

"Ha! ha! ha! there will be a pageantry of another sort, my dear! Do you notice how many Southern men are quietly sending their women and children out of the city?"

"Yes."

"It is to get them out of the way of this other pageantry of which I spoke. My Elfie, Washington is a Southern city, it belongs to us, and a mere sectional President-elect will never be permitted to take his seat here."

"Indeed!" exclaimed Elfie.

"Never!"

"But how can he be prevented from doing so?"

"By force of arms."

"By force of arms!" echoed Elfie.

"Yes. Listen; all over Virginia—all over Maryland —there are bands of devoted and desperate men, organized and sworn to prevent Lincoln from taking his seat. Our people in Washington know this, and are ready to co-operate with us. I bear a captain's commission in one of these bands. Colonel Eastworth is my superior officer. We have three branch and one main rendezvous. And they are near the bridges crossing the Potomac and the Anacostia. Our plan is, on or be

several rendezvous, in the darkness of night; to march at the same time over the three bridges; to surprise Washington, and so take the city by assault," said Albert, warming into enthusiasm with his narrative.

"Oh, Heaven!" muttered Elfie, between her clenched teeth.

He heard her mutter something, but failed to catch the word; and he utterly mistook the cause of her paleness and sternness of aspect. He was, indeed, absorbed in his own subject; and so he continued to reveal his plans:

"Yes; the streets of Washington may run with blood; the houses of Washington smoke in ruins; but on the fourth of March, when Lincoln is expected to take his seat, the Confederate flag shall wave above the Capitol!" he exclaimed, rising in his excitement and pacing the library floor.

"God forbid!" panted Elfie.

Still he was too absorbed in his own subject to hear her. After walking up and down the floor a few times, he came and seated himself by her side, and asked the question:

"Where is your father, Elfie?"

"He went back to Virginia, a few days ago, to look after his interests there."

"When is he expected to return, my dear?"

"Not until the inauguration day. He wishes to be here then."

"Do you suppose he knows what is really to take place before that day?"

"I do not suppose he does," said Elfie.

"No; probably he does not! Certainly he does not! or he would not have left you here exposed to the coming danger! Elfie, my darling! you must not be left here! As soon as I shall have seen Colonel East worth and delivered the dispatches intrusted to me for him, I shall go back to Virginia. And, Elfie, my own girl, you must go with me!"

He had taken her hands in his own, and his face was beaming with love, and his voice was melting with tenderness as she spoke to her, and tried to meet her eyes.

But she withdrew her hand and turned away her face; she loved him and hated him at the same moment; her heart was breaking, and she wished for death. But she never dreamed of flinching from her duty! He continued

"This is no time, my own love, for false delicacy or womanish etiquette! I cannot possibly leave you here exposed to the terrible dangers that are impending over the city! In revolutions, my Elfie, the innocent are sacrificed with the guilty! I cannot leave you here, exposed to the horrors of the coming days! I must make you my wife; take you with me to Virginia, and leave you under the protection of my widowed mother! She is alone, Elfie! She has no other son but myself, and no daughter at all! She will receive my beloved wife as a dear daughter, my Elfie! Come! what say you, my own? Do not avert your head! Let me see your sweet face! Turn toward me! smile on me! Oh, my Elfie! make me happy!"

"Oh! Leave me! Leave me! Leave me!" she exclaimed, in a passion of indignation, as she started up, flung off his hand, and walked across the room.

This time he heard her, understood her, and gazed upon her in astonishment, incredulity and consternation.

"Elfrida! is this acting? Or is it real madness? What do you mean?" he exclaimed, going toward her.

"Keep off!" she said, so shortly, so curtly, so sternly, that he stopped suddenly, like a man on the brink of a precipice.

"Tell me what you mean by this, Elfi?" he cried.

"What I mean by this! I mean to be true to my country! Next to my duty to God, I rank my duty to my country! And I will be faithful to her, though my heart should break in its fidelity!" passionately exclaimed Elfie.

"Your native State is your country! To her alone is your allegiance due. She is about to secede from the Union, and she has a right to do so. And it is your duty to go with your State!"

"I deny that a State has any right to secede from the Union! Set up that doctrine, and see where it would end.

country; for if a State has a right to secede from the Union, a country has the same right to secede from a State; and a township to secede from a county; and a farm from a township; and the barn from the farm; and the husband from the wife, and the child from the father!—and there you have disintegration and anarchy! Bosh! preach State's Rights not to me!"

"Elfie!" answered the Secessionist, hotly, "I am willing to admit your capacity for understanding the construction of a dress or a dinner; but I doubt your ability for comprehending the Constitution of the United States."

"Gammon! The Constitution of the United States is written in just about the plainest English that I have ever read, and I claim to understand my mother tongue!"

"Elfie, you cannot mean to turn traitor to your native State!" exclaimed Albert Goldsborough.

"No! I do not mean to turn traitor to my native State, or native country, or native farm! or to my pap or to my two unks. In being true to the whole Union, I am true to every part of the Union, and to every citizen thereof."

"But Virginia is only nominally in the Union. In a very few weeks she will be out of it, by the unanimous voice of her people, heard through their representatives in the Assembly."

"Fiddle! Virginia go out of the Union by the unanimous voice of her people, indeed! I am one of her people! and I would die before I would utter one syllable in favor of secession! My pap and two unks and a host of our friends are loyal Virginians who would shed the last drop of their blood in defense of this glorious Union of States that makes us one of the mightiest powers among the nations of the earth! And if Virginia is ever voted out of the Union, it will never be by the unanimous voice of her people, or even by the will of the majority of her people!"

"I tell you you are mistaken! Virginia and Maryland, too, will follow the glorious example of their chivalric sister, South Carolina, who——"

"Albert Goldsborough, I am not going to stand here

all day long, listening to you; I warn you that Dr Rosenthal is loyal to his heart's core, so loyal that he does not suspect and could not understand disloyalty in any man! He is as innocent now as I was an hour ago of the plots going on under his own roof. If he knew of them he would denounce them instantly!"

"What! is not Dr Rosenthal a Secessionist?" demanded Albert, in consternation.

"No, sir!"

"Nor your father, nor your uncles?"

"No."

"Elfrida, you have played a very treacherous part with me. You have pretended to be one of us; you have made false statements in regard to your persecutions in the cause of secession, and you have drawn out my confidence, only to turn upon me," said Albert, bitterly.

"Anything more?" inquired Elfie.

"Is not that enough?" demanded Albert.

"Yes, but I would like to hear the whole charge before replying to it. Is that the whole charge?"

"Yes."

"Then I deny it *in toto*. I have played no treacherous part by you. I never pretended to be one of you. It was yourself who took it for granted that I must be a Secessionist. I made no false statements about my persecutions in the cause of secession. I told you that our house was burned over our heads, and we had to escape for our lives. And you jumped to the conclusion that the outrage was perpetrated by the Unionists of our neighborhood. I did not seek to draw your confidence out. You bestowed it upon me freely. If I turn upon you now, it is as a loyal heart turns upon a rebel!"

"Elfrida, I won't stand this!" hotly exclaimed her lover.

"Then if you won't 'stand' it, you had better walk it. Marry you, indeed! Not if I know it. Gammon! If I were fool enough to marry you this week, why, next week, or next month, you might send me to prison

"Elfrida, I will not bear this!" exclaimed Albert, stamping.

"Then don't. There is no reason why you should. You know the way out of the house into the street, and you are at liberty to take it. I strongly advise you to do so," said Elfrida.

He glared at her, and then striding toward her, took her roughly by the arm, and hissed in her ear:

"You have become possessed of our secrets. But beware how you betray them. For if you should, woman as you are, the vengeance of the Banded Brothers will surely find you out."

"Bosh!" exclaimed Elfie, "what do you think I care for the vengeance of the Banded Brothers? I care not for them, Albert Goldsborough, even though they may track and kill me for what I am about to do. The hardest part of my trial, Albert, you will never know, and perhaps could never understand!" said Elfie, and she set the library door wide open, and then went to the corner of the mantelpiece, and rang the bell.

"What is that for?" uneasily inquired Albert.

"It is for a servant to show you the way to the front door, Mr. Goldsborough, since you don't seem to know it. Go! I will give you a few hours to get out of the city and hide yourself. Then I will go to the President and denounce your plan, that immediate measures may be taken to defeat it."

"To the President!" sneered Albert Goldsborough, with a laugh that seemed to say: "Why, he is one of us!"

"Yes, I will go to the President and denounce this plot; and if he won't listen to me, I will go to General Scott, and he will save the city. But in the meantime, Albert Goldsborough, I will give you a few hours to escape in. I believe there is a train leaves for Baltimore and Philadelphia in an hour from this; and there is another leaves for Alexandria and Richmond in an hour and a half. May the Lord bring you to reason! Go!" she said, pointing to the open door.

"Elfrida!" he exclaimed, again advancing toward her. "If you suppose that I am going to submit to the humiliation you have put upon me, you are quite mistaken! I insist——"

At that moment a servant, summoned by Elfie's bell, entered the room, and Albert broke off in his speech.

"Go!" said Elfrida, in a low, stern voice, as she still pointed to the door. "Go! there is no time to be lost, either by you or me! If you do not obey me at once, I will summon Dr. Rosenthal and his two brothers, who are in the house, and have you arrested as you stand!"

"You are a young demon!" hissed Albert Goldsborough, grinding his teeth, as he flung himself out of the room.

"Attend that gentleman to the door, Catherine; and then step round to the livery stable and tell them that I shall want a carriage to be here by two o'clock," said Elfie.

The girl bowed her head and went out of the room, closing the door after her.

And little Elfie, left alone, paced up and down the library floor, as a chafed young lioness might pace her den.

"It is all over between us now," she sobbed; "all over between us forever and ever! And oh! I did love him! I did love him so dearly! And with all his faults he did love me so truly! And he confided all his plans to me so trustingly. And now I must turn on him and denounce him and expose him to capture and death! or else I must hide his secrets in my bosom and let him go on planning the capture of Washington and the destruction of the Union. Oh, my goodness! was ever a poor girl in such a fix as I am!" added Elfie, as she left the library with the intention of seeking her own room, to prepare for her visit to the President.

For in all the ebbs and flows of contending passions Elfie was as true to the country as is a politician to his own interests.

"I never can trust myself to tell the story. I should become agitated and talk slang perhaps, and get myself and my information discredited. Take the city by assault! Turn the streets into rivers of blood and the houses into smoking ruins! Capture the Presi dent-elect and plant the Confederate flag on the dome of the Capitol! Heaven and Earth and the other Place! what a plot!" exclaimed Elfie, as she sat down to her writing-desk and began to write a short, condensed account of the plan divulged to her by Albert Goldsborough.

When it was finished she put it in a blank envelope, saying to herself:

"I will not direct it to any particular individual; for if I do not find one high official dignitary at leisure to see me I must seek another."

Then she put on her outer garments and sat down to wait for the carriage she had ordered.

It came at the hour, and she went downstairs and took her place in it. She gave the order to the President's house and drove thither.

Ah! with what a beating heart she got out of the carriage, ascended the broad stairs and presented herself to the porter. It was almost a relief to her to be told that the President could not receive any one that day.

"After all, I doubt if it would have been of any use to call on him," said Elfie to herself, as she returned to the carriage and gave the order:

"To the War Department."

Arrived at that building, Elfie once more left her carriage, entered the house and inquired her way to the office of a certain "high official dignitary," who must be nameless in this story.

Elfie was shown into an ante-room, where she found herself in company with about half a dozen other persons of both sexes, who were waiting to see the great man.

As she was the last arrival, she had to wait until each of these had been singly received and dismissed.

At last her turn also came, and she was ushered into the audience chamber of the "high official."

And with grim satisfaction Elfie noticed how his countenance changed as he read her letter.

Presently, with his eyes still following the lines, he put out his hand, and rang the bell that stood upon his table.

A messenger answered it.

Then he—the "high"—wrote a few lines at the end of that paper, placed it in another envelope, directed it, and put it in the hands of the messenger, saying:

"Take this to its address."

When the messenger had bowed low and left the room, the great man turned to Ellie.

"You have rendered good service, and I thank you for your zeal. You can withdraw."

CHAPTER XXIII

ERMINIE'S GREAT SORROW

WHEN Albert Goldsborough was turned out of the library by his indignant little lady-love, he did not go out of the house as she had commanded him to do. He passed cavalierly by the staring and stupefied servant who had been ordered to attend him, and saying that he should go to Colonel Eastworth's rooms and wait for his return, ascended the stairs.

Catherine slipped after him, opened Colonel Eastworth's door, and showed the visitor in. And then, thinking that she had literally obeyed orders in "attending" the gentleman, she returned to her duties in the lower regions of the house.

Meanwhile, Albert Goldsborough threw himself into a chair before the fire to wait for Colonel Eastworth.

Three long hours he had to wait. The time hung heavily on his hands. He read a little from the newspapers that lay scattered over the table; he walked restlessly, looking into all the cupboards and out of the windows; then he sat down at the round table to improve the time by writing letters that lay heavily on his conscience. One letter he wrote to his mother, another to some co-conspirator in Virginia, and a third he wrote to Ellie—this last full of complaining love and tender reproaches. He was still engaged in writing this letter, which the   inable as love letters usually are   was suddenly flung open, and Colonel Eastworth strode into the room.

"You here?" he exclaimed, on seeing his visitor.

"Yes, colonel," said Albert, rising and hastily rolling up his love letter and thrusting it into his pocket.

"Have you brought anything?" he inquired, coming up to the table, and speaking in a low voice.

"These, colonel," replied the young man, delivering his dispatches.

Colonel Eastworth dropped into his chair, tore open the packet and read the papers, commenting on their contents as he went on.

"So," he murmured. "L. will do nothing until the Legislature has acted E. also holds back until the ordinance of secession is formally passed. J. is waiting for more light, and making the affair a matter of prayer. But M., S and W are ready to take the field now, each with a following of more than a thousand men! Good! I predict that when Washington is ours, those faint-hearted, purblind fellows who cannot make up their minds, but must needs wait for 'more light,' will be braced up a little, and be able to see their duty, or their interest, which, with such laggards, means the same thing."

The remainder of the document was read in silence and with a lowering brow. Then he drew a quire of paper before him, took a pen, and rapidly indited a letter, which he folded, sealed, and put into the hands of the young man, saying:

"I am sorry to send you off again in such a hurry, before you have even had time to rest, Goldsborough; but it is absolutely necessary that this should be in the hands of S. before to-morrow morning. There is to be a meeting at Witch Elms to-morrow evening, and he must be present; for the final arrangements as to the precise time and mode of the assault will be discussed and decided upon."

Albert Goldsborough received the packet, but instead of starting immediately on his misson, he hesitated and dropped his eyes upon the floor.

"Well, what now? You have something to tell me!" excl

"Yes, colonel, I have! You are no longer safe in this house! A little, prying imp, in the form of a young girl, has discovered our plot, and means to denounce us to the authorities and to our host!"

"The demon! this cannot be true!" exclaimed Colonel Eastworth, in consternation.

"It is as true as truth, colonel! She has threatened to denounce us all! And she will surely carry out her threats!"

"What girl is this?"

"Little Elfrida Fielding!"

"Ah, the little serpent! And to think that such a little, insignificant creature should be able to do so much harm!"

"Ah, colonel! a worm may burrow a hole that shall sink a ship of the line!" said Albert Goldsborough.

"Yes, yes! Now I must hasten my departure. It is very fortunate for my plans that old Rosenthal has gone off to Baltimore to see his brothers thus far on their way to New York. And that he will not be home until late to-night. I can leave a letter of adieu to him. But, Albert, how did this girl manage to discover so much?"

"Who can tell?" replied young Goldsborough, evasively, for not for the world would he have confessed to his colonel his own indiscretion in betraying his secrets to Elfrida before he could be sure of her sentiments on the subject of secession.

"I suppose the little witch has been eavesdropping. There are too many doors to this apartment to make it a safe consultation room," said Colonel Eastworth, moodily.

"There are," admitted Albert, with a sigh.

"Well, in any case, in a very few days I should be obliged by expediency to withdraw from the house, and this discovery has at most but accelerated my action. It is fortunate that old Rosenthal is out of the way!—Well, good-day, Albert. I must really send you off at once," said Colonel Eastworth, holding out his hand.

"And I must really go," agreed young

Goldsborough, respectfully saluting his "superior officer" as he left the room.

Colonel Eastworth, left alone, sank down into his chair and fell into the moody meditation so frequent with him of late. Born of an old historical family, whose names were identified with the chronicles of the country; whose men were all brave, whose women were all pure; nurtured in the highest principles of truth and justice; tried and proved in the legislative halls of his native State and on the battle plains of Mexico, up to within a few months past Colonel Eastworth was a man of stainless honor and glorious fame. But he believed in the absolute sovereignty of each single State in our Federal Union; in the absolute right of each State to secede at will from the Union, and in his own allegiance due solely to his native State. Thus, warped by the Doctrine of State's Rights and tempted by the fiend Ambition, he had been won over to the cause of the Southern Confederacy. Not, however, without a severe struggle did he win his own consent to abandon the old flag that had been the idol of his boyish worship, for which in his bright and blameless youth he had shed his blood and risked his life, under which he had gained a nation's gratitude and a hero's crown. This struggle over, all the rest was easy enough—easy as "the descent to hell" is said to be. The doctrine of State's Rights admitted, the other doctrines of Expediency naturally followed as an excuse for all manner of dishonorable action This Expediency led him to lend the powerful aid of his astute intellect and military experience to the bands who were planning the capture of the city and the seizure of the President-elect.

After some minutes of moody thought Colonel Eastworth arose, went downstairs to seek Erminie. He found her in the drawing-room, toning down the gas which had just been lighted, and putting those last delicate finishing touches on the artistic arrangement of the room of which only the young mistress' hand seemed capable.

"I am happy to find you alone, sweet love," he said, gliding to her si'

"And I am very happy to be alone to receive you," answered his betrothed, with confiding frankness. "I love my friends very dearly; but, oh! indeed I am not so very sorry that the company is gone for the present. We could not have a word apart while they were here, could we, Eastworth?"

"No, sweetest girl, we could not! we could not. And did you miss our *tête-à-têtes* so much, mine own?" he asked, seating himself in a large resting-chair and drawing her toward him, much, very much, as a father might draw a daughter to sit upon his knees.

But the Lutheran minister's child was very delicately shy, and that beautiful shyness was one of her most bewitching charms. Softly and gently, and without offense, she evaded his motion, and passed in behind his chair and bent playfully over him.

"Oh, yes, yes! I missed our *tête-à-têtes* so much! I missed you every day and every hour in the day!"

"Did you, my dearest one! did you, indeed, miss me—such a gray, wrinkled, careworn wretch as I am?" he said.

She bent over him with caressing tenderness.

It was true! Six months before this time there had not been one silver thread in the raven tresses, or one line on the ivory forehead of Colonel Eastworth; but now care had streaked his hair with gray, and the constant habit of frowning had planted deep wrinkles between his brows.

Erminie leaned over him with caressing tenderness, and pressed her lips to that spot on the top of his head where the thin hair indicated swiftly approaching baldness.

"I love you more for every white hair and every deep wrinkle; they are indices of thought and of suffering; and how can I but love you more for them?" murmured Erminie, laying her soft cheek upon his head.

"Come around here, my own! my own! I am your husband, or soon to be so! Sit where I can see your sweet face!" he pleaded, reaching behind him and getting hold

"I will sit here and look up into your face—ever the most beloved face in the universe to me!" murmured Erminie, softly, as she drew a footstool to his feet and seated herself upon it, and placed her hand in his.

"Erminie," he said, bending over her and gazing and speaking with an earnestness approaching solemnity, "Erminie, do you really, really love me?"

She looked up at him with a frightened aspect, and answered slowly:

"Oh, you know I do! You cannot doubt me! What made you ask such a question?"

"Because, my beloved, I am about to put your love to a terrible test!" he replied, with an agitation that powerfully appealed to her sympathies.

"That is just what I wish you to do! what I pray you to do! Put my love to any test—any! so that I may prove to you how truly I love you—how much I would do for you!" she answered, in a low, fervent, faltering voice; and blushing intensely at her own temerity, even while feeling so anxious to reassure her lover.

"Erminie, the test by which I shall prove your love will be the severest test by which the love of a nature like yours could possibly be tried."

"It will not be too severe for mine! I invoke the trial! I invoke it!"

"Erminie, do you love me enough to henceforth cast your lot with mine, for good and evil, for time and eternity?"

"Ah, yes, yes, yes! But that is not the test, for surely every woman loves her betrothed as much as that! But I love you, oh, so much more!" she murmured, hiding her face in his caressing hands.

"You love me enough to forsake all and follow me?"

"Oh, yes, yes! Did I not promise that on the blessed day when my dear father placed my hand in yours in solemn betrothal?"

"You will cleave to me, to me only, forever and ever, through good report and through evil report?"

"As my soul lives, I will!" fervently exclaimed the Lutheran minister's daughter, uttering the rashest vow that was ever spoken by trusting lips.

She did not even add the saving clause: "In all cases not inconsistent with my duty." She did not dream of doing so. Her pledge to her lover was unconditional because her faith in him was unbounded.

Nor was hers the mere blind faith of a loving heart. It seemed to be justifiable, for Colonel Eastworth was a man highly honored by the world, both for his private character and his public services. How could she ever imagine that he would call upon her to forsake her father and her country?

Yet this he was about to do. This was the test to which he meant to put her devoted love. And now he believed that the time was ripe for the disclosure of his plans. Now he felt assured that she was truly and unreservedly his own—so bound to him, body and soul, that she was not only ready to suffer with him, but willing to sin for him, if he should wish her to do so.

"Erminie," he said, looking down into her loving, trustful, fervent face, "Erminie, you have pledged your faith to me by a very solemn oath—'As my soul lives.'"

"Yes! And I repeat it. 'As my soul lives!' And if there could be an oath more solemn and binding than that, without being profane, I would pledge you my faith by it!"

"Erminie," he stooped and whispered, "you are already almost my wife!"

"Oh, yes; I consider myself so. With us, you know, betrothal is as sacred as marriage," she murmured.

"Then, my beloved, what I wish you to do is to become my wife in reality and immediately," he whispered.

"But my father, dear Eastworth! My father would not consent. And besides, he is not here, and will not be here until late to-night," she answered, when at last she was able to reply.

"No, my beloved, your father would not consent. It would be quite useless to ask him even if he were here; and he is not here. We must act, Erminie, without consulting your father!"

"Oh, Eastworth, without my dear father's consent. I could not—I could not strike such a blow at my father's heart," she pleaded, plaintively, not as if she could persistently resist his wishes, but as if she were imploring him to spare her the trial. He saw that and took an ungenerous advantage of it.

"You do not love me," he said, coldly and bitterly.

He had never spoken to her so roughly before. She looked up at him in surprise and affright.

"No, you do not love me, or you would not answer me so," he repeated, with cruel emphasis.

"Oh, I do, I do! Heaven knows how truly and how much!" she said, clasping her hands in the fervor of her feelings.

"Erminie," he said, changing his tone from bitter severity to tender earnestness, "Erminie, I would not ask you to do this were there not the gravest reasons for it. Shall I tell you what these reasons are, my beloved girl?"

She dropped her head upon her bosom. Her gesture might have meant assent or despondency. He took it as an assent and he continued:

"Erminie, I am obliged to leave, not only this house, but this city, to-night—to leave, not only in haste, but in danger!"

"In danger!" she echoed, growing very pale.

"Yes, in danger—and as a fugitive!"

"As a fugitive! Oh, Heaven of Heavens! what has happened?" she gasped, in deadly terror for his safety.

"I have been betrayed."

"Betrayed!"

"You do nothing but echo my words, sweet love!"

"Oh, forgive me! How can I help it? They are so strange and so alarming—your words. And I am all in a maze of bewilderment," she faltered, trembling excessively.

"Do you not surmise what all this means, Erminie?"

"Oh, no, no, no! I dare not—I dare not! I only know whatever the mystery is, you are blameless in it."

"Thanks, sweet love, for your boundless faith. But I am something higher and better than blameless, my Erminie, or I should not deserve your trusted love.

I go out of this city in haste, in danger, and as a fugitive; but I return to it, Erminie, at the head of an army, with beating drums and waving banners!"

She gazed at him in amazement. His words were as unintelligible to her as if he had spoken in Sanscrit.

"Now do you understand?" he inquired, smiling.

Reassured by his manner, she also smiled, as she shook her head and replied:

"I understand that my betrothed husband is all that is good, noble, honorable; but I do not understand his words."

"My beloved Erminie, listen: I am a Secessionist! One of the leaders in this second coming war of independence, which is to be more glorious than the first; one of the builders of this second young republic, whose splendor is destined to eclipse the first! And when I ask you to go away with me to-night, it is to share the fate of one who would lift you up beside him to, perhaps, the highest position in the gift of the young Confederacy!—Why, what is the matter with you, love?" he suddenly broke off and inquired, as she turned from him and dropped her head upon her bosom. "What is the matter with you, Erminie?"

"My heart is broken!" she murmured, in an almost dying voice.

"Nonsense, my darling girl! I know what your professed principles are. I often hear you express yourself strongly in favor of this absurd 'Union.' But I also know that, daughter-like, you take your opinions from your father, and, parrot-like, repeat the words he uses, without attaching much meaning to them. Henceforth, Erminie, you must take your opinions, not from your father, but from your husband. What do you say, my love?"

"I do not think that I took those opinions from my father. I do not remember the time when I did not know that treason——"

"Erminie!" he exclaimed, in a voice so stern as to make her start.

"Oh, pardon me," she said. "I did not mean to speak so rudely. And I did not wish to offend you. And oh, yes, I misunderstood you. Heaven grant that I may have done so. Oh, indeed, I must have done so! I am so stupid and bewildered. You are true to your country, are you not? Oh, tell me that you are, and I will ask your pardon on my knees for my momentary doubt of you!" she pleaded, clasping her hands, and gazing at him with imploring eyes.

"Yes, Erminie, I am true to my country; but not in the sense, I fear, you mean. I am true to my country. I am pledged for the support of the Southern Confederacy, which is the only country I acknowledge!"

"Then, oh, my heart! all is over between us!" she cried, sinking down at his feet, utterly overwhelmed by this blow he had dealt her.

He stooped and raised her tenderly, and drew her to his bosom, murmuring:

"Erminie, my love, my love!"

She turned suddenly and threw her arms around his neck and clasped him tightly, as though she would have held him with all her girl's strength back from the Male-bolge of ruin into which he was about to plunge.

"Oh, Eastworth, I would give my life to find you indeed right! I would rather be wrong a thousand times than you should be wrong once! But I see this all too clearly to deceive myself. I have loved this Union so much! I have thought of her as the Promised Land, the New Jerusalem, the refuge of all the oppressed, the hope of the world! And would you aim a deathblow at her? Oh, think how weak she would be if broken up and divided! Think how the old despotic monarchies of the East would rejoice over her downfall, which would prove self-government a failure among nations. Oh, my dearest, let me hold you back! I would give my life—almost my soul—to save you from this vortex!"

"Erminie, love, you speak from prejudice and from feeling, and not from reason and judgment. Dear love, I will not reproach you, though you have called my devotion to my native State and her confederates treason, but I will say that when a man is charged with treason he has the right to defend himself. Will you hear my defense?"

"Eastworth, if I have said anything offensive to you, I do earnestly beg your forgiveness. But I did not mean to offend."

"Will you hear my defense?"

"Oh, yes, yes!"

Colonel Eastworth began to plead the cause of Secession with all the arguments by which astute leaders influence the opinions of people. These arguments are too familiar to all to need repetition here. But they made no impression on the mind of Erminie Rosenthal. She was not to be deceived by sophistry or persuaded by eloquence, or even won over by love. "Her eye was single, and her whole soul was full of light."

Hour after hour slipped away while he argued, persuaded and implored Erminie to unite her fate with his own, and accompany him to Virginia. And Erminie suffered, wept, but remained steadfast to her principles.

At length, as the time approached for his departure and found her unmoved, he became angry, and gave way to cruel reproaches.

"You have deceived me, Miss Rosenthal. You have played the part of a heartless coquette. You do not love me and you have never done so."

"Oh, Eastworth, I love you more than life! Heaven truly knows I do!" she said, through her sobs.

"Words, words, words! You can talk of love glibly enough. No doubt you could write what school misses would call 'sweet verses' on the theme; but you cannot feel it, Erminie."

"Oh, Eastworth, I would sacrifice my life to save you if I could. Heaven truly knows that I would!"

"Words, words, words again! All that is easily said. You would sacrifice your life to save me. It is very safe to promise that, since no such sacrifice can possibly be required of you. You will sacrifice your life, which nobody asks you to do, but you will not go with me when I leave this place a fugitive—you will not go with me, though I implore you to do it."

"It is because it would be wrong for me to do so, and I dare not do wrong."

"Words, words, words!" he said again, with bitter scorn. "Farewell, Miss Rosenthal."

And he got up and strode toward the door.

Quick as light she flew before him, intercepted him, and clasped him in her arms.

"Oh, don't—don't go! Spare yourself! Oh, Eastworth! oh, my love, spare yourself!" she cried, almost beside herself.

"Will you go with me?" he stooped and whispered.

"No, never! I dare not do wrong!"

"Then let me go alone, false-hearted girl!" he cried, tearing off her clasping arms and flinging her from him with such force that she fell upon the floor.

He rushed up into his room, rang for his servant, sent out and ordered a carriage, and while waiting for it hastily packed up his most valuable effects, and as soon as it came to the door he entered it and drove to the station in time to catch the train for Alexandria and Orange.

Some minutes after the carriage had rolled away, Elfrida chanced to come down to the drawing-room, and there she found Erminie lying upon the floor in a swoon.

In great alarm she rang for assistance, and then flew to the side of her friend and raised her up.

Erminie opened her eyes, and, recognizing Elfrida, burst into tears and sobbed passionately.

"Don't cry—they are not worth tears," said Elfie.

"Oh, Elfrida! oh, Elfrida! If you knew—if you knew!" sobbed Erminie.

"I know all about it. I saw Colonel Eastworth drive away in a cab, with all his luggage packed in and around it. And I know that your lover has gone to help my lover to plot against the safety of the city. But, thank goodness, I have been beforehand with them."

At this moment Catherine opened the door and came in.

"Did you ring, miss?" she inquired.

"Yes—more coal," said Elfie, with great presence of mind.

And when the girl had gone, Elfie whispered to her friend:

"Keep a stiff upper lip; never say die; don't let the servants see us fret."

"I must not let my dear father see me grieve. To prevent that must be my first care. But if it were not for him I should pray—oh, I should pray for death!" sobbed Erminie.

"Can't see it in that light at all! Long life to all true patriots, both men and women, because, you see, the country needs them all! And now, Minie, you are hardly able to stand. Do let me help you up into your room before that sharp-eyed girl comes back," said Elfie.

Erminie yielded, and Elfie took her upstairs and persuaded her to lie down on her bed.

"Now, the governor will not be home until the late train gets in; that will not be until eleven o'clock tonight. I will sit up for him and have his oysters and lager beer ready for him; and I will tell him that you are very tired and have gone to bed."

"Thanks, dear Elfie! And by to-morrow morning I hope to be able to meet my father with some composure," said Erminie.

"And now what else can I do for you?"

"Nothing, dear girl, but to leave me alone with God."

Elfrida stooped over her and kissed her, and then softly left the room and closed the door.

The six o'clock dinner that was prepared that day went away from the table untasted. There was no one to partake of it.

Elfie sent out and got some fresh oysters and lager beer for her kind host, and had a neat little table set in the library ready for him when he should come home.

He came in at eleven o'clock.

Elfie opened the library door and drew him in there, and helped him off with his wrappings and with his overcoat, and placed the easy chair near the fire, and brought him his bootjack and slippers, and performed all the affectionate little services that Erminie was accustomed to render her father.

"Where is my Minie?" inquired the old man, extending his hands over the warm fire, when he had made himself comfortable.

"Gone to bed very tired, leaving me to be your daughter for this once."

"And a nice little daughter you are, my dear. I wish Justin had taken a fancy to you instead of to that Tammany Hall reformer."

"So do I! But he hadn't the good taste to do so, you see," said Elfie, saucily.

"And my Minie was tired. No wonder, poor dear! She has had a great many cares lately, with so much company staying in the house. I am not alluding to you, my dear, for you are a help and a Godsend! And Eastworth?"

"Oh, he has retired too (from the establishment)," added Elfie, in a mental reservation.

"Ah, yes, well. I must have some supper now, my dear, since you are my daughter."

Elfie rang, and supper was served; and then the old man and the young girl separated and retired to their respective rooms.

And dear, unselfish Elfie, now that her fortitude could be of use to no one under the sun, broke down and wept all night, soaking her pillow with her tears.

In the morning, when Dr. Rosenthal came downstairs, the first thing that met him was a letter that Colonel Eastworth had left in charge of Catherine to be delivered to him.

To his unbounded astonishment, that letter revealed to him that his late guest and promised son-in-law was pledged to the support of the Southern Confederacy and had gone away to enter upon his new service.

"Heaven have mercy on my poor child!" was the first thought of the father.

Erminie came down to breakfast as pale as death and almost as still.

"I see that you know all, my dearest child," said the old man as soon as he saw her.

"Oh, my father, pray for him—pray that he may be led back to us!"

"I will, my Minie!—I will, my angel child! God bless you!" said the doctor.

Erminie seated herself at the head of the table, and went through the duties of the breakfast service quietly; and after breakfast she went about her household affairs as usual. Later in the day Elfrida communicated to Dr. Rosenthal Albert Goldsborough's visit and revelation to herself, and also her own visit to the War Department and its results.

"And, ha! that was what hurried Eastworth away. But for Erminie's sake I will not call him ill names, however well he may deserve them. Heavens! to think I should have been so blind!" said the old man, whose astonishment at the conduct of his late guest increased with every hour of thought upon the subject.

In the course of that day a rumor spread through the city which created a great excitement. It was to the effect that the War Department had received certain information of a large and well organized plot to seize the capital and prevent the inauguration of the President-elect.

And everywhere citizens were enrolling themselves in military companies for the defense of Washington; and among the first names that went down upon that immortal roll was the name of Ernest Rosenthal.

CHAPTER XXIV

ON THE DESERT ISLAND

While the stormclouds of civil war, charged with destruction, lowered darkly over our dear native land, all was benign repose on the Desert Island where our young pair had been cast away.

The wreck of their ship still lay high and dry upon the rocks where she had struck. So fast was her position, with her keel impaled upon the sharp hornlike points of the rocks, that neither winds nor waves had as yet power to break her up or lift her off. It seemed as if she must remain there until she should gradually perish and go to pieces by the drying and warping of her timbers in the blazing sunshine. This state of affairs continued for many months.

Every day during this period Justin, Britomarte and Judith passed over the reef of rocks from the island to the wreck, and fed the animals there and brought away as many of the stores as they could carry. But as the way was long and the work toilsome, and as twice in the twenty-four hours the reef of rocks was covered with water, it was impossible for them to make more than one trip a day; and it took them a long time to remove all the stores; a time of much anxiety it was, for they were in constant expectation of some terrible gale that should break up the wreck.

At length, after many weeks of labor, they had brought away from the wreck everything that could possibly be of use to them on their desert island, and this, of course, included all the real necessaries of life, and stores of provisions enough to last them for years. All these things were carefully stowed away in the caves and grottoes of which their mountain was full.

It was not until all the stores were secured that Justin proposed to bring away the animals, for they had been best off on the wreck so long as there was anything there for them to eat, and therefore they had been left there to the last. It was a work of difficulty, almost amounting to impossibility, to get these beasts over the causeway; but finally the task was safely accomplished and the castaways settled down to a monotonous existence on the lonely isle.

In the spring Justin commenced building; but on account of rough material and imperfect tools, and for the lack of help, the work progressed very slowly.

Thus more than a year passed since they were first cast upon the Desert Island.

They had given up all expectation that any roving ship should come near enough their isle to discover the signal flag that they always kept flying from the summit of the mountain, though every day Justin paid a visit of ceremony to that flag and took a look out at sea through his telescope.

Nearly two years had passed, and no incident worth recording had happened, when one night their island was visited by a most tremendous hurricane. It raged all night, and only subsided in the morning.

At midday, when all was over, Justin, Britomarte and Judith walked up to the top of the mountain to see what had become of the wreck that had remained there for twenty months, high and fast upon the rocks, and perishing slowly by the dry rot.

Justin arranged the telescope and took a sight. And what did he see?

Not the wreck! for the last vestige of the wreck was broken up and carried away by the winds and waves in the last night's tempest.

He saw a sail, a strange sail, with a strange flag, bearing down upon the island.

CHAPTER XXV

A STRANGE SAIL

"WHAT is it, Justin? Oh, dear brother, what is it?" eagerly inquired Miss Conyers, almost losing her presence of mind in the vehemence of her anxiety.

"It is a sail—a strange sail! Compose yourself, dear Britomarte," answered Mr. Rosenthal, without removing his eye from the glass.

"A sail!" she repeated, breathlessly.

"Yes, dear!"

"Oh, Justin!"

"It stands in toward the island."

"She sees our signal!"

"No, I think not, unless the captain's glass is better than mine; for with mine I cannot make out her colors yet, and our signal is no more conspicuous."

"Are you sure she is coming in here?"

"Yes."

"But why, unless she sees our signal?"

"She has been driven out of her course by the gale of yesterday; but probably she has safely outridden the storm. She may be coming hither in search of fresh water or wood."

"Oh! Justin, if she should strike that sunken reef of rocks as our poor ship did?"

"She will not do so, dear! She is steering clear of the rocks and for that little cove to leeward of them."

"Oh, Justin, Justin, then she will surely anchor there. And we—we shall be rescued! Oh! we shall see our fellow-beings and our native land again! The thought makes me reel with joy and—suspense!" exclaimed Miss Conyers, really growing dizzy with emotion, and clasping the flagstaff for support."

"Dear sister, calm yourself."

"Ah! how can I? Our case seemed so hopeless! and now the thought that we shall be rescued and taken back to our native country overwhelms me! Oh, to leave this! to go home! it is like bursting the bonds of the grave, and rising from death to life! To go home!—to go home! Oh, Justin, does she draw near? Are you sure that she does not turn her head to steer away again?"

"Sure."

"At what rate does she seem to sail? Is she making rapid progress?" persisted Britomarte.

"She is making very rapid progress, though I cannot tell you at how many knots an hour she is sailing. There! I can see her colors now."

"You can! What are they? English? Dutch?"

"I think they are our own Stars and Stripes—the most beautiful national colors that fly!"

"Oh, Justin—Oh, Justin! Our own dear Star-Spangled Banner! That would be too much joy!"

"I think it is our flag. I am not sure, because I cannot yet see very distinctly. I think it is, because I see the red and the white; but I cannot make out the blue field with the white stars."

"That would not be so conspicuous against a background of blue white and white foam; but you will see the whole presently," said Miss Conyers.

Justin continued to gaze through his telescope at

the stranger for a few minutes longer, and then he spoke:

"Britomarte!"

"Yes, Justin."

"They are not the Stars and Stripes."

"Oh, Justin! I am so sorry! But then we ought to be glad and grateful for any flag that should come to our rescue. What is it, then, Justin? The Union Jack; that would be the next best thing."

"No; it is not the Union Jack."

"What is it, then? Can't you speak and tell us, dear Justin?" said Britomarte, a little impatiently.

"The truth is that I myself don't know! I thought I was familiar with the colors of all nations, but I cannot make these out at all!"

"How strange. What are they like?"

"Like bars—red, white and red I do not recollect them as the colors of any nation on the face of the earth!"

"Nonsense! You have forgotten! Let me look, Justin. I am familiar with the flags of all nations," said Britomarte, impatiently.

He adjusted the telescope for her sight, and she took a long and silent view.

"What do you make of the flag?" inquired Justin, with good-humored sarcasm.

"Red—white—red! I can make nothing of it whatever. I never saw it before."

"Judith, you are an old salt, and have seen many a strange flag in the ports where you have stopped in your voyages to and from India. Take a look at this one, and tell us if you ever saw it before," said Justin, as Britomarte retired from the telescope.

"Sure and so I will. Faix, if it was the flag iv purgatory itself, with Ould Nick at the helm, I'd be glad to hail it, so I would, if it would take us offen this baste iv an island," said Judith, taking her place at the telescope and "sighting" the object.

"Well, can you make the flag out?" inquired Justin

"Devil a bit. I niver saw the likes iv it before in all the days iv me life. Sure and I'm thinking it must be a pirate or a fraybooter," said Judith.

"You may be right, Judith! though Heaven forbid you should be!" answered Mr. Rosenthal.

"Justin!" exclaimed Britomarte, who now replaced Judith at the glass—"Justin, she must be a pirate! She carries guns! I see them!"

"I know she carries guns; but it does not follow from that circumstance that she is a pirate. She may be an armed merchantman."

"Sailing under no recognized flag, Justin? Would not an armed merchantman sail under the colors of her country?"

"Most likely."

"And if this should be a pirate!"

"Yes, if she should! The contingency is not a pleasant one. Judith, we must go down the mountain, my good girl, and hide all the animals in the holes of the rocks; for, if this strange sail should prove to be a pirate coming here in search of wood and water, she would be sure to make very free with all our stores, and especially with the beasts!" said Justin, uneasily.

"Troth would she! And sure if the crew was hungry for fresh beef itself, they'd kill and ate Crummie, the crayture in less time nor I could milk her, so they would!" said the Irish girl.

"Come, let us go!" urged Justin, taking up his telescope.

The three turned their steps down the mountain side, and employed the next hour in driving the animals into the caverns at the base of the mountain; and closing up the openings to these caverns, not with boards—which would have attracted attention—but with green brushwood, arranged in such a way as to seem a part of the natural thicket that clothed the mountain side.

When this was done, they went to Britomarte's grotto, and concealed as many of the most valuable articles there as they could find a hiding place for.

Then they walked down to the beach in the direction from which they expected to see the strange ship. They had no need to use their telescope now. As soon as the reached the sands they saw the ship at anchor in the little cove, while from her masthead flew the strange flag.

While they gazed, a boat put off from the ship and rowed rapidly toward the shore.

In ten minutes it touched the sands.

The six oarsmen laid on their oars; and the one officer, in a uniform as strange as his flag, stood up in the bows and lifted his hat in courteous salutation to the islanders.

"I had not expected to find civilized people in this outlandish place," he said, in English, to Justin, who came forward to meet him.

"You are welcome," said Justin, offering his hand

"I had no idea that there was a European colony here! What is it—English?" inquired the stranger, stepping on the shore, and again lifting his hat and bowing politely to the women

"There is no colony. We are not colonists. We were cast away on this island nearly two years ago." said Justin.

"Cast away!" echoed the stranger, recoiling in dismay.

"Yes. We were passengers in the East Indiaman. Sultana, bound from Boston to Calcutta, and which was wrecked upon these rocks below."

"And so that was the fate of the missing Sultana!" said the stranger, gravely.

"That was her fate," repeated Justin.

"Were any of her crew or passengers saved besides yourselves?"

"We cannot tell! They took to the lifeboats! The first boat that left the ship sailed for the open sea, and we never heard of her fate. The second one attempted to reach the land, and was swamped. This lady and her companion were in that second boat when it went down They were saved by means of the life preservers that had been fastened round their waists. They were thrown on shore by the waves. The remainder of their boat's crew perished, I fear "

"And yourself?"

"The captain and myself were left on the wreck. The captain was washed overboard by a great wave.

I escaped only by clinging fast to the shrouds of the mizzen-mast, which was above water. When the sea went down, I managed to reach the shore over that reef of rocks, at the end of which our ship had struck."

"And where our ship had very nearly been lost in the late tempest! You have been here nearly two years, you say. Good Heavens! how have you subsisted?"

"Partly by the natural productions of the island," said Justin, evasively.

"And how have you got on with the natives?"

"There are no natives except beasts, birds, reptiles and insects."

"Then the island is uninhabited?"

"By man? Yes, except ourselves."

"And you have been here nearly two years. Heavens! And in all that time seen no ship from home?"

"No ship from anywhere! I think this island is out of the usual course of ships."

"Yes, we were driven far out of our course, and clean out of our reckoning, before we saw it! Two years! And yet the dress of the young lady and her attendant is just as neat as though fresh from the hand of the laundress," said the stranger, incredulously.

"We managed to save a few necessaries from the wreck, and clothing, soap, starch, and flatirons were among them," Justin explained with a laugh.

"Humph! nearly two years on this desert island, without news of the world outside! Without telegrams, letters, or newspapers! How, in Heaven's name, have you managed to endure life?"

"Indifferently well! Do we look as though we suffered from ill health, or low spirits?" inquired Justin

"No, that you don't! But your Eden has an Eve! Oh! that the desert were my dwelling place, with one fair spirit for my minister! You have two! Happy man! The Sea Scourge has not one!"

"The Sea Scourge!" echoed Justin.

"My ship out there, of which I am the captain, at your service!"

Justin bowed and then said:

"My name is Rosenthal. If you will give me yours I will present you to the lady."

"My name is Spear, for want of a better."

"Miss Conyers," said Justin, stepping a few paces towards Britomarte, "Captain Spear, of the Sea Scourge."

Captain Spear bowed very low. Miss Conyers bent slightly and then looked up, to see before her a tall, broad-shouldered, stalwart man, of about forty years of age, with prominent features, red hair and beard, and sun-burnt complexion.

"And the young woman with the damask-rose cheeks?" inquired the captain, indicating the Irish girl.

"Her name is Judith Riordan. She is Miss Conyers' attendant," said Justin, coldly.

Notwithstanding which, Captain Spear turned, and honored the maid with a deep bow as he had bestowed upon the mistress, and a bold stare of admiration into the bargain.

Judith turned away, hugely affronted, growling:

"Bedad ye nadent be thrying to come yer comether over the likes if me, so ye nadent! Meself don't like the looks iv ye."

Captain Spear turned with a smile to Miss Conyers, saying:

"I hope you do not share your companion's antipathy?"

"If I did," said Miss Conyers, "I should not show it to a stranger who comes among us, perhaps seeking relief for his own necessities; perhaps to rescue us from our exile."

The captain bowed, and then said:

"Mr.—Rosenfeldt—is not that the name?"

"Rosenthal," corrected Britomarte.

"Mr. Rosenthal tells me that you have been on this lone island nearly two years; and in all this time have had no news of your native land."

"It is quite true."

"You must have suffered intense anxiety."

"No; I left no near relatives in my native land to

mourn for me. I had one or two school friends; but they were too happily situated and to well cared for long to lament my unknown fate."

"And you, Mr.—Rosenthal—am I right?" said the captain, turning to Justin.

"Lord kape yer!" impatiently interrupted Judith—"hev ye got no mimory at all, at all? or are ye afther dhrinking itself, that ye can't remimber a gintleman's name, when ver afther hearing it so often! It's Rosenthal, sure—thal, thal, thal! There! twist that round yer tongue, and lave off staring at me as if ye'd ate me!"

The captain of the Sea Scourge laughed, and once more turned to Justin, saying:

"Mr. Rosenthal, how have you borne this long separation from home and friends, and this utter lack of news from the world outside, for nearly two years?"

"As I hinted before, neither my health nor spirits have suffered materially. I left a venerated father and a beloved sister and many friends. I know that my father and sister have mourned me as dead; and that they continue to remember me with affection; but I also know that religion and time have combined to soothe their sorrows and regrets. As for the world from which I am separated, I feel that the Lord took very good care of it before I was born into it, and can continue to take very good care of it now that I am exiled from it!"

"Mr. Rosenthal, you are a philosopher."

"Nevertheless, I shall be very glad to get back, with my companions in misfortune, to our native country," said Justin.

"And it will confer upon myself more happiness than I ever received in my life to take you all back," said the captain, earnestly.

"Thanks! I can well believe it," replied Justin, warmly.

"Troth, maybe he's not so bad as he looks," muttered Judith to herself.

Britomarte studied him with more attention than before. It was strange, but he impressed the islanders in opposite ways; for while his appearance excited suspicion, his manners inspired confidence—except, perhaps, in the single instance of his bold stare at poor Judith

"Will you——" began Justin, but before proceeding with his sentence he went up to Britomarte and spoke apart to her, asking her permission to invite these strangers to the grotto. She gave it readily; and then Justin stepped back to Captain Spear and said

"Will you do us the honor to come up to our home and take lunch?"

"Thanks—willingly. I should like to see what sort of a home you have contrived to provide on this Desert Isle," said the captain.

"And your boat's crew? Can they not leave their boat to accompany us?"

"By no means! I will not so far trespass on your kindness or the young lady's forbearance."

"Oh!" said Britomarte, earnestly, "believe me that neither Mr. Rosenthal nor myself would consider it a trespass. It has been so long, so long, since we have seen any other human faces than our own that we are more than delighted to welcome you and your whole crew."

"Thanks, young lady. With your kind permission, then, I will call the men off."

So saying, the captain walked a few paces toward the boat, and called·

"Here, Mulligan! Secure the boat, and you and your mates come off and follow us."

Then he came back to where Justin and Britomarte stood, and said that he was ready to accompany them.

CHAPTER XXVI

THE CAPTAIN OF THE "SEA SCOURGE"

They walked on through a grove of palms, and then through a thicket that clothed the base of the mountain, until they reached the front of Britomarte's grotto.

"You see it is to no house that we are able to invite you, captain, but we will make you very heartily welcome to this 'hole in the wall' of the mountain." said Justin, smiling, as he opened the door, and drew aside the curtain that concealed the entrance to Britomarte's grotto.

"A palace for Pan and the wood nymphs, upon my soul!" said the captain, in sincere admiration, as he followed Justin and Britomarte into the grotto, and looked around upon its glistening white walls and brilliant skylight.

"We like it very much," said Britomarte.

"Like it! Who would dwell in houses made with hands, when they might live in a fairy grotto like this?" exclaimed the captain.

Justin drew one of the armchairs forward, and invited him to take it.

And Judith removed the woolen table cover, and replaced it with a damask tablecloth, preparatory to spreading the lunch.

As plates, dishes, glasses, castors, knives, forks and spoons were in turn placed upon the table, the captain of the Sea Scourge looked on with ever-increasing amazement. Turning his eyes from the well-appointed table to the comfortably-furnished grotto, he said:

"It appears to me that you saved a great deal from the wreck."

"Yes," said Justin, cautiously, for he could not as yet feel full confidence in his guest; "yes, the ship was cast very high upon the rocks, and when the sea went down she was almost entirely out of the water, and we saved at least enough furniture from the cabins and dining-saloons to fit up this grotto comfortably. The crockery in the dining-saloon suffered most in the storm, for out of a mountain of broken glass and earthenware, we rescued only a dozen or so of whole pieces; and indeed the whole pieces are not entirely whole, for there is scarcely one that is not cracked or chipped."

"It must have been a stupendous labor for one man to get all these things especially this heavy furniture, from the wrecked ship to the shore."

"It was the labor of months," answered Justin, "but I did not accomplish it alone. Miss Conyers brought all the light articles over, and Judith Riordan, who is a model of strength, assisted me to bring the heavy ones."

While the two men conversed, Judith, under the direction of Britomarte, spread the table with a cold ham, a chicken pie, a loaf of bread, cheese, and a bottle of brandy.

"Brandy, too!" exclaimed the captain of the Sea Scourge, on beholding this last welcome addition to the feast. "Brandy, too! you are very fortunate, as well as industrious. You must have saved a lot of it, to have lasted you nearly two years."

"Nay," said Justin, evasively, "we saved some bottles, but as we kept it in case of illness, and never required its use in that contingency, the store could not give out."

"Then I assure you, if I were going to leave you a settled colonist upon this Desert Isle, I would not touch a drop of your brandy, but as I hope to take you all with me when I sail, I will gladly drink it to your health and happiness," said the captain of the Sea Scourge, suiting the action to the word by helping himself liberally to the brandy.

"Sure if he's not a fraybooter itself, it's fray and aisy he is entirely," muttered Judith, as she passed Miss Conyers on her way to the kitchen. Britomarte smiled, and Judith presently reappeared with a pitcher of water, which she also set upon the table.

And now, all being ready, Justin invited his guest to seat himself at the board.

"But where are the men whom you ordered to follow you, captain?" inquired the host.

"Oh, they are straggling in, I suppose. They will be here presently, doubtless. But, my young friend, pray don't waste this brandy on them, whatever you do. It is genuine old Otard, such as you cannot buy for love or money in the States, though you may pay highly for a lot of drugged Yankee rum that sells under its honored name. Besides, my fellows wouldn't appreciate it, and it is desecration of good liquor to give it to men who don't know it when they taste it. Give them the cheapest whisky that you may happen to have to throw away," said the captain, filling for himself another glass, which he held up to the light with the glance of a connoisseur.

"Indeed, I think I am no better judge of liquors than the mot ignorant of your men. We have a small cask of whisky, and your men are welcome to it, though whether it is good, bad or indifferent, I cannot tell," said Justin, who was busy in cutting up the chicken pie, with which he liberally helped his guest.

"Chicken, by all that's gracious! Did you save chickens enough to stock your poultry yards, my friend?" inquired the captain.

"We saved a few, from which we raised other broods," answered Justin, rather reservedly, for it did not escape his notice that while Captain Spear put his host through a rather close cross-examination, he was not at all communicative on his own affairs.

And neither had Justin lost sight of the mystery of the strange flag, but with something of the old Bedouin sentiment of hospitality, which permits the guest, whoever he may be, to come and go unquestioned, Justin forbore to make inquiries, at least for the present. He hoped that the captain himself would soon volunteer information.

In this he was disappointed. The captain ate heartily of the chicken pie, and passed from that to the ham, and from the ham to the cheese, washing down the whole with abundant draughts of old brandy, which semed to take no more effect on him as yet than so much pure water

At last, when the stranger had eaten enough and was satisfied, and Judith had taken out the remnants of the feast, and divided them among the men who were sitting grouped outside the grotto door, Justin thought the time had come when, without impropriety, he might question his guest. He began in a delicate, distant, roundabout manner, on the common ground of politics.

"I need not ask you if you are a native American, Captain Spear. I see that you are."

"Yes—I am. And yourself? Your name is German; yet you speak English like a native."

"I am a native American of German descent," answered Justin.

"A native American, are you?—of the North, or the South?" inquired the stranger, pointedly.

"Of the South," replied Justin, rather reservedly, and feeling that the tables were being turned upon him, and that from the questioner he was again becoming the questioned.

"Of the South! So am I. Give me your hand again. We shall be friends, I am sure!" warmly exclaimed the red-bearded captain, seizing the fist of his host and shaking it heartily.

"Thanks," said Justin, wincing somewhat. Then, making another effort to enter upon the common ground of politics, he said:

"When I left my native country last October a year ago, the contest was very bitter between the two great parties that divided the nation. Which succeeded in electing their candidate?"

"Good Heavens! What a realizing sense of your long sequestration from the world and your utter ignorance of its affairs your question gives me! I positively never fully appreciated your position until this moment! Man, you might as well have been dead and buried in your grave as entombed alive in this desert of an island!"

"I do not think so," said Justin. "But tell me who was elected President of the United States?"

"Is it possible that you don't know?"

"How should I? I left the United States in October. When I left there seemed to be an equal chance of success between the candidates; the election did not come off until November."

"And you don't know what has happened since?"

"No, I tell you."

"What! did no passing ship bring you the news?"

"If a ship had passed, we should not have been found here," said Justin, impatiently.

"Did no bird sing it? No wave bear it? No breeze waft it?"

"Birds, waves and breezes are not apt to gossip with me," replied Justin.

"Hear it, Olympian Jove! Here is a gallant son of the South that does not yet know that he is free! That he has been free for nearly two years! A man that still believes in the supremacy of the Stars and Stripes and in the existence of the Glorious Union! Ha—ha—ha! ho—ho—ho! Oh! but in respect to the ladies' presence, I could shout with laughter! Come—what will you give me for my news?"

"Nay, friend, if you will not freely impart your news to an exile who has been without any for so long a time, I have nothing to offer you but my thanks," replied Justin, greatly perplexed by the words and manners of his guest.

"Now that appeals to my better nature! I will tell you all. But stay—I must not tell you all at once. It would overwhelm you!"

"In Heaven's name, what has happened? Have we annexed Canada, or Mexico, or both?"

"Neither yet—I tell you I must break the matter to you gently. And first by answering your question as to who was elected President of the United States. And I will do it dramatically as well as gradually. Behold, the curtain rises on the grand drama Act 1st, Scene 1st.—The Election of Abraham Lincoln!"

"Thank Heaven!" said Justin.

"I say so too! We Southerners worked hard for the election of Old Abe; because we knew if he was not elected we could never carry our point with the common people against their superstitious attachment to the Union."

"What do you mean? I don't understand you."

"No; perhaps not, for that was one of the deepest dodges of state-craft that ever was tried. The slave-power working covetly for the election of the abolition candidate! Ha—ha—ha! Ho—ho—ho!"

"Go on—perhaps I shall know what you would be at presently," said Justin.

"Perhaps you will. Shift the scene. Scene 2nd.—The Secession of South Carolina!"

"What!" thundered Justin, in astonishment.

"Yes, sir!" replied the captain of the Sea Scourge, who understood only the astonishment.

"South Carolina seceded?" repeated Justin, now in incredulous amazement.

"Glorious little State! Yes! She alone first flung down the gauntlet of defiance! She, single handed, challenged the whole power of the Federal Government and inaugurated the second great War of Independence!"

"What followed?" demanded Justin, in a low voice; while Britomarte, leaning her elbow on the table and bending forward, listened breathlessly to the next words of the stranger. "Wait and see! Shift the scenes. Scene 3d. This is a very exciting scene. Secession of Georgia, followed by the secession of all the Gulf States! Retirement of the Southern Senators from the Senate of the United States!"

"And were they suffered to depart?" inquired Britomarte, in a soft but thrilling voice.

"Of course they were, young lady! What should hinder them?"

"Their arrest, I should think."

"Ha—ha—ha! Ho—ho—ho! Catch Uncle Jemmy at that game! or any of his Cabinet either! But let me go on with the play. Scene 4th. A very stately scene this—the Confederate Congress at Montgomery! Organization of a provisional government! Election of Jefferson Davis as President of the Southern Confederacy!"

"No!" exclaimed Justin, starting up in almost uncontrollable agitation.

"Yes, I tell you! Now sit down and be quiet! Don't let your feelings overcome you prematurely. For there are more news and greater scenes to come! I see I was right to break the glory on you gradually—as the day dawns. No one could bear the light of the sun if it started up suddenly in the blackness of the night."

"Go on," said Justin.

"I'm going on Scene 5th. A very comic scene this. Executive mansion. Emissaries of the Confederacy inviting President Jemmy to withdraw

United States troops from Fort Sumter. Emissaries from Major Anderson beseeching President Jemmy to reinforce United States troops at Fort Sumter. President Jemmy standing hesitating between two opinions, like the donkey between two bundles of hay —doesn't know what to do, and does nothing."

"The man must have been in his dotage!" exclaimed Justin.

"Probably! We didn't object to that! But let us proceed with the play. Scene 6th. A splendid spectacular scene this—embracing the whole depth of the stage, the full force of the company, brilliant fireworks, et cetera. In short—The bombardment of Fort Sumter! The fall of Fort Sumter! Lowering of the Star Spangled Banner. Elevation of the Confederate Flag! Grand Tableau! And the curtain falls upon the first act of the great drama amidst thunders of applause."

Justin had sprung to his feet, and was standing gazing with starting eyes, distended nostrils and clenched teeth at the speaker.

"What the demon ails you, man? Are you mad?" exclaimed the rebel captain.

"I would return the question! What ails you? Are you mad? Are you drawing imaginary pictures black as the scenes of Dante's Inferno? Are you talking at random? Do you know what you are saying?" demanded Justin, glaring at his guest.

"Yes, I know very well what I am saying; I am saying that we have stormed and carried Fort Sumter! That we have dragged down to the dust the proud Star Spangled Banner that never was humbled before!" said the rebel captain, helping himself to another great bumper of the strong old brandy that was now beginning to affect even his seasoned system, so as to inflame his blood and dim his perceptions.

"Oh! dread God of Battles, where stayed thy thunderbolts?" exclaimed Justin, starting from the table and hurriedly pacing the whole length of the grotto.

He felt an almost uncontrollable desire to take this man by the throat and hurl him through the door;

but he remembered that the man was his own invited guest, and had sat at his board, broken his bread, and drank his health; he also reflected that only from this man could he get the information which he was so anxious to obtain, and so restrained his impulse.

Meanwhile Captain Spear deceived himself with that common delusion which blinded so many Secessionists to the sentiments of loyal Southerners, whom they supposed to be fellow Secessionists, merely because they were fellow-citizens; and his perceptions were still further obscured by the fumes of the brandy he had swallowed, and so he utterly misunderstood the character of Justin Rosenthal, and mistook the cause of his excitement. He believed that the young man, being a native of the South, must be an advocate of Secession, and that his great emotion was in sympathy with his own high exultation over the victory he had just been describing.

"If you will only sit down and compose yourself, my young friend, I will go on with the play. There are greater glories to come than any I have yet described, I can tell you!" said the rebel captain.

"Yes, go on with the play!" said Justin, throwing himself into his chair, but averting his face from the captain.

"The curtain rises on Act 3rd, Scene 1st. There is another grand spectacular scene! Again the whole depth of the stage; the full strength of the company; pyrotechnics—dazzling effects! In a word The Battle of Manassas! The great Federal army under General McDowell—the Great Confederate army under General Beauregard. Tremendous engagement! Terrific fighting! Total rout of the Federals! Complete triumph of the Confederates! Grand tableau!"

Here the captain paused, helped himself to another bumper of the old Otard, swallowed it at a gulp, closed his eyes, and leaned back in his chair.

"Go on," said Justin, scarcely able to speak for the strong emotion that nearly choked his voice.

"That's all. I have finished the bottle, and I have finished the tale; or, rather, all I have to tell. When the curtain dropped on that scene I left the theatre of war, at least in regard to the military branch of action. In short, I received letters of marque from the Confederate Government, authorizing me to cruise in quest of Federal prizes, and I took the command of the privateer Sea Scourge. I have already taken a few Federal merchant ships; but after appropriating their cargoes and money chests, was obliged unfortunately to scuttle and sink them. Hadn't enough men to spare, you see, to man them and send them home."

"And their unfortunate crew?" groaned Justin.

"It was a pity," said the drunken captain, sleepily, "but I had to sink them with their ships! Hadn't men enough to guard them!"

"And now?"

"Now I am cruising about in these latitudes, lying in wait for returning East Indiamen, which are always rich prizes and easy prey, being without guns."

"And so!" exclaimed Justin, no longer able to restrain himself, but bounding to his feet, and seizing the rebel captain by the throat, and shaking him violently—"and so I have been harboring no less a miscreant than a licensed pirate, who takes advantage of his letters of marque and makes war—not upon men-of-war, but upon defenseless merchantmen—seizing their cargoes, murdering their crews, and scuttling their ships!"

"It was a mil—lil—litary necessity, commodore'" spluttered the wretch, gasping and choking in the viselike grasp of the furious young athlete.

"Your instant execution is a moral necessity, miscreant!" thundered Justin, shaking him by the throat as though he would have shaken his sinful soul from his brutal body.

"Justin! Justin! forbear! would you murder the villain at your own board!" frantically exclaimed Britomarte, starting up and seizing the arm of the young man. "Would you murder him before my eyes!"

"I would execute him now and here! for he deserves instant death!" cried the young man, tightening his grasp until the pirate grew black in the face.

"Justin! Justin! spare him! not for his sake, but for

your own honor! He is too much intoxicated to defend himself. He is helpless as a child in your grasp! For your own honor, Justin! curb your just rage and spare a defenseless man!" pleaded Britomarte, clinging to her lover.

"I will obey you, my queen! I will spare the miscreant, though he does not deserve to be spared, never having spared others!" replied Justin, hurling from him the form of the pirate, who fell heavily, strinking his head upon the stone floor.

"Oh, Justin! I fear that he is already dead!" exclaimed Britomarte, approaching the motionless form of the pirate, who, from the united effects of drunkenness, suffocation, and concussion, was now quite insensible.

"He is dead drunk, that is all," replied Justin, turning the body half over with his foot and then leaving it.

He went to the entrance of the cavern and looked out. The men that had been grouped before the door were nowhere in sight; but Judith was walking about gathering up crusts and bones and other litter left by them on the ground.

Justin beckoned her to approach and she came.

"What are you doing, Judith?" he inquired, in a low voice.

"Claning up the yard afther the saymen, sure. Troth, they're as dirthy as pigs at their males, so they are."

"Where have they gone, Judith?"

"Divil a bit iv me knows! They took up the keg iv whisky ye gave them, so they did, and walked off wid it before me two looking eyes. Meself thinks they have carried it down to the boat, and are stealing it off to the ship unbeknownst to the captain! Sure I called to them to stop; but they told me ye gave them the whisky itself, which I couldn't contradict."

"I am glad they are gone, Judith; but I suppose they will come back here presently for their captain. Come in here, Judith, a moment; I wish to speak with you," said Justin, gravely.

Judith came into the grotto, wondering. But when

she saw the insensible form of the pirate captain, she exclaimed:

"Lorrud kape us! I thought how it would be! Sure he's afther dhrinking a whole bottle iv that strong old brandy, and has fallen down dead dhrunk, so he has. Sure, sir, where will we drag him away to?"

"Nowhere, Judith! he must remain just where he is until his men return to take him! But draw near and listen to me. This man is not a Confederate officer, nor is his ship a Confederate privateer. Neither would be acknowledged by the Confederate States. The Southern people would not tolerate piracy. This man has taken advantage of civil war to become a pirate. You have heard and read enough to be able to know and dread the lawlessness and cruelty of these pirates——"

"Pirates! Lord betune us from harrm, are they pirates?" exclaimed Judith, open'ng her mouth and eyes and suspending her breath.

"They are pirates, Judith. Now compose yourself, my good girl. And, dear Britomarte, attend. You must take Judith with you and leave this grotto. You must both go up the mountain to my hole in the rock, which is the safest hiding place on the whole island. You must conceal yourselves there until these men have finally left the island and their ship has sailed. If they do not see you again they may not think of you. Or even if they do think of you, they will never be able to find you in that secure retreat. Go at once!"

"But you, Justin—but you," exclaimed Miss Conyers, anxiously.

"I can take care of myself."

"Oh, how? Oh, how? Think of the fury of that wretch when he recovers his senses, and remembers the punishment you inflicted on him. Think of the vengeance of his crew. What could you, one man, do against the pirate and all his band?"

"Britomarte, you who have no fears for yourself, should have none for me. Only death can come to me. Worse, infinitely worse, might reach you. Go, dear

Britomarte, Go at once. These miscreants may be even now on their way here," he urged.

"Justin, once before I was forced from your side in an hour of deadly peril. I will not be so again," she replied, looking white, and firm as marble.

"Dear Britomarte, you shall be forced to nothing, but you shall be convinced of the necessity of following my advice. The peril you dread for me is nothing—nothing. That drunken brute whose recovery you dread so much, will not come to his senses for many hours. His men, when they come for him, will have to carry him off in his present state of unconsciousness. And even when he does recover, it is not likely that he will remember anything about the choking he got from me. As to the crew, I have treated them kindly. They will be contented with helping themselves to everything they want, and they will leave me in peace. It is you and Judith only who will be in peril from them—in awful peril, if they see you. Go, Britomarte. Oh, dear Britomarte, hasten!"

"I cannot bear to leave you alone to meet that desperate band!" she cried.

"Britomarte! I can take care of myself by staying here, but I can only take care of you by concealing you in the cavern. Britomarte, listen! In that horrible Sepoy insurrection in India a few years ago, when the banded fiends invested the Tower of Dpl and carried it by storm, the young English officer commanding the place shot his young bride through the brain, to save her from falling into the hands of those demons! Britomarte, if you do not follow my counsel and conceal yourself in the cavern, that may be the only means left me to save you from worse than death!"

Still she hesitated.

"I would rather fall by your hand than be forced to leave you in an hour of danger!" she said.

"Britomarte, I repeat you shall be forced to do nothing—not even to save yourself; but if you persist in remaining here, you will drive me mad!" he exclaimed.

"I will go, then," she answered, reluctantly.

Not to give her time to think the matter over, he

slipped her arm in his and led her from the grotto, calling to the panicstricken Irish girl to follow them.

Holding her hand, he helped her to ascend the almost inaccessible height where his "hole in the rock" was situated.

He put her and her attendant in there; and then he closed the opening with fragments of rock, so loosely put together as not to exclude the air; and then he stuck green brushwood in between them in such a way as to make it look like growing bushes and conceal the entrance from the most prying eyes.

Having completed his task, he put his head down among the brushwood and his lips to a small crevice between the fragments of rock, and whispered:

"Good-night, dear Britomarte! Trust in Providence and keep up your spirits. As soon as the pirate ship has gone I will come and release you, and all will be well."

CHAPTER XXVII

AT BAY

JUSTIN returned to the grotto and busied himself with putting out of sight all Britomarte's and Judith's little personal effects that might have tempted the cupidity of the pirates or reminded them of the presence of women on the island.

Having done this, he went to one of the caverns where the stores taken from the ship were kept, and he selected from them tobacco, pipes, whisky, greatboots, sticks, guns, pistols, swords, sabres, a little of everything, in fact, that looked like a man's peculiar property and suggested only the presence of man, and he brought them into the grotto and scattered them about in careless disorder.

Then he sat down to rest and to wait for what should come next.

With rest came the opportunity of reflection, for up to this moment he had acted from impulse only. But now in the midst of his clear sense of the danger that threatened not only himself, but her who was dearer to him than his own life, he thought with keen anxiety of his beloved native country, plunged in all the horrors of civil war and menaced with destruction. And, oh! the intolerable longing that filled his soul to get back to her, to fight for her, and, if need were, to die for her. But this could not be, he knew. The ship that he had hoped would have borne him and his companions back to their homes was now discovered to be a pirate, sailing under false colors, and making prey of unarmed merchantmen. He and his party, if they should escape death from the crew, must remain on the lone island waiting for the improbable event of another vessel's arrival to take them off. But even in his deepest distress Justin did not despair; his trust in Divine Providence was too strong to permit him to do so.

While thus reflecting, he suddenly became conscious of the approach of the pirate crew.

He arose to his feet, and standing over the unconscious form of the drunken captain, waited to receive them.

They reached the front of the grotto; but they did not come in immediately, they stood about in groups and seemed to be waiting a summons, until at length one of their number advanced to the door of the grotto and touched his hat.

"Well, my man, what is wanted?" inquired Justin, assuming a calmness he was far from feeling; and yet his disturbance was not upon his own account, but solely upon Britomarte's.

"If you please, sir, we wanted to tell the captain that the tide serves," replied the man, civilly enough.

Justin pointed at the insensible form at his feet, but even before he had done so the man's eye had fallen on it, and the man's disgust broke out in an oath.

"By ——! There he is again, as drunk as ——!"

"If you are going to make sail, my man, you and your mates will have to take your captain and carry him off in his present state," said Justin, speaking with a forced quietness.

"By all the ——, ——, 'd serve him right to

leave him here! And a precious good opportunity to get rid of him; and a glorious riddance it would be, too!" said the man, stooping over and staring at the fallen captain.

"You would not surely abandon your chief in his present helpless state of unconsciousness?" remonstrated Justin, who had no desire to receive the pirate permanently.

"Oh, wouldn't we, though? I don't know why we come back for him at all, that I don't! If anybody had stated the proposition to sail without him, I'm sure we would have done it. If we leave him here it will save his life and save us the trouble of cutting his throat, which we would be sure to do before long," said the man, coolly, as with his hands on his knees he stooped low and stared intently into the stupid face of the captain.

"Is he so very unpopular on his ship, then?" inquired Justin, as with difficulty he repressed the disgust and horror awakened by the man's words and manner

"Unpopular! Why, shiver my timbers, if we have ever been in a fight or storm yet that he hasn't got as drunk as Julius Cæsar, and left the ordering of the fight, or the working of the ship, to Mate Mulligan. And Mulligan we want for our captain. And Mulligan we mean to have!" said the man, suddenly turning and leaving the unconscious captain and going out to his companions, to whom he began to talk in a low and earnest voice.

Justin did not attempt to follow or to interfere with him. Upon reflection he was glad that a subject so full of interest and excitement as the disposition and desertion of their captain by his crew should have arisen to engage their thoughts and prevent them from remembering the existence of the women on the island. He watched the man who was haranguing his mates outside; he saw how, with eager eyes and fierce gestures, they crowded around him; and so he was not surprised when the speaker at length left his turbulent hearers and returned to the grotto door and

"Master, the boys mean to leave that lubber here and elect Mate Mulligan captain and me first mate. But, master, we will take you off, as you have done the handsome by us in the matter of the keg of whisky; if you don't mind cruising round a bit with the certainty of a fight now and then, and the chance of some day or other getting into port somewhere."

"Thank you; but I am colonized here for the present, and do not wish to leave just yet," said Justin.

"Just as you please, master! Have you got any more of that good liquor left?"

"Yes, there it is; help yourselves; you are quite welcome to the whisky, tobacco, pipes, or anything else you may see here in my Robinson Crusoe establishment," said Justin.

"Now that is what I call handsome! Here, mates, lend a hand and help to carry some of this liquor and 'bacco to the boats!" said the man, once more going to the door and calling to his companions.

They all came in at his summons.

Justin noticed that the man whom Captain Spear had called Mulligan was not among them. And thus he knew that Mulligan had no part in the mutiny, and had been elected captain of the pirate ship in his absence, without his knowledge, and possibly against his will.

The men touched their hats, civilly, to their host, and then began to take up the articles pointed out, and to carry them off.

"Good-bye, master! Sorry to leave so kind a host! Call again when we pass this way! Meantime, wish you joy of the new comrade we have left you!" said the ring-leader of the mutiny, as with a bottle of whisky in each of his pockets and one in each of his hands, he followed the last sailor from the grotto.

Justin went to the door and watched them out of sight, and then he took his telescope and climbed the mountain to the tableland on the summit and watched them as they entered their boat and rowed toward the ship.

With the aid of his glass he saw them embark, unload the

davits; and still he watched them while they got up their anchor, spread their canvas to the breeze and made sail; and still further he watched until the ship had sailed away from the island and waned in the distance.

Then he hurried down the mountain side and into the grotto to look after the pirate captain, his late guest, who was henceforth to be his prisoner.

He found Captain Spear still in the heavy sleep of intoxication.

He left him and went to one of the caverns where articles rescued from the wreck were kept, and looked up a set of fetters, consisting of handcuffs and anklets, such as are often kept on board East Indiamen for the restraint of a possible mutineer or other criminal. He had brought them off the wreck, not with the most distant idea that he should ever be obliged to put them to their legitimate use, but for the same reason that he saved every portable piece of iron that he could find—namely, because he knew that it would be valuable on their desert island, where they might remain for years, or for life, cut off from all supplies from without.

Having found the fetters, he returned to the grotto, and, stooping down fastened them upon the wrists and ankles of the sleeping pirate.

CHAPTER XXVIII

THE CAGED TIGER

WHEN Captain Spear awoke his rage knew no bounds, but Justin firmly made him acquainted with the state of affairs, whereupon the captain became sulky and refused to take any food, saying that he preferred to die and that his death would be laid at the door of Justin, who would meet his due reward when his crime was discovered.

Next morning he had so far relented as to drink a cup of Judy's tea, given with reluctance by the Irish woman, who vowed that hanging was too good for him.

In the course of a few days he came sulkily out of his cavern and crept about through the groves and by the streams, or along the seashore of the beautiful island. He had a limited use of his fettered limbs—enough to help himself in all absolute personal needs; for instance, he could walk slowly, wash his face, or feed himself; but he could not inflict the slightest injury upon either of the women, if he happened to meet them together or singly in his rambles about the island.

Whenever he met Judith, she mocked him.

When he met Miss Conyers, she returned his greeting kindly. If the arch enemy of God and man had been their prisoner she could not have treated him unkindly.

Justin always used him humanely, and encouraged his companions in exile to do likewise.

"The man has forfeited his life by every law of every civilized land! but we are not warranted to become his executioners. We have only to deprive him of the power of committing more crime, and then to treat him with Christian charity," he argued.

Justin Rosenthal was now a very busy man. In the two years that he and his friends had spent upon the island he had made what progress was possible in "making the wilderness to bloom and blossom as the rose." The first few months had been spent in the stupendous labor of getting the stores, the animals and the furniture from the wreck over the long, rugged, almost impassable reef of rocks to the island.

By the time that nearly incredible work had been successfully accomplished, the rainy season, the winter of these latitudes, had set in, and all further outdoor work was suspended for several months.

When spring and sunshine had come again, it was necessary, first of all, to build fences to guard the fields and gardens that were to be cultivated from the intrusion of the cattle and poultry; then to till the ground and plant the seeds, of which he had found a great variety in the stores of the missionaries, con sisting of wheat, rye and Indian corn among the field grains, and beans, peas, potatoes, turnips, cabbage, lettuce and so forth among the garden seeds.

Of course, the planting of all these seeds, many of which were indigenous to the north temperate zone only, was a questionable experiment, to be tried.

All this—fence building, soil tilling, seed planting and cultivating—was a long labor for one pair of hands, and it occupied the whole spring and half the summer.

But the labor was crowned with all the prosperity that could be hoped. At least half the garden seeds produced good crops of table vegetables. Among the grain the wheat did very well, the Indian corn still better, but the cotton was the greatest success of all. Justin had traveled all over the cotton growing States of his native country, but never had he seen such great white pods of such rich, fine fibre anywhere.

The early autumn months were occupied in harvesting these crops.

In this work Britomarte and Judith were able to help Justin. While Justin cut the wheat, Britomarte picked the great pods of cotton from their stalks and housed them in the grotto, and Judith pulled the ripe ears of Indian corn and stored them in her kitchen.

The end of this work had brought the beginning of their second winter on the island, and again all outdoor labor was suspended.

Those wintry days and evenings were spent very profitably.

Judith and Britomarte picked the cotton, separating the seed from the wool with their fingers.

Justin, who possessed great mechanical ingenuity, constructed a wheel for Judith. A pair of cards had been found among the stores of the wreck.

Judith carded and spun the cotton wool into fine yarn, and Britomarte knit it into hose for her two friends and herself.

Justin also began to try to construct a loom for weaving, but as the task was a difficult one to a man not brought up to the trade, he had many failures before he had any prospect of success.

Thus had passed the second winter of their sojourn upon the island. It was near the end of the second summer that the pirate ship had anchored near their island, and the captain, by a strange turn of fate, had become their prisoner.

And now Justin was very busy getting in his second summer's crops and building up his long delayed dwelling houses.

CHAPTER XXIX

BRITOMARTE'S NEW HOME

BEFORE the end of the autumn Britomarte's house was completed. A rough house it was, indeed; not at all like those of the north temperate zone, yet possessed of some advantages peculiar to itself.

Its architect was limited in the matter of hand tools and of building materials; for the first he had to depend upon the carpenter's box rescued from the wreck, and for the second upon the cocoa-palm trees and the mountain rocks.

Its site was selected in front of the cocoa-palm grove, facing the sea, and looking westward toward their native hemisphere.

Its plan was simple enough, and had first been drawn by Justin upon paper. It was a low, square, spacious house, all of one story, to keep it safe from destruction by the tornadoes that sometimes visited the island.

It contained four large rooms, separated by two long passages that ran, one from front to back and the other from end to end, crossing each other at right angles in the centre of the house, so that each room was completely divided from the others. It had four doors, one at each extremity of the two passages. The rooms had each two windows in the outer walls, and two doors opening into the passages.

The walls were built of the long, straight, smooth trunks

of a sawmill, formed the very best substitutes for planks. The roof was made of transverse poles cut from the trunks of very young trees and covered with the broad, strong, featherly palm leaves laid one over another in rows, and kept down by other transverse poles securely fastened. This rustic roof afforded a complete protection against the rain and the wind

The kitchen chimney was built of fragments of rock joined with a strong cement made by mixing the sap of the cocoa tree with lime burned by Justin from the shells and bones collected from the island.

There were no floors, except the ground, which was leveled and beaten hard. The walls inside were made smooth by a rude plastering of moistened soil packed in between the logs. And then both floor and walls were covered with the cement, that gave them the appearance of cream-colored stone.

I said the house fronted west. The windows of the two front rooms only were glazed with glass, taken from the sashes in the cabin of the wreck. They had also shutters. The two back rooms had shutters only.

The northwestern front room was the family parlor. It was neatly fitted up with the furniture rescued from the saloon of the wreck. It had a red carpet on the floor, a centre table and a lamp, a side table and bookshelves, a sofa, a rocking-chair and four common chairs, and lighter articles too numerous and trivial to mention.

The southwestern front room was Britomarte's bedchamber, which was also shared by Judith. It was daintily fitted up with furniture saved from the ladies' cabin and berths of the wreck. It had a neat carpet on the floor, white curtains at the windows, and two little white beds, in opposite corners. It had also a chest of drawers surmounted by a looking-glass, flanked by a workbox and a dressing case; a washstand provided with a white china basin, ewer and soap dish, only a little the worse for being knocked about in the wreck; a low chair, a footstool, a little candlestand, and other small conveniences.

The southwestern back room was Justin's sleeping apartment. It was fitted up with severe simplicity.

The windows were not even glazed, but were only provided with rough wooden shutters; the hard floor was bare; the bed was a narrow mattress laid upon a rude bedstead; the washstand was a broad wooden shelf, with a tin basin and a stone pitcher; the chair was a three-legged stool, and the wardrobe a few strong pegs driven into the walls, upon which he hung his clothes. All these primitive articles of furniture were of his own manufacture, from fragments of the wreck.

This rude seaside dwelling place was fenced in by a low wall made by driving short stakes, cut from the cocoa trees, closely together into the ground after the manner of a stockade; and two rude gates, one front and one back, gave entrance and exit to the premises.

At the back of the yard there was a small storehouse, or pantry, built to keep a limited supply of provisions—the great bulk of their provisions being still kept in the mountain grottoes, where they could best be preserved.

A few tropical vines had been transplanted from the thicket at the base of the mountain to the soil in front of the house, and had really taken root, and were now trained up to festoon and shade the windows and doors.

At the end of the first autumn month all was ready.

It was on a certain Wednesday afternoon that our friends first took possession of their new home.

Justin, having seen the women established, went to his outdoor work, which was just now the transplanting of some young fruit trees that he had raised in a nursery from the seeds, and that now needed to be set out.

Britomarte took her needlework—some shirts that she was neatly repairing for Justin—and seated herself beside the front window of her bedchamber, looking out to the western sea, and across toward her own native land.

It was a novelty and a delight—perhaps the greatest novelty and the greatest delight of the whole change—to be able to sit sewing at an open window, and looking out upon the land, sea and sky.

Heretofore, since she had been on the island, she had not been able to do so.

Her grotto had been a beautiful place—a wood-nymph's bower, a fairy queen's palace; but it had no windows, and its lofty skylight, though it illuminated the whole place, afforded no outlook whatever, and gave but a limited glimpse of the sky. When she had sat there and sewed her vision had been bounded by the walls of solid rock, which had given a prison aspect to her dwelling-place.

Now all this was changed.

She sat sewing at a cheerful, open, white-curtained window, letting her eyes rove, whenever she raised her head, freely over land and sea and sky, with a buoyant sense of liberty and—a touching sense of gratitude also!

Who was it that had changed her life so happily? Nay, who had saved, sustained and blessed her life, ever since she had been cast, a helpless creature, on this desert island?

Justin Rosenthal, a man, one of the common enemy, one of the hated sex, one of the despots, the oppressors and despoilers of women!

They spent their first evening in the new house, around the center-table in the parlor. The lamp was not lighted; for the windows were open, and the full moon was shining so splendidly as to make all the land and sea and the sky almost as bright as noonday—quite as bright as a London day.

It was a new delight to Britomarte, on rising in the morning, to be able to throw open a window shutter and gaze out upon the broad expanse of sea and sky; another to eat breakfast in a large parlor, with the cheerful light of the morning sun shining in at the eastern windows; and still another to change from room to room and enjoy the aspect of each in turn.

"Sure this is house-kaping at lingth, ma'am, isn't it? It's having a home iv our own, 'if it's iver so homely,' as the song says. It's domestic happiness intirely, so it is," said Judith, as she was assisting Miss Conyers to set the bed-hangings in order.

"We have to thank Heaven and Mr. Rosenthal for it all, Judith."

"Sure, and so I do, ma'am. And day and night I wish myself was a praist so I could marry you two togither, an' faix it's the only thing I'm unable to do for ye."

After breakfast every day Justin went out to his outdoor work. He set out a large number of young fruit trees that he had raised from the seed—plum, peach and apricot trees. Their cultivation upon this new soil, in this new climate, was an experiment which only time could decide to be a success or a failure.

His next work was to gather in and store the late crops of grain.

By the time this was done the wet season set in with great severity; and the castaways were confined for the most part to indoor occupations.

But they were not idle.

Justin would not lumber up the women's apartments—as he called the parlor, kitchen and best b'd chamb'r—with any of his cumbersome working materials; but he gathered them all into his own Spartan room, and there he busied himself through the first wet days with grinding, mending and arranging his tools; and then he took a great quantity of palm leaves that he had collected during the dry months and he occupied himself with stripping them up and weaving their fibres into mats of every description—large, thin mats to lay before the doors to wipe shoes upon in muddy weather, and small fine mats to put on the table to set dishes on.

As these mats were completed he delivered them over to Judith to be stored or to be used. The girl was especially delighted with the door mats, which she declared would save her a "dale iv scrubbing," and she was profuse in her expressions of gratitude to Justin, whom she declared to be always saving her life entirely with his thoughtfulness.

After having made a quantity of mats of all sorts, Justin commenced the manufacture of baskets. First he made a fine large

the pride of Judith's life; and then a dozen or more of fruit and vegetable baskets of all sizes; and, lastly, a workbasket for Britomarte, on which he expended his finest materials, and all the taste, skill and ingenuity he possessed. It was a miracle of convenience, if not of beauty. It was rather large and oval in form; the middle space long enough to contain a good-sized garment folded up; and all around that middle space little divisions like smaller baskets, to hold buttons, hooks and eyes, cord, tape, thread, etc., and to keep them separate and in order; each little division had its little movable top; and the whole basket had its cover and its handle. I have been particular in describing this little affair, because its invention was a work of love, and its usefulness every woman among my readers will appreciate.

Britomarte valued it not upon account of its beauty or its usefulness so much as because its every mesh and fibre had been woven by those beloved hands that were dearer to her than all others; yes, deny it to herself as she might, dearer to her than all others upon earth!

Judith was in rapture with the basket.

"It's a beauty iv a basket! a darlint iv a basket! a little angel iv a basket! And sure meself wishes I was clever at the nadle, so I could use one, too. But faix if I can manage to put a patch in an ould tablecloth, it's as much as meself can do," she said.

"Never mind, Judith. You can weave, and that is what neither Miss Conyers nor myself can do. I shall make another attempt at the construction of a loom this winter; and I think between my recollections of my grandmother's loom and your suggestions, I shall be able to construct one."

"Ah, thin, if ye'd only do that same, sure I could waive beautiful cloth out iv the lovely cotton and woolen yarn I carded and spun last winter, or last wet season—if that's winter—though I'm thinking it's hot as the dhry season itself; and faix I can't tell winther from summer in this haythen iv a climate."

Justin kept his word with Judith and labored with the loom, putting it together and taking it to pieces, doing and undoing his work, hammering and tinkering at it all day long—when he had nothing better to do—for, in fact, the experiment of loom building was not sufficiently full of promise of success to justify the wasting upon it time that might be more profitably employed.

In the evening he joined Britomarte in the parlor, and read aloud, while she sewed and Judith knitted.

Thus passed their in-door life during the wet season.

CHAPTER XXX

THE OLD FAMILIAR FLAG

When spring and sunshine came again, Justin began to lay out new garden beds and to put in the seeds for early vegetables.

And Judith, to her heart's delight, began what she called her "spring claning." But first of all, as their boxes of hard brown soap had nearly given out, Judith showed her skill in the manufacture of soft soap from lye made of wood ashes, and grease melted from kitchen fat.

When she had succeeded in this, she commenced her "claning." Every housekeeper knows what that process is in the hands of a skillful woman; so it is enough to say that Judith accomplished the task in the best possible manner; and that at the end of a week's work, the house and all within and around it was as clean and neat as human skill and human hands could make it. White curtains replaced the red ones at all the windows; and the winter carpets were stowed away and the floors were covered with the matting that Justin had manufactured from the long fibres of the palm leaves during the winter months.

While Judith had been engaged in the housecleaning Britomarte had employed herself in laying out the front yard in parterres and planting them with flower seeds.

And Justin, in the intervals of his field and garden work, built a neat cover over a clear spring at a short distance from the house; he built it of stone for coolness, and dug a channel for the spring to flow through, and paved and cemented it, so that the pans of milk and cream and pots of butter could be set in the running water. Adjoining the dairy was a temporary shed, where the cow could be driven to be fed and milked in bad weather.

"Sure, it's all beautiful entirely; and I wish Crummie could go on giving millik foriver, so I do! But that can't be expicted, and sure she must go dhry some day, and thin whativer shall we do? Och-hone!" cried Judith, as she contemplated her new dairy, and felt herself divided between delight in its acquisition and dread of the calamity she had foreshadowed.

"Never mind, Judith. 'Sufficient unto the day,' you know. And we cannot tell what may happen before Crummie goes dry. We may all be safe at home in our dear native land by that time," said Justin, soothingly.

"Ah, Lord send that same! But aven so, all our labor here will be lost! Och-hone! whichiver way one looks it's heartbreaking, so it is!"

"Nonsense! whichever way one looks the prospect is encouraging! If we are to spend our days here, we shall grow more and more comfortable every day of our lives; if we are to be rescued from here, we shall return to our own country. Be reasonable, Judith."

"Yes, all that's aisy said! But if Crummie goes dhry, what thin?" whimpered Judith.

"We must do without milk. But Crummie is not dry yet, Judith," laughed Britomarte.

And then all returned from their inspection of the dairy and walked toward the house.

On their way thither they stopped at the sheepfold to look at a young lamb whose advent Justin had announced that morning. When they had sufficiently admired the pretty little creature, they went on a little further and paused at the poultry yard to see the broods of young chickens newly hatched that were

"The darlints! look at thim! iviry little teeny rolypoly looking like a little pod of cotton wool! forbye they are gold-colored instead of white! And to think afther watching and feeding and caring for thim all the summer, I shall maybe have to wring their necks in the autumn. Faix meself thinks I shall niver have the heart to do it at all, at all!" laughed Judith, as she gazed upon her favorites with a strange blending of pride, pity and affection.

They turned from the poultry yard and continued their walk toward the house.

As they went on Britomarte noticed that Justin kept his eyes fixed uneasily upon the southwestern quarter of the heavens, where a few wild feathery black clouds flecked the burning crimson of the sunset.

"What is it, Justin?" she inquired.

"I think we shall have a tornado to-night," he answered, gravely.

And, even as he spoke, the clouds were driven up higher and blacker, and the moans of the rising wind swept over the sea and land.

"Yes, we shall certainly have a tornado! Hurry on to the house, dear Britomarte! I must go back and put the animals under cover," said Justin, suddenly turning back and hastening toward the sheepfold.

"And sure I must go and see if all the little chicks are safe in the henhouse, and lock the door and stop the hole to keep them in it," said Judith, as suddenly hastening after him.

Britomarte, left alone, pursued her way toward the house, while darker grew the sky and deeper moaned the wind.

In the few minutes that passed before she reached the house, the heavens had grown black as night and formed a wild contrast to the ocean, which, as far as the eye could see, was one mass of boiling snow-white foam, across which the rising wind moaned and wailed as a prophetic spirit lamenting the woe to come.

Britomarte hurried into the house and began to let down the windows and close the shutters, hoping and praying all the time that Justin and Judith might return be

When she had securely fastened up the house, as it was now pitch dark, she lighted the lamp and sat down to wait for the return of her friends.

The thunder rolled and broke, crash upon crash, like the explosion and fall of a world overhead, at the same instant that the lightning shot like shafts of fire through every crevice in the house, and the rain came down as if the "windows of heaven" had been opened for another flood.

"Heaven protect them!" exclaimed Britomarte, clasping her hands and thinking of her friends.

Then she suddenly started up and ran to the door to listen for their coming.

As she got there she heard rapid steps and hurried speech, followed immediately by loud knocks.

She tore the door open, and they rushed in, Justin, Judith and—the pirate captain—followed by the raving storm.

Justin, exerting all his great strength, closed and barred the door against the wind and then turned to Britomarte and whispered hurriedly:

"Dear sister, go into your parlor. I will join you there presently and explain."

Britomarte followed his advice, and went back to the parlor, attended by Judith

"Judith," as soon as they had reached the room and closed the door, "tell me how Mr. Rosenthal came to bring that man here to-night? I am glad that he has done so, but I wish to know how he happened to do it."

A blinding flash of lightning that shot arrows of fire through every crack and seam of the house, and a deafening crash of thunder, like the explosion of a planet overhead, interrupted Judith in her answer. Instead of replying, she muttered a pater and told her beads. And it was not till all was temporarily silent again, and Miss Conyers had repeated her question, that Judith answered:

"Divil a bit iv me knows at all, at all. Sure I was running back to the house as fast as me two heels could fetch me, to get out iv the storm, when I fell over thim both, close to the door here. And niver a woord was spoken anyther side. And now, ma'am, wid your lave, I'll just go and change me clothes, for divil's a dhry thread is on me at all, at all, wid the rain that came down by bucket fulls."

"Go at once, Judith. Hurry, or you may catch cold."

"And so I will hurry, ma'am. Sure it's a fray shower bath I've had entirely—Glory be to Moses!"

This last exclamation was struck from Judith by a thunderbolt so much more tremendous than anything which had preceded it, that there is no simile to be found for it in heaven or on earth.

"That must have struck very near us," said Britomarte, as the thunder rolled down the abyss of space and died away.

"Mary, Star iv the Say . . . S'int Pater, pray for us sinners!" . . . muttered Judith, invoking all the saints she could think of in an emergency.

"I think you are in more danger from damp clothing than from the thunderbolts, Judith. Go and change," said Miss Conyers

"If we had only a blessed candle itself, this haythen iv a storm couldn't hurt us," whimpered Judith.

"You have your Heavenly Father, who is the Lord of the heavens and the earth Appeal to Him It is an awful storm!" said Miss Conyers, as another blinding flash of lightning pierced every crevice of the closed house, and another peal of thunder rolled and crashed over their heads, and died away in the distance

Judith told her beads as fast as she could pass them through her fingers. She was shivering alike with terror of the tempest and chilliness from her wet clothes. And Britomarte again urged her to go and change them

"Sure I daresn't lave the room If I'm to be sthruck down dead, I'd like to be wid some one to pick me up and spake a good worrd to me parting sperrit," moaned the panic-stricken girl.

"Come, Judith, if you are afraid to go alone, I will attend you with pleasure," said Miss Conyers, kindly.

But just as she spoke Justin Rosenthal opened the door and entered the room.

"I have come to explain to you how I happened to bring this man home," he said.

Before Britomarte could answer, another thunderbolt fell, seeming to shake the very island from its foundation. When the noise of the report had rolled away, Justin repeated his words, and Britomarte answered:

"Oh, Justin! as if the humane act of bringing a wretched man in out of a storm like this required any explanation among Christians."

"But has it not occurred to you that I might have put him into one of the caverns?"

"Perhaps you came upon him at some distance from the mountain."

"Yes, that was just the case. I met him near the house, just before I met Judith. He was wet to the skin, shivering with cold, and tottering with weakness. I think that he is very ill. I have brought him in, taken off his fetters and his wet garments, and given him a change of dry clothes and put him on my bed."

"You did right, dear Justin, quite right. I could not like you if you could treat even a bad man badly," said Miss Conyers.

"Sure the wicked should be thrated according to their wickedness," put in Judith.

"If that were the rule, which of us would go unpunished?" inquired Miss Conyers.

Again a blaze of lightning, a crash of thunder, a blast of wind and a torrent of rain suspended their conversations. When this burst of the storm was over, Justin said:

"Now, as soon as possible, I want Judith to prepare some gruel, or panado, or broth, or whatever is good for a sick man."

"Troth, Judith, will set him up with it, and you too. Divil a bit iv me will stir a fut to go nigh the iron stove in this baste of a storm, for any cause, at all, at all, let alone to make gruel for a morthering divil like that, which same would be a thepting iv Providence," said Judith, decisively.

"I will go," said Miss Conyers, and she arose to leave the room, followed by Justin.

"Och hone! Ow-oo!" howled Judith, running after them. "Sure will the two iv ye lave me here, to be sthruck down alone wid the lightening, and all for the sake iv a haythen iv a pirate? Faix, if ye must return good for avil to yer enemies, ye needn't do it by returning avil for good to yer friends, sure."

Britomarte, unmindful of the storm that must have frightened a less brave woman from the proximity of the iron stove, went to work and prepared a bowl of nice hot gruel, which Justin took to the sick man.

After that, Justin, with the help of Judith, moved the sofa from the parlor into his room, for his own accommodation, while the pirate occupied his bed.

And then, though the storm was still raging with tremendous violence, Justin persuaded Britomarte and Judith to retire, assuring them that they would be safer from the lightning in bed than anywhere else.

The storm raged through all the night.

The two women suffered great disturbance to their sleep.

At one moment they thought the tremendous thunderbolts that fell so near must crash through roof and ceiling, and bury them in the ruins of their dwelling; at another, that the wild wind which howled along the heavens must lift their frail house, with all its inhabitants, and hurl it away before the furious hurricane; at another, that the heavy sea which cannonaded the rocks below must rise and overwhelm their home, and bear it off to destruction.

But the mad night of tempest and terror passed at last.

Neither Judith nor Britomarte knew exactly when they dropped asleep, except that it must have been near day, when the storm had expended its violence, and they had exhausted their strength with watching.

It was late in the morning when Britomarte awoke. She arose without disturbing Judith, who was still sleeping. She opened the blinds and looked out. The sky was clear and bright, and the sun was shining down upon a scene of ruin indeed.

was still high and foaming. But a thousand birds were singing their morning songs of joy at the passing of the storm.

At first, dazzled by the brilliancy of the scene, Britomarte saw nothing of the damage that had been done. But as her vision cleared, she saw that trees had been torn up by the roots, or blown down, or shred of their branches that strewed the ground. Their outhouses and fences, indeed, for their very lowliness, had escaped the fury of the storm, and were standing safe. Such was the aspect of the land.

The sea, as far as the eye could reach, was one vast expanse of foam; but it was evidently subsiding.

While Britomarte gazed from the window, Judith awoke with a start, exclaiming:

"Lorrd forgive me, ma'am, are you up, and meself snoring away here in bed? Why didn't ye call me, sure?"

And with that she jumped up and began to dress herself in great haste.

"There was no such imminent need to break your rest after such a night of disturbance, Judith," said Miss Conyers, leaving the window and beginning her own morning toilet.

"Sure it was a storm to be remimbered all the days of one's life, so it was," said Judith.

"It is past," answered Britomarte.

When they were dressed Britomarte went into the parlor to open the windows and set the table, and Judith into the kitchen to make the fire and get the breakfast.

Soon Justin came out of his room.

"Good-morning, sister! The dreadful night is over, thank Heaven! How did you pass it?" he inquired of Britomarte.

"As Macbeth passed the night of Banquo's murder, in 'starts and flaws,'" said Britomarte, smiling. "How is your sick man?"

"In a fever. We shall have to keep him here for a few days until he gets better. I hope that Miss Riordan will not object to giving him a cup of tea and a round of dry toast this morning."

"Oh, no! Now that Judith's panic has passed, she has come to her senses," said Miss Conyers, going into the kitchen to give the requisite orders.

"I'll jist tell ye what, ma'am! There was only eight barrels iv flour saved out'n the wreck, and for nearly two years we three people have been eating of it; and for more than six months we four, counting the pirate, have been using it! And, though I've eked it out as well as I could, wid using mele and rice and vigitables, still it is getting low! We've opened the last barrel, and this is the last loaf iv bread made out iv it; and I want it to last till to-merrow, so I do! And now you want to throw away a lot iv it in dhry toast for that haythen!" said the indignant Irish girl, as soon as she had received Miss Conyers' orders.

"Judith, I am ashamed of you! If it was our last loaf we should divide with a sick man, though that sick man were the greatest miscreant on earth! And with a whole barrel of flour, and when the flour gives out, a whole hogshead of wheat in the grain."

"Yis; but how is the whate to be ground at all, at all? Sure it will be slow work grinding it in the coffeemill! Troth it's to your own interests I'm spaking—not mine!"

"I know it, Judith. But now do an act of charity, and procure the tea and toast for the suffering sinner."

"Sure I'll do it to plaze ye, and for no other raison in life," said Judith, as she went about to execute the order.

When this refreshment was ready, Justin took it in to the sick man and served him carefully before coming to his own breakfast.

Britomarte waited for Justin, and when he returned, the coffee, rice muffians and broiled birds were brought in and they sat down to the table to enjoy their morning meal.

After it was over, Justin took some books and carried them in to the sick man, who seemed to be suffering from a severe cold and debility more than any other illness. And then Justin went out to his work, which upon this day consisted of clearing away the litter strewn all over the ground by the storm of the past night.

Britomarte went into her chamber and sat down at her favorite window to sew and to watch the sea.

She was turning a dress for Judith, and she pinned the end of it to her apron while running up a long seam. Every time she found it necessary to change the place of the pin, she raised her head and looked out at the ocean.

How monotonous and solitary looked that ocean! No change ever came over it except the change from storm to calm or from day to night, and *vice versa*. No living thing ever appeared on it or above it except the plunging fish and the sailing water fowl. But she loved it; and she watched its gradual subsidence from passion to peace as she would have watched the falling to sleep of some sufferer who was dear to her.

All the long forenoon she sat sewing and watching the ocean. Towards noon it had become wonderfully calm, considering the recent storm.

Once, on changing the place of the pin that held her work, she looked up and gazed far out to sea—far out to where the western horizon touched the water. She held her breath—she strained her eyes—and then with a cry she started up, threw down her work, ran into the parlor, caught up the pocket telescope, rushed back to the window, kneeled down, drew out the cylinders, rested it upon the window sill, trained it toward the western horizon, and put her eye to the glass.

"Yes, it was a ship!—a ship of war; for she could see the guns—a ship of the Union, for she could see the Stars and Stripes! And it was standing in directly for the island!"

With a great cry of joy she dropped her head upon her hands and thanked God.

Then she sprang up and ran out of the house to look for Justin. She ran up and down, and all about, calling him at the top of her voice—calling him as if she had lost her senses!—calling him until he heard her from his distant post of labor; and came rushing in great alarm to meet her.

"What is it, Britomarte? Compose yourself, dear sister! I am here at your side! You are safe. But what has happened? Has that man——"

"It is a ship!—it is a national ship!—bearing our own Stars and Stripes! And she is steering for our own cove! Oh, Justin!"

And Britomarte threw herself upon her brother's breast and burst into tears of rapture.

Justin pressed her to his heart again and again. Not even the arrival of the long-desired, long-prayed-for ship could make him release her until Judith came flying toward them to know if her young lady had gone mad or what had gone wrong.

"It is a ship, Judith! Oh, Judith, it is a ship! And it bears our Stars and Stripes!" said Britomarte, raising her head from Justin's breast, and releasing herself from his embrace.

"Praised be to all the saints!" piously ejaculated Judith.

"Praise be to the merciful lord of heaven and earth!" said Britomarte, reverently.

Justin lifted his hat and said "Amen."

And then all three hurried down to the beach by the cove to look for the ship.

She was coming very fast. She was entering the cove! They could see her colors well with the naked eye. When she had got a little into the cove, where the water was smooth, she dropped anchor and let down a boat, which was soon manned by an officer in the naval uniform of the United States. A flag-staff, bearing the Stars and Stripes, was planted in the stern. And the oarsmen pulled stoutly for the beach.

As the boats neared them, Justin raised his hat to salute the colors. Britomarte waved her handkerchief. Judith followed suit, and all three simultaneously cried out:

"Hail! hail! hail! to the flag!"

Their salutation was answered from the boat. The men rested on their oars a moment, while they raised their hats

"Hurrah! hurrah! hurrah!" three times three. And then they pulled faster than ever for the shore.

The excitement of our party verged upon the madness of joy.

Britomarte's rapture burst forth in song—the glorious "Star-Spangled Banner!" and when she came to the chorus her companions by her side joined her in singing:

" 'Tis the star-spangled banner! Oh, long may it wave
O'er the land of the free and the home of the brave!"

And the men in the coming boat responded:

" 'Tis the star-spangled banner! Oh, long shall it wave
O'er the land of the free and the home of the brave!"

And the next instant the boat touched the strand, the officer sprang on shore, and the men waved their hats with another prolonged:

"Hurrah!"

CHAPTER XXXI

THE GUESTS

"WELCOME."

This was the first word that sprang alive from the heart to the lips of Justin Rosenthal, as he held out both his hands and cordially grasped those of the young officer who stepped on shore.

He was a very handsome fellow, this young sailor, of slight but elegant figure, of dark olive complexion, dark brown hair and mustache, and dark, hazel eyes. His expression of countenance was gracious, his movements graceful and his manners courteous. In a word, he had the air of a true gentleman.

"Thanks," he answered, lifting his cap and announcing himself as: "Lieutenant Ethel, of the United States sloop of war Xyphias."

"I am rejoiced to see you, lieutenant—truly rejoiced," said Justin, with smiling emphasis, as he heartily shook the hands of the newcomer. "I am Mr. Rosenthal, late of Washington City," he added.

"I am very glad to know you, Mr. Rosenthal."

"And this young lady," said Justin, turning the lieutenant toward Britomarte, "is Miss Conyers, also late of Washington."

Again the young sailor lifted his hat and bowed profoundly.

"And this other young person," said Justin, smiling, "is Judith Riordan, Miss Conyers' attendant, and our companion in exile, and as such as dear to us as a sister."

"I am glad to make her acquaintance," said Lieutenant Ethel.

"And now," said Justin, eagerly, "will you walk up to our house, while we become better acquainted?"

"With pleasure," answered the young officer, and he immediately offered his arm to Britomarte, as the way was rugged.

But with a courteous smile she declined the assistance; and they walked on in an irregular group.

Under all these civilities there had been on both sides a half suppressed eagerness of curiosity. On that of the young officer, to know how these American citizens happened to be found on the desert isle in the Indian Ocean. And on that of Justin to know how the war went in his native land; and also with him it was something more than curiosity; it was almost an agony of anxiety. And it broke forth as they went on.

"Outward or homeward bound?" he inquired.

"Outward," replied the young lieutenant.

"I am sorry for that! I had hoped that you were going home. Nevertheless, you are as welcome—as welcome as—what shall we say, Miss Conyers? What simile shall we find to express how welcome he is?" said Justin, turning to Britomarte.

"None so strong as the simple fact," answered Britomarte, and then, turning with a smile to the visitor, she added: "You are as welcome, sir, as friends from home to exiles on a desert island."

Lieutenant Ethel bowed.

"From what port are you last?" inquired Justin.

"From New York."

"And where bound? You must not take exceptions to my asking many questions. I shall have many as a Yankee in the pursuit of information under difficulties. Remember that news is scarce here. In fact, the morning papers are not delivered with the regularity we could wish."

"Oh, pray question me as much as you like. I am ready to give you all the information in my power. If I forget to volunteer any, ask me."

"Then, where are you bound?"

"Oh, I beg pardon. We are cruising in search of privateers, reported even down as low as these latitudes, lying in wait for our returning East Indiamen, which offer them a rich and easy prey."

"Ah!" exclaimed Justin, breathing hard, "if you are just from home you can tell us—how goes the war for the Union?" he eagerly inquired.

"Fast and furious!"

"Ah, Heaven! and I not there to take a part! Which side has the advantage?" he breathlessly questioned.

"The South. Heavens! what a great fight those Southerners are giving us! By the soul of Washington! none but our own people could have beaten us so thoroughly as we have been beaten at Big Bethel, Bull's Run, Ball's Bluff, and the battles that have followed those fatal fields!" fervently exclaimed the young sailor, with that generous admiration which every true hero feels for heroism, even in a foe.

"And I not there to strike a blow!" fumed and fretted Justin.

"Well, hundreds of thousands of brave men are there, striking hard blows in the good cause."

"But still the rebels have the advantage you say?"

"Yes; for in every battle they fight as Leonidas fought at Thermopylæ—as Roland fought at Roncesvalles. But this state of things cannot last. It is only a question of time. We shall overwhelm them by numbers at length, if in no other way. There is something pathetic and tragical in the aspect of the South now, in the midst of her delusive victories. It is sad to see so much heroism and self-devotion wasted upon a cause as evil as it is hopeless."

Britomarte turned to look at the young speaker,

and thought that she had never seen a face or heard a voice more interesting or more eloquent.

"You have a broad vision and a large heart. You are brave and patriotic, but you are also just and generous. You might gallantly for your country, yet you feel deeply for the brave, misguided men who have brought all this woe upon her. And you would willingly be the Curtius to plunge living into this yawning gulf of disunion if that act would cause it to close above your life!" said Britomarte, gravely.

"Heaven knows how willingly I would, lady," earnestly answered the young man, reverently raising his cap.

"We are lingering too long in the sun," suggested Justin; "let us hurry on to the house."

"Pedad he's jealous! and with good reason," muttered Judith to herself.

"Let us get into the house. We have a house, even on this uncivilized isle," said Justin, as the whole party increased their rate of speed.

"Yes; but all this time I am struck with astonishment to find my fellow-citizens here, beating about the walls of the universe like the lost spirits of the two lovers in Dante's 'Inferno,' and I am consumed with curiosity to know how they came to be thrust outside the world," said the young lieutenant.

"And, unlike myself, you are too polite to ask questions. Well, you shall know all about it. But here we are at the house. Please to walk in," said Justin, leading the way through the rustic gate, up a graveled walk, between borders of fragrant flowers, to the vine-shaded portico that roofed the door.

"Welcome to our island home!" he added, as he opened the door and conducted the guest into the hall, and through that into the parlor.

"Thanks," said the young stranger, removing his cap, and gazing around upon one of the pleasantest summer rooms he had ever seen in his life. Straw matting was on the floor; snow-white curtains at the vine-shaded windows; fresh flowers on the mantel-shelf and on the tables, and coolness, comfort and beauty everywhere.

Justin handed him a chair.

Judith ran out to prepare refreshments.

When they were all seated, the young lieutenant said:

"Everything I see around you increases my astonishment and curiosity. You seem really to be comfortable and permanently colonized here!"

"Heaven forbid!" exclaimed Justin, quickly. "We have been here over two years, and passed a not unhappy period. But we have had enough of it, and want to get home."

"But — how — came — you — here?" inquired the young man, slowly and emphatically.

"Ah! you have really asked the question at last. I thought I should bring you to it!" laughed Justin. Then, growing suddenly grave, as he thought of the shipwreck, he said:

"You remember the ill-fated Sultana?"

"East Indiaman? sailed from Boston for Calcutta last October was two years ago? Yes, I should think I did. I was on the sloop of war Penguin at the Cape of Good Hope when she touched there. She remained two days, and then sailed, and was never heard of afterward."

"We were passengers on the Sultana. After leaving the cape she encountered heavy gales, and was driven entirely out of her course and out of her reckoning, and finally upon the reef of rocks below here, where she was wrecked."

"Great Heaven! And you were cast away here?"

"Yes."

"And your fellow-voyagers?"

"They were but too probably all lost."

"Tell me the particulars.

Justin settled himself in his chair and told the tragic story of the shipwreck.

The lieutenant listened with deep interest. He was much too young a sailor to be very familiar with such disasters.

When the narrative was finished, and he had expressed all the horror and the pity that was naturally inspired by the tremendous calamity, he said:

"But in the midst of all the desolation it was very fortunate for you that the ship struck so high and fast between the rocks, and held so long together."

"Yes; it enabled us to save nearly all her cargo, provisions, and even furniture and live stock," said Justin.

"It was a stupendous undertaking to remove them all."

"Yes; but it was successfully accomplished; and it enabled us to establish ourselves comfortably here."

"Yes, indeed!" assented the young man, looking approvingly around upon the pleasant room. "That was more than two years ago. And you have lived here ever since, quite isolated from the world?"

"Yes."

"And in all that time no ship has passed?"

"Yes! one ship! But of that hereafter. Tell me now, lieutenant, how you come to be so far out of your course as to touch this island?"

"We are not out of our course. We are cruising about these latitudes on the lookout for rebel privateers, as I told you. We were just as likely to find one lying to in your cove as anywhere else hereabouts."

"Just," answered Justin, emphatically.

"But we did not exactly come in here to look for them. In fact, we suffered some injury from the gale last night, and this morning we steered for this cove, that we might be at anchor here while repairing. It was while we were letting go the anchor that the captain, to his unbounded astonishment, saw you and your companion on the beach. He immediately sent a boat on shore to see who you could possibly be; for, up to the moment at which we discovered you, we had supposed the island to be entirely uninhabited."

"Then, of course, you did not see our signal?"

"Signal? What signal? Had you a signal?"

"We have had a pennon flying from a staff at the highest point of land on the island ever since we have been here. We have renewed it from time to time during the last two years. There it is."

"Where?" inquired the young man.

"There!" said Justin, going to the window and pointing to the top of the mountain.

But there it certainly was not.

"I suspect that the wind made free with your flag of distress, friend; for certainly not a vestige of it remains," said the young lieutenant, leaving the window and retiring to his seat.

Judith reappeared and laid the cloth, and spread the table with coffee, rolls, butter, fried fish and broiled chicken.

"It is our luncheon hour," said Justin; "draw up and partake."

The young lieutenant frankly accepted the invitation.

They gathered round the table, and while they ate they talked of the war for the Union.

The young officer gave his host a detailed account of all those disastrous engagements that had followed the first fatal field of Bull Run. But always he spoke hopefully of the future. When luncheon was over the young man arose and thanked his host and prepared to return to his ship

"The captain will come on shore to see you, I am sure. How long we may have to remain here for repairs I do not know; a few days, I suppose; but when we sail, of course, you and your party will go with us?" he said.

"Of course we shall, with your captain's kind permission," replied Justin, with a smile.

"We are not homeward bound, as I have already told you. We are cruising in search of rebel privateers. We may be some months longer in these latitudes, and we may have a sea fight or so. Still I think, upon the whole, your prospects will be better in going with us than in staying here."

"Immeasurably better! Besides, we can stock your storeroom with a large quantity of fresh provisions which may be acceptable to your crew. And, if there should be a 'sea fight or so,' as you say, why, I shall be happy to take part in it."

"Troth sc ... '. .rt 'n Judith, "if ye will put me

behind a safe place entirely, with a little hole convanient for me to shoot through."

"Thank you, Miss Riordan. You are another Moll Pitcher," replied the young man, laughing. Then, turning to Justin, he said:

"Why cannot you accompany me back to the ship? Our captain, I know, will be very happy to see you. And he would probably like to return on shore with you."

"I thank you, I should like very much to go on board in person and invite your captain to visit us here. But, are you sure it will be convenient for you to carry me?"

"Convenient for me to carry you? Why, certainly. And not only convenient, but delightful. And not only you, but you all. Will Miss Conyers honor us by making one of the party?" said the young sailor, turning toward Britomarte.

"Will you, Miss Conyers?" inquired Justin.

"Thanks! no, I think not this morning. Some other time," answered the young lady.

So, with a courteous bow, the young lieutenant lifted his cap and left the house, accompanied by Justin.

They walked down the beach, where they found the boat waiting. The young officer motioned Justin to precede him and then followed him into it.

And the oarsmen took their oars, pushed off from the land, and struck out for the ship.

Five minutes of rowing brought them alongside.

The captain stood on deck waiting to receive the stranger.

The young lieutenant stepped on board, accompanied by Justin, saluted his superior officer, and then presented his companion.

"Captain Yetsom, Mr. Rosenthal."

The two gentlemen thus introduced to each other, bowed somewhat informally.

"Wrecked from the Sultana, some two years since, and cast, with two companions, on this desert island," the young officer went on to explain.

"Lord

cabin and take a glass of wine," said the captain, as if the calamity had just then occurred, and the sufferer was in immediate need of a restorative.

Captain Yetsom was what might well be called a stout man. He was of medium height, but thickly set and solidly built, with a large head, broad shoulders, deep chest and strong limbs. He had a florid complexion, blue eyes and sandy hair and whiskers. He wore the undress uniform of a captain in the United States Navy.

"Come—come down into my cabin and take something to drink. It will help you."

"Thanks, captain. I will go down into your sanctum with pleasure; but as we have just risen from the luncheon table, I do not require any refreshment," said Justin.

"Nonsense, man, you must need something to drink! A glass of generous wine would set you up. Come down and take—— Lord bless my life and soul, what a calamity! Were they all lost?"

"All but three," answered Justin, as he followed the hospitable and obstinate sailor down into the cabin.

And there, over some rich old port, Justin had to tell again the tale of the woeful shipwreck, and to hear again the story of those fatal fields of Bethel, Manassas and Ball's Bluff.

This talk wore away a good part of the afternoon; and then Justin arose to go.

"I came on board in the hope of persuading you to return with me and spend the afternoon and evening at our rustic dwelling," said Justin, standing, cap in hand.

"Not to-day. To-morrow, perhaps. We shall be here three or four days, at least. The ship's carpenter reports our injuries from the late gale much more serious, or, at least, more extensive, than we had supposed them to be. He says it will take the best part of a week to get her ready for sea again. When we sail I hope you will go with us I dare say you have no desire to colonize here?"

"Not the slightest. I and my companions in exile will very gladly take passage with you," said Justin.

"And I shall be very glad to have you. But mind! I do not promise to take you home immediately. We may have a bout or two with the rebel privateers first," explained the captain.

"'So mote it be!' I should enjoy a bout or two with the rebel privateers; and bear a hand in it as well as I could."

"I'll warrant you!"

"And now, captain, I have a large quantity of provisions, consisting of live stock, fresh vegetables, fish, eggs, fruits and so forth, which I would like to place at your disposal," said Justin.

"Oh, I wouldn't like to rob you of them! In fact, I couldn't think of doing so," said the captain, while his palate, almost pickled with a surfeit of salt food, fairly watered at the mention of fresh meat and vegetables.

"But," said Justin, smiling, as he noticed this, "if we are to be your passengers, where will be the robbery?"

"True—I didn't think of that! Surely it would do you no good to leave all the fresh food here to go to loss after you are gone."

"Certainly not. Therefore, captain, if you can spare any of your hands from duty on the ship, perhaps you had better send them on shore to employ the days while you remain here in taking the provisions on board."

"Certainly. That is good advice," said the captain, smacking his lips.

"And—I shall hope to see you and as many of your officers as you please to bring, to dine with us to-morrow at four."

"Yes—thank you. We'll come."

"Then I will bid you good afternoon, captain."

"Ahem! I beg your pardon! Stop!"

Justin stopped.

"Mr. Ethel!"

The young lieutenant answered the call.

"Is the boat ready to take Mr. Rosenthal on shore?"

"Ay,

"Then I will take leave of you," said Justin.

"Ahem! wait one moment," said the captain.

Justin waited.

"Ahem! Ahem! Ahem! You say that you have plenty of fresh provisions over there?"

"Plenty, captain; and they are heartily at your service," said Justin, suppressing a smile.

"Beef?"

"No, I am sorry to say, not beef. We have but one milch cow."

"That's bad. Mutton?"

"Running; not killed. You see we never kill sheep at this season, for one would spoil before we three could eat it."

"Humph! that's bad again. But a slaughtered sheep wouldn't spoil before we could eat it here on shipboard."

"You shall have your choice of the flock to-morrow, captain."

"Thank you; I will take it then. Have you chickens?"

"Yes, I am happy to say that we have chickens in our larder already prepared to cook."

"Ahem! send me a pair for my supper by the boat when it returns; there's a good fellow."

"Certainly, captain. It was my intention to do so," said Justin.

"And now I'll not detain you, since I see you are in a hurry to be off," said the captain.

And Justin bowed and left the cabin.

On deck he found Lieutenant Ethel waiting to see him on shore. And they entered the boat and were rowed back to the island.

"You will be so kind as to send one of your men with me to take back a basket which I promised to send the captain," said Justin to Lieutenant Ethel, as the boat touched the sands.

"Yes, certainly; go, Jones," said the young officer.

And the sailor to whom he gave the order arose and followed Justin on shore and then up to the house.

And then before even giving Britomarte an account of his visit to the ship, he ordered bring a large covered basket, and with his own hands he filled it with chickens, eggs, fresh butter, cheese, milk, fruit and fish, and gave it to Jones, directing him to take it with his compliments to the captain of the Xyphias.

And Jones touched his hat and went back to the boat.

Justin passed into the parlor, where Britomarte, with tea ready, waited for him.

"Oh, Justin! what a joy to think that we shall leave this lonely isle, and sail for our native land once more!" she exclaimed.

"Yes, an unutterable joy!" replied Justin.

"Ah! what a change has a few hours brought about. This morning, when we arose, we had no more idea of being rescued from this island than we had had on any day in the two years and a half that we have spent here!"

"No, indeed! Let us thank the Lord for this great deliverance."

"Oh, I do! I do!" said Britomarte, fervently.

Then a silence fell between them for a few minutes—a silence which Britomarte at length broke by asking:

"Our prisoner, Justin—what about him? Have you told the captain of him?"

"No, not yet. I have concluded to defer all mention of our prisoner until to-morrow, when the captain and his officers are coming to dine with us."

"Yes; that will be the best opportunity of introducing the subject," assented Britomarte.

After tea they spent the evening in planning for the entertainment of the captain and the officers of the Xyphias. And then they separated and retired to bed—not to sleep, but to lie awake with the joy of thinking about their voyage home.

CHAPTER XXXII

THE PIRATE SPEAKS FOR HIMSELF

The next morning was one of pleasant bustle in the island home. The little household was astir early. And directly after breakfast they went about preparing to receive their company.

Justin went out with his tackle to the little creek making up from the cove, where at this season he could catch fine fish.

Britomarte began to sweep and dust the parlor, and to arrange the furniture and put fresh flowers in the vases. These vases, by the way, were of wickerwork, woven by Justin from the fibres of the palm leaves, and provided with wooden cups hollowed out from blocks of palm logs, to hold the water for the flowers.

Judith, in the kitchen, was up to her eye in pastry, jelly and custard.

"Sure it is a blissing intirely that I was so saving of the sugar, using the sweet sap from the canes in the swamp as offen as iver I could to make it last. And a notable favor iv Crummie not to go dhry. True for ye, ma'am, wid the sugar, and the milk, and the eggs, and the fresh fruit itself I can make a dessert fit for the royal family to sit down to, let alone the dinner that will go before it, wid fresh fish and ham, and roast chicken and pigeon pie. And the idea iv our having company to dinner, ma'am. Sure it's in a dhrame I'm thinking I am all the time. Plaise, ma'am, will ye be so good as to pinch me, to see if I'm awake itself?" said Judith to Miss Conyers, who had come into the kitchen for more water for her flowers.

"Don't you think if you were to put your finger to the hot stove, it would do as well, Judith?" laughed Britomarte.

"Faix, no, ma'am. I niver could abide a burn. And troth if it is a dhrame itself, I don't know as I care to wake. To think I used to say, whin we came into this new house, that if we had only one neighbor living across the fields there some ers, where we could go and take tay oncet in a while, it would be pleasanter like. And sure now me words are coming thrue, for if we haven't a neighbor itself to come and take tay wid us, we have a company iv gintlemen and officers coming to dine wid us. Troth, it is a dhrame, sure enough."

Miss Conyers left Judith to her work and her wanderings of fancy, and returned to the parlor to complete the decorations of that pleasant room.

By and by Justin returned with a large string of fresh fish, which he took into the kitchen and handed over to Judith.

As he left the kitchen, he met, coming out of the opposite door, the pirate captain.

"Ah, you feel better to-day. You feel able to be up?" said Justin.

"Yes. Come in, I want a word with you," said the man.

Justin went into his bedroom, which, for the last two days, had been almost entirely given up to the prisoner.

"Well?" said Justin, taking a chair and seating himself.

"Well," said the prisoner, throwing himself into another chair, "there is a Yankee man-of-war in the cove below."

"The United States sloop of war Xyphias, commanded by Captain Yetsom, is out there."

"Exactly. And the officers are all coming here to dine to-day?"

"The captain, and as many officers as he can bring, are coming."

"Precisely. So I understood from the gabble of the women flying past my door. Now I tell you what, Mr. Rosenthal, I wish to surrender myself to the captain of the Xyphias."

"You will do well," said Justin, with a feeling of intense relief; "that will be your best possible coarse, and it will save me from the distressing duty of delivering up a man whom I have sheltered in his need and nursed in his illness."

"And shoke—an't choked in his cups, and handcuffed and locked up in his sleep, ha! ha! ha! ho! ho! ho!" laughed the man.

"It was the monster who proclaimed himself a rebel and a pirate, boasted himself a throat-cutter and a ship-sinker, that I took care of in that way. Such a monster was not to be let loose upon two helpless women, who had not even the means of securely barricading their doors against him," calmly replied Justin.

"Ha! ha! ha! Ho! ho! ho! Yes, when I'm in liquor I'm always a monster by my own account. I have then a mad delight in inspiring fear, horror and detestation."

"Then you must expect unpleasant consequences from indulging in such a mad delight. But how could I know then, how can I know now, whether you spoke the truth of yourself or not?"

"By my word of honor to the contrary, given in my sober senses, if you choose to take it. If you do not, I have no other way at hand to convince you. Did even my mutinous crew accuse me of anything worse than taking a little too much?"

"No!"

"And then again, the lady saw through me better; but it is true that women are keener sighted than we are."

"Why did you not say all these things to me long ago? If you had, your captivity would have been very much ameliorated," said Justin, regretfully.

"Why? Can a brave man ask? Do you suppose that I was going to explain and apologize and supplicate my captor? I'll tell you what, so far from that, if I could have got loose I should have killed you!"

"Or tried to do it, you mean. You used some bad language on waking up and finding yourself fettered."

"Yes, I 'cussed some,' as the darkies say; that's a fact."

"Why do you make now the explanations you have withheld to your hurt for six months?"

"Why again? Can a good man ask? It is because you brought me in from the storm, struck the fetters from my wrists, gave me your own clothes, laid me upon your own bed, and nursed me like a brother. That's the reason why I have explained to you first. In any case, I should have to give a true account of myself to the captain of the Xyphias, to whom I intend to surrender."

"Then you are not really what you reported yourself to be?"

"What exactly did I report myself to be—Captain Kidd?" laughed the man.

"A pirate! throat-cutter! ship-burner!"

"Ha, ha, ha! Rebel I am, since you dub as such the commanders of all Confederates privateers. But I never cut a throat or burned a ship in my life! I never harmed a woman or child in my life, or man either, for that matter, except in fair fight!"

"I am glad to hear you say so. I hope you will be able to convince Captain Yetsom of the truth of your statement. You had better surrender to him as soon as he arrives. I will give you an opportunity of doing so in the parlor! After you have made your case clear to the captain, I shall be glad to have you join us at dinner. There is my wardrobe—a limited one, indeed—at your disposal. All that can be expected of us Crusoes is cleanliness. We have none of us swallow tailed coats or kid gloves to go to dinner in," laughed Justin.

"Thank you; they would be an inconvenience if we had them, especially the kid gloves. Do you know when the ship sails again?"

"In three or four days. She is anchored here for repairs of injuries received in the late gale."

"And your party goes with her, of course?"

"Yes. We shouldn't like to stay here and chance the coming of another ship."

"Whither goes she?"

"Cruising after privateers."

"After privateers! I'll be——" (and here the captain swore a tremendous oath) "if I don't hope she'll overhaul the Sea Scourge! That has turned pirate unquestionably, and I should like to see all those mutinous r.. .. . . and arms."

"The arms would break with their weight," laughed Justin.

"Then they'd be killed by the fall, and that would be just as well."

The cheerful bustle of a numerous arrival startled Justin, and with a nod to the rebel sailor, he left the room and hurried to the hall door to receive his guests.

There was the florid captain, the two lieutenants, the chaplain, the surgeon, the doctor and the purser—a party of six, come to dine with Justin.

"How do you do? how do you do?" said the captain, heartily shaking Justin's offered hands. "That pair of fowls was delicious, I tell you; and the fish and eggs were a fine addition to my breakfkast this morning. Let me introduce these gentlemen: the Rev. Mr. White, ship's chaplain; Lieutenant Ethel, you know; Lieutenant Robins; Dr. Brown, ship's surgeon; Mr. Bruce, ship's purser. Gentlemen, Mr. Rosenthal."

Having accomplished this introduction with a great deal of ceremony, the captain, with his officers, followed his host into the parlor, where there was another introduction—namely, to Miss Conyers, who received the party with graceful courtesy

"And now, Mr. Rosenthal," said the captain, as soon as they were all seated, "my men with the boat are down below there waiting your orders concerning the shipping of those provisions you talked of. If you will send one of your hands to show them where they are, they will go to work immediately."

"You forget," said Justin, smiling, "that I have no hands but those with which nature has provided me. I should not like to part with either of them. But, if you will be good enough to excuse me for fifteen minutes, and allow Miss Conyers to entertain you, I will go and show the men where the provisions are stored, and set them to work."

"Do so, then, my young friend! Of course, we will excuse you for so good a work," said the captain.

Justin bowed and left the room. But, before leaving the house, he put his head into the bedroom door and looked to see if the rebel captain was ready for the interview with the Union officer. He saw Captain Spear, with his head in the wash-basin, engaged in a very much-needed ablution.

"You will be ready in fifteen minutes?" inquired Justin.

"Yes, or in twenty."

"Then I will come for you."

"Thank you."

Justin hurried down to the beach where the boat was waiting, called the men to follow him and took them to the mountain grotto, where his provisions were stored; set them to work at its removal, and then went back to the house.

He found the rebel captain all ready to go in the parlor.

"You will remain here a few minutes while I go to Captain Yetsom and prepare him to see you. Remember that he has not even heard of your presence here yet."

"And my sudden appearance might kill him with joy! Is that it? Well, go and break the news gently, Mr. Rosenthal," laughed the rebel, sarcastically.

Justin went into the parlor.

"Back already!" exclaimed the jolly captain of the Xyphias.

"Yes, and I have some news to tell you!"

"'News' what, on this place? It must be that Columbus has discovered America, or the Dutch taken Holland."

"No; but it is that we have taken the captain of the Sea Scourge!"

"Lord bless my soul and body! man, are you mad?"

"No, nor dreaming. We have taken the captain of the Sea Scourge!"

"Taken the captain of the Sea Scourge? We know that he was reported cruising about in these latitudes, lying in wait for East Indiamen; but we have seen nothing of him; there was no Sea Scourge nor any other ship in sight when we anchored here, or when we came ashore."

"And yet we have the notorious sea rover."

"Spear?"

"Yes, Spear."

"Bosh, man, you are jesting with us! You mean that you have him in his photograph, or something."

"No; I mean that I have him in person."

"Then there must be some other play upon the words. Have Spear personally present on this remote Indian isle! You might as well boast that you have Davis here!—as you may have in his ambrotype, just as you have Spear."

"I assure you that the captain of the Sea Scourge is on this island, in this house, and waiting to surrender himself to you!"

"For Heaven's sake, explain yourself! Read me the answer to this riddle before my head goes!" said Captain Yetsom, while his officers listened with the same sort of curiosity they might have felt in an ingenious enigma, or as if the case had been put to them in conundrum style, as: "Why have we the captain of the Sea Scourge here?" and they were trying to guess the answer, or expecting one from the propounder of the question that should set the room in a roar.

"I will explain," said Justin, and turning to Lieutenant Ethel, he continued:

"You may remember, lieutenant, I told you yesterday, in reply to an observation of yours, that the Xyphias had not been the only ship which had passed here, in the two years and a half we have spent on this island—that there had been another ship?"

"Yes, I remember."

"That other ship was the Sea Scourge, driven out of her course by a furious gale. She came into our cove sailing under the rebel flag, which greatly perplexed us, as we had never seen or heard of it."

"Yes? Well?" exclaimed the captain and several of the officers, listening eagerly.

"The captain landed here; brought us the first news of the war which, you may judge, much astonished and grieved us He proclaimed himself a Confederate privateer, sailing under letters of marque from his government. He drank more brandy than was good for him, and went to sleep on the floor. In the afternoon his crew mutinied, deposed him from his command, put another man in his place and sailed without him."

"Good! Where did you say the fellow is now?"

"On this island! in this house! He has been here ever since he was abandoned by his ship, of course He is now ready to give himself up to you. You will treat him, I hope, as a prisoner of war."

"That, as it may be, I must see and question the fellow first," said the captain of the Xyphias.

Justin went out and returned, accompanied by Spear.

The prisoner walked straight up to the captain of the Xyphias, whom he recognized by his uniform, saluted him, and said,

"Sir, I am Captain Spear, of the Confederate ship Sea Scourge. I surrender myself to you, claiming the usage of a prisoner of war If I had a sword I would hand it over; but I have none."

CHAPTER XXXIII

LEAVING THE ISLAND

The next day was a busy one to our islanders.

Justin was engaged in packing up and sending off his stores of fresh provisions to the ship. And the jolly boat plied all day long between the ship and shore to transport them.

Britomarte and Judith were employed in packing such clothing, books and household effects as they meant to take with them from the island.

It had been determined, in solemn consultation between the three, that some of the live stock, some of the household furniture, and even some of the provisions—such as would be likely to keep for a length of time—should be left on the island, in case any other ship should be wrecked upon its rocks, or any other passengers cast away upon its desolate shores.

In the fields they turned loose a few sheep and pigs and fowls.

They would have left Crummie, the cow, too, but that Judith raised such a howl as never had been heard from her before, not even on the occasion of the shipwreck; and vowed that to leave Crummie behind would break her heart entirely.

To comfort Judith, and, above all, to stop her deafening howls, Britomarte promised that Crummie should go. And Britomarte's promise was her bond; and, moreover, her word was law.

The day that our islanders spent in consulting, deciding and packing, the officers of the Xyphias passed in preparing for a great feast to be held on board the ship in honor of their new acquaintances and in return for their hospitality. And on the second day our islanders were invited to partake of it. They went early, fared sumptuously, passed a very pleasant day, and returned late at night to their island home.

The remaining days of the week were spent in repairing the injuries of the ship and transporting the stores from the island.

The captain of the Xyphias thought the ship would be ready to sail on the following Monday

When Justin heard this, he invited the captain and all the officers to come and spend Sunday—the last Sunday and the last day on the island—at this house, to hold divine service there.

And early on Sunday morning, the parlor, now dismantled of half its furniture, was converted into a temporary chapel, and hymns were sung and prayers said and sermons preached, both in the morning and in the afternoon. The sermon in the morning was preached by the ship's chaplain; and in the afternoon by Mr. Rosenthal; and the officers and the crew attended both services, and the captain of the Xyphias slept comfortably in his seat through both sermons; but let this be said for him—that he would not have slept, or even winked, during a sea fight, though it had lasted day and night.

When the afternoon service was over, the crew and some of the officers returned to the ship; but the captain and others remained and spent the evening, and only left at a late hour.

FAIR PLAY

Wind and tide favoring, they were to sail early in the morning.

The jolly boat was to be at the landing by sunrise to take the last load of our friends' effects to the ship. It was then to return for Justin, Britomarte, Judith, Crummie and the little dog.

And though this was their last night on the lonely island that they might never expect to revisit again, and they were on the eve of embarking for their dear, native land, and thoughts and feelings were busy alike with tender regrets and joyful anticipations, yet—in consequence of the bodily fatigue they had endured that day, they fell asleep as soon as their heads had touched their pillows, and slept profoundly until morning.

The daylight, creeping in at the windows, woke Justin first.

When breakfast was over they went to work at their final preparations for departure.

I said that they intended to leave the house with a portion of the furniture, clothing and books, for the benefit of any future shipwrecked sufferers who might possibly be cast away upon the island.

So Britomarte went into the bedroom, and made up the beds, and tidied the washstands, and set the chairs straight and closed the windows, and fastened the doors.

And while she was doing that, Judith washed up all the crockeryware and cooking utensils, and put them away in the cupboards, and then she cleaned up the kitchen, and put out the fire, and shut the windows and doors.

In the meantime, Justin went into the parlor and set the chairs, tables, lamps and vases straight, and laid a Bible, a hymn book, an old copy of Shakespeare and an old almanac, a slate pencil and some paper, pens and ink upon the book shelves. Then he fastened the windows and doors.

Finally, the three friends, having completed their work, met in the front passage.

"Troth," said Judith, "whoever comes afther us can't say

they'll find everything convanient to their hands, so they will."

No one answered the girl. But Justin, with a grave face, summoned the two women to his side, and then, reverently lifting his hat, returned thanks to Divine Providence for their long preservation on the desert island, and for their present happy deliverance, and invoked his blessing on the isle they were leaving, that it might yet become the cultivated and populous habitation of civilized and Christian man, and on their own coming voyage, that it might have a prosperous course and happy end.

And then the three went out of the house, closing the front door behind them, and taking their way to the beach, followed by the faithful little dog. Justin carried on his shoulder the last box, which came out of Britomarte's room, filled with combs, brushes, towels, etc.

Down on the sands they found the boat waiting for them under the command of Lieutenant Ethel, who, to do them honor, had come in person to take them on board.

Crummie was already in the boat, to which she had been enticed by Judith's old device of a pail of "warrum male and wather."

And now, with her nose in that delicious mess, she remained quiet enough while the boat was still.

Lieutenant Ethel stepped on shore, bowed profoundly to Britomarte, and held out his hands to Mr. Rosenthal, with a hearty:

"Good-morning."

"I hope we have not kept you waiting," said Justin.

"Not a moment. We have only just got Mistress Cudd in here," laughed the young man, pointing to Crummie.

They all then got into the boat.

Judith went immediately and stood by the head of the cow, with her hand on the creature's neck, ready to soothe and control her in case she should become frightened and restive when the boat should begin to move.

But Crummie had seen too many ups and downs in

this world to be disturbed by trifles, and so she made the passage to the ship with great composure.

CHAPTER XXXIV

THE CRUISE

The captain of the Xyphias stood on deck to receive his passengers.

The deck was a scene of great bustle, with the seamen getting ready to make sail. Some were weighing anchor, some loosing the topsails and courses, and others coiling down the ropes.

Through the crowd the captain led his passengers to the head of the gang-ladder, and took them down below to the gundeck where his own quarters were situated, and he assigned them berths in his own cabin.

Britomarte and her attendant had a stateroom to themselves, and Justin had a share in the captain's stateroom. It appeared from all this that they were to be received as the captain's own guests, and have seats at his private table as well as berths in his cabin.

Having introduced his guests to their new quarters, the captain returned to his post on deck. And the noise of getting under way roared and thundered overhead!

Britomarte and Judith went into their stateroom to inspect it and lay aside the small parcels that they had brought from the house in their hands. And then Britomarte asked Justin to attend them up on deck that they might watch their island as long as it should continue in sight.

They went up and stood in the stern of the ship, leaning over the taffrail, and looking upon the island, until the Xyphias began to heave and turn, and then, as the wind filled her canvas, to sail away from the open sea. They watched the lonely isle as it gradually receded from their sight, until palm trees, rocks and caverns were all lost to view and indistinguishable maze of color—they watched it until it dropped lower and lower down toward the horizon—until its outline became confused with the boundaries of sky and sea—and then they turned away. Britmarte drew her veil to hide her fast-falling tears.

When she lifted it again there was nothing around her but the lonely sea and sky.

The second day of their voyage was a pleasanter one than the first, principally because the captain, having discovered the temperate habits of his passengers, did not insist upon their making five meals a day.

They were steering for Cape Town, where the captain hoped to anchor by the end of that current week.

"We may meet a homeward-bound vessel there," he said; "if so, we will put you on board of her."

"It is you who are now anxious to get rid of us, captain," said Miss Conyers, archly.

And the jolly captain put on the air of a very much injured man, and vowed that Miss Conyers did him great wrong.

The ship was constantly on the lookout for rebel privateers, and kept a man at the mast-head day and night, relieving him every two hours. But night followed day, and day succeeded night, and still no sail of any sort was to be seen on all the lonely sea.

Nevertheless, this was one of the happiest periods that our three friends ever passed. The weather was charming, the sky clear, the sea calm, the wind light, and the ship flew on over the waters at the rate of ten knots an hour. The ship's captain and officers were all extremely pleasant companions, and unaffectedly glad to have these guests along with them to break the monotony of their sea life.

During the continuance of the fine weather, the three passengers spent every day on deck and every evening in the captain's cabin.

Usually the captain, the chaplain, Justin and Britomarte formed a party, and played a rubber or two of whist.

Sometimes, to vary the evening's pastime, Miss Conyers would exercise her talent for dramatic reading, and on these latter occasions, all the officers that could be spared from the deck would be invited into the captain's cabin to receive their share of the entertainment.

Sometimes, also, Miss Conyers sang for her friends. And this singing was perhaps the greatest treat she could give them. A woman's sweet voice caroling their favorite songs on the blue water was a novelty and a delight indeed.

Thus pleasantly passed the days until Saturday morning, when they made Table Mount. And on Saturday noon they anchored in Table Bay.

Justin and Britomarte went on shore to call upon their friends at Cape Town.

They went first to the South African College, but learned there that their old acquaintance, Professor Jack, had gone to Europe to collect certain rare scientific works for his library.

Then they went out to Silver Tree Villa to see their esteemed friends the Burneys.

They found the reverend doctor and his family at home and in good health, but immeasurably astonished and delighted to see Mr. Rosenthal and Miss Conyers, for they had heard of the wreck of the Sultana, and had supposed their young friends to have been lost.

And next it was the turn of Justin and Britomarte to be equally astonished and delighted for they learned that the lifeboat containing the missionary party, after drifting about the ocean for several days, had been picked up by a Dutch merchantman bound for the Cape of Good Hope, and all the passengers rescued; that the Elys and the Bretons had remained guests at Silver Tree Grove for a month, during which subscriptions had been taken up in all the churches to raise a fund for their relief, and at the end of which, being entirely refitted out, they had sailed in the East Indiaman Djalma for Calcutta, en route for their distant field of missionary labor, where in due time they had safely arrived.

Mrs. Burney was able to assure Miss Conyers that her friends were all well and doing well, for she heard from them by every Indian mail.

Great was the surprise and joy of Justin and Britomarte on hearing this news.

"Then, after all, the crew of that boat must have relented and taken the two men on board," said Justin.

"I suppose when Captain McKenzie refused to leave the ship he left room in the boat for one, and they managed to make room for the other," observed Britomarte.

They dined with the Burneys, but were obliged to decline all further hospitality, as the length of their ship's stay at Cape Town was very uncertain.

So they took an affectionate leave of their friends, and returned on board the Xyphias, in good time for the captain's early supper table, which was spread with all the luxuries to be obtained at Cape Town.

"I have news of the Sea Scourge. She touched here on the day before yesterday, remained a few hours to get in wood and water, and also to pick up a few seamen, and then she sailed again," said the captain, as they sat down to supper.

"Where?" eagerly inquired Justin.

"East and north. Going, no doubt, to meet returning East Indiamen from Calcutta. We must go in pursuit of her, and lose no time about it either. So, Mr. Rosenthal, we sail with the first tide to-morrow."

"I am rejoiced to hear it," said Justin.

"I have caused inquiries to be made, and find that there are no homeward-bound ships in the harbor. So this young lady, I am selfishly glad to know, has no option but to go on with us for the present," added the captain.

"Unless she prefers to accept the hospitality tendered her by the Burneys; in which case she can remain at Silver Tree Villa, and wait for a homeward-bound ship. What do you say, Miss Conyers?" inquired Justin, turning toward her.

"I say that, with the captain's kind permission, I will stay where I am," replied Britomarte.

And so that matter was settled.

CHAPTER XXXV

THE CHASE

WITH the first tide the next morning the ship sailed. The weather kept its promise and was very fine.

The ship steered northeast, flying before a fresh wind at the rate of ten or eleven knots an hour.

And all day long our passengers lounged upon the deck, reading, promenading or chatting; and all the evening they played whist in the captain's cabin.

And day and night the captain kept a man at the masthead on the lookout, and relieved him every two hours, that his vigilance might not slacken.

But days and nights went by and there was no sign of the Sea Scourge, or any other ship, on all the lonely sea.

At length one evening when the tropical full moon and great stars made all the sky and sea almost as bright as day, and the officers off duty were lounging on the deck, and the captain and his party were playing whist in the cabin, there came a cry from the man at the masthead:

"Sail ho!"

It roused the officers on deck like the blast of a trumpet does the war horse. They "snuffed the battle afar off."

It startled all the whist players in the cabin, except the phlegmatic captain, who went on counting his points:

"Two by tricks and two by honors; and five before! We're nine to their nine, Miss Conyers. And now all depends upon the odd trick. So we must look sharp! —I knew we should overhaul her at last! Parson it's my deal."

But no one listened to the captain. Every one was straining their ears to catch the voices from the deck.

"Sail ho!"

The cry rang through the night air like an alarm.

"Where away?" called the officer of the forward watch.

"About three points off our weather bows."

"What do you make of her?"

"Can't make her out yet!"

While this bawling was going on aloft, the captain of the ship sat quietly over his rubber of whist.

Presently Lieutenant Ethel came below, touched his cap, and said:

"If you please, sir, we have made a strange sail."

"What do you make of her?" inquired the captain, without ceasing to deal his cards.

"We can make nothing of her as yet, except that she appears to have seen us and is running away."

"That proves her to be the Sea Scourge, or some other pirate! Clap on all the sail we can carry, and chase!—— Diamonds! Parson, it is your lead, and we are waiting for you. Miss Conyers, look sharp! We are playing for the odd trick," said the captain, as he turned up the trump and sorted his cards.

The young lieutenant went on deck with his orders. And soon the ship flew under the pressure of her sails.

The captain went on with his game, and played well; and as none of his excited companions could give sufficient attention to the business in hand fairly to compete with him, he won the odd trick.

"We've beat them in the rub, Miss Conyers. Shall we try to beat them in another one?" inquired the captain, as he gathered up the cards.

"Oh! no! pray don't! let us go up on deck and look after the chase!" eagerly urged Britomarte.

"You!" exclaimed the captain, in laughing astonishment.

"Yes, I!" answered Britomarte, as her eyes widened and brightened.

"Lord bless my soul alive, here is a young lady as eager for the fray as any of us?" laughed the captain. "I'll warrant you, when you get back to your native country, if the war is not over, to take an active part in it!"

"That I shall!" answered Britomarte, emphatically.

And all the while she looked her eager impatience to get upon the deck.

"There is no necessity for haste, my dear young lady! We shall see nothing when we get there—except what we have seen for so many days and nights—an expanse of sea and sky!" laughed the captain.

"But the strange sail?" eagerly questioned our amazon.

"Ay, the strange sail! You'll not see her, at all events! The men have made her out only through their glasses! She is miles away! and we shall not overhaul her before morning," said the captain.

And he set the watch and went below, and turned in for a short nap, leaving Lieutenant Ethel to manage the ship.

Justin stayed on deck a little while longer, and then followed the captain's example.

But none of them, except the phlegmatic captain, rested very well that night. The thought that they were chasing a privateer, whom they would probably engage in battle next morning, was not likely to rock them to sleep.

Britomarte certainly never closed her eyes; she was awake no less by her own excitement than by the "tireless tongue" of Judith, who talked of nothing but the coming fight and the share she would like to take in it.

"Sure, meself hopes they'll find something for me to do in it! Troth, if they'd put me to one iv the big guns, I could fire it off wid the best iv them. And if they'd not trust me to do that same, I could hand patridges as well as the powdy monkeys thimselves!"

"Cartridges, Judith," said Miss Conyers.

"Sure, that's what I'm maning! And, troth, I'll find something to do in it, or me name's not Judy Riordan!"

"I am glad and proud to see so much spirit in a sister woman, Judith, whether you find an opportunity to exercise it or not," said Miss Conyers.

At which Judith was so delighted that she went off into another fit of boasting more extravagant than the first.

To have heard Judith talk then, you would have imagined her to be Boadicea, Joan of Arc and Moll Pitcher rolled into one.

So passed the night in the cabin.

Just before the dawn of day, Lieutenant Ethel came below to the captain and reported the chase within range of their lee-bow gun.

"Fire a blank cartridge into her," said the captain, immediately turning out.

Britomarte and Judith overheard every word of this short interview; and Judith clapped her hands for joy, exclaiming.

"Now they're going to begin. Sure meself is happy as Paddy at Donnybrook Fair! And, oh! that I was up on deck wid the seamen! Wouldn't I——"

"Boom-m-me!" thundered the cannon over the sea, with a report that shook the ship

With a violent bound, Judith leaped up, clapped her hands to her ears, and, shaking and screaming with the extremity of terror, hid her head in Britomarte's lap.

"Why, what's the matter, Judith?" inquired Miss Conyers, as the sound rolled away. "Is this your heroism?"

"S'int Pater and all the Holy Apostles! Mother Mary and all the blissid virgins!" gasped the panic-stricken girl.

"Boom-m-me!" roared an answering gun from the chase.

"Ow-oo!" screeched Judith, burying her head in Britomarte's lap; "kiver me up! kiver me up! I'm kilt entirely!"

But Miss Conyers started up, threw the girl off her knees, hurried on her clothes and hastened out into the cabin, where she met Justin leaving his stateroom.

"The action has commenced!" exclaimed Britomarte.

"Yes, dearest one. Stay where you are, I beseech you. You can do no good on deck," urged Justin.

"If I can do no good, I can at least risk my life with the others," persisted Britomarte.

"But to what end? Britomarte, you will not only

do no good by going on deck, but you will do much harm by being in everybody's way," said Justin, bluntly.

She looked intently in his face to see if he spoke in earnest, before she answered.

"If that is so, I will stay here. But oh, how unwillingly."

And she sat down, only half resigned to her inactivity, and meditated how she could change it into good service.

While they spoke, another shot was exchanged between the ships.

Justin hurried up on deck.

Everything there was in admirable order. None of the confusion that too often precedes an engagement appeared.

The deck was cleared for action.

The men were all at their quarters, the officers at their posts.

The captain was standing on the quarter deck, leveling his glass at the chase, which was, moreover, in full sight about two miles ahead.

The firing ceased for the time being.

"What is the meaning of this lull, captain?" respectfully inquired Justin Rosenthal, coming to the side of Captain Yetsom.

Sailors will swear, more is the pity, and Captain Yetsome, dropping the telescope to his side, blew off a tremendous oath, under the impression that he had a sufficient provocation to do so, and then he added:

"We are on a false scent, sir; we have been chasing an English ship."

"Are you certain?" doubtingly inquired Justin.

"Humph! these infernal pirates sometimes show false colors. This is what has happened, Mr. Rosenthal. When I came up on deck I found her within good range of our lee bow chaser. I ran up the Stars and Stripes and sent a blank cartridge into her by way of a visiting card. She returned the compliment by firing a salute from her stern-chaser; but did not show her colors, and did not cease to run."

"And then?"

"I sent a more urgent message to her in the form of a round shot from our lee-bow chaser. She returned the fire in kind and hoisted the English Union Jack."

"But didn't heave to?"

"No, nor cease to run away from us. Whatever she does, she does not cease to run."

"But an English ship, or an honest ship, scarcely would do that."

"Scarcely. And that is what makes the affair doubtful and awkward. If she is an English ship we have no business to pursue her; but if she is a rebel privateer sailing under English colors we must take her."

While the captain spoke, Mr. Rosenthal had been attentively regarding the chase. Now he said:

"The longer I look at that ship, the more familiar she seems to me. Will you lend me your telescope, captain?"

Captain Yetsom handed the glass and waited the result of Justin's inspection.

Justin pointed the instrument and took deliberate sight at the chase. He viewed it attentively for a minute and then returned the telescope to the owner, saying quietly:

"You are not on a false scent, captain."

"Eh? What do you make of her?"

"The Sea Scourge."

"Are you quite certain?"

"Quite. I cannot be mistaken. Indeed, I recognized her by naked eye from her general appearance. And when I brought the glass to bear upon her, I knew her also by individuals marks."

The captain of the Xyphias waited to hear no more. He laid down his telescope, sprang upon the poop deck, and drew out his speaking trumpet.

As the men had scarcely taken their eyes off their captain during the fifteen minutes of suspense in which they stood idly at their quarters, there was no need to call their attention.

The captain put the speaking trumpet to his lips, and thundered forth the words:

"My lads! the prize that we have been seeking, the

Sea Scourge, is before us. And please Heaven she shall be ours before night!"

Tremendous cheers from the seamen responded to the captain's pithy speech, and proved their good will to the work before them, and their confidence of victory.

CHAPTER XXXVI

THE FLIGHT

"Stand to your guns men!" thundered the captain of the Xyphias.

And the deafening cheers sank into silence, and the order was promptly obeyed.

"Mr. Ethel!"

The young lieutenant came quickly at the captain's call.

"Pass the order to fire at the enemy's mizzen mast Strike it as low as possible, for the lower you carry it away the more unmanageable the Sea Scourge will become The heavy press of sail she carries forward will then lift her stern high out of the water and render her less obedient to her helm."

"Ay, ay, sir!" responded the cheerful voice of the young officer, as he touched his cap and went forward to see the order executed.

The gunner in charge of the lee bow chaser was an old and experienced one.

The lieutenant gave him the order, word for word, as he had received it from the captain

"We'll try, sir," said the veteran, with a confident smile and pat on the breech of his gun, which satisfied the lieutenant that the gunner knew his business The gun was now ready. He sighted her, and gave the command

"Fire!"

Out poured the deafening discharge, and two hundred pairs of eyes were tracking the course of the ball through the air, each in impatient suspense to see the effect.

It struck close under the stern of the enemy.

"A good shot! a capital shot!" exclaimed the captain. "A little more elevation on your next, and you will splinter his mizzen mast."

Meanwhile Lieutenant Ethel raised his telescope and took sight at the chase. And it seemed that the captain of the Sea Scourge, finding that his false colors did not protect him, and having a ball drop so close under his stern, concluded that he was known, and determined to fight the battle out under his true ones. Down fluttered St. George's Cross and up flew the Stars and Bars. And the next instant his stern chaser answered the iron messenger from the Xyphias.

The shot plunged into the sea close on the weather quarter of our gallant ship, doing no other harm than copiously sprinkling the jolly tars on that side.

"A free shower bath in hot weather is a pleasant and a wholesome thing!" exclaimed a young midshipman, who had received his full share of that blessing.

But another good fellow, a landsman recently shipped from Cape Town, who had been standing gaping and staring with mouth and eyes open, received a deluge on his face and chest, striking him with such a shock that he lost his balance and his reason at the same moment, and fell flat upon his back, rolling over and over, imagining that the ball had struck him, and that the water gurgling back from his throat was his own lifeblood, and bawling at the top of his voice:

"I'm shot! I'm shot! My head's off! My head's off! Take me down! Take me down!"

Amid roars of laughter from his companions, an old salt caught up a pair of shell hooks, similar in shape to fire tongs, and, reaching forward, brought the ends together over a piece of flesh under the fellow's pantaloons with an unmerciful squeeze.

The dead man sprang up with wonderful agility, and amid piercing shrieks, bawled out:

"I'm shot again! I'm shot again! Take me down below! Take me down below!"

Such peals of laughter followed this that the lad opened his eyes, looked about, came to his senses and realized his position.

At the captain's command he went forward and slunk out of sight.

The next shot from the Sea Scourge took off the head of the brave old salt, spinning it round and round until it struck the deck, while the headless body sank quivering down upon the very spot where but a moment before the form of the coward had rolled.

But—

"The coward dies many deaths,
The brave man dies but once."

Shot after shot was now exchanged between the ships with little effect; the Xyphias all the while gradually drawing nearer the Sea Scourge, and the chase growing more exciting.

At length a lucky shot from the Xyphias struck the enemy's mizzen mast, just above the mizzen top, and down came the wreck.

Cheers upon cheers went up from the crew of the Xyphias.

Yells of defiance answered them from the decks of the enemy.

Lieutenant Ethel again leveled his glass at the chase.

The Sea Scourge still minded her helm, as her spanker and crotchet were still standing and drawing. The wreck of her mizzen mast was promptly cleared away. And she doggedly answered gun for gun, shot for shot, though the Xyphias was now gaining rapidly upon her, and her case was well-nigh hopeless.

At last a shot from the Xyphias struck the taffrail of the enemy, close by the wheel, scattering the splinters in every direction. One struck the helmsman, driven to his very heart. In his death agony and delirium he clutched the spokes of the wheel with the grasp that could not be loosened, and he slowly sank windward to the deck, turning the wheel with him. The Sea Scourge, in obedience to her helm, rounded sharply to the wind.

Seeing his ship breaching to, the captain of the Sea Scourge ran aft, yelling.

"What d'ye mean by that, you —— sea cook? Luff! Luff!"

There came no response from the helmsman; and indeed in the same instant that he ceased speaking the captain perceived that the man was past hearing He reached the helm too late. The ship was already taken aback and lying directly across the course of the Xyphias, and not two cables' length from her. He gave the helm to a seaman near, and, springing upon the poop deck, yelled forth the order:

"Rake her with your port battery!"

Then issued forth a tremendous discharge that shook the privateer from masthead to keel, so that she trembled like a living creature struck with palsy. Then he braced her yards and put her wheel hard down, so as to bring her again upon her course.

Meanwhile, from the deck of the Xyphias, Captain Yetsom, observing the privateer in the act of broaching to, first looked, expecting to see her haul down her colors. But as they continued to fly, he put up his helm to clear the Xyphias from the raking fire that he foresaw would be poured into her from the port battery of the enemy.

But so quickly did the Sea Scourge broach to, that the Xyphias could not get away in time, and so she received the enemy's whole broadside obliquely over her lee bows, with disastrous effect.

The roar of the cannon, the crash of falling timbers and the shrieks of the wounded were appalling.

Many poor fellows lost their lives and many more their limbs.

But now, above all the noise and confusion, the voice of Captain Yetsom rang out clearly and firmly:

"Man the starboard guns! Clew up the courses! And so we cross the privateer's bows, take good aim and pay her well for this!"

And before the Sea Scourge could veer round upon her course again, the Xyphias came across her bows. A long line of fire belched forth from the starboard guns, sending iron missles crashing and tearing into the Sea Scourge, and dealing death and destruction everywhere among her crew.

Here Justin's clear and ringing voice was heard high above all others in the cheers that rose heavenward from the deck of the Xyphias.

Again these cheers were answered with yells of defiance from the deck of the privateer, whose sails now began to fill rapidly, so that she quickly wore round.

This brought the ships opposite to each other.

And now commenced a murderous exchange of broadsides. Roar followed roar! Crash came upon crash! The shrieks of the wounded on both sides mingled with each other and with the cheers of their unhurt companions.

Justin was everywhere—inspiring the brave to still greater deeds of valor, encouraging the faint-hearted till they outrivaled the most heroic, helping all by precept and example, and serving at the guns where men had fallen, until relieved.

And now the foremast of the Sea Scourge was seen to totter and fall!

While the enemy was encumbered with this wreck, Captain Yetsom set his courses and, shooting ahead, took up a raking position, from which he poured into the Sea Scourge a galling fire of grape and cannister.

The privateer persistently returned the fire with her bow chasers, and promptly cleared her deck from the wreck of the foremast.

Captain Yetsom seeing that with the indomitable courage of his countrymen she would sink before she would surrender, and seeing also that she was manoeuvring to get into position again, determined to carry her by the board.

He stood off for a short time and gathered his officers and men about him and said:

"That privateer is well fought. Her commander will go to the bottom with her colors flying, rather than haul them down. He cannot have many men remaining fit for duty. So, to save the lives of my men, as well as those of his also, I am resolved, by the help of the Lord to carry her by the board."

This announcement was received with tremendous cheers.

"Enough! To your quarters, men!" thundered the captain.

The order was immediately obeyed.

"Mr. Ethel!"

The young lieutenant sprang to his captain's side.

"Get ready the boarding party!"

Ethel sprang to execute his order.

Captain Yetsom then put his ship about, and as she came in collision with the Sea Scourge, poured into the enemy a broadside from her port battery, and then, cutlass in hand, leaped on board, followed by Justin and the whole boarding party.

Here they were met by a set of men, few in number, but desperate in resolution, and a terrible conflict ensued. Foremost among the boarding party might have been seen the tall form of Justin, cheering on the men and striking good blows for the flag he loved so well.

In the meantime, what was Britomarte doing? Where Justin had left her, she had sat studying what she might do to help the good cause. Suddenly she found out her mission.

"There will be wounded men," she said, "and no one to attend to them in the excitement of the action."

And she arose and opened her trunks and boxes, and took from them all the soft old linen she could find, and sat down to tear it into bandages, and having done that, she began to pick the shreds that were left into lint.

While Britomarte was engaged in this humane work, her panic-stricken companion lay in one of the berths, with her head under the cover, trying to deafen herself to the sound of the battle.

When the shrieks and groans of the wounded and dying began to mingle with the roar of cannon and the crash of timbers, then Britomarte gathered up her linen bandages and lint, and put them in a little basket with a pair of scissors, a flat knife, and needles and thread, and with the basket on her arm, she went up on deck.

Everybody was too busy there to see or stop her.

Through the black and sulphurous smoke, through pools of blood, between dead bodies, heedless of the cannon balls that tore crashing past her, she made her way to that part of the deck where the ship's surgeon stood among the wounded, having them carefully carried below.

"Doctor, I have come to take care of these brave fellows," she said, pausing at his side.

The surgeon looked at her in dismay.

"Young lady, for Heaven's sake——" he began; but she took the word from his lips.

"Doctor, for Heaven's sake forget that I am a 'young lady,' and look upon me only as a human being, able and willing to be useful," she said.

"Boom-oom-m-o! crash! splash!" came the cannon ball from the Sea Scourge, tearing its way over their heads, and dropping into the sea before them.

Britomarte stood like a statue, absolutely unshaken by the tremendous shock.

"Were you not frightened?" asked the doctor, in amazement.

"No; why should I be?" she coolly demanded.

"Nay, why should you not be?"

"In the first place, because I have no fear of death; in the second, because I have no great love of life. If I could feel fear, I should rush to the very front of danger to cure myself of the weakness."

"I believe you would. You are formed of the metal of which heroes are made!"

"Let me help you," said Britomarte, feeling impatient of his praise, and pointing to the basket of linen bandages and lint that she carried in her hand.

"Well, my child, you can help me, and you may. And at least you had better be down below with me binding up wounds, than up on deck with the gunners helping to make them, as I think was your first aspiration," replied the doctor.

"Yes," said Britomarte, "I should like to serve at one of the guns, but since I am not permitted to do so, I am w... you will f... I shall not d... brave sailors' wounds any the less tenderly because I should prefer to make wounds for other people to dress on the bodies of the foemen!"

And saying these words, she followed the doctor down into the cockpit, where the wounded lay, some in hammocks, some on sail cloth, and some on the naked planks.

And there her curage, her humanity, and, above all, her divine purity, so impressed the ship's surgeon, that he did utterly forget that she was a young lady, and he made her as useful as if she had been a medical student.

At the surgeon's orders, with her sharp scissors and steady hand she ripped up the sleeves of the sailors' wounded arms, or the trousers of their wounded legs, with equal promptness. She cut sticking plaster into long, slender, strips, and watched the doctor to see how he brought the gaping lips of mere flesh wounds together, and closed them, by laying across them, at right angles, these delicate strips of plaster, and then bandaged them up with linen.

She watched him perform this simple operation once. And then she assured him that she could do that as well as he could. And after that, while the surgeon attended to the more serious cases—probing wounds, extracting balls, and even amputating limbs —Britomarte closed and bandaged all the simple flesh wounds with a skill equal to that of the surgeon himself, and with a tenderness that drew from her rough patients many thanks and blessings.

And all this time the roar of battle went on overhead and all around her. Occasionally a ball struck near

At length, however, the cannonading ceased, and a noise and confusion of another sort was heard above —a mighty cheering and hurraling and running to and fro.

"What does that mean?" exclaimed the doctor

But nobody could answer him, and he was too busy with his wounded to go and see for himself.

Britomarte had dressed the last wound of her last patient, and was holding a glass of brandy and water to his lips, for he was faint from the loss of blood, when another injured man—a young midshipman—was brought down.

And he reported that the captain had resolved to carry the enemy by the board.

"And that brave young fellow, Mr. Rosenthal, is foremost among the boarding party, fighting like another Paul Jones," he added.

Britomarte listened breathlessly; but waited quietly until her patient had drained the glass that she held to his lips, and then she gently laid his head back, put down the glass, and rushed up on deck.

She reached that horrible deck—the scene of the late carnage. It was slippery with human gore, and spattered with brains, and littered with the splinters of shivered timbers and shreds of rent canvas, and fragments of broken weapons, and obstructed with dead bodies; and over all hung a sulphureous smoke of gunpowder that obscured the vision and blackened all the sails and rigging; and above all rang the clash of steel, the report of firearms, the screams of the wounded, and the yells and cheers of the combatants.

Through all these horrors Britomarte rushed to the starboard side of the ship to which the Sea Scourge had been clawed up so closely that any one might easily pass from one to the other.

On the deck of the Sea Scourge the battle was raging fiercely.

At first, her senses all bewildered with horror, Britomarte perceived before her only a pandemonium of clanging, clashing, thundering, smoking, blazing, bleeding, screaming, yelling chaos! But presently her straining eyes made out the figure of Justin.

Conspicuous above all the rest by his great height and strength, and by the grandeur of his inspired countenance, which seemed as that of a god of war, and flinging himself wherever the fight was fiercest, he soon became the one target of the enemy, who struck at him from all sides.

Seem'
ing, Bri

"Oh, Heavenly Father protect him! In Thine infinite mercy protect him!"

Then, no longer able to restrain herself, on seeing him in the most imminent peril, she caught up a cutlass from an arm-chest near, and crying:

"Oh, God of battles! give strength to my weak woman's arm this day!" she rushed over to the deck of the Sea Scourge, in the midst of that hell of war, and stood by her lover's side.

Meanwhile Justin had singled out the pirate Captain Mulligan, as his own; and also Mulligan, who was a brave man, had sought out the mighty champion of the Xyphias.

And at the moment in which our amazon, cutlass in hand, boarded the Sea Scourge, these two met; and Justin's other assailants fell back at a signal from their captain. And now, between the two, stroke followed stroke in rapid succession, each very adroitly parried. At length Mulligan lost his temper, and with that his presence of mind, and made a fierce lunge at his adversary's heart, which was quickly parried, and before he could come to his guard again, Justin brought down a crushing stroke upon his head that felled him to the deck.

But as he was in the act of leveling this fatal blow, he caught a glimpse of a seaman with a cocked pistol pointed close to his head. He thought that his time had come; he mentally prayed that his soul might be received in heaven; he heard the report of the pistol, felt the ball whizz through his hair, and thanking the Lord for his preservation, he turned and saw—what? The seaman's pistol arm resting on the cutlass with which Britomarte had struck it up!

To her, then, he owed his life. But there was not an instant of time to think of that now. Quick as lightning his arm flew up and his steel fell, crunching through the brain of the seaman, who dropped lifeless to the deck. Every act in this passage of arms passed with the rapidity of thought. There was not more than a minute occupied in the felling of Mulligan, the aiming of the pistol, the striking it up by Britomarte, and the braining of the assassin by Justin.

Now heedless of the battle storm that raged around them, Justin dropped upon one knee, as a knight before his queen, and, seizing the hand of his beloved he exclaimed with deep emotion:

"I owe my life to you!"

"I have owed mine many times to you. Thank Heaven that you are saved!"

After the fall of their captain was known to them, the pirate crew submitted, crying for quarter.

The Sea Scourge was now the prize of the Xyphias.

And down came the Stars and Bars, and up ran the glorious old flag!

CHAPTER XXXVII

VICTORY

As soon as the crew of the Sea Scourge had surrendered, Captain Yetsom ordered them below and closed the hatches.

Then he detailed a small party of his own men and placed them under the command of Midshipman Bestor, to take charge of the prize, and ordered the others to their own ship.

As soon as he regained the deck of the Xyphias he sent for Lieutenant Ethel, and passed down into the cabin.

A strange weakness, dizziness and dimness of sight was creeping over him.

"Why, what is this?" he said to himself. "It can not be from that scratch! Bosh! I must get a glass of brandy."

But in the act of crossing to his locker, he turned giddy, reeled, grasped at the nearest object for support, and then fell forward upon his face to the cabin floor in a deep swoon.

At the same moment Lieutenant Ethel was in the act of

He instantly ran to his assistance, exclaiming anxiously:

"Captain! what is the matter? Are you ill?—wounded?"

Receiving no answer he placed his hands under his captain's arms to lift him up, and in doing so perceived that his coat was saturated with some warm glutinous matter. Instantly withdrawing his hands for examination, he found them covered with thick blood. In serious alarm now, he turned the captain and drew him gently to a spot where the fresh air could blow upon him, and then he ran to the head of the companion ladder, and, calling to the sentinel stationed near, he said·

"Scribner, pass the word to the cockpit that the captain requires the presence of the surgeon immediately in his cabin."

Ethel, for his part, rushed back to the side of the captain and began rapidly to unbutton his coat and vest. When he came to his underclothing he found it crimson with blood, that had flowed so freely as even partially to fill the space between his top-boots and the limbs they covered.

The young lieutenant groaned in anguish of spirit, for he loved his captain as man seldom loves man.

The surgeon now came down the companion ladder. Seeing Ethel bending over the prostrate form of the captain and tearing away the blood-stained clothing, he rushed forward, exclaiming:

"What's all this? What's the matter? The captain wounded? Good Lord! he is one clot of blood! In Heaven's name, sir, why was I not told before?"

"I came in here but a moment ago and found him lying flat on his face," replied the young man, in a heartbroken voice. "Oh, doctor, is he dying?"

"I hope and trust not. He has fainted from loss of blood."

"I loved him as a father! he was so good, so kind! Oh, doctor, is he wounded mortally?"

"How can I tell until I examine the wound? Here, take hold of this sleeve of his undershirt while I take the other. Now draw gently. There, the wound.

And what a wound! I fear it is all over with our poor captain! Come, Ethel! stop that! This is no time for blubbering like a woman, my boy! A minute, as we use or waste it, may save or lose our captain's life. Here, take the water in this basin and gently swab the blood away from that wound, which I perceive has nearly stopped bleeding, while I run for my instruments," said the doctor, rushing out of the cabin as fast as his fat legs could carry him.

No braver man than young Ethel had boarded the Sea Scourge that day; yet as soon as the doctor was gone, he burst into sobs that shook his whole frame; and his fast-falling tears mingled freely with the water with which he washed his captain's wound. He did his work as tenderly and as thoroughly as possible, and had perfectly cleansed the wound by the time the doctor returned. And even to the young man's unprofessional eye the wound looked less formidable than at first.

The doctor got down upon his knees and made a very careful examination, and then he lifted his head and exclaimed:

"Thank Heaven! it is not near so bad as I had expected to find it! It is an ugly flesh wound at worst, and he'll weather it. You see, a pistol ball has entered here on his right side and furrowed its way clear across the chest and come out under the left arm. No wonder he bled so much. But he could bear it. He could bear it!"

While the doctor spoke he lost no time; he was busy cutting low, slim strips of sticking plaster, with which he gradually brought the ragged edges of the wound together, securing them by laying the strips at right angles with the length of the wound, and then carefully bandaging.

When this was done, with young Ethel's assistance, he washed his patient thoroughly, put fresh clothes on him and laid him on his bed.

Lastly the doctor administered restoratives, that soon brought the captain to himself.

On recovering ... om
looked his ... his

bed, and, seeing Dr. Brown and Lieutenant Ethel bending anxiously over him, he feebly inquired:

"Why am I here? What has happened?"

"You have been wounded, but not seriously. You fainted from loss of blood and fell upon your cabin floor. Lieutenant Ethel found you and called me. And we have dressed your wound, and undressed you and put you to bed, where you are to remain for the present."

The captain writhed and frowned. Of all things he abhorred to lie inactive in bed at this crisis. But he recognized the truth of the doctor's words, and he submitted to necessity; the more readily because he felt that the few words he had spoken had already exhausted him. He rested to recover a little strength, and then he beckoned young Ethel to stoop close to his lips.

"Mr. Ethel," he whispered, "you will take command of both ships. See the prisoners secured according to your best judgment. Make all necessary repairs. Then—shape for Cape Town."

Having with difficulty given these orders, Captain Yetsom turned his face to the wall, and, from sheer exhaustion, fell asleep.

Dr. Brown and Lieutenant Ethel left the cabin. The doctor went to attend to his other cases. The lieutenant hastened to attend to the important duties that now devolved upon him.

Meantime, where were our two young friends, and what were they about? Justin and Britomarte had returned to the Xyphias with the officers and crew. As soon as the general congratulations upon the victory were over, Justin walked apart with Britomarte, and taking her unresisting hand in his, looked upon it with intense affection for a while, and then, in a low and earnest voice, he said:

"You have gloriously redeemed your word, my sister. You have borne a heroic part in this engagement. You have passed where the cannonading has been heaviest, and you have risked your life in the thickest of the fight! But the ——— oh, forever and forever thank God that this white hand has been raised only to save and to heal, and not to slay."

His voice, his whole frame so shook with emotion as he uttered these last words, that she caught the contagion and dropped her head upon his shoulder and burst into tears. He drew her closer to his heart and leaned over her.

The rough sailors passing near saw all this, but they had long ago set this pair down as betrothed lovers, and their only feeling was of sympathy with them.

"By ganny!" said one gray old sea dog, as he passed, "if I could find a gal as spunky as that one, I'd spark her myself, old as I am!"

Justin bent over Britomarte, delicately soothing her, more by looks and touch than by words. At last he said:

"Do you know—can you imagine, dearest, how deeply, doubly grateful I am to Divine Providence that it is to you I owe my life? A good gift is always precious, but more precious from those we love and most precious from the one we love most!"

"Brother Justin," she said, raising her head and smiling through her tears, "do not make more of this matter than it really is. I, too, am deeply grateful that I was enabled to save one who first saved me, and who for two long years toiled hard to keep me from starvation on that desert island. Say no more about that, brother; but oh! devoutly thank God with me that he has protected you through all the dangers of this dreadful day!"

"I do—I do, Britomarte! that He has protected, not me alone, but us, for you have been exposed to as great danger as any here. Oh, Heaven, when I think of that I——"

"Brother Justin," interrupted Britomarte, recovering her old tone, "whatever we do, don't let us grow sentimental."

"We will not. But this I will say, and you must hear: By one of the most heroic acts that man or woman ever dared, at the most imminent risk of your own life, you have saved mine. But I tell you now, Britoma[rte, the life you have saved] is worhless, and worse than worthless to me, unless you will allow me to devote it henceforth and forever to you!"

Again his voice and his whole frame shook with the intensity of his emotions. She, too, was deeply agitated, but with a queenly effort she regained the sovereignty over herself and answered gravely:

"I am ashamed of you, brother Justin That sentiment was quite unworthy of the mighty champion of the Xyphias, who carried terror into the hearts of the Sea Scourgers. Devote your life to God and to his suffering humanity, and leave me to do the same."

And she was about to leave him to return to her wounded in the cockpit, when something in his aspect, that was not sentiment, or passion, or anything like either, alarmed her.

"Justin—brother! how ill you look! What is the matter? Is it possible that you are wounded?" she breathlessly demanded.

"Fatigued, dear sister, fatigued."

"But you are so pale?"

"Have you not seen me as pale as this after a day's work on the island?"

"Yes, sometimes, when the weather was very warm "

"Well, the work has been very warm to-day. Never heed me, sister. A little rest will set me all right, and then I shall be able to give some assistance to the officers, until they reduce this chaos to order again."

Very slowly and reluctantly Britomarte left him, and went down into the cockpit to send a messenger to look for Judith, while she herself gave her services to the wounded.

As soon as Britomarte was out of sight, Justin tottered to the nearest gun carriage, and sat down upon it, utterly unable to move a step further.

In the hand to hand fight on board the Sea Scourge, he had been half conscious of receiving a wound, though in the excitement of battle he had paid no attention to it; but when the fight was over and the excitement subsided, he was made fully aware, by a sharp pain under his right arm, and a trickling sen sation, that he was wounded and bleeding. Even then, not wishing to part with Britomarte, he had retained her at his side until an approaching faintness warned him that to save her from the knowledge of his condition, he must let her go. Therefore he spoke of Judith, that Britomarte might go in search of her and give him the opportunity to look to his wound. His lifeblood was flowing fast away, his strength was failing him, yet he gave no utterance to suffering, lest he should distress her whom he loved more than life.

Now that she had left him, it was with a sigh of intense relief he sank down upon his rude seat. He felt that he had not power to reach his cabin, and that he must look to his wound as he sat.

He called to a seaman passing near, and desired his assistance. He also sent word to the sentry at the cabin door not to let the women out until he should give the word.

Then, with the help of the seaman, he took off his clothes and came to the wound.

It was not a severe one, though it had bled so freely. He had been struck from behind with some long, sharp weapon that had entered near the armpit, passed through the flesh of the right side, and come out through the skin near the breast bone.

The other sailors, seeing Justin stripped to his waist and covered with blood, came running to him with expressions of alarm and sympathy, for by his bravery and kindness he had become a general favorite.

They were all vociferous in their demands for the surgeon. But Justin checked them with a word.

"My good friends," he said, "there are many poor fellows who need the surgeon much more than I do; let him attend to them first." And then he sent a cabin boy for some water, towels, and clean clothes from his stateroom.

At this moment Lieutenant Ethel came out of the cabin. Seeing the men grouped idly around the gun carriage, he came up to order them to their duties when, perceiving the state of Justin, he exclaimed:

"Good heaven, Mr. Ross...! You wounded, too?"

"Yes; but very slightly. Give yourself no uneasiness, lieutenant."

"Has the surgeon been sent for?"

"No, and pray do not send for him. Leave him to attend to the poor fellows who need him more than I do."

"I insist upon sending for him. All our badly injured men have been looked to. And now that I see your hurt is not the trifle you would make it out to be. Here, Jones, go down to the cockpit and desire the surgeon to come up at once. Men, to your duties!"

The messenger went on his errand. The seamen dispersed at the order. And soon the good doctor came.

"Ah! Mr. Rosenthal wounded? I thought it hardly possible for you to have escaped, if all were true that I had heard of you. Not badly hurt, I hope? Let me see! This fellow had struck at you from behind, and with a dagger, too. May Satan fly away with the cowardly assassin! If he can be identified, he ought to be hanged!"

"Never mind him now! I don't care to have him identified. And I don't think the wound severe."

"No, it is not severe! A few days' rest and regimen will set you all right."

The doctor soon closed the wound, and then told Justin to lean on his arm while he led him to his stateroom.

But Justin asked the doctor first to send down to the cabin, and get the women out upon some pretence, as he did not wish to distress Miss Conyers with needless fears.

"Miss Conyers! Why, bless you, my dear fellow, I left Miss Conyers in the cockpit hovering like an angel of mercy over the poor wounded sailors there, ministering to their wants, alleviating their sufferings and bringing smiles to faces that before her coming had been wrung with anguish! She is a lovely woman," said the doctor.

The doctor now supported his patient to the state-room, laid him in the berth, and after a few moments left him in a refreshing sleep.

CHAPTER XXXVIII

EXPIATION

Among the killed on board the Xyphias was Captain Spear.

Whether it had been owing to his long enforced abstinence from his bane, strong drink, or to the long hours of solitude giving him ample time for reflection on the desert island, or to earlier and holier associations revived, or to all these influences combined, I do not know; but it is certain that a gradual change for the better had been stealing over this man for some time before the sea fight.

Up to the day of the engagement he had had the freedom of the ship. On that day, however, in the beginning of the action, Captain Yetsom, meeting him on deck, had said:

"I know how hard it is for a brave man to be cooped up in his quarters while a battle is going on, but prudential considerations oblige me to send you to yours. Were you at large here unforeseen accidents might place it in your power to do us much injury."

"Captain Yetsom," said Spear, speaking earnestly and seeking to meet the eye of the commander of the Xyphias, "if you will give me the freedom of your deck during this engagement, I promise you upon my sacred honor that I will take no part in it against you or for your enemy. I owe the dogs who deserted me no love or service, Heaven knows! And even should circumstance place it in my power to harm you or aid them, I will do neither. I swear it in the hearing of high Heaven!"

Captain Yetsom looked into the eyes that had been seeking his so earnestly, and saw there such good faith as won his confidence.

"Well—I will trust you," he said, and hurried off to his duties.

Spear had promised no more than this.

All through the exciting chase he had remained a silent, inactive spectator, brooding mournfully over—what?

Officers and men, passing rapidly on their hurried errands, sometimes glanced at this sombre figure like a statue there, and wondered carelessly what his thoughts and feelings might be.

And what were they in truth? Who could tell? Was his love for the old flag stealing over him? Did he remember how his father, now in his grave, had sailed and served under it for more than forty well-spent years? How that brave and patriotic father had taught him to love and honor it as the emblem of his nation, the safeguard of liberty, the ægis under which the oppressed of all the earth found or hoped to find protection? Or did he remember his own stainless and promising youth when he had been the pride of his father, the joy of his mother, the idol of his brothers and sisters, and the very life's life of her, the fair one, dearer than all the rest, who was to have been his wife, but from whom the sins of his manhood had utterly divided him.

Ah, seduced by evil counselors, misled by specious arguments, tempted by ambition, and weakened by that growing vice, he had suffered himself to be drawn in and hurried down into that malebogle, in which so many brave, misguided spirits perished! He had deserted the old Flag—he had raised his hand against it!

I cannot speak here with assurance, for I gathered these antecedents of this man from another source than his lips; but I think it must have been memories like these that caused the sobs and tears that shook his broad chest and flowed down his bronzed cheeks as he stood again under the old Flag, among the men who were fighting for it. I say no one could read his heart or tell his thoughts and feelings; but many saw his actions and heard the few words he uttered.

"God have mercy on me, what have I been doing? God forgive me, for I have been mad, I think.'"

While he had been standing thus absorbed, entranced, by the memories of the past and the pains of the present, the storm of battle had been gathering all around him.

The ships had been manoeuvring and were now abreast of each other, pouring in their broadsides

The tremendous crash of the reports aroused him. He started up, his eyes kindled with a new resolution, and he watched his opportunity to put it in practice.

It came. He saw a brave gunner fall. He sprang to fill his place, and served the gun until he was relieved. After that he threw himself into the action with all his soul, now serving a gun that was short handed, now, cap in hand, cheering on the men. He drew attention from all. Many a brave old soldier, in the midst of the battle, found time to grasp his hand, saying

"You are one of us still, God bless you!" or words to that effect. One earnest old gunner of the order of men who prayed and fought gave him a grip, exclaiming, with more cordiality than coherence:

"'There is more joy in Heaven over one,' et cetera, and 'go thou and do likewise.'"

On seeing his zeal and devotion, Justin found time once to dart to his side and say:

"Heaven bless you for your noble example! I had done you injustice in the past! Forgive me now!"

"You did me no injustice, Mr. Rosenthal I had given you too much reason by word and deed to think the worst of me. I was never so evil as I made myself out to be, however; though evil of late have been my days Enough! that is past! And I am offering up my life in expiation now"

He was indeed He never shrank from duty or from danger. And, not ten minutes after these words had left his lips, a cannon ball from the enemy struck and cut him in two. And thus at last was his promise to his dying father grandly redeemed.

To return from this episode.

Lieut . . . . the forehold of the X;pnies . . . . the prisoners. Then he mustered his men under arms, passed over to the Sea Scourge, ordered the hatches to be taken off and the prisoners to come up on deck

One hundred and nineteen men responded to the call, and were all marched to their place of confinement, with the exception of the officers, who were furnished quarters with the officers of the Xyphias.

As soon as the prisoners were secured, a portion of the ship's company were set to putting the Xyphias in order. The decks were swabbed, the rigging righted, and all traces of the late conflict so effectually removed that she began again to look like one of our tidy men-of-war, and not like a cross between a shipwreck and a butcher's shambles.

Lieutenant Ethel, with the surgeon and another portion of the crew, went over to the Sea Scourge to attend to her remaining wounded and to put her to rights.

The injured men on the upper deck having been already removed and relieved, the lieutenant and the surgeon passed at once to the lower deck, where a sight of horror met their eyes.

The wounded, dying and dead lay scattered thickly around. The groans of the living were more appalling than the ghastliness of the dying or the dead.

All that were still breathing were at once tenderly removed to the cockpit, where the surgeon of the Xyphias, assisted by the surgeon of the Sea Scourge, dressed their wounds, administered opiates, or in other ways sought to alleviate their sufferings.

Body after body of the dead was brought up, sewed in a sail-cloth winding sheet, with a weight at head and foot, and solemnly consigned to the deep, to remain until that dread day when "the sea shall give up its dead."

This sacred duty having been performed, the deck was swabbed and put in as good order as circumstances would admit.

The carpenter now reported that he had plugged all the shot-holes of both ships under or near the water lines, and sounded their pumps, and that neither of them

Lieutenant Ethel then ordered that the further repairs needed by both vessels should be continued by watches both day and night, so that the benefit of the present calm might not be lost.

And then he went below and turned in to take the rest he so much needed.

Britomarte, on leaving Justin, had gone, as I said, down into the cockpit to look after her own especial cases among the wounded, and also to dispatch a messenger in search of Judith. An hour passed away, during which Britomarte had ministered to the wants of all her patients, and at the end of which her messengers returned without any news of Judith, who was nowhere to be found.

Miss Conyers now felt seriously alarmed lest some fatal accident had happened to the girl, or lest she, under delirium of terror, had cast herself into the sea. In the midst of this anxiety, however, it occurred to her that at the cessation of the cannonading Judith might have returned to the cabin. With this hope Britomarte repaired thither.

She had scarcely reached the foot of the companion ladder, when she thought she heard a groan coming from the direction of the stateroom occupied in common by herself and Judith.

She hurried thither, and opened the door, and there lay the girl tossing and moaning in high fever, brought on by excitement.

"Lord bless ye, ma'am, is it yerself sure? Troth I thought you had forgot me entirely, and left me here to perish alone. Foix I'm burning up, so I am. May the divil fly away wid all say fights, for this has been the death of me, so it has. Sure, I'm murthered complately—from head to fut. And you left me to me fate so you did."

"Hush, Judith! You must be quiet, or you will grow worse. Try to compose yourself now, while I go and get something that will do you good," said Miss Conyers, laying a towel wet with cold water upon the girl's burning head.

Then she went in search of a surgeon and procured

Then she renewed the wet towel, rearranged the disordered bed, darkened the room and left Judith to repose. If any of my readers imagine this portrait of Judith to be overdrawn, I can assure them it is not. I knew this girl for years. She was just the "medley of contraries"—the mixture of wit and folly, good sense and absurdity, spirit and cowardice, selfishness and self-devotion, that I represent her to have been. I lost her, and could have better spared a better."

From the cabin Miss Conyers returned to the cockpit, to her wounded, bringing smiles to the faces of the poor sufferers, as she tenderly eased their positions, turned their pillow, bathed their faces and hands, or held cooling drinks to their feverish lips.

It was while Britomarte was engaged in this humane work, that the surgeon was summoned on the upper deck. But little did she imagine that he was called to attend Justin or that Justin had the slightest need of his care.

Britomarte did not confine her attentions to the wounded on the Xyphias. But when she had done all she could for them she visited the Sea Scourge and ministered to the sufferers there.

The next morning the repairs upon the Xyphias were completed, so that she was once more in good fighting order.

The men were then transferred to the Sea Scourge to expedite the work there. Lieutenant Ethel found the decks of the prize clean and sweet, the wounded men in their hammocks, and the work progressing so rapidly that the privateer would be fit for sailing in twenty-four hours.

Britomarte, worn out by her arduous labors of the day before, slept very late that morning; and upon entering the cabin she found that the breakfast had been long set. She was very hungry, but not knowing the condition of her companions, she patiently waited for their appearance, only wondering at their prolonged absence.

At length the steward entered the cabin, and she inquired what detained the gentlemen

The masters desired not to alarm her, answered

that neither Captain Yetsom nor Mr. Rosenthal had risen yet.

So Britomarte, amazed at their self-indulgence and unsuspicious of their true state, breakfasted alone, and then took in a cup of tea and a round of toast to Judith, whose fever was now gone, but who still kept her bed from the weakness of reaction.

Finding still that her companions did not appear, she became uneasy and went to seek the surgeon and inquire of him the true reason of their absence.

Dr. Brown informed her that they were both wounded, though not dangerously; and that he had ordered both of them to keep quiet for a day or two.

"My Brother Justin wounded! And I not know it until now! Oh, Dr. Brown, I must go to him at once!" she exclaimed, in excessive agitation.

"No, Miss Conyers, you must not—you of all persons."

"But I will go! Who shall hinder me? And why should I not? Why shouldn't I, who have cared for so many wounded seamen who had no claims upon me but those of common humanity, go and wait on my own—" her voice broke down in tears.

"Sweetheart?" said the doctor, archly, finishing her sentence in his own way.

"No, sir! my own soul's brother!" flash'd Britomarte.

The doctor shrugged his shoulders.

"I ask you why I may not minister to my brother, as I have ministered to scores of strangers?"

"Because your presence would agitate him as it could not possibly agitate strangers. He must be kept quiet to-day. His wound is not a dangerous one, as it is now, but there are incident upon even slight wounds such things as irritative fevers, which are bad, and erysipelas, which is worse."

Britomarte sank down upon a coil of rope and covered her face with her hands.

"Now don't do that! You, the 'Battle Queen' of yesterday, to give way to-day because your—ahem! well! brother, since you will have it, brother—is wounded! I tell yo

The worst of it is he concealed it too long. He concealed it until every other case was attended to—noble fellow! Now see here! I told you of what might possibly happen in case he should be excited, only to prove to you how necessary it is that he should be quiet. Now I will tell you what I will do with you. I will promise that if he is kept still today, he shall see you for a few minutes to-morrow or next day."

But Britomarte was too much agitated to trust herself to speak. She started up, flew to her stateroom, flung herself upon her berth and burst into tears.

"Justin wounded," she sobbed, "and concealing his wound from all others until even the humblest sufferer was served! And concealing it even from me, to save me pain! How patient, how noble, how self-sacrificing he always is! Justin wounded! and ah! much more seriously than the doctor will admit. And if he should die! disappear from the earth forever! I could not live on it! I could not! Heavenly Father spare him and save me this dread trial that I could not bear!"

Yes, truly the "Battle Queen" of yesterday was a weeping woman to-day.

The next morning, on waking, both Captain Yetsoen and Mr. Rosenthal found themselves much better, though still so heavily oppressed with languor and weariness that they dozed away the whole day, indifferent to all that was going on around them and unconscious almost even of their own existence.

Britomarte again breakfasted alone, feeling very miserable. She had never realized so keenly how vitally necessary to her happiness Justin's presence was. And she was not permitted to see him that day.

In the course of the forenoon Judith came out of her stateroom, cross and sulky, and muttering maledictions upon the sea, the ships, the guns, and most things in general.

Meanwhile the calm still continued and the works on the prize were all but finished.

On the third morning our two wounded friends were very

Justin especially, whose hurt was the least severe, felt his strength so much revived, and his wish to see Britomarte so urgent, that in the afternoon he arose and dressed himself and crept out into the cabin.

Britomarte was seated with her elbow resting upon the center table, and her forehead bowed upon her hands in deep thought.

Justin came quietly to her side, and resting his hand upon the table, whispered softly:

"Britomarte!"

Like a deer she sprang up, her hands extended, her whole face beaming with joy, as she exclaimed:

"Oh, Justin! I am so glad to see you! I have missed you so much! I wished to go and nurse you, but the doctor would not allow it. How is your wound? And why did you conceal it from me?"

"Dear Britomarte, I did not wish to distress you with groundless anxiety. My injury was slight. I am nearly well now, and I owe more than I can tell to my short confinement by the welcome you gave me. But yourself? I see that you have been a ministering angel among the wounded. How have you escaped ill?" he answered, bowing down upon her with infinite tenderness and solicitude.

"I have borne everything well, except your wound and your concealment of it from me. Oh, Justin—"

"Well, well dear, see, I am all right now, quite right," he answered cheerily.

But even as he spoke, she saw his lips grow pale and a film pass over his eyes, but she governed her alarm, and said gently:

"Justin, come and lie down there on the sofa, hush! you must not speak. I will help you to lie, and I will get a book and sit down by you and read to you, but if you attempt to talk I will leave you."

"Well, I submit myself to you, my gentle nurse," said Justin, willingly enough obeying her directive, for he felt that he was not strong enough to sit up or self denying enough to leave Britomarte's company.

So she led him to the sofa and eased him gently down upon it, and arranged the cushions under his head and

Then she drew a chair to his side, and sat down to read to him. Her right hand held the book on her lap, her left hand lay softly on his forehead. She read purposely in a low, monotonous tone.

Presently, as if her touch and tone were mesmeric, his eyes grew heavy, then closed. She shut her book, and continued to watch him until gradually her head drooped lower and lower, until her forehead rested on the arm of the sofa, and her beautiful, heavy, dark hair, slipping from its fastening, fell down and mingled with the auburn curls that shaded his pale forehead.

Both were asleep.

Judith came in and found them so. She stood contemplating them a few minutes, and then her Irish enthusiasm burst forth.

"Och, sure, what a beautiful picter entirely. It's like the babes in the woods, so it is, or Adam and Ave in the garden iv Aden, before the sarpint entered it. Sure it's made for aich other they are, the darlints. Troth meself wonders the chaplain did not marry thim out iv hand, the jewels. Faix it's a pair iv slaping beauties they are, the angels. And meself will sit down and guard thim."

And Judith drew a chair up to the sofa, and set herself squarely before them, losing all consciousness of her own pains, injuries and misadventures, in the satisfaction with which she contemplated this picture of beauty and repose.

CHAPTER XXXIX

A GHOST APPEARS TO JUDITH

The ships were now both repaired as well as they could be at sea. Passed Midshipman Bestor was placed upon the Sea Scourge with a prize crew, and ordered to sail when the Xyphias should, and if possible, to keep her always in view, or if he should lose sight of her, to shape for Cape Town and meet her there. The prisoners were then divided, half of them being sent back to the Sea Scourge.

By eight bells every preparation was completed for sailing. But there was no wind. A dead calm still prevailed. All that night and the next day it continued. But on the ensuing morning, just before dawn, Lieutenant Ethel was awakened, and notified that the wind was rising.

He sprang up and hurried on deck, where he found the men all alert, and in the highest spirits. And soon both ships were bounding on their course.

From this day everything went on smoothly; wind and weather favored them; the ships kept in consort, and no unpleasant event occurred to mar the prosperity of the voyage.

Justin, under Britomarte's fostering care, rapidly improved. It was strange to see with what a motherly tenderness and solicitude this young girl guarded and guided the sick man who was at least ten or twelve years her elder. She would not permit him to overexert himself in any way; she forestalled all his needs; she walked with him, sang to him, and amused his waking hours or soothed him to repose.

Poor Justin! this was a great joy and a great trial to him. He idolized her, but he was forbidden to tell her so. He was in raptures and he was in despair. He considered himself the happiest man alive, and he wished himself at the bottom of the sea.

Notwithstanding which he got well so fast under Britomarte's fostering care, that on the seventh day from his sailing his name was stricken from the sick list.

Captain Yetsom also improved very rapidly under the skillful treatment of the surgeon.

On the tenth day, at night, every one was awakened by the lusty cry

"Land ho!"

And on the morning of the eleventh, coming on deck, they found themselves anchored in Table Bay.

Here the captain announced that they should remain for twenty-four hours, as he had to see the American consul, and parole a portion of his prisoners.

Under these circumstances, Justin and Britomarte,

taking Judith with them, went into Cape Town, and spent the day with their hospitable friends, the Burneys, at Silver Tree Villa.

In the meantime Captain Yetsom, who had now resumed command of his ship, went on shore, and made arrangements with the American consul there concerning the prisoners of the Sea Scourge, who he proposed should be paroled and put ashore at Cape Town. This measure, when made known to the prisoners, was met by different individuals in different ways. Some among them who were vagrants belonging to no particular country, such as might be picked up at any seaport to serve under any flag, were willing enough to be turned loose at Cape Town, where they would be sure to find employment.

Others, chiefly American and Irish, rather than be left in a foreign port, were willing to take the oath of allegiance to their own or their adopted government, and to ship as seamen on board the Xyphias, which, by reason of the large number killed and wounded, was now short handed

Others again were neither willing to remain at Cape Town nor to take service on the Xyphias, and they earnestly exclaimed against the enormity of Captain Yetsom's cruelty in turning them loose upon a foreign shore.

Captain Yetsom, when he good naturedly condescended to notice these grumbling remonstrances, answered them in a few words "Military, or rather naval necessity!" The Xyphias, going on her cruise after more privateers, could not be encumbered with prisoners—could not be converted into a floating gaol; and the prisoners could not be trusted on the Sea Scourge, which was to be sent home.

So these malcontents were left with the others.

The prisoners thus disposed of, Captain Yetsom turned his attention to other and equally important matters.

He relieved Passed Midshipman Bestor of his charge, and ordered Lieutenant Ethel to take command of the prize to take her home to New York. He reinforced the crew of the prize with the best seamen from the Xyphias, and he wrote his dispatches to the Secretary of the Navy, describing the capture of the privateer, praising the conduct of his officers and crew, especially recommending Lieutenant Ethel for promotion.

Britomarte, Justin and Judith were to go home on the prize. So on the afternoon of that day all their luggage was transferred from the cabin of the Xyphias to the quarters prepared for them on the Sea Scourge. But they themselves, yielding no less to their own inclinations than to the solicitations of the captain, determined to remain with their friends on the man-of-war all that night, and up to the hour of sailing the next morning.

Very early the next morning all was cheerful bustle on both ships, making ready to sail.

Lieutenant Ethel came on board the Xyphias to receive his captain's last orders, and then immediately returned to the Sea Scourge.

But not until the last hour, when the sails were set and the anchor was weighed, did Britomarte and Justin take a last leave of Captain Yetsom and his officers, and amid many mutual good wishes leave the deck of the Xyphias for the yawl boat that was to take them to the Sea Scourge.

When all was ready for sailing, the two vessels fired their signal guns and stood out to sea, the Xyphias shaping her course to the northeast, and the Sea Scourge to the northwest.

Britomarte, Justin and Judith stood in the stern of the Sea Scourge, leaning over the taffrail, and watching the Xyphias as long as she continued in sight.

On board the Xyphias the doctor and the chaplain stood in a similar position watching them. At intervals Captain Yetsom appeared with the other two, and waved his hat to his friends on the Sea Scourge, and was answered by the waving handkerchiefs of our party.

And this was kept up long after they failed to distinguish each other's faces, and until the ships themselves were out of each other's sight.

One   hich

they left the Cape, Lieutenant Ethel, Justin, Britomarte and a young midshipman were seated around the cabin table engaged in a rubber of whist, when they were all startled by piercing shrieks, followed immediately by the form of a girl, who came pitching, tumbling and rolling down the companion ladder, and fell upon the cabin floor.

All the company around the table sprang up simultaneously. And Justin rushed to Judith and raised her up, while Britomarte eagerly inquired what the matter was.

"Oh, it's the ghost! the ghost!" gasped Judith, beside herself with terror.

"What ghost, girl? Are you mad?" said Justin.

"Oh, the ghost iv me swateheart, sure!" sobbed Judith, white and shaking in her panic.

"Nonsense," laughed Justin; "ghost, indeed! I'd like to see one, for once. What does a ghost look like, Judith?"

"Och, a raw head and bloody bones it was! Ow-oo! Ow-ootch!" she screamed, covering up her face and falling into spasms.

"Give her some brandy," suggested the young midshipman.

And Lieutenant Ethel called the steward, and had a glass of brandy brought immediately and poured down her throat. It seemed to do her good. They set her back in an armchair, and Britomarte said:

"Now, Judith, tell us what alarms you so."

"Lorrd bless ye, ain't I afther telling yez? It was the ghost, sure—the ghost iv me gay Tom, as was dhrowned in the dape say more'n two wears ago!"

"The ghost of Foretop Tom! Judith, you were dreaming!"

"Faix, I wish it was a dhrame itself. But I was wide awake, sure, sitting at the head iv the ladher there, and gazing at a great star, and wondering how far it was off, and what it would be like if one could take howld iv it. And sure I got tired iv that, and I riz up, so I did, and seeing there was none iv thim bastes iv saymen about, I thought I'd take a turn on the deck. And sure I hadn't walked tin steps afore, happening to rise my head, there I saw the ghost iv me gay Tom standing right foreninst me own two looking eyes. Ow-oo! Ow-ootch!"

"Hush, Judith; don't scream so. Tell me what he looked like," said Miss Conyers, convinced in her own mind that the girl had been dreaming.

"Troth, ain't I afther telling yez before? Sure a raw head and bloody bones he was! Thin as a skillippin' pale as a spicter! and tall as the mainmast, wid a white linen cloth bound round his head, and his right fut tied up in a rag! and his left arm in a sling! and he a-laning on a crutch!"

"Judith, it was one of the convalescent wounded men you saw."

"Divil a bit! It was the ghost iv me own Foretop Tom. Sure wouldn't I know it when I saw it standing there foreninst me own two looking eyes! And didn't I like to die wid the fright? And didn't I wish the ship would open and let me down into the say?"

"Did it speak to you, Judith?" laughed Justin

"Spake to me? Lorrd help ye' do you think I was going to wait there for it to spake to me? No, I ran down into the cabin here as fast as me hales would bring me!"

"What do you think the ghost wanted of you, Judith?" inquired Lieutenant Ethel.

This was an unlucky question for Judith's equanimity. It set her speculating in horrors.

"What it wanted iv me, is it? Ah, Lorrd kape us, who can tell! Maybe to warn me iv another shipwreck, whin we would all be dhrowned. Or another say fight, whin we should all be murthered. Or at laste of me own death itself. Sure a ghost niver appears for nothing"

"Never," said Lieutenant Ethel, mischievously.

"Ow-oo! Ow-ootch!" screamed Judith, falling into fresh spasms.

And it became necessary to give her more brandy. And then Miss Conyers coaxed her off into her stateroom and made her go to bed, and sat with her until, under the influence of the brandy she had taken, Judith fell asleep.

"What could have frightened her so?" inquired Miss Conyers, as she came out into the cabin.

"It was as you suggested, either a dream or the figure of one of our convalescent wounded men, I suppose," said young Ethel

And this explanation seemed so plausible that it was adopted by all.

"You have very little good of your attendant, I fear, Miss Conyers. Since I have known her she has certainly been more trouble than use," said the lieutenant.

Britomarte laughed and answered:

"That is because since you have known her she has been in circumstances to draw out all the faults of her character. No one is perfect. But Judith would be a treasure if it were not for her absurd tears—fears of everything—beasts, guns, ghosts—what not."

Saying which Miss Conyers sat down to the table and they finished the rubber of whist.

Next morning, under the influence of the cheerful sunlight, Judith herself was half inclined to laugh at her own superstitious terrors of the preceding night, and to admit that she might have been dreaming or deceived by an accidental likeness. But when evening came again she kept closely in the cabin, and nothing would induce her to leave it

On the next afternoon, being the third day from the first appearance of the mysterious visitor, Miss Conyers left Judith engaged in tidying the cabin, and went up on deck to sit and read. She had not been there more than ten minutes when, with piercing shrieks and streaming hair and wild eyes, Judith came flying toward her and dropped at her feet, and buried her face in her lap.

"In the name of Heaven, Judith, what is the matter now? Are you really going mad?" exclaimed Britomarte.

"It appeared to me again! It appeared to me again!" screamed the girl.

"What?"

"The ghost! It looked in at me through the cabin windys! It had its head tied up in a cloth and its arm in a sling! I know it's come to warn me in me death! I know it has!"

"Judith! you will drive me out of my wits if you go on so. Be quiet," said Miss Conyers, sternly.

"Ow-oo! Ow-ootch!" screamed Judith, clasing Britomarte firmly, and burying her head in her lap.

Miss Conyers beckoned a cabin boy who was passing by, and sent him to ask Mr. Rosenthal to come to her.

And when Justin obeyed the summons, Britomarte pointed to Judith and said, laughing:

"She has seen the ghost again, and is senseless and helpless with terror. Assist me to take her down into the cabin."

With an impatient shrug of his shoulders, Justin complied with the request. And they took Judith down and laid her on the berth of her stateroom.

"It is worse than useless to be dosing this girl with brandy. We shall teach her to drink. Go and bring me a glass of cold water," said Miss Conyers.

And when Justin brought it she made Judith swallow it all.

"What can ail the girl, Justin? Is she losing her reason, do you think?" impatiently inquired Britomarte.

"I think she labors under an optical illusion, incident upon an abnormal condition of the nervous system. She has an excessively nervous temperament, which has been severely tried in the last fortnight," answered Justin.

"Then I must try to have patience with her," smiled Britomarte.

But Judith did not get over her panic till the next morning, and then several days passed without a reappearance of the ghost or the illusion.

At length one evening when the moon was bright, Miss Conyers, instead of going down into her cabin, sat in the stern enjoying the beauty of the night; and presently feeling chilly, she told Judith to go to her stateroom and fetch a shawl.

The girl started to obey; but the next minute uttered a terrific shriek.

Miss Conyers sprang to her feet; and there, not

three yards from her, stood Judith, struck, statue still, with terror, gazing upon—what?

A figure just as she had described the apparition to be—thin as a skeleton, pale as a spectre; and if not as tall as the mainmast, certainly looking preternaturally tall from being so preternaturally lean; his head was bound up in a white cloth, his foot tied up in a rag, his arm in a sling, and himself leaning on a crutch—the ghost of that Foretop Tom who had been drowned more than two years ago.

An icy chill of superstitious horror, that all her will and intellect could not prevent, shot through the veins of Britomarte Conyers.

But the next instant she had governed this feeling; and saying to herself, "I will find out what this means," she walked straight up to the figure and laid her hand on its shoulder.

CHAPTER XL

HOMEWARD

"Who are you, man?" inquired Miss Conyers, looking in the face of the mysterious stranger.

"Me? Ou, I'm just naebody!" answered the apparition, rather sulkily.

"What is your name?"

"Just Tam McAlpine."

"Foretop Tom!"

"Ay, just himsel'."

Miss Conyers sank down upon a coil of ropes, and drew the trembling Irish girl to her side, and then said.

"You have surprised me very much, and you have terrified this girl nearly out of her senses, but I am glad to know that you were saved from the wreck;" then turning to her agitated companion, she said, "Judith, you see it is Tom himself. Why don't you speak to him?"

"Sure I see it now. And I'll spake whin I'm able.

I can't yit!" sobbed Judith, covering her face with her apron, and rocking herself to and fro

"Ay, that will be the way she has treated me ever sin' I foregathered wi' her on the deck. Screeching and rinning fra me as if I had been Auld Nick!" complained the Scotchman.

"No wonder. We all thought that you were drowned more than two years ago. And she took you for your own ghost How were you saved?"

"E'en by a miracle—nae less. When the boat capsized I laid hold of an empty cask, and whilk buoyed me up all night until the tide turned, when I was floated far out to sea. I gave mysel' up for lost, but held on to the cask till my strength was weel nigh spent At length I was seen and picked up by the ither lifeboat, whilk had been beating about all that time. Three days after, when our bread and water was nearly gane, our boat was picked up by an outward bound Dutch merchantman, and we were saved."

"An almost miraculous preservation, indeed. You must have been astonished to see Judith here. Our preservation was quite as strange as your own."

"Ay, and I might e'en ha' ta'en the lass Judith for a ghaist, if I hadna' been tauld by the sailor lads of the castaways lost from the Sultana, and ta'en off the Desert Island by their captain."

"Oh, then you were prepared to see us," laughed Miss Conyers "But still, I don't see how you should be here?"

"I was taken prisoner from the Sea Scourge."

"Oh, ye were, were ye, ye born divil!" exclaimed Judith, uncovering her face, and speaking **for the first** time "And so ye turned pirate and murtherer, did ye? Troth, I'd rather ye'ed been dhrowned in the say, so I had, than ye should have turned cutthroat on me hands."

"Ay! that's the way she's guided me, ever sin' I met her on the deck," grumbled the Scotchman "Will ye hear a mon speak for himsel' before you accuse him, lass?"

"And sure what can ye say for yerse'lf at all, at all,

afther being found upon the Say Scourge among a lot iv divels?"

"Young leddy," said the Scotchman, appealing to Miss Conyers, "will you condescend to speak to the lass and bid her be reasonable?"

"Indeed, McAlphine, I am so pained to hear that you were one of the crew of the Sea Scourge, that I have nothing to say against Judith's natural indignation, said Miss Conyers.

"Ou, ay! a mon gets it on baith sides! May be, young leddy, ye'll let me expleen before you judge me."

"If you can explain to Judith's satisfaction, I should like to hear you do it, McAlpine," said Miss Conyers, gravely.

"Aweel then, after our boat was picked up by the Dutchman, I took service with the captain and went the voyage to Calcutta, and then back to England. After whilk I shipped on a merchantman in St. Catherine's docks, calling hersel' the Sea Scourge, bound for the Indies, and sailing under the Stars and Stripes. And here I will take leave to say that being a native of Ayrshire in Scotland, I owe nae mair allegiance to the Stars and Stripes than I do to the Stars and Garters or to the Stars and Crescent—whilk last I take to be the emblem of the Turk; or to the Stars and Bars, whatever they may represent, or to the stars in conjunction with ony ither creature. It was na, however, until we overhauled a Baltimore clipper that the Sea Scourge ran up the Stars and Bars, and I kenned for the first time that I was shipped on board a preevateer. I had nae choice but to bide where I was, whilk I did until the engagement wi' the Xyphias, when the preevateer was captured."

"And ye fought ag'inst us, ye murthering divil," put in Judith.

"Nay, lass, that was na my duty; I was on the foretop, and na at the guns. I helped to work the ship, that was a'; and e'en that' wi' nae guid will; for I aye argued wi' mysel' that I had been entrapped intil the service of the preevateer; but I could na help mysel' till the fig't was over. I was wounded, as ye see, by a bit splinter that struck my head, and I fell to the deck, breaking my arm and spraining my ankle."

"Tom, is it the truth ye're afther telling me?" inquired Judith, through her tears.

"Ay, lass; what else? D'ye think I would tell ye a lee?"

"Thin, Tom, darlint, I beg your pardon entirely for thinking ill iv ye. Troth——" And here Judith broke down and sobbed.

"Hout, tout, lass! dree your een and sae nae mair," said Tom.

"Tom, ye're a jewel, sure; but how came ye here at all, at all, whin all the prisoners were left at Cape Town except thim that took the oath of illaygiance and shipped on the Xyphias?"

"I tould my tale to the captain, and said I would like to take service on the prize. And when I was able to leave my hammock he granted my petition and put me here."

"Och, Tom, jewel, sure my heart's broke entirely wid the thought iv how I misthrusted and abused ye," said Judith.

"Hout, lass, sae nae mair. D'ye think a bit hard word is gaun to part you and me after a' that's come and gane?"

Miss Conyers had been for some time dropped out of the conversation. And now honest Tom became so extremely sentimental that she really felt herself one too many; and so she arose, and leaving the sweethearts together, she slipped away to her seat in the stern.

There presently her own ill-used lover joined her. And she gave him the solution of the ghost riddle by describing her meeting with Foretop Tom.

"It is singular that I have never chanced to meet him," said Justin.

"I fancy that he has been below in his hammock until lately. He looks scarcely fit for duty now," said Britomarte.

And then as the night was growing damp and chilly, and the lights in the cabin looked cheerful and inviting, Miss Conyers proposed to go below; and they went and finished their evening in music and conversation.

The next day Justin had an interview with Foretop Tom, who was able to tell him much more relating to the rescue of the missionary party than he had learned from the Burneys.

Tom related all that he knew, either from observation or hearsay—how the crew of the lifeboat, finding all their arguments and persuasions vain to induce their captain to desert the ship and join them, and being moved by the tears and prayers of the missionaries' wives, had at last consented to receive the two missionaries, who, being of slight form, they said, would not both together take up much more room than that left vacant by the stout captain. So they had been rescued from the wreck of the Sultana, picked up by the Dutch merchantman, and afterward taken on board by the East Indiaman, which was luckily bound to the very port of Calcutta for which they themselves had sailed in the aill-fated Sultana.

From this time no event occurred to vary the monotony of the sea voyage.

As they drew nearer to the shores of their native country, Justin and Britomarte began to experience an intense and ever deepening anxiety. How, after so long an absence, should they find the friends they had left at home? Were they well? Were they even living? Who could tell? How slow was their approach to their destination! how torturing their suspense!

There came a day when Lieutenant Ethel said:

"In three weeks, if we have good luck, we shall make New York harbor."

And then they counted the weeks, until the morning came when the young commander said:

"If this weather holds we shall be in port in four days."

And then they counted the days until the night arrived in which the lieutenant announced:

"We shall be in New York at dawn to-morrow."

And then they counted the hours. They sat up on deck until a late hour, hoping to be able to make out their native shore before going to rest. But there was no moon; and though the sky was clear and the stars bright overhead, yet the western horizon, on which their line of coast should appear, was veiled with clouds and fogs.

At length, weary with watching, they bade each other good-night and retired to their respective staterooms. Yet even then and there they could not sleep. The keen anxiety as to how they should find their friends, if indeed they should find them at all, and how they should find their country, if civil war had left them a country undivided—chased slumber from their eyes, until near dawn, when, as often happens to night-watchers, they fell asleep from sheer exhaustion, and slept profoundly until a late hour of the morning.

Britomarte was then aroused by a loud rapping at her stateroom door.

She started up, only half awake and much bewildered, and demanded:

"Who is there?"

"Sister, it is I. I have come to tell you that we are anchored in New York harbor," answered the voice of Justin.

With an irrepressible cry of joy Britomarte sprang up, and with hands trembling with delight, began to dress herself. She was as much overjoyed by the announcement as though she had not been confidently expecting it. She was soon dressed and out on deck, where Justin advanced to meet her.

"And all the land is rejoicing in the news of the glorious victory just gained!" he said as he led her on where she could see the forest of shipping in the harbor, and the forest of spires in the great city beyond.

"Thank Heaven! Thank Heaven!" she fervently exclaimed, with a heart too full to utter another word.

"The tide of war has turned, my sister. And the whole city is rejoicing in the news of a glorious victory," repeated Justin.

"You told me that before. Yes, I heard you, and I

thank Heaven for that also. This victory, Justin! Is it a final one?"

"I dare not say that. But the precursor of a final one, we may venture to predict."

"And where was it gained?"

"At Gettysburg."

"At Gettysburg! Why, that is in Pennsylvania."

"Yes, my sister. Lee has invaded Pennsylvania; but has been met at Gettysburg by the Union army under General Meade, and driven back with tremendous loss. The news of the victory has just reached New York, and the city is mad with joy!"

"This is glorious news to greet us on our arrival!" said Lieutenant Ethel, coming up. "Good-monring, Miss Conyers. Let us congratulate each other."

"With all my heart!" exclaimed Britomarte, cordially grasping the hand that was extended to her.

"Here are the morning papers, Rosenthal. A boat has just come alongside and brought them," continued the young lieutenant showing a half-dozen of the journals of the day, which he immediately divided between Justin, Britomarte and himself.

But all three were really too much excited to compose themselves to reading. They did but devour the telegraphic news containing the brief announcement of the victory of Gettysburg, and then they began to talk about it, and they continued to talk until the stewart came to say that breakfast was on the table.

They went into the cabin and sat down to the table. But who could eat? They drank some coffee and made a pretense of nibbling some bread and meat. But even the fresh eggs and beefsteak, rare luxuries to the voyagers, that the boat had brought alongside that morning in time for their breakfast, could not tempt them.

They soon arose and made preparations to go on shore.

The principal part of Justin's, Britomarte's and Judith's effects had been packed up for several days. All that they had to do now was to put up the few articles that they had left out for their last use.

When this was done they put on their outer garments and were ready to leave the ship—only waiting for Lieutenant Ethel, who had a few last orders to give before accompanying them on shore.

Justin and Britomarte sat in the stern.

"My sister," said the young man, "let me be a brother to you in reality. We are about to leave the ship which has been our home so long. The greater part of our effects has perished in the using, and the greater part of our means is lost. Tell me now, as you would tell your brother, what are your plans for the future, Britomarte?"

"I will," she answered, frankly. "Certainly my wardrobe is rather dilapidated, and nearly three years behind the time; but still, as it is clean and whole, I hope it will be considered decent and passable. For the rest I have about thirty dollars in gold, which you saved with my other effects from the wreck. This will suffice to take me to Washington, and keep me for a few days.

"And then?"

"As Heaven wills."

Justin groaned.

"Oh, Britomarte, my beloved! that you would give me a legal right to protect you!"

"Justin! no more of that I implore you, if we are to retain even the semblance of friendship," she exclaimed.

"It is but a semblance on your part, at least, I sometimes think," said Justin, bitterly; then quickly repenting the injustice of his words, he added—"But no! you saved my life at the most imminent hazard of your own. Yes, your friendship, Britomarte, passes the love of other women. Yet, oh, my soul! why is it, why, that you abjure the only relation in which we can rationally stand to each other? Well, well—I will not ask you. I will try to be silent on that subject— silent forever! I——" his voice quite broke down and he covered his working features with his hand.

She looked at him and turned pale with the excess of her own emotions. She laid her hand tenderly upon his.

"Justin! b   t   st brother! I am n t worth

all this feeling! indeed, indeed I am not, Justin. I would die to give you content—Heaven knows that I would. I would die, but I cannot marry you, Justin! I cannot!"

"I shall never again ask you to do so," he mournfully replied: "I shall—as soon as I see you safe to Washington, and meet my father and my sister—I shall enlist in the army, and in discharging the high duty that I owe my country I shall seek to forget my private griefs."

"Yes, do so, Justin! do so, dearest brother! and my prayers will follow you, and the favor of Heaven shall be upon you! And if you are not happy, you will still be blessed, since all who do their duty are so."

"But it is not of myself that I think; it is of you— of you! So young, so beautiful, and—forgive me, Britomarte—so poor and friendless! When I think of that, and of your obstinacy, all my strength and manhood desert me!"

"Nonsense, Justin; I have health, intellect, freedom and—thirty dollars in gold to start with. Now, what would you think of a young man in my place with all these advantages? Would you make such a moan over him? Not a bit of it. You would think his prospects exceedingly promising. Now I assure you, Mr Rosenthal, that—all other things being equal—a young woman is quite as well able to take care of herself as a young man."

"But this war! this war!" groaned Justin.

"Exactly. This war will open to me, as to others, a field of duty and usefulness."

While they spoke Judith and Tom had been standing at a short distance away, conversing together.

Now the girl approached Miss Conyers, and stood rolling the strings of her bonnet and blushing deeply.

"What is it, Judith?" the young lady asked, kindly.

"Sure, ma'am, ye know I towld yez that when we landed I should go to me aunt, who keeps a ship chandler's shop on Wather street, and she'd give me a home or get me a service?"

"Yes, Judith; are you not going there? Have you changed your mind?"

"Yes, ma'am, sure; but——"

"But what, Judith? Out with it," said Justin.

"Me gay Tom wants me to marry him," said the girl, turning as red as a cabbage rose.

"Well, Judith?" said Britomarte.

"Well, ma'am, sure you rimimber I promised you nivir to marry any man till the laws was changed so the women could get the upper hand iv the men entirely."

"Not exactly so, Judith; but you promised me never to marry until the cruel laws are changed so that we women may have our rights," amended Britomarte.

"Well, ma'am, and sure ain't that all the same?"

"Not precisely. But what is it you wish to do now, Judith? Do you wish me to protect you aga'nst the importunities of your lover? I will do so effectually."

"Ma'am?"

"Do you wish me to speak to Lieutenant Ethel to order Tom McAlpine to let you alone?"

"Och, no, sure, not for the world, ma'am!" exclaimed Judith, in dismay.

"What do you want, then?"

"Sure, ma'am, I want ye to relaise me from me promise."

"I thought so," laughed Justin.

"To release you from your promise, Judith?" questioned Britomarte, with a mortified air.

"Yes, ma'am, plaise," said Judith.

"You had better do it at once, sister, or she will break through it," said Justin.

"Why do you wish to be released from a promise so freely and deliberately given, Judith?" gravely inquired Miss Conyers.

"Well, you see, ma'am," answered Judith, blushing and looking down and twirling her bonnet strings, "whin I made that same promise nivir to marry a man till the laws was changed, sure I was on that baste iv an island, where there was nivir a man to marry at all, at all—let alone belaiving me gay Tom was dhrowned. So you see it made no differ. But now I'm back in a Christian counthry, and me gay Tom alive and well, and now sure I want to be relaised from me promise."

"Well, Judith, I release you from your promise; but I do it only because I feel sure that if I did not you would break it."

"Sure, ma'am, I thank you kindly, so I do; and so will me gay Tom," said Judith, much relieved, as she turned and walked to rejoin her lover, who stood waiting for her in evident anxiety.

"I never could understand why Judith should call that grave and stolid Scotchman her 'gay' Tom," said Justin.

"She did it first in covert sarcasm, no doubt. And she has since continued it from habit," answered Britomarte.

Lieutenant Ethel now joined them, saying that the boat was ready to take them ashore.

They immediately arose and went to the starboard side of the ship and descended to the boat, followed by the lieutenant.

When they had all taken their places the boat was pushed off. A few rapid strokes of the oar brought them to the pier, where they got off, hailing with deep and heartfelt gratitude their native land.

CHAPTER XLI

NATIVE LAND

"Now," said Lieutenant Ethel, on taking a temporary leave of them, "I have some official business with the authorities here which must be attended to at once; so I shall have to leave you for a while; but I will send a man with you, and when you have found, and are settled in your hotel for the present, you can send him back to the ship with your address, and I will forward all your luggage without further trouble to yourself."

"You pursue us with benefits," said Justin, cordially pressing his hand.

"And if I succeed in seeing the parties I wish to see, and getting my business through in time, I will join you and spend the evening with you. By the way, when do you go on to Washington?"

"By the first train to-morrow. I should go on to-night, but it is abslutely necessary that I shuld write to a friend there to prepare my sister for my arrival. You know that she must long have looked upon me as lost."

"Yes. Then, if you go on to-morrow, I think that I shall be able to accompany you. You are aware that I am the bearer of dispatches to the Secretary of the Navy."

"Certainly."

"Well! Good-morning! I hope you will find pleasant quarters. Martin, do you go with Mr. Rosenthal's party," said the young lieutenant. And then, raising his cap to Miss Conyers, he struck into a by-street and was soon out of sight.

The sailor left in attendance upon Mr. Rosenthal stood hat in hand, waiting orders.

"Martin," said Justin, "go and call a carriage."

The man started on the errand.

Miss Conyers turned to Judith, who was standing with Tom McAlpine by her side.

"Judith," said the young lady, "will you go with me to the hotel for the present?"

"No, thank you kindly, ma'am. When the carriage comes, and I see ye into it, sure Tom will take me to my aunt's. And whin I've seen her, I can go back to the ship and find out from Mr. Martin where yez are stopping. And I will come up this evening to take leave iv yez."

"Very well, Judith," said Miss Conyers, with the tears starting in her eyes, for the companionship of more than two years had very much attached her to the girl.

In a few moments the sailor returned with the carriage, and Justin put Britomarte into it, followed her, and gave the driver an order to drive to a certain hotel, where he had once been in the habit of stopping.

It was

still neighborhood, and it happened to have some pleasant rooms vacant and at the disposal of our party.

As soon as Justin had seen Britomarte comfortably ensconced in her apartment, he went down and dispatched the sailor back to the ship with his address for Lieutenant Ethel.

Then Justin started out on foot to visit his uncle, Friedrich Rosenthal, the great importer, at his place of business in Chambers street. Besides his earnest desire to see a kinsman whom he sincerely loved and esteemed, he felt a great anxiety to hear such news of his father and sister as Mr. Friedrich Rosenthal would probably be able to give him, and also he needed funds to defray his hotel bill and his expenses to Washington, and which his wealthy uncle would readily advance to him.

Justin walked rapidly down the street, sharply turning the corners at the imminent risk of upsetting old ladies and running over little children, until he turned into Chambers street, where every step that brought him nearer to his uncle's house, and to certain news of his beloved relatives, increased his anxiety and took away his breath.

He came in sight of the house and looked up. A strange name occupied the signboard:

Steinfeldt.

There was a sudden pause in all his pulses, and then he hurried into the house, and glanced up and down the long lines of bales upon bales of goods, and upon the strange array of faces behind them.

One of the strangers advanced to meet him.

"What would you look at, sir?"

"Is—has Mr. Friedrich Rosenthal retired from business?" faltered Justin.

"Mr. Friedrich Rosenthal? I am not able to say, sir."

"How long have you been here?"

"Nearly a year, sir," replied the young man, looking surprised at the question.

"Is the—is Mr. Steinfeldt in?"

"Yes, sir; in the counting room I think."

Justin had no cards, but he took a scrap of paper from a writing-table near, and wrote his name, and handed it to the young man, saying:

"Will you take this to Mr. Steinfeldt?"

The youth started off on the errand, and presently returned, accompanied by a stout, respectable-looking, middle-aged man, whose rubicund countenance expressed much concern.

"You are a relative of the late Mr. Rosenthal, I presume?" said this gentleman.

"The late!" echoed Justin, starting back.

"Ah! I am very sorry, exceedingly sorry, to have spoken so thoughtlessly. But, bless my soul, I supposed—— And it has been so long—over a year!" stammered Mr. Steinfeldt, with a face full of sympathy.

"I have been absent from the country for more than two years. I have just returned from India," said Justin, not wishing then and there to enter upon the particulars of his shipwreck.

"Bless my soul, yes! And yet knew nothing of what had happened here. Letters, perhaps, miscarried, or passed you. Dear me! yes, it must be a great shock. Come into my counting-room and recover yourself. Here, Perkins, wine—quick!" said Steinfeldt, leading the way to the back of the warerooms, followed by Justin, who accepted his invitation only that he might learn the particulars of his uncle's death, and if possible, also, some news of his father and sister.

The kind-hearted merchant made him sit down in an easy chair, and, when the wine came, pressed upon him a glass of good old port.

"Yes, it is a great shock. You say that it is more than a year since my uncle died."

"It has been—about fourteen months."

"What was the cause of his death?"

"An attack of pneumonia, that carried him off after about ten days' illness."

"Were any of his family with him?"

"He had no family of his own, as you probably know. He had one brother in Germany, but of course there was no time to summon him. His orphan niece, a young lady from Washington, was with him when he died."

"But he had a brother in Washington—a Lutheran minister," said Justin, feeling his heart stand still.

"Ah, yes—the father of that niece who was with him in his last moments. But he went before. He fell in the first battle of Bull's Run."

"Oh-h-h!" groaned Justin, dropping his head upon the table with such a moan of unspeakable agony that the good merchant sprang to his feet and leaned over him, exclaiming:

"Lord forgive me! And you—you are his son, and I have blurted this dreadful news so suddenly. I was thinking that you were the son of the brother in Germany."

Justin did not answer. His shoulders rose and fell with the great sobs that shook his frame.

The merchant went and closed the door of the room, and drew the bolt, so that no other eyes should look upon the anguish of his fellow-man.

"My sister; where is she?" at length asked Justin.

"She returned to Washington, enriched by the will of her uncle, who constituted her the sole heiress of his immense wealth."

"Enriched in fortune, but, oh, how impoverished in home!" groaned Justin. Then rising, he held out his hand to the merchant, saying, "I thank you, sir, for the information you have given, as well as for your delicate kindness to a heavily-stricken man; and I will bid you good-day."

"Have you a carriage at the door?" inquired the practical merchant.

"No."

"Then I must order one for you. You are not in a condition to walk through the streets, Mr. Rosenthal."

Justin bowed his thanks and resumed his seat.

And when the carriage was announced, he took leave of the friendly merchant and drove to his hotel. He went at once to his own room, and gave way to the sorrow that was almost bursting his bosom.

Some hours later, when he had attained some degree of calmness, he entered the sitting-room, occupied in common by himself and Britomarte.

Miss Conyers was deeply engaged reading an "extra," with further details of the great battle of Gettysburg. On hearing the door open, she looked up, and was at once shocked by seeing Justin enter, looking pale as death, and wearing the traces of deep grief upon his brow.

She threw down the paper and started up to meet him, exclaiming, breathlessly:

"Justin, what is the matter? What have you heard? Erminie?"

He crossed the room and threw himself upon the sofa.

"Erminie!" again gasped Miss Conyers, in breathless anxiety.

"Britomarte, Erminie is alive and well, but—fatherless!" he groaned, covering his face with his hands.

"Oh, Justin! Oh, Justin! Oh, my dear, dear brother!" she cried, and forgetting all her pride, she hastened to his side, put her arms around his neck, drew his head upon her bosom, and bending her face upon it, wept with him.

And her sympathy was an unspeakable consolation.

Later in the day Justin nerved himself to write a letter to his sister, and this letter he inclosed in another one directed to a clerical friend in Washington, to whom he announced his return, and whom he solicited to go and break the news cautiously to Erminie, and prepare her for his arrival. Having posted this letter with his own hand, to insure its going by the evening mail, he returned, and dined alone with Britomarte in their sitting-room.

Lieutenant Ethel, true to his engagement, came to spend the evening with them.

He entered at first, full of a project to take the whole party to the Academy of Music, to see a new opera that was creating a great sensation. But as soon as he saw the faces of Justin and Britomarte, he knew that some distressing intelligence had met them on their arrival, and he forbore to mention his plan. He greeted them both gravely, and took a chair offered him by Justin, and looked from one to the other in mute, respectful sympathy.

"I have received ill news since I saw you last. I have to mourn the death of my father," said Justin, in a low voice, while Britomarte turned away her face to conceal "the teardrops that from pity fell."

"I am very much grieved," said the young lieutenant, simply and earnestly. "Is there anything that I can do for you? If there is, pray order me. It will be a satisfaction to me to be of service to you in any way."

"Thanks, thanks," murmured Justin, earnestly pressing the hand that he had extended to him; "I do not know that you can do anything."

"And now tell me frankly—I came with the intention of spending the whole evening with yourself and Miss Conyers, either here or somewhere else, no matter where—but now tell me candidly, would you rather I should remain here, or go away? Speak freely. If you wish me to remain, I will do so with comfort, or if you wish me to go, I shall not take offense," said young Ethel, earnestly.

"I do not wish you to go, good friend, for your presence will be a comfort to us; neither dare I press you to stay, for the evening will be as dull to you as it is sad to us."

For an answer Lieutenant Ethel took off his gloves and put them in his pocket, and drew his chair nearer to that of Justin.

Britomarte arose and rung for tea to be brought up.

"Will you tell me more? How did your honored father die? That he died the death of the righteous I know, as a matter of course; but was he ill long?"

"He was not ill. He was in the army; he fell at the first battle of Bull Run," answered Justin, gravely, adding: "That is all I know as yet. I learned that much only from the man who has succeeded to my uncle's business. My good uncle, too, has passed away; but that lesser grief is swallowed up in the greater one."

"Ah! yes, yes," sighed the young lieutenant.

A few minutes passed in silence, during which a

waiter appeared with the tea service. When he had arranged the table, Miss Conyers dismissed him, and presided herself over the tea-urn.

"I hope you succeeded in completing your business to-day," said Justin.

"Yes, thank Heaven, that I did," especially as I am now doubly anxious to bear you company on to Washington," replied the young man.

"You are a good fellow, Ethel," said Justin, gravely.

As it was decided that they should leave for Washington by the first train in the morning, it was thought advisable that they should all retire to rest at an early hour that night; so Lieutenant Ethel, at nine o'clock, arose to take his leave.

"I shall go on board again to-night, so as to give my last instructions to Passed Midshipman Allen, whom I shall leave in charge of the prize. But I shall be sure to meet you at the train to-morrow," he said, as he shook hands with Justin and Britomarte, and bowed himself out of the room.

A few moments longer the two friends remained in conversation, and then Britomarte bade Justin good-night and withdrew to her chamber.

There she found Judith waiting for her.

"Ah! is it you, my dear girl? I am glad to see you. I was afraid that something had prevented you from coming, and that I should not see you again before leaving," said Miss Conyers.

"Troth, sooner than that should have happened, I would have gone to the gates iv the station, so I would, and watched every living soul that came in and every train that wint out till I saw you. But sure I got the name iv the house from Martin, and troth I made me gay Tom tetch me here! and here I've been staying, waiting for you, these three hours," said Judith.

"I am sorry. I didn't know that you were here, or I shouldn't have kept you waiting."

"Bother the odds, asking your pardon, ma'am, for I was very comfortable entirely. But now it's only to say good-bye and good luck to you, ma'am; for it's getting late too o'clock, and I must be going, for me aunt can't abide late hours, so she can't," said Judith, rising to go.

"You found your aunt well?" kindly inquired Miss Conyers.

"Divil a bit betther at any time iv her life; only whin she saw me, as she thought me dhrowned many a long day ago, she wint off into the highstrikes, so she did, and had fits so fast that we had to give her four glasses iv rum before she would come round. But sure she's all right now, ma'am, except in the matter iv a pain in her temper, as she is subject to; and be the same token, I mustn't bring it onto her by staying out late, so I will bid you good-bye, and God bless you, ma'am."

"Good-bye! and may the Lord bless you also, Judith," said Miss Conyers.

"But sure I'd like to take lave iv Misther Rosenthal before I go."

"You will find him in his sitting-room, Judith. Any of the waiters will show you where that is," said Miss Conyers.

And she drew the girl to her bosom and kissed her before she let her depart.

CHAPTER XLII

HOME AGAIN

AFTER a very early breakfast, Justin and Britomarte, with all their luggage, set out by the first omnibus that left the hotel for the early train to Washington. After paying his hotel bill, Justin had scarcely five dollars left, but he knew that he could get an advance from Lieutenant Ethel, whom he could reimburse immediately upon his arrival at Washington.

They met the young lieutenant on the ferryboat. He advanced smilingly toward them, saying:

"You see that I am punctual, and more than punctual, for I meet you on the ferryboat, instead of at the station. We could not have had a finer day for our journey," he added, cheerfully, as he shook hands with Justin and with Britomarte.

For you see, Lieutenant Ethel was not one of those mistaken individuals who imagine that they must always continue to wear a long face on a bereaved friend. He had earnestly expressed his sympathy and heartily offered his services; and his action stood good for all times; and now he meant to be cheerful, and to try to cheer them.

They reached the station in good time.

Leaving Miss Conyers in the ladies' room, they went together to the office to procure their tickets; and there Justin told the lieutenant of his dilemma.

"Draw on me, my dear fellow, for any amount in my possession. I have a hundred dollars in my pocketbook, and you are welcome to ninety of them," said the young man, cordially.

"Which would leave you just money enough to take you to Washington. No, thank you. Twenty dollars will answer my purpose, if you will let me have the use of that sum until I get home," smiled Justin.

"I wish it was twenty thousand, instead of twenty dollars, and that I were as able to give you the big sum as I am willing to lend you the little one," said the lieutenant, placing a note in Justin's hand. Justin thanked him, and got the tickets for himself and for Britomarte.

Before leaving the hotel, Miss Conyers had placed her pocketbook, containing thirty dollars, in the hands of Justin, with the request that he would keep it to pay her traveling expenses until they should reach their journey's end, when he might return it. And Justin, to prevent, or rather to defer a dispute on the subject, had accepted the trust; but neither for her hotel bill nor for her railroad ticket had he touched her little hoard. He was resolved to return the pocketbook intact as he had received it.

Having secured their tickets and checked their baggage, they rejoined Britomarte and took her to the train, and found comfortable seats in the ladies' car, to which Britomarte's companionship admitted them both.

They were scarcely seated, when the newsboys came into the car, crying the morning papers.

"Times, Herald, World, Tribune, *et cetera*. Full particulars of the Battle of Gettysburg!—Capture of the Pirate Sea Scourge!—Wonderful rescue of three shipwrecked passengers from a Desert Island!—Tribune, World, Herald, Times!"

"Now, who on earth could have put our adventure in!" exclaimed Justin, half amused and half annoyed at the circumstance.

Lieutenant Ethel blushed and then laughed, saying:

"I am afraid I am responsible for that! though I never supposed it would get into the papers. You see, yesterday I told the whole story of the cruise of the Xyphias to some friends and strangers that I met at dinner at the Astor House. I dare say there were some gentlemen of the press present, though I did not think so at the time."

"That accounts for all, then," said Justin.

And the party bought half-a-dozen papers. And the train started.

They had a swift and pleasant run to Washington, where they arrived safely at seven o'clock in the evening.

On reaching the station, Lieutenant Ethel left the car first, to go and secure a carriage for his friends.

"Britomarte! my dear, dear Britomarte, you will come home with me to Erminie? Don't wound me by refusing! Say that you will come," urged Justin, when he was left alone with Miss Conyers.

"No, no, no! not this evening, for the world! For this evening you and your sister should meet alone," she earnestly replied.

"To-morrow, then?" he inquired.

"Yes! to-morrow I will see Erminie."

As every one was now leaving the cars, they arose from their seats and went out. Lieutenant Ethel met them with a carriage.

"Where, then, shall we take you to-night?" questioned Justin, as he handed Britomarte into her place.

She named the hotel where she wished to stop. And Justin gave the order to drive there.

On arriving at the house, he took care to secure a good room for Miss Conyers; but not until he was on the point of taking leave of her did he hand her her pocketbook. And he was relieved to see that, without examination, she put it in her pocket.

Then he bade her good-night, and re-entered the carriage and drove to the house of that clerical friend to whom he had written to prepare Erminie for his arrival. He did not leave his carriage, lest his friend should detain him too long from his sister. He merely sent in a request that the Rev. Mr. Sales would come out and speak to him for a moment.

And when that gentleman came out, full of wonder and welcome and warm congratulations, Justin eagerly inquired if he had received his letter and delivered the inclosure to its destination.

And being answered in the affirmative, and informed that his sister was prepared to receive him, Justin cordially thanked Mr. Sales for his kind offices.

The clergyman would willingly have detained Mr. Rosenthal, and made a lion of him for the evening. But Justin excused himself upon the ground of his great impatience to meet his sister.

And so Mr. Sales, with many expressions of amazement and thankfulness that Justin and his companions should have been so providentially preserved and happily restored to their friends, suffered him to depart.

Justin gave the order to drive to the parsonage, and then threw himself back on his cushions.

Ah! who can imagine the emotions with which, after so long an absence, he drew near his father's house?

As in a dream, he saw the lights of the shops whirl past each side, as his carriage rolled through the streets. In a dream he perceived that it stopped before the gate of his old home. In a dream, he found himself going up the shaded walk, standing under the vine-wreathed portico, ringing the bell, and entering the door. Still in a dream, he found himself in a lighted drawing-room, and saw before him his sister Erminie, dressed as he had never seen her in his waking hours—in the deepest mourning. With a great cry:

"My brother! Oh, my brother!" she ran to him and threw herself upon his bosom.

And then he awoke! He clasped her closely to his heart. And they wept in each other's arms.

Erminie was the first to recover herself. She lifted her head from his bosom and murmured the question:

"You know, my brother, you know that—that——" her voice again broke down into sobs.

"I know all, sweet sister, all!" he answered, tenderly caressing her.

"He died—as he wished to die—cheering on his men to the charge!—to that gallant charge which, for the time being, turned the tide of battle and almost redeemed the day, even on that fatal field of Manassas!" she sobbed.

"He died a hero's death; he fills a hero's grave; he leaves to all posterity a hero's name!" murmured Justin, lovingly soothing her.

"Oh, Justin, I think, had there been many leaders like him in our army that day, the defeat had been a victory."

. . . .

With the departure of the shipwrecked lovers from the deserted island, that had been their refuge for so long a time, closed the most singular phase in their lives.

With their arrival in their native country to find it in the horrors of civil war, commences for them a career of activity and adventures full

"Of moving accidents by field and flood,
  Of hair breadth 'scapes i' th' imminent deadly breach,
  Of being taken by the insolent foe——"

All of which, together with the after fate of all the persons mentioned here, is told in the sequel to this story, entitled, "How He Won Her."

THE END

Good Fiction Worth Reading.

A series of romances containing several of the old favorites in the field of historical fiction, replete with powerful romances of love and diplomacy that excel in thrilling and absorbing interest.

A COLONIAL FREE-LANCE. A story of American Colonial Times. By Chauncey C. Hotchkiss. Cloth, 12mo. with four illustrations by J. Watson Davis. Price, $1.00.

A book that appeals to Americans as a vivid picture of Revolutionary scenes. The story is a strong one, a thrilling one. It causes the true American to flush with excitement, to devour chapter after chapter, until the eyes smart, and it fairly smokes with patriotism. The love story is a singularly charming idyl.

THE TOWER OF LONDON. A Historical Romance of the Times of Lady Jane Grey and Mary Tudor. By Wm. Harrison Ainsworth. Cloth, 12mo. with four illustrations by George Cruikshank. Price, $1.00.

This romance of the "Tower of London" depicts the Tower as palace, prison and fortress, with many historical associations. The era is the middle of the sixteenth century.

The story is divided into two parts, one dealing with Lady Jane Grey, and the other with Mary Tudor as Queen, introducing other notable characters of the era. Throughout the story holds the interest of the reader in the midst of intrigue and conspiracy, extending considerably over a half a century.

IN DEFIANCE OF THE KING. A Romance of the American Revolution. By Chauncey C. Hotchkiss. Cloth, 12mo. with four illustrations by J. Watson Davis. Price, $1.00.

Mr. Hotchkiss has etched in burning words a story of Yankee bravery, and true love that thrills from beginning to end, with the spirit of the Revolution. The heart beats quickly, and we feel ourselves taking a part in the exciting scenes described. His whole story is so absorbing that you will sit up far into the night to finish it. As a love romance it is charming.

GARTHOWEN. A story of a Welsh Homestead. By Allen Raine. Cloth, 12mo. with four illustrations by J. Watson Davis. Price, $1.00.

"This is a little idyl of humble life and enduring love, laid bare before us, very real and pure, which in its telling shows us some strong points of Welsh character—the pride, the hasty temper, the quick dying out of wrath. . . . We call this a well-written story, interesting alike through its romance and its glimpses into another life than ours. A delightful and clever picture of Welsh village life. The result is excellent."—Detroit Free Press.

MIFANWY. The story of a Welsh Singer. By Allan Raine. Cloth, 12mo. with four illustrations by J. Watson Davis. Price, $1.00.

"This is a love story, simple, tender and pretty as one would care to read. The action throughout is brisk and pleasing, the characters, it is apparent at once, are as true to life as though the author had known them all personally. Simple in all its situations, the story is worked up in that touching and quaint strain which never grows wearisome, no matter how often the lights and shadows of love are introduced. It rings true, and does not tax the imagination."—Boston Herald.

For sale by all booksellers, or sent postpaid on receipt of price by the publishers, A. L. BURT COMPANY, 114-120 East 23d Street, New York

Good Fiction Worth Reading.

A series of romances containing several of the old favorites in the field of historical fiction, replete with powerful romances of love and diplomacy that excel in thrilling and absorbing interest.

DARNLEY. A Romance of the times of Henry VIII. and Cardinal Wolsey. By G. P. R. James. Cloth, 12mo. with four illustrations by J. Watson Davis. Price, $1.00.

In point of publication, "Darnley" is that work by Mr. James which follows "Richelieu," and, if rumor can be credited, it was owing to the advice and insistence of our own Washington Irving that we are indebted primarily for the story, the young author questioning whether he could properly paint the difference in the characters of the two great cardinals. And it is not surprising that James should have hesitated; he had been eminently successful in giving to the world the portrait of Richelieu as a man, and by attempting a similar task with Wolsey as the theme, was much like tempting fortune. Irving insisted that "Darnley" came naturally in sequence, and this opinion being supported by Sir Walter Scott, the author set about the work.

As a historical romance "Darnley" is a book that can be taken up pleasurably again and again, for there is about it that subtle charm which those who are strangers to the works of G. P. R. James have claimed was only to be imparted by Dumas.

If there was nothing more about the work to attract especial attention, the account of the meeting of the kings on the historic "field of the cloth of gold" would entitle the story to the most favorable consideration of every reader.

There is really but little pure romance in this story, for the author has taken care to imagine love passages only between those whom history has credited with having entertained the tender passion one for another, and he succeeds in making such lovers as all the world must love.

CAPTAIN BRAND, OF THE SCHOONER CENTIPEDE. By Lieut. Henry A. Wise, U.S.N. (Harry Gringo). Cloth, 12mo. with four illustrations by J. Watson Davis. Price, $1.00.

The re-publication of this story will please those lovers of sea yarns who delight in so much of the salty flavor of the ocean as can come through the medium of a printed page, for never has a story of the sea and those "who go down in ships" been written by one more familiar with the scenes depicted.

The one book of this gifted author which is best remembered, and which will be read with pleasure for many years to come, is "Captain Brand," who, as the author states on his title page, was a "pirate of eminence in the West Indies." As a sea story pure and simple, "Captain Brand" has never been excelled, and as a story of piratical life, told without the usual embellishments of blood and thunder, it has no equal.

NICK OF THE WOODS. A story of the Early Settlers of Kentucky. By Robert Montgomery Bird. Cloth, 12mo. with four illustrations by J. Watson Davis. Price, $1.00.

This most popular novel and thrilling story of early frontier life in Kentucky was originally published in the year 1837. The novel, long out of print, had in its day a phenomenal sale, for its realistic presentation of Indian and frontier life in the early days of settlement in the South, narrated in the tale with all the art of a practiced writer. A very charming love romance runs through the story. This new and tasteful edition of "Nick of the Woods" will be certain to make many new admirers for this enchanting story from Dr. Bird's clever and versatile pen.

For sale by all booksellers, or sent postpaid on receipt of price by the publishers, A. L. BURT COMPANY, 114-120 East 23d Street, New York

Good Fiction Worth Reading.

A series of romances containing several of the old favorites in the field of historical fiction, replete with powerful romances of love and diplomacy that excel in thrilling and absorbing interest.

GUY FAWKES. A Romance of the Gunpowder Treason. By Wm. Harrison Ainsworth. Cloth, 12mo, with four illustrations by George Cruikshank. Price, $1.00.

The "Gunpowder Plot" was a modest attempt to blow up Parliament, the King and his Counsellors. James of Scotland, then King of England, was weak-minded and extravagant. He hit upon the efficient scheme of extorting money from the people by imposing taxes on the Catholics. In their natural resentment to this extortion, a handful of bold spirits concluded to overthrow the government. Finally the plotters were arrested, and the King put to torture Guy Fawkes and the other prisoners with royal vigor. A very intense love story runs through the entire romance.

THE SPIRIT OF THE BORDER. A Romance of the Early Settlers in the Ohio Valley. By Zane Grey. Cloth, 12mo, with four illustrations by J. Watson Davis. Price, $1.00.

A book rather out of the ordinary is this "Spirit of the Border." The main thread of the story has to do with the work of the Moravian missionaries in the Ohio Valley. Incidentally the reader is given details of the frontier life of those hardy pioneers who broke the wilderness for the planting of this great nation. Chief among those, as a matter of course, is Lewis Wetzel, one of the most peculiar, and at the same time the most admirable of all the brave men who spent their lives battling with the savage foe, that others might dwell in comparative security.

Details of the establishment and destruction of the Moravian "Village of Peace" are given at some length, and with minute description. The efforts to Christianize the Indians are described as they never have been before, and the author has depicted the characters of the leaders of the several Indian tribes with great care, which of itself will be of interest to the student.

By no means least among the charms of the story are the vivid word-pictures of the thrilling adventures, and the intense paintings of the beauties of nature, as seen in the almost unbroken forests.

It is the spirit of the frontier which is described, and one can by it, perhaps, the better understand why men, and women, too, willingly braved every privation and danger that the westward progress of the star of empire might be the more certain and rapid. A love story, simple and tender, runs through the book.

RICHELIEU. A tale of France in the reign of King Louis XIII. By G. P. R. James. Cloth, 12mo, with four illustrations by J. Watson Davis. Price, $1.00.

In 1829 Mr. James published his first romance, "Richelieu," and was recognized at once as one of the masters of the craft.

In this book he laid the story during those later days of the great cardinal's life, when his power was beginning to wane, but while it was yet sufficiently strong to permit now and then of volcanic outbursts which overwhelmed foes and carried friends to the topmost wave of prosperity. One of the most striking parts of the story is that of Cinq Mar's conspiracy; the method of conducting criminal cases, and the political trickery resorted to by royal favorites, affording a better insight into the statecraft of that day than can be had even by an exhaustive study of history. It is a powerful romance of love and diplomacy, and in point of thrilling and absorbing interest has never been excelled.

For sale by all booksellers, or sent postpaid on receipt of price by the publishers, A. L. BURT COMPANY, 114-120 East 23d Street, New York

Good Fiction Worth Reading.

A series of romances containing several of the old favorites in the field of historical fiction, replete with powerful romances of love and diplomacy that excel in thrilling and absorbing interest.

WINDSOR CASTLE. A Historical Romance of the Reign of Henry VIII, Catharine of Aragon and Anne Boleyn. By Wm. Harrison Ainsworth. Cloth, 12mo. with four illustrations by George Cruikshank. Price, $1.00.

"Windsor Castle" is the story of Henry VIII., Catharine, and Anne Boleyn. "Bluff King Hal," although a well-loved monarch, was none too good a one in many ways. Of all his selfishness and unwarrantable acts, none was more discreditable than his divorce from Catharine, and his marriage to the beautiful Anne Boleyn. The King's love was as brief as it was vehement. Jane Seymour, waiting maid on the Queen, attracted him, and Anne Boleyn was forced to the block to make room for her successor. This romance is one of extreme interest to all readers.

HORSESHOE ROBINSON. A tale of the Tory Ascendency in South Carolina in 1780. By John P. Kennedy. Cloth, 12mo. with four illustrations by J. Watson Davis. Price, $1.00.

Among the old favorites in the field of what is known as historical fiction, there are none which appeal to a larger number of Americans than Horseshoe Robinson, and this because it is the only story which depicts with fidelity to the facts the heroic efforts of the colonists in South Carolina to defend their homes against the brutal oppression of the British under such leaders as Cornwallis and Tarleton.

The reader is charmed with the story of love which forms the thread of the tale, and then impressed with the wealth of detail concerning those times. The picture of the manifold sufferings of the people, is never overdrawn, but painted faithfully and honestly by one who spared neither time nor labor in his efforts to present in this charming love story all that price in blood and tears which the Carolinians paid as their share in the winning of the republic.

Take it all in all, "Horseshoe Robinson" is a work which should be found on every book-shelf, not only because it is a most entertaining story, but because of the wealth of valuable information concerning the colonists which it contains. That it has been brought out once more, well illustrated, is something which will give pleasure to thousands who have long desired an opportunity to read the story again, and to the many who have tried vainly in these latter days to procure a copy that they might read it for the first time.

THE PEARL OF ORR'S ISLAND. A story of the Coast of Maine. By Harriet Beecher Stowe. Cloth, 12mo. Illustrated. Price, $1.00.

Written prior to 1852, the "Pearl of Orr's Island" is ever new; a book filled with delicate fancies, such as seemingly array themselves anew each time one reads them. One sees the "sea like an unbroken mirror all around the pine-girt, lonely shores of Orr's Island," and straightway comes "the heavy, hollow moan of the surf on the beach, like the wild angry howl of some savage animal."

Who can read of the beginning of that sweet life, named Mara, which came into this world under the very shadow of the Death angel's wings without having an intense desire to know how the premature bud blossomed? Again and again one lingers over the descriptions of the character of that baby boy Moses, who came through the tempest, amid the angry billows, pillowed on his dead mother's breast.

There is no more faithful portrayal of New England life than that which Mrs. Stowe gives in "The Pearl of Orr's Island."

For sale by all booksellers, or sent postpaid on receipt of price by the publishers, A. L. BURT COMPANY, 114-120 East 23d Street, New York

Printed in the USA
CPSIA information can be obtained
at www.ICGtesting.com
LVHW020748140923
757966LV00024BA/209